We Came as Angels

*Our journey from
celestial beings
to human beings
and back again*

Kenneth W. Brown
A novel based on true experience

We Came As Angels
Our journey from celestial beings
to human beings, and back again
by Kenneth W. Brown

Published by:
Waterwoods Press
PO Box 1354
Minnetonka, MN 55345
http://www.waterwoodspress.com

Published 2002

Printed in the United States of America
Library of Congress Cataloging-in-Publication Data
Brown, Kenneth W.
    We came as angels : our journey from celestial beings to human beings, and back again / Kenneth W. Brown
       p.   cm.
ISBN 0-9716079-0-7
1. Spiritual life--Fiction   I. Title
PS3552.R689 W4 2002
LCCN 2001098980

Cover:
Karen Anderson; original photograph
Kenneth W. Brown; original concept and design
Randon L. Brown; draft digital front cover
Paul Andrea; graphic artist, full cover

This book is dedicated to the caring guardian within you.

This book would not have been possible without the following people.

Lon, who guided me through perhaps a hundred past-life regressions. He made sure that I brought the past to the present, skillfully avoiding the tragedy that occurs when it happens the other way around.

Larry, who taught me how to sing with frogs while standing knee deep in star lit bogs, with an open heart. His acceptance and persistent encouragement helped motivate me to build a room in the back of the garage for a place to write. Then, he was excited to read what I wrote.

Donna, who for more than two decades has shared her friendship, caring and wisdom. She continues to teach me the difference between fantasy and vision, hearing and listening, how I get lost in time tunnels and most importantly, how to accept my humanness. She provided valuable comments on the manuscript, and is a dear blessing in my life.

Renee, my wife, who gave needed feedback, perspective, and homemade soup, while balancing the difficulties of a career and motherhood. She also co-authored her own book, *The Conscious Consultant,* which I proudly mention here. Her insights on this journey of life are as enriching as her spirit.

It is the connection to friends and fellow seekers that made laughter, and completing this book, possible. In addition to the four above, heartfelt appreciation goes to Michael S., Jessica B., Carola May W., Betsy B., Carol W., Leslie B., Shannon H., Dick B., Doris B., and Larina B., who provided thoughts and suggestions to help me bring this story into the world of words.

Thank you.

To the reader,

Tears sometimes fell as I wrote the visions down that are now within this book. Visions which coalesced around a simple, late night climb up the Great Pyramid in February of 1990. The images I offer to you are quite real to me, as real and vivid as any picture I may wish to recall from yesterday.

Initially, I wrote the visions down as a simple chronology of events, much as common history books are written. But that style did not convey the richness or intensity of those who walked the Earth in ancient days. My attempt to place those events within a novel is my attempt to bring that intensity to you. I cannot know the accuracy of my inner visions, and make no claim that they are the "truth." I only know that I offer them to you from deep within my chest, and that it feels good to let them go.

Sincerely,

Kenneth W. Brown

"There is free will in each choice we make, in each action we take." *Guardian*

Chapter 1 *Giza*

I inhaled. A mixture of odors assailed my nostrils. Oil on the dark, desert road under my tired feet released the scent of its ancient, black tarpit. A rotting cantaloupe attached its fermented odor to dry air. The leaves of a road-side palm plant smelled like parched eucalyptus, and my perspiration, strong from a hard day's travel, joined with the hot aromas.

My pace quickened as the hill grew steeper, and my pulse began to throb. Without warning the long forgotten image of the African storyteller came to mind. "Senegal," I said out loud. "So many years ago. Seems like yesterday." Feelings flowed from the years I'd traveled and seemed to manifest in the image of this one individual. His dark skin reflected an eerie shine from the glow of kerosene lamps which hung from long, thin wooden poles. His unusually broad face was framed by white hair that shone like fine spun wool in the lamplight. Wide-set eyes, like enameled beads of tiger's-eye, flashed at me time and time again as he whirled like a figure skater on dark ice.

My mind focused on the road under my feet once more, then began to wander again. Why am I so compelled to see what lies on the other side of a hill? Why can't I be happy with one view? I kicked a small stone out of my way. A slow, deep sigh escaped my chest as I took another step. Why do I feel like something is missing? What am I looking for?

My mind turned to recent events that had brought the value of my own life into question. William's death was a shock. A drunk smashes into his car and he's dead. His business, his wife, his kids, his friends left behind without warning. I kicked at another rock but missed it. Took a step back, kicked again and it exploded into a puff of dust. I loved his zeal for life. We spent an evening together last month. Now he's gone. It makes no sense. I glanced at the stars and down to the black road again. I started to kick a pile of dust in the road but stopped short, realizing just in time that it was camel droppings.

I spoke to the night, halted before the dung. "This is silly to walk up here. Why can't I just be happily asleep in my hotel right now?"

In my next step up the long road, the piercing eyes of the African storyteller once again formed in my mind, riveting me to my place in the village crowd. Though his body rotated, with each revolution his eyes only left mine for a short moment as he quickly turned and found me again. The very thought I had so many years ago returned, "It must be because I provide an easy target as he spins, the lone white face in the gathering."

The beat of his small drum increased as his legs, fixed like a stork's with one foot held high, blurred into the image of a cobra ready to strike. "Look away from him," my mind said, but my body couldn't. The timeless sound of the drum continued. I was entranced, as though his sound and gaze held me with an unknown power. Then, seemingly all in the same instant, the storyteller barked a sharp cry, jumped into the air and came down with his bare feet spread wide in the desert sand, his eyes fixed upon mine as if in tight embrace. My body was frozen in the hot night. Slowly, ever so slowly, his hands traveled upward to the top of his head, his elbows out at right angles to form the silhouette of a triangle. "Like a pyramid," I said to him at the time. He laughed.

His voice cracked like a whip as he pointed to the stars with weathered hands. His gesture compelled me to follow it into the Eastern night's sky. *You want me to go to the pyramids?* The teeth in his wide smile flashed like stones framing a friendly cave. In that moment I knew I would see the great pyramids someday. When I looked down from the stars to see him again, he had gone, blended into the village throng without a trace.

My reminiscence was cut short as my foot slid through something and the odor told me what it was. I scraped it off on the broken rocks by the side of the road.

I'm crazy. I should be in bed. I traveled all last night and today. I'm having flashbacks, and I'm stepping in camel shit. I should go back and get some sleep. If I've waited fifteen years to see the pyramids, I can wait till morning. And daylight. But softly, gradually, the face of the African storyteller appeared once more. The lines in his broad face formed ravines across its ebony, weathered landscape. His eyes glistened as their gaze penetrated mine. "Go now," they seemed to say.

I placed one foot in front of the other and peered ahead into the night. The cracked asphalt road wound up a steep hill that would eventually take me to Cheops, the largest pyramid in the world. I tilted my head upward and stopped to stare again. Its upper half was still outlined above the palm fronds, but it seemed no closer. It teased me onward.

Why didn't I make it here from Turkey fifteen years ago? I saw myself in a coffee house in Antalya, gazing out over the deep blue Mediterranean Sea as I made the decision. "Guns and fighting to the south. The Syrian border is closed. I'd better head east toward India instead." Egypt had to wait for another day.

That decision to travel east instead of south had been easy. Just like my decision to backpack around the world after working through college. I needed to see more. See how other people lived and thought. Some inner voice convinced me to trade in my worldly goods for a bank account and spend three years roving the world.

Has it really been fifteen years since I finished that journey? By the time I got back to the States, I was ready for a long-term relationship instead of the short-term relationships I'd had on the road. It seemed natural and right for marriage and children to follow such a trip. A different kind of journey. Longer term. I smiled. I still made it to Egypt.

My gaze fell upon a low stone wall that ran like a snaking vine next to the road. I leaned over its edge to peer down into a dark courtyard. An old man squatted next to a small charcoal fire and gently stirred its coals. As they flared, a shimmer of light reflected off the stubble on his face as faint pinpricks of deep orange. In a gesture that seemed unanchored in time, he stirred the contents of a blackened teapot over the fire and slowly sat back on his heels. My mind hurled thoughts. I could choose to go and sit by his comfortable fire and drink tea with him. Why not? I'm tired. What difference would it make? I sighed, and felt the warm pull of the amber glow. The man picked up the teapot and poured into a small cup. The smell of mint tea flowed into gentle currents of air. Mint tea, the welcoming brew that sustained me across Africa those many years ago. I stared longingly down at the man again. He appeared so peaceful, so content. *Keep moving.* I turned and walked on.

To distract myself from my reminiscent mood I gazed at the pyramid. Its massive triangle blotted out the stars. "I am closer," I said, trying to be positive, and returned to inner thoughts. Could we build something like Cheops today? I don't think so. I don't think anyone thinks so. And what about those strange chambers inside? What were they for? All empty except for a vacant sarcophagus. I brushed uncombed hair back from my forehead and felt fine grit.

Its thirty-foot cap stone is missing. Why? The tops of the other pyramids are there. And what about that engineer who in 1859 discovered that an electric current came from its top? Why would that happen? Electricity isn't emitted from the other pyramids. I watched starlight play across the grainy asphalt as I walked on and on.

I stopped again to rest and leaned my head back to stretch my weary neck only to suddenly feel that the massive pyramid seemed to have grown from the ground as if upthrust from the bowels of the earth. I walked toward it more quickly, eyes cast upward, darting from feature to feature in the dark light. Was the height of each row of blocks the same? Some looked higher than others. I strained my eyes for more detail and felt a wave of excitement pass through me as I saw giant steps of stone disappear as if into the heavens. "I'm almost there," I said with satisfaction, and my pace quickened again.

"Stop!" a harsh voice called out. With a start, I glanced down to see a pole extended across the narrow road. My eyes followed it to a small guard booth where a man wrapped in dark cloth peered at me from a dilapidated doorway. "The Pyramid is closed."

I gathered my wits and mustered energy for the debate. "But I've been traveling all day and last night, too. I just want to see it!"

The guard approached me, plodding as if taking steps repeated countless times before. "You can go around to the Sphinx," he said dispassionately, waving his hand around to the right. "The entrance to the Sphinx is still open. It is the entrance to see the light show."

"I just want to touch the pyramid," I replied earnestly, but felt desperation.

"All tourists like to see the light show," he asserted. Then, as if feeling a need to appease my disheartened expression he added, "It's too dangerous to walk here at night." The guard waved me on in a casual and clearly dismissive gesture. "Bandits. Snakes."

I turned around obediently, feigning appreciation for his concern. How silly. It's safe here. And a light show? Give me a break. Travel all day and night to sit with a horde of tourists in neat rows of chairs? I don't need to sit in an outdoor theater watching colored lights flash to melodramatic music. Tonight I need to touch the Great Pyramid.

As soon as I walked a respectable distance back down the road and sensed that the guard had returned to his rickety wooden shelter, I darted behind a forlorn scrubby bush. I squatted and leaned around its edge and cautiously peeked toward the obstinate man. A faint light flared as the guard lit a cigarette. Good. If he saw me dart to the side of the road, he wouldn't be lighting a match in front of his eyes. If I moved far enough away into the barren landscape, and moved cautiously, it was possible this bored sentry would be too apathetic to care about a distant figure should he even see one. Besides, as long as he held that glowing cigarette, I could track his movements a lot more easily than he could track mine. A lazy guard is no match for a dedicated sneak, I thought, and was suddenly energized.

I struck a path due west. With the pyramids aligned perfectly along the cardinal points, keeping bearings was easy. Darkness and the desert landscape's rolling features concealed my movements. My feet picked their way through the rock-strewn terrain to approach Cheops from the deserted south rather than from the guarded north. I'll come in past the smallest pyramid, Mycerinus. He'll never suspect it.

No lights betrayed my movements. Outfoxing the guard was easy, and I proudly took the last few steps toward Mycerinus. The desert, the darkness, and I all seemed to greet the huge rectangular stones at once. I placed my hands on one of the many slabs that formed the foundation of the smallest pyramid, closed my eyes and welcomed the faint odor of limestone. I breathed it in and after holding that breath, relaxed. I opened my eyes. The individual stone I touched was over four feet high and seven feet long. How far it stretched under the ascending stones resting on top of it I could not tell. But it was big, skillfully shaped, and very heavy. Slowly, I raised my head to see tall steps rising into the night sky. How did they do this? I sat down on the block and leaned against Mycerinus. The smallest pyramid felt as massive as a mountain range.

How could people build them? So precise, yet so immense. I moved my hands back and forth across the stone. How many millions of human lifetimes have come and gone while these pyramids stood, silent messengers of our distant past?

I lay face down against the stone. Its coarse mass pressed against my chest, and I once again drew in the deep smell of earth's limestone. Caring, as if from ancient tenderness, grew within me. Motionless against the stone, I asked, "What are you?" I slowly rolled onto my back and stared up the staircase to the heavens. A soft desert breeze blew a caress of invisible night air. I said in a whisper, "If only I could hear you speak."

The absolute stillness of the night eluded time. Questions washed rhythmically through me as though my mind lay sleeping on a distant shore, the waves seeking to caress and awaken it. Questions, felt rather than thought, ebbed to and fro. I lost track of where I lay as the cool earthy mass pressed against my back and I peered up into the night. If I have a soul, where is it? Starlight reflected off minute crystals in the limestone like a thousand brilliant mirrors. Is there life after death? For William? For me?

Suddenly, I opened my eyes and sat up. Dizziness and confusing images swirled through my mind as I struggled to regain my bearings. How long have I been here? I squinted to read my watch in the darkness. To my surprise, only ten minutes had passed. "Ten minutes?" I said out loud, stood slowly, and dragged my hand across the stone. *Strange dream. Angels hurling great beams of light. Were they fighting? Against what?* I took a deep breath and sighed. I'd better get going. I'm starting to hallucinate.

As I rounded the corner of Mycerinus, Chephren, the middle pyramid, stood not a football field away like a monolithic mountain of stability. It rose to only meters below Cheops, but it still retained some white marble sheathing at its top. Grinning all the way, I reached it and gazed upon its rows of solid blocks. As I passed them I felt like a man reviewing steadfast troops, each one fitting neatly to form the whole. Each strong in its place. My feeling for the mass of the structure transformed into a feeling for the individual stones, linked together through wonderful orchestration. The individual stones touched each other, supported each other as if cells of one body.

I turned the next corner and now saw Cheops, its silhouette once more outlined in the distance against the night. Its mysteries mocked me as I hurried toward it. The legions of Roman, Islamic, Christian, French and German soldiers that marched through the centuries could only pass beneath its shadow. Built by slaves? With precisely honed blocks weighing over thirty tons? What about the Grand Gallery with its inexplicable twenty-eight-foot-high polished ceiling? How could slaves build such a majestic mountain? There was love in the hands that made this. I stopped and examined its sheer staircase and a new thought emerged, "I wonder if I could climb-"

"Stop!" a voice barked. Ripped from my thoughts, I wheeled around to see a different man, this one wearing a wrinkled khaki shirt and dark baggy pants. "The pyramids are closed," he said with certainty.

Caught. "Closed?" I asked, feigning a calm I did not feel. "How can things so large, and so old, be closed?"

He smiled wryly, but his demeanor was certain. "My friend in the guard booth," he pointed down the road, "said to watch for you. He said you walked around through the desert to get past him."

I stood dumbfounded. "I...I just wanted to touch the pyramids," I replied, caught like an errant child.

"So you touched them. You should go."

"Why?" I asked directly. "I'm not going to hurt anything."

"No," he responded slowly, studying me. "I don't think you have a hammer to chip a souvenir."

"I wouldn't do that!"

"Some do," he replied as his eyes flashed with momentary fire. Then, he grinned incongruously and studied me again. "So, you care for our history?"

"I care very much," I replied, sensing an opening. A long silence fell between us as he gazed at me and I at him. "I need to climb Cheops," I blurted out, surprising myself as well as him.

His chin wrinkled, but his expression didn't show shock. Instead he turned away from me to look at the monstrous peak. "Maybe not a good idea," he replied quietly. Another pause. "Last month, three tourists died on that pyramid."

"Died? How?" The idea seemed absurd.

His piercing eyes held me in place. "They came very late in the night, just before dawn, and managed to avoid us. The pyramid is steep. We don't know how they fell. We just know that in the morning all three were found dead at the bottom."

We both stared back to the silent mountain, and then he added, "Once you begin to fall, it is very difficult to stop."

"So that is why you close the pyramids at night?"

He laughed and I felt some of the tightness in my chest lift. "The pyramids are never really closed. Too big. This one covers thirteen acres." He looked again toward Cheops. "They are just open to fewer people at night." His grin made me grin. "But we must be very careful who we let climb the pyramid."

I will climb it, I thought to myself as inner excitement grew. But then he continued speaking with an intense stare, seemingly reading my thoughts. "No one climbs without a guide. Many more tourists than those three have died. Several a year. It is as if the pyramid hurls them off." He waved his arm in the air, flicking his wrist casually. Then, evidently suspecting I hadn't gotten the point added, "It is dangerous. You must know how to speak with it."

"I see," I responded seriously, feeling the chance to do a solo climb evaporate, but climbing with him wouldn't be so bad if he kept out of my way. Then he added, "These deaths are very bad. It is forbidden to climb the pyramid."

Forbidden or not, it was clear that some people still did. "I'm a good climber," I insisted. "I've climbed many high mountains."

"I watched you circle though the desert...From just up there." He pointed thirty feet up the side of Chephren. Then he added, "You did well. You didn't let my friend, the snakes or the bandits stop you."

Snakes and bandits? I felt my face flush as I recalled the certainty with which I made my secret, perhaps foolish, approach.

He scratched the stubble on his face. "They both prowl the ravines for easy prey."

I regained my composure after a deep breath and said, "I need to climb."

His head turned side to side, and he replied thoughtfully. "This is not a good time. It is too early in the night." His head turned to me. After a heartbeat, he added, "I can see your desire is deep. Come back at two o'clock in the morning. Fewer soldiers. Also the light show is starting soon. There will be too many lights...and eyes."

I considered. Returning later would mean less chance of getting caught by soldiers, but it would also mean walking back to the hotel, going to sleep and waking up for the walk back. I looked down at my feet. Once I was in bed there was little chance I could make myself get up, not after getting no sleep last night and traveling through such a long, hard day. Besides, I was here now. Isn't it best to seize the moment?

"I'm here now, you're here now." I looked at Cheops. "The pyramid is here now." I fixed my tired eyes on this interesting man, who smiled now, and repeated, "I'm a good climber."

"You make things difficult for me." He shook his head. "It is not good to climb during the light show. The lights shine on one side of the pyramid, then in a flash are on another. We would have to climb the spine and jump from side to side to keep out of the light."

We, I thought. He said, we would have to climb. "But I bet you have the light show memorized," I countered with optimism. "You know when the lighting changes. You tell me when, and I'll jump."

He gave a quiet laugh. "You are very determined." He rubbed his stubbled chin once more, then fell silent as he looked at the triangular mountain. A strange sense of calm enveloped us as I, too, gazed at Cheops and let the silence grow. At last he said, "I will be your guide," and as if to convince me of the value of his services added, "My name is Hamar; I will make sure you do not die."

I allowed him his drama. "I'm sure I'm in good hands. You know what you're doing," I said to give him reassurance about his decision, but to myself thought, "There is no way I'll fall off this. It's easy compared to climbing the rock faces of the Sierras."

"I know you need to climb." He cocked his head upward and a slight smile flickered on his weathered face. Then his tone changed to address business. "You will have to give me enough money to pay two guards for the risk they take. The one you spoke to and another over there will be in trouble if we are caught." He pointed toward the northeast corner of Cheops.

"What about you?" I asked.

"As payment, you give me what you feel is right." Then he added seriously, "You say you are a good climber. You need to be. We will climb very fast."

I reached into my front pocket and brought out several Egyptian dinar notes. "Is this enough?"

He scanned the notes. "It is enough for us to receive." Then after a pause he added, "Is it enough for you to give?"

I peered at Hamar. As the starlight revealed the deep creases in his face I felt suddenly strange, as if things were not as they seemed. I shook off the feeling with effort, and re-focused on the man before me. He was not young. Though his eyes gleamed with fiery life, his leathered skin told of the years he'd spent in bright desert sun and strong wind. My hand reentered my pocket and touched the secret flap of the money pouch. As if he could read my mind he said, "You will know what is right after the climb."

I glanced at the pyramid and felt a ripple of fatigue. *I wonder what this is really worth?*

"We must hurry," he said. "The light show will be starting."

He scurried across the dark bedrock like a goat, and I was surprised how difficult it was to get my body into similar quick, responsive motion. After a five-minute scramble, he left me in an excavated pit near the southwest corner of the Great Pyramid. "Wait here," was all I heard before noticing he was gone.

Tired and exhilarated in the same moment, I reflected on the evening. All I'd planned was a stroll to touch the pyramids before returning to my hotel for a much deserved sleep. Again, I studied the rocks towering above me. Thousands of stone blocks the size of small cars rose before me like a giant's staircase. What am I doing?

I took a deep breath of hot air, exhaled slowly, and tried to comprehend the adventure I'd chosen. I took cautious steps to reach the first, foundational course of stones that had been set by meticulous hands thousands of years before. Standing next to it, I rubbed I my hands over the side of solid block, unfractured through time. "If only you could talk," I whispered.

I pressed my face against it to draw in its earthy aroma. I closed my eyes and thought of the green and blue paleozoic seas that gave birth to the hard limestone. My thoughts carried me deep, deep into the earth, under the continents that float on heavier, yet molten, orange stone, hot and alive with slow motion, immense currents of molten rock pulsating with the heartbeat of the planet itself. Suddenly, I stepped back, disturbed that my feet were actually tingling with heat.

This is a weird place. I looked around the pit that held me. It measured about twelve-by-twelve feet. One ramp of crumbled stone led out. What if this guy went to get the soldiers? What if he's taken my Egyptian money and is going to just leave me here? I could be here for hours! Soldiers could find me and then what will I do? Say I'm waiting here to climb the pyramid? I refocused on the massive staircase, slowly walked over to its base and gingerly placed my hand on a foundational stone once more.

"This is magnificent," I whispered.

"Psst," a voice hissed. "Come now."

I turned to see Hamar. No longer did he appear the life-worn guard casually talking of his work. Now ready for the climb, he had transformed into a gymnast.

"Come!" he exclaimed in a hushed tone.

Although I was taller, much younger and seemingly more muscular and fit, I climbed out of the hole with a grunt as loose stones rolled under my feet.

"We must go quickly," he said. "Stay near me. Put your feet where I put my feet. Do not look down."

The first block was chest high, and I watched with anticipation as Hamar swung to its top with ease. I attempted to scramble up the rock as adeptly and was surprised at the strain. "Use the footholds," Hamar said as he scampered ahead.

What footholds?

After only a few minutes my leg and arm muscles burned with a bone-deep fire. I swallowed, and a pithy dryness that felt like chalk filled my mouth. "How long has it been since I've had water? Or mint tea?" I looked upward to see Hamar ascending like a rocket. "Can't stop now," I grunted out, "got to move!" My legs and arms seemed to pull me upward with a will of their own, automatically finding places to grasp.

The height of the stair courses varied. Rows of large, chest-high blocks unexpectedly appeared after three-foot-high ones, and I couldn't settle into a comfortable stride. Climbing this slope was more like climbing boulders than the even stairs I'd assumed. I climbed and climbed.

"Be ready to jump to the other side!" Hamar pointed around the corner we had scaled. "The lights will soon be bright here!" I glanced toward the Sphinx, so far below it looked small, and a crescendo of sound burst from gigantic speakers.

I pushed upward and paused to see Hamar leap across a pile of broken stone that lay like a scree slope in our path. Poised to make the same move, I heard only the sound of my pounding heart echoing through my body. I pushed off without conscious thought and cleared the pile of rubble, but my momentum carried me directly into solid stone. My head hit it with abrupt force and knocked my glasses across my nose. I struggled to regain composure, and cautiously freed one hand from its hold to straighten them. "This way!" Hamar said quietly. "We must get to the top before the lights shift to this side again!"

"Holy shit," I breathed.

He ran up the pyramid like a man with fire in his belly, adrenaline in his veins. My adrenaline, on the other hand, flowed from a need to get to the top alive. Minute hand and footholds seemed to appear from nowhere. One step at time, I thought. One step at a time. Without warning, my fingers slipped from the slab above me and grazed the edge of a sharp calcified shell. Pain shot through my hand.

"Damn!" I held my hand tightly against my chest, both pressed to the stone. I had no choice but to stop and catch my breath.

"The lights change soon! We're almost to the peak." Perspiration stung my eyes. I raised my face to see Hamar point toward the other side which still glowed with light, backlighting the pyramid for the crowd below. In an instant the lights went out. I turned my head toward the base of the side I was on to be greeted by a burst of blinding orange light. "Jump!" I heard as I felt myself twist, claw my way to the top, and drop into blackness.

Chapter 2   *Souls of Light*

Where am I? I looked down, but could not see my body. Just a void beyond blackness; all an abyss without boundary. *Did I fall and die?* Stilling my thoughts, I strained to listen. Something was coming. Slowly, a distant tremor penetrated the emptiness. Like a tonal wind so soft it didn't yet sound like a sound. Then, as sudden as clashing cymbals, an avalanche of pulsing chimes filled the dark void. My head swam.

A hole of light appeared, and I fixed upon it: a point of reference in the nothingness. But before my eyes could focus, it swelled to a brilliant fireball, seemingly everywhere at once. I lost all sense of where I began or ended. A shocking streak of blue lightning shot through the hot-orange current. Then flashes of yellow, green, now more blue branched like gargantuan electric trees growing within an ethereal sea.

I was lost, without bearings; a single element of something so vast it was nameless. I began to dissolve. "God help me," I thought plaintively.

After a long, torturous moment, I felt of breath of air, a soft breeze. I took a breath. As I let it go I knew that I was not alone. "Pretend you're watching a movie," I thought whimsically.

Watching a movie. *Why not?* I felt solace for the first time since the vision began. I smiled, and started to view the scene as though it was on a surrounding screen, rather than from a lost mind. I watched fascinated and transfixed, as orbs of light darted and danced in a streaming, rushing torrent.

Words came. Words that crystallized from within the saturated solution; and they resonated without end. "Go forth, go forth and create. Touch Me with all you become." Feeling a stronger sense of self now, I watched as the moving picture showed millions of new souls touch fertile dark ocean and sing.

I saw orb-like souls stream by, and an iridescent violet ball became clear in the foreground. It paused, as if also watching the flooding tide of spring along with me. "I have a name," it said, filled with curiosity. "What is my name?" The question was earnest, yet, not desperate. "Yawri. My name is Yawri," he proclaimed with a new-found voice. Suddenly, an electric surge of light swept him on, and confusion rang in his echoing sound.

"Am I separate now? How can I be separate? Where is the Creator?" The entity began to spin and careen. "Where is the Creator?!" it called out as it searched for something substantial in the electric, cascading mist. "Am I separate? I don't want to be separate." He strained to listen, to connect. "Was that a scream? Did I hear a scream?"

A breath of light touched him as though with a kind hand. "I am with you," a quiet, yet firm voice said. "The Creator has sent forth souls, particles of Itself, to add more to All. We must keep moving."

Yawri looked around for the source of the voice, but saw only the sparkling torrent. "Is the voice inside me? Why was there a scream?" Vague shapes moved through the light and he saw other beings in the bottomless ocean that brimmed with particles of the Creator.

The voice came again. "You are not separate, because the Creator is All."

Excitement filled Yawri's voice as he decided to leave restraint behind, and join the melee. "I'm free!" he exclaimed. "Free to create, free to explore, free to move and expand." He bounded through the cascading mist deciding that it was something to embrace rather than fear.

Time passed - millions of years passing like minutes. As the sending-forth matured, ever more ethereal reality was filled with beings seeking wisdom through co-creating with the Creator. Beings pooled to form nodes of light which gave depth and breadth to the fluid cosmos. Galaxies sprang forth as though grown from thought. Yawri roamed and explored, taking delight in observing the myriad of creations. As he'd done countless times before, he considered what to explore next. "I wonder what that is," he said as he spied a nearby opening to a strangely translucent tunnel. "I haven't seen one of those before."

He approached confidently, rushing toward it like it was a prize. Without warning, he began spinning as if in a whirlpool, and was sucked inside. "Help!" he managed to call out, but the current swept him down the strange tunnel. His sight blurred as he sped through a maze of veins that forked to unfathomed directions, the membrane-like walls pulsing as if they were part of an immense body. Startled and fascinated in the same moment, he saw branching veins of transparent pink and violet shoot by. Again without warning, the living tube opened and seemed to eject him into a new place and time. He hovered outside of the strange Creation, transfixed, as he stared back at the opening. "What happened?" he asked.

"Your first trip through a time tunnel?" another being answered. Yawri did his best to regain his bearings as he saw another ethereal soul near him. A golden orb of light framed by distant stars addressed him again. "I am called Muran," the being said.

Yawri focused upon the mouth of the tunnel once more, then back to Muran. "A time tunnel. What's a time tunnel?" Yawri moved toward it slightly, as if trying to discern more for himself.

Muran flowed toward the tunnel entrance with him. "Time is a Life form, a Creation." His orb shimmered a soft gold and his manner was unhurried. "It's a structure that adds a temporal quality to Creations. If you know how, you can travel through the tunnels, through time, and experience the many dimensions of temporal reality at will."

Yawri viewed the entrance with curiosity. "I think it just chose to send me here. I'm in a different place from where I was, and I think it pulled me in on purpose."

Muran moved closer to Yawri and spoke in a friendly tone. "When in the presence of something conscious I've found it best to communicate with it, otherwise it may play a joke upon you."

Yawri projected his caring connection to the tunnel entrance. As it glowed a welcoming orange in return, he made a silent commitment to learn how to navigate time tunnels. But as he turned his attention to Muran, distant round objects which floated in the velvet space behind the golden orb captured his attention. "What are those things?" he asked.

Muran's color slowly pulsed between yellow and gold. "You're viewing physical reality here," he said as though it was obvious. "Those things are planets."

"Physical reality? Planets?" Yawri reached out with his senses toward the distant spheres, and felt the weightless although physical particles of Life. "This space is filled with a living dust!"

"Yes," Muran commented. "Beings co-create with the Creator to utter the correct tones to call particles of Life together. A swirling of particles begins, and depending upon the tones, different types of planets and stars are formed. The physical Creations are as conscious as you or I."

Yawri beamed as he gazed from the nearest planet to distant pricks of light. They shined like sun-soaked diamonds floating in a black sea. Then, opening himself to perceive more, he saw pastel veils of purple wave through space like vast curtains rippling in a soft wind. "Physical reality is filled with very different energy than I've ever seen before." He focused his attention on the nearby planet again. Thrill grew as he willed himself to move toward the intriguing ball. "Let's go see it," he called to Muran as he rushed away.

"Wait!" Muran called after him, but he was gone.

As Yawri neared the planet he was surprised to see the complexity of its whirling dance and rapid journey around its star, and he was puzzled. "It's complicated. I wonder how souls help form these physical things?" He stopped to observe the frozen icy blue planet. Its surface moved in slumbering undulation. "What's that pull?" He wondered as he felt the presence of yet another new energy. "That planet is pulling particles of physical reality to it like a suction. Maybe I could join them," he said as he felt himself accelerate toward the mass.

"Stop!" Muran's voice called after him. "Don't blend your thoughts with the physical particles! You can't join with them the same way you do ethereal energies!"

Yawri shifted his thoughts away from the particles and toward Muran. He slowed, then stopped, then traveled to hover next to Muran. "I got a little caught up in the excitement," he tried to explain.

Muran pulsed a bright yellow before settling down to a soft golden color. "Do you always rush off like that into things you're just learning about?"

"Usually. It's never been a problem before. Part of the adventure is learning how to get out of things I don't understand."

Muran's voice resounded with concern. "Well, you might move a little slower with physical reality. A soul's ability to co-create in this dimension is the same as it is in the ethereal realms you're used too. But if you use your free will to join with a physical Creation, like you were doing with those particles, you might find yourself thinking that you *are* physical. Then where would you be?"

Yawri's gaze didn't leave the planet. "Learning how to get out of things I don't understand, I suppose."

Muran considered his response. "Well, although they are part of the same whole, physical and ethereal Creations have important differences. There is gravity for example. Do you hear its tones?" he asked. "Different combinations of soul-sound and soul-light create different levels of gravity. The beings that are uttering those tones are doing so to draw the particles they need to co-create a physical planet."

Yawri moved slowly toward the gaseous planet. "These physical things are conscious," he said, getting used to the idea.

The being drifted alongside Yawri, and studied the celestial sphere before speaking. "The souls that work with the Creator to make planets are very conscious and have been learning how to do it for billions of years."

The relevance of the statement seemed lost on Yawri. "This planet does make its own sound, just as you and I do. I hear it. It's fascinating."

After several minutes of listening to the tones Muran said, "Come, I'll show you how to be on a planet without merging with its mass."

Yawri watched as the golden orb began to move closer to the planet, and always drawn to see more, happily followed. Muran glowed with increasing light as he descended. "Increasing your soul-light reduces the pull of gravity just as increasing your soul-sound increases it. It's all in how you connect."

"Of course," Yawri replied with more certainty than he felt. "It's all in how you connect."

Muran continued. "The souls co-creating this one are very skilled with joining ethereal and physical realities. I'm just learning how to do it with a much simpler Life form, trees." He said the word respectfully, as though paying tribute.

"Trees?" Yawri didn't have the vaguest idea what they were.

"Trees," Muran replied. "They grow on some planets, and although they're all different, they all bring stability to support diverse Life. That's a purpose I certainly agree with, and they are an excellent Life form to teach me about joining with physical reality."

Yawri's attention was distracted upward as he saw a swirl of cosmic dust stream toward the planet. "That makes sense," he said.

Muran shone like a transparent, miniature golden sun as he spoke again. "I'm going to speak with the souls who are co-creating this planet, and see what more they can teach me about co-creating with trees."

Yawri now gazed out to the stars to locate the other planets circling this sun. "I think learning about physical Creation is a good idea, too." He felt resolution with his new idea.

Muran's color suddenly rippled with waves of light yellow and gold. "Fine as any choice is." His color became a more constant gold again. "But be thoughtful. As I have said, beings can be become lost in physical reality if they don't keep their perspective. Remember, the Creator gave us free will. Our Creations will not be controlled by It at all."

Yawri was positive. "No matter what we create we'll have more to take back to the Creator. All will be more. It's just learning."

"I suppose," Muran said mindfully. "I suppose."

The golden orb continued descending to commune with the souls who had co-created to form the gaseous planet. "If you're interesting in joining ethereal with physical energy you won't find better teachers. Do you want to speak with them, too?"

Yawri focused his perception toward the undulating surface. It looked dull yellow. He gazed skyward toward the brilliant star filled sky. He scarcely looked back at Muran. "I want to investigate other planets in this solar system first. And I want to learn about time tunnels," he replied eagerly. With a hasty goodbye and an exuberant spiral, he bounded off. Muran watched him streak away for a long moment before he once more moved toward the planet, and the teaching he sought there.

Yawri wasted little time exploring the remaining planets of this solar system before he left to explore another. Some contained all the shades of blue, another the reds, another the grays. Occasionally planets held two colors, blue and green or brown and yellow. He learned that the more colors, the more sounds and diversity of Life.

Over hundreds of years, he mastered travel through time tunnels and found that they truly did provide the fastest means to explore the many dimensions of temporal reality. He learned that the solar systems were intimately connected, as a watery planet's islands are connected by an actual sea. An idea from one solar system flowed through the universal ocean to another solar system so that similar Life forms appeared in both. Although each planet was unique, they were similar, too.

He entered the arm of a small spiral galaxy and his attention was drawn to a large number of souls flowing toward a particular star. Curious, he followed them and as they drew closer to the star, he heard tones he'd never heard before. Each of the star's planets sang a different song, yet combined their ensemble into a symphony unique to his experience. Groups of beings broke away to sing with the planet's song that they wished to join. Some went to a planet of gasses, others to fire, others to a planet of ice, some to moons. Several came to a planet which called the elements of water to it through its own vibrant sound.

Pausing before this planet, he joined other souls listening to its call drifting through the heavens. "Come the waters. Come the Life. Come and join me in co-creation." Comets streamed toward it. Yawri knew instantly that souls who had chosen to learn about physical reality by joining their energy with the icy comets, were sailing to it to offer their water. The planet received them, and a blanket of silver steam reflected star rays back to the heavens like a prism.

"There are so many different sounds here." Yawri said to the group of other souls watching the display. "This planet is bound to have a lot more diversity than most."

One of the other orbs of light responded. "It is rare to find a solar system that has received so much of the Creator's own touch. This planet's beings are co-creating with It directly."

The group began to descend toward the planet. "Wait for me!" Yawri called. The radiant souls floated through the atmosphere, and all sensed the sanctity of physical Life springing forth in spontaneous Creation. Yawri was completely enthralled as he descended through the thick layer of clouds to find out what lay below.

A warm, earthly sea stretched from horizon to horizon. Rain streamed like silver strands of silk from a cocoon-covered sky. Yawri moved through the falling water with glee as rain passed through his non-physical form, caressing him. The churning sea below rolled up to greet the soul, and he dove into the sea's body as one molecule joining a sacred pool of others. He flowed and danced with an explosion of Life that moved effortlessly, yet with a sense of purpose. Thriving, towering plants, anchored by long, jointed stalks to the seabed waved like giant, green flowers toward a liquid blue heaven. Fish with bone-sheathed heads darted to avoid nautiloids whose squid-like tentacles moved rhythmically as they waved outside their orange striped spiral shells. An immense forest of sea grass sheltered brilliant blue neon shrimp as the string-like arms of pulsating jelly fish whimsically beckoned them to their doom. Armored bottom-dwellers moved like walking rocks around uneven yellow and red coral terrain. Hot vents of water created columns of waving, nutrient-rich excelsior, mixing the fire in the earth's belly with comets' water to create the fertile medium for Life's cauldron.

"Now, this is Life!" Yawri said as his violet orb went even lower. The sea bottom teemed with shellfish and aquatic worms which feasted on the death of the menagerie. Every molecule of rock and water brought forth Life, more Creation. Every atom of the rich seabed vibrated with a robust excitement; the sediment itself was alive.

Since Yawri was not physical he discovered that he could flow through the sediment like fine oil through water. Touching, connecting to it, yet moving on. Down, down into deep Earth he went. After passing through a thousand feet of rock he came to a subterranean cavern which opened like a giant womb before him. He hovered respectfully as he saw that it was illuminated with a phosphorescent light of its own. Miniature plants and creatures shone with glowing yellows and blues. Immense pools of warm, crystal clear water bathed Life, and wrapped it in a sacred cradle. Shimmering crystals the size of asteroids grew like mammoth, radiant ice plants along the subterranean shore. An encompassing rapture of Creation played around and through the living rock, each voice adding dimension to the other. Each voice a note connected to other notes which sounded throughout infinity. "Such beauty," he said with awe.

As Yawri descended further, he realized that the rock was not solid at all but was made up of energy surprisingly similar to his own. It just moved more slowly, vibrating with the pulse of the deepest of drums. Rock flowed with its own currents, not unlike the currents of the sea, the air, or the solar winds above. *Each is a reflection of the other.* Atoms vibrated with thought.

"Who are you?" a voice asked in the One Language of all Creation.

Yawri turned his attention to the source of the sound. The wavering shape of a strange creature hovered not five feet away and looked at him expectantly. "I'm a soul from the ethereal oceans," Yawri said, his curiosity piqued. "I heard the song of this place and came to listen." The creature looked dragonfly-like, but wasn't physical, not in the same way as the stone at least. It looked like a thought form.

"I've never seen your kind before," the dragonfly said playfully. "Are you on your way to the land's surface, too?"

"On my way to surface? What do you mean?"

"You know. The soul of Earth creates thought forms. We migrate to the surface to see if there's Life there that we can join with. If we can join with it, we will evolve with it." When Yawri didn't respond the spirit continued. "You know. Life must evolve. If existing Life forms can't accept new thoughts from Earth they'll stop developing and become extinct. It's Earth's law."

"I'm not a thought form," Yawri replied. "I'm a soul."

The dragonfly-spirit sounded perplexed. "I don't know what you're talking about. Earth is the source of all the physical forms here. I don't think you're going to have much luck joining with physical Life on the surface if you don't even know that." The creature went on its way, floating slowly upward toward its destiny.

"Are you confusing thought forms of Earth now?"

Yawri turned. "Muran! What are you doing here?" Yawri's violet glow shimmered with unanchored excitement as he greeted the golden orb he'd met so long ago.

Muran spoke with measured pace. "I understood that you were going to spend time speaking with other planets and learn how they created physically."

Yawri moved closer. "Well, I have. I've visited thousands of them."

"Communicated with them? Or just visited?" Muran asked.

"They've all been so plain," Yawri said as if the answer was obvious. "Just one color or two are slightly interesting, but this one! This planet teems with diverse colors and sounds. Much more interesting, don't you think? What are you doing here? I thought you were helping planets by working with trees."

"I still am. I'm here checking with this planet to see how its thought forms of trees are coming along. I've co-habited with giant red trees in a number of solar systems now, and heard this planet's call. Earth wants help stabilizing its cycles of fire and ice. Trees are great for that."

"What are you talking about? What do trees have to do with fire and ice?" Yawri was perplexed now.

"So many volcanoes erupt, emitting so much ash, that the atmosphere cools and great ice ages are born. The cycle is so extreme that few Life forms can survive. Trees bring stability to air, water and land. The planet is seeking souls with my kind of experience because we help trees."

Yawri was still unclear as his violet orb pulsed with a tinge of blue. "But you're ethereal, like me, how can you affect the physical? It's so dense."

"You're right, ethereal-souls can't balance anything physical by ourselves. You have to be physical to do that. But trees are physical. When we create a union, together we can more effectively bring stability."

"But how? What do you mean, create a union with a tree?" Yawri was more perplexed than ever now.

"You didn't actually talk with many of the planets you visited, did you?" Muran stated rather than asked.

"Well, I didn't stay long on each one. There were so many to see. If I'd stayed somewhere else I wouldn't be here now." Yawri was always in the mood for a debate.

"If you'd stayed longer with any of them, you might have learned that a thought form like the one you spoke with is a part of the soul of this planet. It has no separation from it."

"It did seem confused to see me," Yawri volunteered, as if losing track of exactly what he was debating about.

"Confused was it? It's not really so different from us." Muran answered clearly, although affection showed in his tone. "In a sense, we're thought forms of the Creator just as the spirit you spoke to is a thought form of Earth. Souls like us have been given the free will to create from our thoughts, just as the soul of Earth has."

"Yes, I understand that. We're all different parts of the Creator. But I still don't see how you join with a tree," he said, recalling a point he was trying to make.

Muran was silent for a long moment before he spoke. "It does take a lot of learning to co-create a planet, or even join with a tree. You can't play with physical matter and treat it like a thought form. It's solid. It has mass, density. If you don't know what you're doing, you can become as solid as a stone."

Yawri caught sight of another thought form, this one a dinosaur-like creature floating gently upward with a steady stare back at Yawri. "Yes, I know," he said.

Muran waited for his concentration to return before continuing, his gold a more intense yellow now. "As I join with a tree, I listen. I offer just enough of my energy so that the tree-body can receive what's needed to help more effectively stabilize the atmosphere. It's a connection of pure ethereal to physical energy, a joining of mutual respect. The wisdom we each obtain through the partnership is priceless."

"But how can I nurture physical Creation? I don't want to put my energy into a tree." Yawri found the thought of joining with something so solid distasteful.

Muran considered his question. "Well," he said, pondering. "You don't have to be physical to nurture physical Life." Muran spoke with a measured pace. "The dimensions of Creation are limitless. You don't have to create physically. Purely ethereal realities are very diverse and interesting."

Yawri scanned the surrounding resonating mist and pulsing stone. "But they aren't so vibrant with stark color, so poignant."

Muran seemed to sigh in agreement. "It is beautiful, I know."

"And you just said to impact physical things you need to be physical."

"Not exactly. I said to stabilize a physical atmosphere I need to join with a physical body. All energies have impact. Your ethereal presence can be nurturing. It's a choice." The thought form of a large, feathered lizard eyed them casually as it floated by.

Yawri watched until it disappeared into the earthly mist and then said, "Well, how can I nurture...this?"

Muran was steadfast. "By caring for the planet's development as much as your own. If Earth's Life forms can know the Creator through your ethereal touch as well as through Earth's, all will be enriched. All-That-Is will be enhanced."

"Do you think I can really help?" Yawri seriously considered the effect he could have on physical Creation for the first time.

"Of course. Just listen to the voices around you." Muran paused for a moment to allow Yawri to hear the melodic tones. "Do you hear them? That's why Earth called souls like us here. Earth seeks to expand Creation not only through itself, but through connection with the Creator's other sacred particles." Several seconds passed before Muran added, "If you want to help this planet, then agree to bring the Creator within you to its Life. Doing that will also bring Life to the Creator."

Yawri turned bright violet as excitement bubbled up within him. "I agree," he replied, joy in his voice. "I'll be a gardener, a guardian, of Life."

"Then All will be more," Muran said. "All will be more." Then he paused before adding, "Just be careful."

Yawri strained to see another approaching thought form with renewed curiosity, excited about this new adventure with physical reality.

Chapter 3   *Angels of Ur*

Yawri followed the practice of others and used his thoughts to change his orb-like appearance into another form better suited to serve as gardener and guardian. Energy could be much more effectively sent to aid life forms from etheric arms and legs than from an orb shape, and his etheric body was large, at least twenty-five feet tall and glowing with radiance. His angelic head's cobalt blue eyes were portals to the universe and saw the world as if through infinity. Ears heard sounds; sounds of the first vibrations uttered from Creation, sounds that kindled universes of singing planets, rocks and birds. His own sound blended with the orchestra. The angelic form he chose to manifest suited his work well.

He bent down upon the large outcrop of sandstone on which he stood. It was filled with small nooks and crevices sculpted from a thousand years of falling rain. His translucent arms stretched forth as long sensors toward the Life form of concern. Applying what he had learned over the last hundred years of being a guardian on Earth, one of his shining hands gracefully received communication from the fungus. He wanted to be clear about its needs. After a moment, his other hand gently sent the energy the fungus requested back to it. Poised in anticipation, Yawri was ready to see what would happen.

One of Earth's thought forms would soon come up through the rock at this place, a place which had been carefully prepared. The planet deposited sediments millennia before, and slowly raised them above the sea. Rains were called to sculpt the nutrient-rich stone so that small crevices would provide shelter for Life. Everything was ready.

Small comb-like fungus grew here and as it lived and died it fed vibrant viruses and bacteria, the foundation of plant and animal life. Death constantly gave to life, as life gave to death, in an uninterrupted circle. Now, at this place, Earth was about to birth a thought form that would use the fungus living here to foster more complexity, more dimension. Yawri listened for the planet's request, "Help me fulfill my law of development. Help me bring Life to Life." The request reverberated through his being.

"I connect and call to other dimensions, and ask for help to bring Life forward here." Yawri stood as an open door without the barrier of judgment, to form a link to distant life forms on other planets so they too could touch the new one emerging here.

A chorus filled him and the rock, as if music written long ago just released its sound. Majestic and minute in the same moment, a purple spark appeared in one small nook of the stone. Will the more primitive life form that is already here be able to receive it? Will it be able to accept the new thought? Will evolution or extinction take place? Yawri stared in fascination. As if transformed from spontaneous creation, the new feather-like fungus was grand.

"Ye-es!" Yawri called out with glee as his angelic form soared into the vaporous air and then down into the ground to celebrate with the living rock. "The Creator Itself blesses this place!" he bellowed as he once more rocketed up into the air. He stopped and hovered above the moist, sandstone outcrop to see other beings at work. "How's it going, Aviea?" he called out to another angelic gardener.

"I love this!" Aviea exclaimed as she waved an ethereal hand. She had chosen to manifest a feminine form to better utilize the feminine rather than the masculine part of Earth as Yawri had. "Lichens, liverworts and complex mosses are arriving like an explosion! I never knew co-creation could be so much fun." Delight filled every atom.

"I'm going to go work with the trees now." Yawri gestured toward a distant valley, his face beaming. "Want to come?"

Aviea took a step with her slender etheric body as if to join him, then glanced back down at a lichen. "No, I'm just really fascinated by these plants. They look so simple, but as I work with them it feels like each one is a planet unto itself."

"I know!" Yawri was unable to contain his excitement. "But the trees are so...so simple and complex too. And they're big."

Aviea laughed. "They're big all right." Then she added, "I'll see you later when we meet with Pergaine to learn about the crystals."

"Wouldn't miss it," Yawri replied as he moved away and soared to an immense forest of towering trees. Acres upon acres of woodland passed beneath him until at last he heard the tone which meant that the joining of an ethereal-soul with a tree-spirit was at hand. He descended and although his ethereal body was tall, the two-hundred-foot trees towered over him. "Much more fun than plants," he murmured as he looked up toward the arching red branches and bright green leaves as delicate as fine-grained rice.

One of the older trees called to him. "Come here," it sang. "After all, I can't come to you." Yawri smiled and floated over to it. He hovered a good four feet above the ground to better appreciate the tender ferns that grew there.

"I know you," the tree-being said after thoughtful reflection. "I know you from a time before we had tree-bodies here. You're not lost in physical reality yet, are you? "

"Muran?" Yawri asked, uncertain. "Are you Muran?"

"You remember me!" the tree-being exclaimed. "That's hopeful. I remember you, too, of course. You're the one who liked to visit planets."

Yawri took a step back and tilted his luminous face toward the towering branches. "Not just visit anymore. I've been guiding thought forms into plants on this same planet for ages now."

"So, experienced with physical life now, are you?"

"Experienced enough to know that ethereal-souls benefit from my guidance as they try to join with young tree bodies," Yawri countered triumphantly.

Muran enjoyed the baiting. "Guidance is it? You give them guidance? I thought your kind just gave them nurturing." His humor was increasingly obvious.

"Well, yes. Of course it's nurturing. I just meant..."

"It's okay, Yawri." Muran's voice was deep and relaxed. "Trees like to discuss things, you know. When each lifetime means that you stand together in the same grove for a few thousand years, it's important to have humor." Yawri studied the trunk of the giant tree. Its bark resembled red ripples of water. "Would you like to guide one of my ethereal friends into the tree-body that Earth has prepared for it?" Yawri saw a young redwood tree, perhaps forty feet tall, standing in a shaft of light. "We moved our branches so the sun would find it."

Yawri went over to the small tree and let his angelic form sink into the ground so that his translucent head was near its base. He considered the young tree. "Well, the tree body has been schooled well by the other trees. It seems to know its source for strength comes from Earth, not you," he said with another try at banter.

"The young tree's healthy. We don't begin connecting until a tree is at least a hundred years old, so that it knows its home," Muran said. "It's a little older than that now, and found a place to grow when others did not. We believe that it's mature in its identity with its parent, Earth, but asking others for their opinion seems a good idea. Do you think listening to the opinion of others is a good idea?"

"Of course I do," Yawri replied instantly.

Muran continued with a slow, steady pace. "We must be sure that it's mature enough to maintain its relationship to its parent so that it cannot be overwhelmed by a direct connection to ethereal reality. Please ask it. If it's time, I'd like to witness this guardian-gardener thing I keep hearing about, and see if the rumors are true."

"Rumors?" Yawri asked.

"The wind brings us messages. Who knows what to believe?"

Yawri laughed, then he focused on the young tree and its connection to Earth. "What is your purpose?" he asked it through the voice of his connected caring, the One Language of Creation.

The tree-spirit of the young tree responded. "Our source is Earth. We are cells of this planet. We grow to help other organisms to grow. We help Earth breathe. We hold the waters."

"Do you wish to join with an ethereal-soul?"

"If it will help our parent Earth," the tree-spirit replied.

Yawri rose out of the ground to speak to the ethereal-soul which hovered like a spherical beacon above the tree. It maintained its orb shape because it sought only to join its energy with a tree, not serve as an angelic gardener like Yawri. "Who are you and what is your purpose?"

"I'm an ethereal-soul that has spent many cycles of life and death on a distant planet full of trees. I learned how to join with physical life there without harming it. For me, physical life and death is a part of the uninterrupted continuum, one feeding the other."

"And your purpose?" Yawri wanted to be clear, especially in front of Muran.

"I seek to learn how to nurture the physical life here with my ethereal source, as I learned to do on the other planet."

Yawri listened to the sounds and watched the light which emanated from each source. After a long moment he was satisfied that all was correct. "I'll help you with your first joining on Earth." Yawri moved to a point between the ethereal-soul and the base of the tree, and used his beneficent hands to receive and direct energy. A warm, nurturing glow pulsed from his fingers. "Come and touch the roots of this tree with your essence," he said to the orb, "first with your sound and then with your soul-light. The roots are your doorway in and out of this tree-body. See how fine its roots are, always in motion. Enter them gently, so the tree can receive you." Then Yawri addressed the tree-spirit. "You who are the We, a part of the soul of Earth, receive this being the same way you receive the wind, the water and the sun. Receive it as yet another touch from the outside world to help you become stronger in who you are. It agrees to care for you and help develop Life."

A tone which sounded like a deep base gong, gently, vividly, emanated from the tree. Another tone with the vibrancy of delicate, chiming bells issued from the ethereal-soul. Then, the two tones joined to form a third new sound, so that where only two tones existed before, now an additional third entered the wind. One plus one was three. The branches of the tree developed a faint, yet wondrous yellowish-green glow.

The young tree waved its branches in graceful motion. "The ethereal oceans!" the tree-spirit said. "I feel the ethereal oceans."

The ethereal-soul spoke next. "And you give me vision beyond all of my visions! With you, I know each strand of Life. I can understand the genetic history of every plant and animal!"

"This circle is complete." Yawri moved back with satisfaction. "This new, third life form that you both share is connected to the Creator through an Earthly soul and also through an ethereal-soul." He left them with the excitement of the union, and floated upward to speak with Muran. "So what about these rumors?" he asked the old tree-being.

"Good things are possible," Muran replied affectionately. "It doesn't look evil to me."

"Evil? What's evil?" Yawri had never heard the word.

"Evil is what you have when you separate your actions from the Whole."

Yawri chuckled. "It's impossible to separate from the Whole. You've been in a log too long." He scanned the grove. "Other than developing a strange sense of humor, how has it been going for you? I haven't seen you in so long."

"Don't be such a stranger, then," Muran pretended to scold. "You could have called to me any time. More and more of these joinings take place. The red trees cover almost half of the land's surface now. We must cover three-fourths of the land before the stabilization of fire and ice is complete. After that point, many of us will leave. But don't worry. I'm planning on staying for the duration."

"Oh, I was worried." Yawri teased in return.

Muran continued softly. "We are very pleased, very pleased with the work."

Yawri had the slightest tension in his voice. "The ethereal-souls that are coming to blend with the tree-bodies are able to enter them without much difficulty then?"

"Well, I wouldn't say that." Muran chuckled. "Some of the beings are more experienced with joining than others. A few arrive thinking they can do it the same way they did on another planet. They learn quickly that they can't. The tree-bodies here are well prepared for us. If you try to dominate them they simply kick you out."

"That seems for the best." Yawri gazed again at the glowing branches of the young tree as they moved with the air. "If you're going to be a guest in someone's home, you should follow house rules."

"We try to respect a sacred place." Muran was steadfast. "If you ever need a reminder, come and visit."

Yawri's aura ruffled. He looked away to see a pond where brilliant yellow blossoms of water lilies shone like miniature suns atop tender, green stems. "I'm not likely to need reminding that this is a sacred place."

"Just a thought," Muran said. "A harmless thought. I've seen forgetfulness on other planets, and it can lead to disaster."

"Well, not from me." Yawri started moving away, already anticipating the next adventure. "I've got to go. Some other guardians are working to help bring ethereal-souls into crystal-bodies and I want to see how it's done."

"Minerals, eh? Well, if you like to live in rocks." Then Muran added, "Don't forget to slow down sometime. Do you good to spend a few lifetimes as a tree."

"Not likely," Yawri said and cast a glance back.

"Right. In your case inside rocks would be better. They live millions of years, these tree bodies only live a few thousand. Yes. I think rocks are best for you. Teach you patience."

Yawri moved more rapidly.

"Why not? You've got eternity," Muran boomed.

"Too much to do!" Yawri called as he accelerated upward and let the fog swirl around and through his angelic form. He danced with the tops of the trees, and he touched them with exuberant regard before he sped away for his rendezvous.

When Yawri approached the meeting place he saw Aviea. The high cheeks and straight dark hair that she'd chosen for her angelic form projected inner strength. Another being, he noticed, hovered near an outcrop of mica schist. "Hello!" he called in greeting. "How goes your co-creation?"

Aviea looked up as he neared. "Look! I told you that Pergaine is helping ethereal-souls who are learning to join with the mineral form." He decelerated and came to rest near them as Aviea continued talking. "The souls seeking to join with them are coming from a planet whose surface is completely covered with crystals and minerals. Pergaine says that these beings have learned how to help balance the electrical nature of planets. See the crystal-bodies?" She pointed toward a large family of the deepest green emerald crystals, glistening with mist.

"They're wonderful." Yawri was in rapt attention. "Like a rich garden inside stone." He watched Pergaine, who'd also manifested a feminine nature for her form, send and receive energy to and from the emeralds. "How do these crystal-bodies work with the Earth's electric fields?"

Pergaine finished her work in silence, then rose. "It's actually pretty simple." Reflecting her disposition, she'd chosen a mature, fair-haired, sharp-featured shape for her angelic body. "Earth created the crystals from fluid. Even though the crystal bodies appear solid now, they carry memory of their fluid state. So the ethereal-souls that blend with them can work the fluid multidimensionality of time. That gives them the doorway to work with the planet's electrical balance."

"Oh. I knew that." Yawri leaned toward Aviea. "What planet has she come from?"

Pergaine seemed a little surprised. "Oh. Sorry. I've worked on many planets."

Yawri looked chagrined. "I've visited a lot of them."

Pergaine continued with a crisp, feminine voice. "I spent eons working with physical reality on other planets and know how much there is to learn. The first time I tried to help join an ethereal-soul with the spirit of a crystal mountain I ended up scorching some trees."

"Ouch." Yawri had a pained expression on his face.

She smiled gingerly. "The trees forgave me and I forgave myself. They had the wisdom to know that sometimes even a well intentioned touch can do harm. I had the experience to know how to help heal them. How else can we learn?"

Aviea chimed in. Her etheric form had wider-spaced eyes and long fingers designed to see and manipulate the fine energies needed to work with small plants. "I told Yawri that you knew about the crystal islands coming to the surface."

"You haven't seen crystal islands?" Pergaine asked, puzzled.

"No, but I've seen the crystal caverns deep within the planet. Are they on the surface now?" Yawri sounded rueful. "Been too busy with trees."

Pergaine spoke as though making a pronouncement. "I know an island that will show you more than you can learn from me. It's filled with crystals. Emerald, apatite, celestite, all kinds of quartz. You've got to see it." Although her voice was crisp, her joy was evident.

One glance at Aviea's and Yawri's eager eyes was all that was required to confirm that they were ready to go, and the angelic trio flew off through low clouds. When they reached the ocean that lay between their common working ground and the island, they flew down to its surface, almost skimming the waves to look into its rich repository. After an hour's entertaining flight they saw the island. Its crown of crystal peaks poked into the cloud bank as if it purposefully wore them like a shroud.

"This is it," Pergaine said through the wind as they slowed and descended toward a five-foot-round, pale pink, hexagonal crystal near the island's center. After they landed, Yawri approached it and gazed at its glassy surface. The mineral faces reflected the images that surrounded it like a two-way mirror. Within the crystal, phantom-like shadows and minute bubbles appeared to float as if suspended in a sea.

A multitude of tones emanated from the crystal. As they studied it, a deep voice called out from behind them. "Welcome, Pergaine!" it boomed, and they turned to see another gardener step out from behind a clear quartz taller than he was. Then they saw yet another gardener, stooped near the base of the clear crystal outcrop, but he did not look up.

"Gamon, it's good to see you." Pergaine exclaimed, obviously surprised to see him. "I thought you were working with the animals on the mainland. What are you doing out here?"

"I heard the new sounds on the winds, so Shahitam and I came to see what was going on." He pointed to his friend communicating with the large clear quartz, then his eyes moved across Aviea and Yawri.

Aviea spoke first. "I'm Aviea. I've worked mostly with plants." Then she shot a glance toward Yawri who was beginning to move toward the clear quartz. She cleared her throat.

"Oh. Hi." He spoke distractedly. "I'm Yawri. I help guide souls into trees." As Gamon moved closer it was evident that he was taller than the others, and the white hair he'd chosen for his angelic form gave him a distinguished air. "As Pergaine pointed out, I work with animals, mammals mostly. Some are able to receive ethereal-souls, just like the great trees and some of these crystals. Earth is creating more and more life forms that have the ability to join with souls."

Yawri reached the massive quartz and began to look into it. "Not too close!" Shahitam exclaimed. "I'm trying to get clear information about this crystal's abilities." Shahitam bent back down and returned to work. The whole party looked at Gamon with curiosity.

"Oh." Gamon sounded apologetic. "Shahitam tends to be a little serious at times."

"He's abrupt." Pergaine was unruffled.

Shahitam straightened and his ethereal form quivered with silver iridescence. "I apologize for my abruptness, of course, my friends," he said evenly. "It's just that crystals are extremely powerful. They impact gravity as well as the electrical balance of planets. Working with them is not like working with plants or trees." He cast a glance toward Aviea and Yawri. Obviously he'd been listening. "If you make a mistake with crystals, you can harm an entire planet."

"I see," Pergaine said coolly.

Shahitam stood like an angelic monument. "I'm interested in finding out what abilities these crystals have. They might be the key to unlocking great potential for this planet."

"Potential?" Yawri was confused by the statement. "It's developing fine. What potential?"

Shahitam gazed at Yawri, then spoke simply. "Why, potential for fulfilling the Creator's command to go forth and co-create, of course." Yawri still looked confused but didn't say more.

Gamon ran an ethereal hand through his luminous white hair and added, "We came to this island because the crystals here are making tones that are carried around the world by the winds, and into the universe too. Earth moved them from deep caverns to its surface so they could sing about the abundance of this planet, and call more and more Life to it. This world is becoming a beacon for Life."

"Yes, quite a beacon for Life." Shahitam said in a low monotone. The mist suddenly parted to the right where several other outcrops glowed.

"How do the crystals work with gravity?" Aviea asked, trying to figure it out.

Shahitam, as if returning from a vision, spoke with a commanding voice. "By altering the degree of soul-light to soul-sound, of course."

"Altering what?" Yawri asked, trying to remember what Muran had told him about it long ago. The mist lifted to the left, and more crystal families shone in the distance.

Shahitam drew up. "When we bring soul-light, gravity decreases because our light is completely ethereal, weightless. When we bring soul-sound, gravity increases because sound is physical. The beings that do this work must work very closely with the soul of Earth itself, and as you know, the soul of Earth is touched by the hand of the Creator."

Aviea joined Yawri at the crystal of Shahitam's interest. Aviea peered gently into it as Yawri moved a sensitive hand across its shiny, faceted surface. "But from my journeys deep into the planet long ago," Yawri said as he dropped his hand, "I know that crystal caves there were stabilizing Earth centuries before I came. Why is it that the planet has decided to bring them to the surface now?"

Aviea and Yawri stepped back as Shahitam casually moved between them and the crystal. Then he moved toward them as if it would make the explanation clearer. He answered, "Because life forms on Earth's skin are becoming advanced enough to receive from them, Yawri. Earth is providing more and more life forms that are capable of blending with ethereal-souls. The great trees are one example but there are mastodon, sea turtle, great birds, whales, the sabertooth cat, wolf and bear-like creatures all of whose bodies are now mature enough to seek union with us. Earth is bringing great crystals to its skin so that all can hear the sound of both, the liquid ethereal oceans and the physical planet together. As ethereal-souls and their physical forms hear them, they will each be reminded of their true sources. That's important, don't you think?"

"Of course." Yawri nodded almost automatically. "Everything needs to remember its source."

Shahitam looked into the depths of the crystal. "Yes," he said pensively. "I think crystals will hold the key to this planet." The rest of the party gave no response. "Great glory for our mission is possible here," he murmured. The others looked on as his smile reflected back to them from the smooth crystal face.

Chapter 4 **Angels among Humans**

Shallow warm seas and wetlands covered low-lying ground
like a soft blanket covers a newborn child. One drop of water
from the vast swamps contained a billion microscopic forms of
Life. Marshes offered nurturing havens for freshly budding
Creation. Yawri flew gently past the expansive wetlands to
enter the familiar mist-shrouded treetops. He stopped above a
dew-drop-filled evergreen and movement caught his eye.
Another angelic gardener hovered over tall grass below, and he
called out.

"Pergaine!" Her tall, radiant body rose from its inspection
of some large-grained granite and a smile graced her fine lips.
"How goes the work?" Yawri boomed, happy to see her again.

"Come here. Look at this." She responded studiously.
Yawri's misty body flowed down through the branches to hover
near her. "What do you think of it?"

He saw depressions in the rich soil and studied them.
"Footprints."

"I know that. But of what?"

He stooped to look closer. "They're not from an ape. Look
how the toes are formed."

"I believe these are from human bodies," Pergaine
ventured, her hands gently clasped together below her waist.
"I've been told of them."

"Told of them? What have you heard?" Yawri stood up to
face her, feeling like he'd missed out on something.

"I understand that these are the physical Life forms that
are being prepared for us," she replied with an uncharacteristic
tone of anticipation.

"For us?" Yawri looked down at the sodden footprints
again and back up to radiant Pergaine.

"Evidently. The transformation of Earth's Life is proceeding so well through our guardianship that provision is being
made for a physical way for our work to continue here. You
know that the vibratory rate of this planet is continually
changing. All new planets do. It's congealing and solidifying. As
ethereal beings we are getting less and less able to affect the
increasingly dense Life here." She said with an edge of tension
in her voice.

Yawri's face showed concern. "Sure. I know."

Pergaine continued in her crisp voice. "Our days of helping are numbered. If we don't find a physical form like the souls who have joined with the great crystals or trees have, we might as well leave."

"True." Yawri's mouth showed a twist of sorrow. "I do sense the coming of that time, and it's sad to think that my work here will have to come to an end. I briefly visited with some ethereal-souls that are leaving even now because they say their time here is past, that Earth is becoming too solid. Angels are leaving. But you say these human bodies are being prepared for us? What makes you think that?"

A shaft of sunlight broke through the clouds and turned the long grass bright green. "You remember Gamon, the friend of mine you met at the crystal Atlantean island? The one who works to join souls with the higher animals? He's been working with mastodons lately."

"Sure. I remember him." Yawri nodded, recalling.

Pergaine continued briskly, sunlight flashing in her misty hair. "He says he's heard from guardians who have been watching the humans develop. He's heard that unions have taken place with similar forms on other planets and that because the bodies are mobile, the work of guardians like us can continue as planets solidify."

Yawri felt a curious need to explain why he'd heard nothing on the topic. "I have spent my time working with the trees. The new species that are coming have kept me very busy. But I guess I could be talking more with the other guardians, too. This possibility of uniting with a physical form is fascinating. I haven't considered it for myself, but it works for the ethereal-souls that have joined with the great trees and crystals." *Is there a way for me to keep working here?* He glanced down noticing a delicate lichen dripping with dew and wondered if Aviea, his friend who loved the small plants, was facing similar concerns. "But taking a physical form myself? I don't know."

"But Yawri, what if the Creator is giving us the opportunity to continue work here? What if these physical bodies are being prepared for us?" Pergaine's ethereal face showed a struggle with the question. "These human forms can swim in water, swing through air and run on ground. They don't stay fixed to one place like the trees or crystals. They don't have to wait for Life to come to them, they can go wherever Life is and help it." They stared down at the footprint again. Pergaine shook her head.

"Have you seen them?" Yawri tried to narrow the subject to something more tangible.

"No, Gamon has," She said with certainty, clearly more comfortable speaking about Gamon than about her own feelings. "But as I said, he's never joined with one himself. He's heard of beings on other planets that have." The two guardians peered into the forest, and tried to see where the footprints led.

Yawri spoke absently. "What about Aviea? She spends a lot of time looking at the soil and small plants. Has she seen any sign?"

"The last time I spoke with her was down in the waterwoods," Pergaine turned back to Yawri. "She told me she'd seen footprints, but like me, she hadn't seen actual humans." When he gave no response, she followed Yawri's gaze back down the path. "Why don't we ask Gamon if he knows where we can observe some humans? I know where he's working."

Yawri brightened at the thought of a mini-adventure. "Let's go!" he exclaimed simply.

As they moved away she added as if to herself, "I hadn't considered it myself until I saw the footprints."

Yawri was absorbed in his own thoughts as they both took to the air. *Muran's tree-body can't walk, but human-bodies can.*

They ascended into the hovering clouds and within minutes came down into a broad valley filled with tall, leafy plants and thick prairie grass. "Gamon!" Pergaine called out in her soprano voice. "Gamon, is that you?" The angelic being turned toward them.

"Pergaine. Greetings! How goes the work?" he called out.

Yawri and Pergaine settled near him. "Our visit has everything to do with how the work is going," she replied, getting right to the point. "You remember Yawri?" The two bowed heads in greeting.

"I work mostly with the trees," Yawri said by way of reintroduction.

"I remember." Gamon had an air of certainty, which was complemented by his chosen manifestation of a white beard. "I've had good success here lately," he waved a wide, etheric hand to the broad valley, "helping many souls blend with larger mammals. The mastodon is one of my favorites. Did you know that they not only use the One Language, but can talk to each other using physical tones? They make very low tones that travel through the ground. They can communicate with each other across miles that way." Gamon's excitement revealed his fascination at working with large mammals.

Yawri turned eagerly to hear more, but Pergaine interrupted. "Gamon," she began with a serious tone. "Yawri and I saw human footprints today. Have you heard any more about them?"

Gamon lowered his voice. "I've heard guardians talking a lot about them, all right. But I'm not convinced that any of us knows much about them."

"What do you mean?" Pergaine prodded, her form shimmering in the morning light.

Gamon considered the question and then began to explain. "They haven't been studied enough yet. The human has a head with eyes, ears and a mouth that sits upon a torso, has arms for working and legs too. Similar to us, except they're solid."

"They're created to look like us?" Yawri, his curiosity aroused, was filled with questions. He glanced around as if expecting to see one.

Gamon addressed the question. "It might be that we both chose forms that are best suited for what we do. They search, they gather, they tend. Just like we do. What better form would you have?"

Pergaine wanted more clarity. "But it does seem quite an amazing coincidence, doesn't it? I mean, if they weren't created for us, why would they look so similar to the forms we adopted to work here? It's as though they're a physical imitation of us."

"Maybe they are being created for us." Gamon cast his gaze to the ground, then to the familiar herd of mastodon he had been tending before addressing the fact known by all of the guardians. "It's just hard to be certain because the vibratory rate of the planet has become so dense, that no one can get clear communication with Earth anymore. It has all become so physical."

Pergaine followed the turn of his bearded face. Both were quiet a moment as they watched the grazing mastodon as if trying to discern some answer there. Yawri interrupted their thoughts. "But I'm ethereal, not physical, and it's getting more and more painful for me to lower my vibratory rate to work with things that are so solid." All eyes jerked to the sound from the sharp, hoarse cry of a monkey as they saw it being carried away by a bird with a twelve-foot wing span.

The three considered their situation as the bird flew over the ridge with its prey. "Gamon," Pergaine said as she recovered her focus, "have you actually seen any of them?"

Gamon seemed hesitant but admitted, "I know where a tribe of humans lives, probably those footprints you saw. Would it help you to see them? I can take you there." He volunteered.

Pergaine replied without hesitation. "We were hoping you could do that." Yawri nodded in rapid agreement and the trio took to the air, flying above cypress trees whose branches were curtained with long strands of airy moss. A large white egret dove into a clear pond and left it with a thrashing, silver fish. Minutes later they came to an area of the forest where the trees were more widely spaced. They stopped to hover among the branches of a deciduous tree, and Gamon pointed down through the leaves. "There they are." He almost whispered as if they were spying rather than observing. "Let's stay hidden so we don't disturb them."

Pergaine said clearly, "I count fourteen." Then she added, with slight distaste, "They're so short."

"Kind of like apes," Gamon added. "Except they have very little hair and when they walk they stand erect." Though their bodies were naked, two had slung pouches made from animal skin over their shoulders which evidently held food they had just gathered.

"I see two types of bodies," Yawri commented, moving forward for a better view.

"Yes," Gamon nodded agreeably. "Just like all the mammals, they express both the mother and father characteristics of the planet. They connect to co-create." Serendipitously, two of the bodies fell down together. "There, see that? Just like all the animals. They're mating." Soon the two were coupled in a rolling, laughing, rhythmic embrace.

"But," Pergaine mused, "I've seen animals mate before. They don't laugh. These humans are having fun."

"They have humor and are intelligent." Gamon revealed that he'd spent a good deal more time than this observing them.

"They seem so eager for each other," Yawri said.

Gamon attempted further explanation. "They're very few in population, and to survive as a species they must multiply. It takes nine full cycles of the moon for them to give birth, and then the infants are helpless for years. If they were not eager, I don't think they'd survive. Unlike other animals that can mate only at certain times of the year, humans can anytime. Earth obviously wishes them to multiply."

Pergaine looked down thoughtfully, her sharp eyes clearly focused. "I don't see how we could connect our energy with them. They're so...diminutive."

"I know." Gamon replied with a reasoned tone. "Human bodies the size of mastodons would make more sense to me. These are not a quarter of our height. How could we do anything with such a small body?" The beings watched the tribe for an hour before returning to their work.

"I'd like to learn more about these creatures," Yawri admitted as the guardians began to move back through the trees.

Then, as the group sailed through the low clouds Pergaine spoke up, "Gamon, if you get further information about these humans, please call for me."

"Same for me," Yawri echoed.

"I will," Gamon declared as they each turned to go back to their own enterprise. "Aviea came by last week. She's interested, too." Before Yawri could ask about her, Gamon called a common, parting greeting as he soared away. "Create with Creator!"

"Create with Creator," Pergaine and Yawri replied in tandem as they moved through the treetops, each with new and serious thoughts on their minds.

Over the next centuries guardians continued to tend the planet, and species flourished with unprecedented rapidity. Even though pulses of extinction took place, the timing of them assured that the information learned went back to Earth, and ever more capable thought forms were sent forth. Life evolved.

But even as the uninterrupted cycle of Creation continued around the ethereal guardians, they slowly, painfully became a smaller part of it. Aviea and Pergaine spoke to each other as they stood on a basalt cliff which overlooked a waterfall cascading into a fern-rich gorge. The sound of cascading water mixed its mist with a thousand smells, each the fragrance of a different plant.

Aviea swept her dark hair away from her broad eyes with a smooth and graceful gesture. "I remember that when I first came here the ground itself seemed a part of the ethereal oceans. Now I can swim in a lake, but not through the ground or rock. I can't descend to join with the underground lakes and caverns. I can hardly hear the voices of my plants."

Pergaine watched a small, bristle-haired rodent scurry through the underbrush. "I know. I have to keep willing myself to be denser so I can continue my work here, and look," she held her arm up for Aviea to see. "My body's no longer a translucent mist, it's more like a silty stream. I can't keep this up."

Aviea's long black hair framed an increasingly opaque, bronze face. "Let's take a break from co-creation for a while," she said. "Let's visit the crystal islands. The crystals sing, they recharge me. They remind me of the ethereal soul that I am."

Pergaine stood up at the suggestion, happy to let the waterfall's mist fill her chest. "The souls that live inside the crystals are so lucky. They bring ethereal reality into crystallized fluid. I wish those human bodies could do that." The two guardians left their perch and sailed over the water, but the joy of past journeys was absent. The trip to be recharged had become too routine. They approached the healing island with uncertainty. More and more ethereal-souls were congregating there. They came to rest next to Gamon and Yawri, who were not at all surprised by their arrival.

"It's time to leave Earth. It's continuing to congeal, as it must." Aviea and Pergaine heard another angelic gardener say as they settled down. "Altering my form from an orb to this limbed shape when I came to work here was good. But I can't continually densify my own ethereal body to stay. I'm afraid I'll become so physical that I could hurt the ethereal connection to my own source."

"We could leave, but what about all the Life here? Who will be its guardian?" Yawri asked.

"And what about the human bodies Earth has prepared for us?" another being asked. "They are multiplying quickly, and appear ready for us to join with them."

"I don't know that they are ready," the first speaker countered. "We could leave, give them time to develop, and come back to seek a union when we know they're ready. I think we should leave."

A very tall being that shimmered with layered, silver opalescence joined in the discussion. "I am Shahitam, and I too feel the struggle of the choice."

Gamon alerted his friends. "He's here! The one who worked with the crystals."

Shahitam raised the volume of his voice so that all could listen. "I don't know what choice will be made here. That is for each of you to decide, but I can share what I have learned on other planets." He paused and all conversation stilled. "I have blended with human forms on them." A murmuring commotion rolled through the assemblage.

"I didn't know he'd done that." Gamon's said, clearly surprised.

Shahitam raised a vibrant hand to regain attention. "I say to you that from my experience the human-bodies here are ready for what must be done. Earth itself tells me this."

Pergaine's voice cut in. "How can you be sure? If the timing isn't right we could harm them, and we haven't been able to get definite communication for ages."

Shahitam persisted. "I can speak clearly to it because of my experience. Listen. Listen to what I share with you." All guardians turned to him, their voices stilled once more. "Earth needs our continued help to develop as is needed for Creation. We were given the Creator's command to go forth and learn and come back and touch It. Who among you would go against the Creator's command?"

Pergaine's voice called out again. "But because things are getting so dense, the only way to continue our work here seems to be to join with a physical form. But human bodies are young. Are you sure they are mature enough to maintain connection with their own source, Earth and an ethereal-soul too?"

"You know that to blend with physical forms is difficult, and now that the planet has densified to the point that it is uncomfortable for you, do you want to abandon Earth in its moment of need? From my knowledge of blending with the humanoids on other worlds, I know the gift the Creator offers us through Earth. And these bodies are mature enough to fill the need. You must understand, that by being mobile in *physical* form we can take our ethereal connection to every mountain, river, sea, plant and animal. Not just some Life forms, but *all* Life forms of Earth, can have the capacity to know All-That-Is. They can know it through the planet's soul and through our touch as well. How can such a goal be ill-advised?"

Another being, called Tisbero, spoke up. His ethereal body's long, reddish hair and fiery skin reflected his person-ality. "It is not the goal I am concerned about," he said in a firm, clear voice. "Only the timing of it. Joining with physical reality is very different from tending it."

Shahitam addressed him with cool probing. "Are you sure that you don't fear for your own comfort?" he asked. "It won't be comfortable. Learning to share space with another is never comfortable." Tisbero brushed his fingers through his hair and stewed on the question. "Besides, you just move a small portion of your energy into a human body. Just enough to have a connection with it. You as a soul are still free to come and go as you please. It's just a small part of your energy, that's all." The assemblage considered his words.

"You see the human bodies multiply," Shahitam continued gently, his silver opalescence rippling as he spoke. "Are the ethereal-souls who blended with the great crystals and trees leaving the planet? No. They accepted the physical bodies Earth prepared for them so that they could stay and continue to supply the Creator's ethereal connection for physical Life. They have chosen to nurture the physical manifestation of the Creator Itself. We can, too."

Gamon spoke up, his voice carrying across the crowd. "You say that you have successfully blended with bodies on other planets. How do the bodies here compare with those?"

"They are comparable. We have had our learning together and have each moved on. I don't know how else to tell you," Shahitam replied with an edge of exasperation. "I know the bodies here are ready because, feeling the pain that this planet has at the thought of us leaving, I put my pain aside and with the courageous willingness of two other guardians, I guided them in the blending with two humans."

"They joined with humans? No!" a startled voice cried.

"Yes!" Shahitam confirmed. "Yes! Do you think I would counsel you to do what I did not know to be right? I sought permission. I asked Earth and the humans, naturally. I only seek to aid what is best for the Creator we love." Shahitam eyed the crowd as if checking for anyone that would challenge his love for the Creator. Seeing no challenge, he continued.

"The human-spirit within the body welcomed their touch. Welcomed it! And why not? They were ready to receive the touch of the Creator through the ethereal oceans. Now, the human bodies know the Creator through Earth *and* ethereal-souls. We can once again speak with all the Life of Earth through the body's own human-spirit. Those voices are not only clear, they are once again crystal-clear. That is how I know the blending is right." The faces received his words as if they were rain upon parched soil. "And, the two human bodies are thriving. They are thriving because they are connected to the waters of the universe and the fire of Earth in the same moment. They are blending these poles into a new strength in their bellies. The joined humans now have the courage to seek new ways of doing things, new ways of asking questions. They're able to solve problems. I say to you that if you choose to abandon Earth after it has prepared these bodies for us then you are as the gardener who only picks fruit without regard for laboring with the soil."

Gamon turned to address his friends, a hand kneading his bearded chin as if trying to find solace there. "What do you think?"

"I know I can no longer hear the voice of Earth like he describes," Tisbero fired, joining the discussion as he swept back his ethereal red hair.

Aviea spoke next. "I love to hear the voices of plants, to know which ones need to grow where and next to what, and what healing they can be used for. I hardly understand their tones anymore."

Pergaine cast a gaze to her opaque feet, then raised her sharp eyes. "But what if the bodies aren't mature enough? We could overwhelm them with ethereal energy and break their connection to Earth. Then what?"

Yawri turned his attention from Shahitam to Gamon. "To leave the creations we have helped bring forth is so painful," he said almost mournfully. "I don't think it's right to abandon our connection, but I don't know what to do."

Tisbero was fully engaged with the foursome now. "I don't know either," he said, almost angrily. "No being can look upon this jewel and say that our work here has not been good. It grieves me that my participation may have to end. I just don't know if the human bodies are mature enough yet."

Separate groups of beings congregated, but the questions were the same. Many sought out Shahitam's counsel, for he was one who had joined with the humanoids on other planets before. A group went off with him to see the two humans which were in union with the two etheric-souls that he spoke of. Most left the healing island with more uncertainty than when they arrived.

More years passed, and slowly, but clearly, the choice of many became evident. The number of souls who joined with human-bodies was increasing.

Yawri, Aviea, Pergaine, Gamon, and Tisbero, invariably drawn together by their common concern for the Life of Earth and their escalating desire to remain with it, met often over the years. Early one spring after they had just returned from watching a tribe of humans, most of whom had now formed a union with angelic souls, they discussed what to do. Pergaine was first to speak as they came to rest on a promontory that overlooked a grassy plain filled with rhinoceros-like creatures. "The humans that have partnered with souls are growing much taller than the others."

Gamon spoke his thoughts, his white hair shining more dimly than in years past. "Yes, and they do solve problems more easily than the others. Did you see how one of them used the broad leaves to make a shelter? The way she formed branches for a frame and tied on leaves?"

Aviea chimed in. "I've heard that the souls who have joined with them can once again communicate clearly with plants, with Earth. Just like Shahitam said they would."

"I'd love to be able to hear Earth's voice clearly again. The gap between us is so wide now." Pergaine's sense of loss lowered her voice.

Yawri looked away from the roving herd and toward his companions. "Did you notice how that female human presented herself to the male with the radiance? He'd obviously joined with an ethereal-soul. He was larger, and more confident. The female wanted his children, all right."

"It's certain that the females desire to mate with males who have formed a union with a soul," Pergaine agreed. "For a Life form to survive, it must develop. It's Earth's law that all Life must develop. The females are just seeking to fulfill that law by arousing the males who are superior."

A soft wind blew, its touch seeking to greet their forms. "I can't deny it," Aviea turned to face the group. "The humans who have formed a union with souls are prospering."

"And I can't deny that the souls like us that have joined with them are able to communicate with Earth again," Tisbero added, arms folded tightly across his broad chest. Above their heads, sunlight painted the clouds like foaming sea.

Yawri's spry form swayed in place. "I can't imagine leaving. I saw thousands of planets before I found this one. Where else is there so much Life?" A stronger breeze rippled the grass, and color flickered from dark to lightest green.

Gamon spoke with reason. "Perhaps it is time to seek a union. Perhaps the humans are ready to become human-beings. The Creator knows I've helped a lot of souls who were experienced with physical forms on other planets join with animals here. I just never thought I would be one of them. I've always been happy just being ethereal."

Yawri spoke again. "But they must have had a first time, too. How else will we be able to continue our work?"

Tisbero raised his fiery eyes, his angelic form reflecting a pale, reddish tint in the late afternoon light. "It's time. The bodies look like they're ready. Let's seek out a tribe and ask permission to join with a human body." All nodded in agreement. A saber-toothed cat streaked toward a bull and scattered the massive rhinos into a thunderous stampede.

Chapter 5   *Joining with humans*

Yawri decided to seek union with a male. It seemed to him that the males traveled more freely, enjoyed the act of creating offspring, yet were not slowed down by pregnancy or nursing. "I don't think I'm ready to join with a body that makes a baby," he told Aviea as he parted from their earnest discussion.

"Suit yourself," she replied. "I think it will be fascinating and very creative."

Yawri felt both excitement and trepidation as he hovered in the high branches of an ancient cedar. Far below, he watched a human animal wade into a rushing creek to catch fish with his bare hands. The hunter stood perfectly still and waited for one of the larger fishes to swim between his fingers so that he could quickly close his grasp. "This one seems intelligent," Yawri murmured.

With sudden movement the hunter grabbed a fish, but it moved so swiftly he caught it near its tail. He jerked it out of the water and tossed it up on the bank where it flopped violently as it struggled to re-enter the stream. In one stride the human gained the bank, picked up the thrashing fish and dashed its head against a rock. He smiled joyously at his good fortune. Yawri moved slowly and silently down through the branches.

As the etheric gardener hovered in plain sight a few feet in front of the great tree, the human looked up and the smile faded from his lips. Although Yawri's opaque body stood over twenty-five feet tall, the hunter exhibited no fear. With a deliberate gesture, he gently raised the glistening fish as if thanking Yawri for his good fortune. Yawri knew that the catch was completely due to the human's own skill, but uncertain about the appropriate response, he nodded gracefully.

Yawri decided to try to communicate telepathically as was his custom with all of the plants and animals, for they all understood the One Language. "You are a good hunter," he endeavored.

The human stared at Yawri for several seconds, to the point that Yawri was becoming concerned, but then he replied, "Others in my tribe have talked of you giants which shine like the stars. You are different from the great spirits who live inside the trees and clear rocks." He tipped his head toward the towering cedars without taking his eyes off the apparition. "You travel freely, like us."

"I travel freely," Yawri replied, moving a little closer.

"I am Kunuta, a great hunter." He held up the long, silver fish proudly for him to see once more.

"I am called Yawri and I come from the stars." He tilted his luminous head upward.

Kunuta followed Yawri's glance at the sky, but then brought his eyes back down to the ground. He tapped his callused, bare foot on the fertile soil. "Earth is my source."

Yawri responded thoughtfully, "The stars are my source. I come from them, just as Earth's great soul does."

Kunuta looked perplexed, then said, "You and Earth are of the same source?

"Yes, the same. We are both particles of the Great Creator."

Kunuta laid the fish down carefully on the stream's bank, and standing proudly, turned his sun-tanned face upward. "What do you wish of the We?"

He knows he is part of the one body of Earth. He's mature enough. Yawri moved closer. "I seek to bring my connection with the Creator to you, and to unite the law of Creation with Earth's law of development."

"I live in the law of development," the human replied. "We must continue to develop or we'll become extinct. We must blend with the Earth's new thoughts."

Yawri struggled to be patient, and not show how excited he was. "By living together, joined as a human and a being, we will both become more. I seek to help you and your tribe develop." *I'm going to be able to continue working with Earth.*

Kunuta turned his head in the direction of his tribe's camp and then back. "This would be a good thing." After worrying his lip for a moment, added, "I have seen that males who have joined with your kind are preferred by females."

"I see the same," Yawri said.

Kunuta still stared up at Yawri's imposing angelic form. "What must I do to become like other humans who are developing with your kind?"

"We join together," Yawri said as he flowed further down the small hill, "in the same way that the big tree and it's ethereal-soul do." He nodded toward the cedars and redwoods nearby.

Kunuta scanned the wooden giants and turned back to Yawri. "To be such as the great trees is beyond hope." His eyes glistened with excitement. "Let us do this thing."

"In time." Now that Kunuta agreed, Yawri felt less sure. "In time."

They shared many hours communicating, and Yawri observed Kunuta for several days. With each visit, Kunuta became more eager to join energies. At last, Yawri felt he had enough information to know how to enter the human with a small part of his essence. The souls which entered the trees did so through the tree roots; however, human bodies received ethereal energy through the top of the head. Yawri wanted to be sure he did this right, and was cautious about the human's brain because it, like he, was electrical in nature and he did not wish to harm it.

"Kunuta," he called out, a month after their first meeting. The human looked up expectantly as he dug tubers among fleshy leaves. *Have I thought this through enough? Once I've joined energies, what will it mean?* Kunuta stepped toward him. "Let us seek the joining," Yawri said.

Kunuta stepped forward, a tuber still in his hand. "You are from the same source as Earth. With you I will develop and be strong."

"We will both be stronger," Yawri replied as he moved slowly over the human's head and after a long moment, gently connected a small tendril of his essence to the body's energy system. Yawri felt the tender filament move down and connect to the electrical circuitry in the human.

It was as if a window opened for Kunuta and Yawri in the same moment. As Yawri looked through Kunuta's eyes he saw a scene so rich in physical texture, sound and color that he was stunned. Kunuta was surprised, too, and neither of them noticed that he dropped the tuber. Kunuta glimpsed the vast ethereal oceans opening before him, and he saw his own beloved Earth floating in it like a sparkling white and blue jewel. His eyes grew wider and wider until Yawri, suddenly alarmed, decreased the size of the ethereal connection to the Universes. "I mustn't overwhelm you with such a flood of awareness that it weakens your relationship to your own source," he said. "We go slowly, Kunuta. We will let the seed grow slowly. We will join cautiously, respectfully." Kunuta seemed awestruck.

Yawri monitored the windows of perception that he opened for Kunuta carefully for months. Each week the amount of energy he was able to join with the human grew. *Because of you, I won't have to leave the planet. I will continue my work.*

Through Kunuta, Yawri slowly touched and connected with every life form, every thought form, of Earth, and he beamed with satisfaction. *The knowledge of physical Creation is now mine, and because I see physical Creation from the inside out, I will be more able to...to do what? To tend it. I will be more able to tend it.*

Two months later, Yawri, Aviea, and Tisbero stood in their angelic forms at the base of a waterfall. Except for the small, woven threads of ethereal energy that connected them with their humans like fine, silver cords of water, they looked the same. The guardians watched the falling waterfall massage the rocks and although their hard surfaces looked impenetrable, the rock was destined to be dissolved. Beyond the swirling pool, the water flowed more gracefully and a lioness took a long drink before she disappeared into the dark undergrowth.

Tisbero's eye caught the sight of a broadwinged hawk as it came to rest on a promontory overlooking the cascading stream, and his fiery voice sounded forth with its own current. "My human is doing very well. Although I have only the slightest amount of my energy in him, he's asking questions and solving problems much better than the unjoined." Fondness showed in his tone. "I can see the world though his eyes at any time. I'm amazed at the texture and flavors of food. It bursts on his palate with such intensity. When he was eating berries yesterday I was totally absorbed in their flavor. I've never experienced anything like it."

"And running!" Aviea cut in with her own excitement, her long fingers waving through the waterfall's mist. "To run, bound across a stream, hunt and make tools is thrilling. It's so odd to see the world through the human's eyes. I feel like a stowaway, watching as it travels across the landscape. It's like I have two lives, me here and now, and the me viewing the physical world through my human."

"And mating," Yawri's words popped out. "For me, all the other sensations pale in contrast to the explosion of energy and emotion that happens when the human mates. It's so intense! Have you experienced it yet? The body's drive to reproduce is so strong that one thought from me and his body joins with females often; several times a day on some occasions. Such emotion! I never knew emotions could be so intense!"

"I know." Tisbero's eyes were wide with agreement. "Mating *is* intense. And what are emotions about? My human has emotions about everything. The amount of compassion they have for each other was a shock to me."

Aviea chimed in again, almost singing. "I think the language of the body is its emotions. With each different experience a feeling arises and flows through the blood so that every cell is aware of the feeling. By listening to them I can share the experience, and whisper my observations to the body."

"Right," Yawri seemed to determine. "By listening to its feelings, I help the body solve problems. When my human felt frustration because a fish escaped his grasp, he just accepted it. I gave him thoughts of a net. My problem-solving thoughts found fertile ground. Kunuta gathered grasses and wove a crude sort of net. He caught more fish than ever. And when he brought them to camp the others celebrated the bounty. I felt his satisfaction!"

Tisbero's etheric red hair looked tousled. "I also help my human ask questions. I thrive on searching out new things, and I've learned he can, too. When he is satisfied to do things the way they've always been done, I whisper questions. He's thriving because this questioning increases his ability to develop."

Aviea ran her opaque fingers through the leaves of a long, juice-rich plant. "I'm learning how far I can push the body by listening to its emotions. When I press the human too hard, her frustration, and sometimes fear, make her ineffective. She seems to just get confused and freezes up. She really likes stability and knowing what's safe before she moves. I'm practicing the balance between having her try new things and maintaining stability. But it's getting easier for me to understand this language of emotions. They pass through the body in a similar way to its blood. Always moving."

"How much energy do you think we can put into them?" Yawri asked, quizzically.

"I don't know." Tisbero jumped to another question that had clearly been puzzling him for a while. "Does anyone know how we retrieve our energy from the bodies when they die? All of a human's essence has simply gone back to Earth before. But now I'll need to get my energy out of the body, too."

Aviea nodded in recognition of the question. "I was speaking to Pergaine about it a few days ago," she replied. "It should be no problem. The bodies know that their source is the Earth. Our energy that is within them belongs to us. When the bodies die, information will naturally go back to its own source."

"I can't see a problem." Yawri's excited angelic form rippled and changed color like prairie grass in the wind. "I would like to continue indefinitely, matching up lifetime after lifetime with the same human-spirit. Each of its new bodies will be more conscious. I'll be able to put more and more energy into them over time. Those gardeners who left the planet because they didn't want to join don't know what they're missing."

The three, all smiles, went back to their humans, tending them as was their custom with all Life.

Chapter 6   **Lemuria**

Yawri shifted the weight of his twelve-feet-tall physical body on the hovering skystone as he delivered instructions to the young pilot. "Add more soul-light to decrease gravity," he instructed. The five-by-fifteen-foot slab of stone rose further into the air. "That's good. Now communicate with the crystals to increase propulsion." The young man closed his eyes and asked the crystals nestled into receptacles at each corner of the skystone to connect to the planet's magnetic flow. In response, the crystals harmonized with the magnetic currents to attract or repel them, which in turn, propelled the weightless platform as silently as a soaring bird.

After the skystone sailed for several minutes without losing altitude, Yawri gave another instruction. "Now ask the air-spirit to braid a shield of air to protect us from the wind."

The skystone wobbled, recovered, then suddenly began to plummet. "No!" Yawri shrieked. "Don't increase soul-sound! That increases gravity!" The young adult fell to the slab's surface and clung on for life as the stone dropped. "Release your link with the crystals! Let me have full contact!"

"I can control it!" the youth wailed.

Yawri's physical body glowed as he inserted his energy between the young adult and the crystals, and decreased the amount of his soul-sound while increasing soul-light. The change restored weightlessness to the skystone and it halted its descent, floating one hundred feet above the rocky ground. The youth stood up, abashed, as he stared over the edge. "We must have fallen six hundred feet," he croaked.

"What happened?" Yawri was stunned.

The youth swallowed and wiped his moist brow before responding. "I don't know. I connected with the crystals to increase soul-light and gravity decreased like it's supposed to. I asked the crystals to hook into Earth's magnetic flows and we moved forward like we were supposed to. Then I told the wind to braid itself so that we would be sheltered from the-."

"You *told* the wind?" Yawri's mouth hung open.

"I mean asked, I asked the wind," the youth said defensively.

The two said no more until Yawri brought the skystone to a gentle stop upon a flat outcrop of gray shale next to a village of woven grass homes. "We'll work again next week as planned," he reassured the youth. "You just need to practice your connection, and your neutrality." The young man nodded agreement as he stepped off the skystone.

Yawri lifted the skystone crystals out of their receptacles and carried them into a small cave under a lip of shale that served as a home for all the crystals in the village. He nodded thoughtfully. *All life forms need their own kind.* Then he walked back out toward the village center and was comforted when he saw Aviea working near her drying racks. They were, he knew, filled with leaves and roots of healing plants. Reaching her, he stopped near a basket of slender orange roots, picked up one, and began chewing it casually.

"Feeling a need to calm your nerves?" She asked as she noticed his selection.

"These are also quite filling," he said as he waved it gently. Then with a more serious tone added, "Well, okay, something strange did happen today. After all my years of teaching young adults to fly skystones, I've never had an experience like this one."

She stopped placing dried herbs in a leather pouch and turned to face him. "That's saying something. What happened?"

Yawri related the sequence of events, and noted the youth's comment about telling versus asking the air-spirit to weave a protective shield for them.

Aviea tilted her head back. Her long dark hair fell from her shoulders down her back, and then with a caring sigh, she fixed her golden eyes upon Yawri. "There is a first time for everything. A few days ago one of our honey gatherers returned with a bee sting."

Yawri's forehead tightened, as did the sound his voice. "That's interesting."

She went back to placing herbs into the pouch but easily sensing his tension added, "You know as well as I that joining with the same human-spirit of these physical bodies for all of these lifetimes has given us nothing but joy. Strange things are bound to happen once in a while."

"I know," he said. "It was just a shock, that's all."

"Well...shocks happen sometimes, I guess," she said as she gave him a warm smile.

Yawri, recalling the root in his hand, finished with a bite. "Life is so perfect as a human-being, I think I forgot about shocking things."

"Hey, you two!" Pergaine's voice rang out. "Do you want to go with Gamon and me to work with some mastodons?" Yawri and Aviea grinned in response but shook their heads a polite no as they watched Pergaine walk by in the distance. She waved acknowledgment as she continued to Gamon's arching hut, her long, white linen smock flowing just above her graceful feet. Pergaine smiled as well. She enjoyed problem-solving as was her task this morning, and she enjoyed bringing in just the right amount of energy from Earth's core to keep her body pleasantly warm on this cool morning.

"Gamon!" she called out in a clipped, alto voice. "Are you ready to go?"

Gamon ducked his head as he walked though his ten-foot doorway and raised it again to look at her. A white mustache and head of rippling white hair did not disguise his tawny appearance. "I found the right herd on the astral last night," he said referring to the guardians' common practice of traveling out-of-body with their etheric astral selves as their physical ones slept.

She smiled appreciatively. "Glad you did because I didn't. My muscles were so stiff from swimming with Aviea yesterday that I had trouble getting into a deep sleep. My body would wake up and I'd have to return to it to see what the matter was. It was just sore."

"We've all learned that Aviea will keep you swimming to find water plants just like she'll keep you hiking to find herbs. The herd we need to visit is about an hour's flight southeast. I saw the topography clearly. They're near the rivers' junction." In unison they walked to the group of about ten skystones resting on their landing pads. "Which one do you want to take?" Gamon's voice sounded formal, but Pergaine knew it was always that way.

"Let's take the white sandstone." Pergaine decisively stepped toward the skystone. "It has functioned well lately with my amethysts." She placed two crystals into circular indentations at the front corners of the slab as Gamon placed two more crystals in the receptacles at the rear. "Ready?" She asked, then she noticed that Gamon's aura already glowed.

As the crystals joined with their etheric energy, the weightless slab rose quickly. It was time for the next request. "I'll send a mental image of our destination." Gamon said as he sent the mental picture of the river valley to the crystals. After receiving the image, the conscious crystals connected into Earth's magnetic field and the skystone began to move toward it.

"There they go." Yawri rested a hand on a drying rack as he stood with Aviea. "I think they'll succeed."

"I sure hope they'll find out what's killing the mastodon," Aviea's pale tan robe showed grass stains from kneeling to tend plants. "I'll bet it's a disease of some kind. Nothing else seems to bother them."

"They're bound to get some good communication going between the bacteria or virus, and the mastodon." Yawri stared in the direction of Gamon and Pergaine and the sight of their disappearing craft made him wonder where he should go.

"I think it would help them to ask the devas there. Those little earth-spirits certainly help me a lot when I'm trying to find out what's going on with plants."

The sound of Aviea's voice brought Yawri's gaze back to her. "You're the best at communicating with elfin-kind. I'm more comfortable with big things."

"Well, I know Gamon's upset. I just wonder if they've thought of working with the earth-spirits, that's all." Concern flashed across Aviea's sun-bronzed face. "With so many of the elder mastodon dying, there aren't enough left to parent the young ones. They're not being trained about their culture. He told me that without parenting, the young ones have no knowledge of how to best use Earth's raw energy and they rampage."

Yawri was sympathetic. "Gamon and Pergaine will find out what's going on." He tried to sound encouraging. "Balance is the natural state after all."

"Yes, but balance in nature can mean extinction for some." She sounded rueful.

Yawri, always a spring in his step, moved closer to her. "I don't think it will come to that. We've been helping species after species receive thoughts of evolution from Earth for millennia. Only those that can't receive the new thoughts are going extinct. The mastodon listen very well, and they're too conscious a creature to stop receiving. They have no real enemies. I wouldn't worry."

Aviea brushed her straight, black hair away from her high cheeks and fixed her golden-brown eyes on Yawri. "Where are you off to today?" She knew him well. Yawri considered the many destinations of need. "I'm taking one of the small sky-stones to visit a friend. Haven't seen him in a long time and on the astral I heard about a group of trees that are in trouble. I think he can give me some insight into the problem." Then he added a bit awkwardly, "You want to come?"

"Yawri, the friend you're talking about is a tree, right?"

"How'd you guess," he said more as statement than question.

"How'd I guess? You love helping the trees. Sometimes I think they're more a family to you than guardians are." She gave him a kind, yet level gaze.

"Not quite," he said with lowered voice, then playfully raised it again and added, "When I get back, can we work with some plants together?"

Her eyes sparkled impishly. "Are you kidding? You'd step on anything smaller than a tree."

Yawri laughed as he walked toward one of the skystones that still had its complement of crystals aboard. "Called your bluff, didn't I?" he said over his shoulder. "You don't really want help with your plants. Getting a little possessive of them, aren't you?"

"Me? No. It's just that I know you're busy with so many new species of trees." Then, reconsidering his question, she added, "Okay. We should work together more."

Yawri bounded aboard the skystone. "We will. I can feel it coming." He was still grinning as the skystone rose and accelerated toward the west, and Aviea went back to her drying racks.

Of all Life forms, trees were the great communicators. With their physical roots in soil and their crowns in the misty sky, they constantly listened to messages that were in the ground and on the wind. Occasionally Yawri visited his old friend Muran with his astral body, while his physical body slept. However, personal visits as a human-being were rare. After a four-hour flight over percolating wetlands and towering cypress trees, the guardian lowered his skystone to the ground and stepped jauntily among the ferns to greet his friend.

"Muran, how goes the grove?"

"Hello, Yawri. The grove grows well. The sun and soil give us much Life." Then he added teasingly, "It's good to see you, at last."

Yawri enjoyed their banter. "Just because you're used to seeing your tree friends around you all the time doesn't mean I'm as root-bound as they are. I do a lot of traveling."

"But it's been three hundred years since your last visit," Muran replied. Sunbeams fell like liquid light as his branches moved in the sky.

Yawri realized the truth of the statement but wasn't going to let Muran have the last word. "Well, I've visited you on the astral. Besides, three hundred years isn't a long time when one lives four thousand like you do."

"Oh, so you're telling me what's a long time? Your fine human-being bodies are living what, eight or nine hundred years a lifetime? Let's see, at this rate you'll make it to see me three times with that body you've got there? That doesn't seem very often to me," Muran countered.

Yawri relented, "Okay, okay. It's just that I've been very busy helping all those deciduous trees, and there have even been some fine, new evergreens. And there are even trees that look like evergreens except they're deciduous."

"Short. They're all short." Muran joked. Yawri grinned as he looked up at the towering giant, more than two hundred feet tall. Muran got back to his point. "Trees are very connected. Three visits a lifetime are not enough."

"Oh," Yawri said, finally hearing the point of seriousness under the banter. "You missed me?"

"Of course. It takes effort to be connected. Your species moves from place to place a little too easily, if you ask me. Learning intimacy comes from the depth of a relationship. How can you have depth if you're always leaving?"

Yawri laid his hands upon the tree's rough, red bark. "I do apologize," he said sincerely.

"Well, I understand that legs are different from roots. Still, you could learn from a tree." Muran released a seed cone and, well-aimed, it landed on the top of Yawri's head.

"Hey!" Yawri squawked, and rubbed his head dramatically.

"I apologize," Muran chuckled.

Placing his hands back on Muran's bark, Yawri closed his eyes and opened his senses to feel the physical as well as the many ethereal dimensions in which the tree lived. He let currents of pastel blue, violet, green and brown flow through him as he savored the fullness of Life-giving essence the tree lived in each moment. After a long minute, Yawri opened his eyes and stepped back. He wanted to bring Muran up to date. "I remember when you told me that you'd learned a lot with a tree-body. Well, I'd like to tell you what I've learned living in a human one. Our village has worked hard at bringing more and more consciousness into the human form."

"So tell me what you've learned," Muran said, genuinely interested. A short-haired shrew poked its tiny black nose out of a hole in the ground and stared up at Yawri.

Yawri took a deep breath, and let it go slowly, not exactly knowing where to begin. Muran gave him a starting point. "You look different from the last time I saw you. Something must be happening."

"You don't mean physically. Have I aged? I'm still twelve feet tall and handsome." Yawri smiled as he stepped forward, avoiding a moist, light green sponge moss. "You mean energetically?"

"Yes. I see energy, not matter. I don't have eyes like yours you know. But that's an advantage. I'm never deceived by appearances."

"So, what is different?

"Well..." Muran sounded uncertain at first, but once he began to explain his thoughts he continued methodically. "I can see that you've been helping a lot of living things. Their thought forms are inside you, you know. If you look beyond the physical dimension into the fourth dimension, you'll see all the hundreds of species of plants, animals and insects that you've helped. It looks like you're kind of a miniature planet to me, carrying and nurturing lots of things. Since a part of them is inside you, that's why you can talk so easily to the ones outside of you."

"Yes, I feel they're part of me. I love the connection." Yawri was trying to understand the point.

"Thanks to your human body they're a part of you, the part of you that's a part of Earth. They're not from this grand part of you that's an ethereal-soul." Muran was playful again.

"Grand? I'm not grand." Yawri scanned the other tall trees in the grove. A red-winged bird flew onto one of Muran's top branches and perching there, stared curiously down at Yawri.

Muran replied seriously. "So what are you doing in this village of yours to make sure this human body you live in remains conscious?"

"Oh, the village is great." Yawri approached Muran and leaned his back against the tree to better take in the landscape. "Thanks to the way we're working, each body I've had since the joining has been more conscious than the one before."

Muran waved some of his branches in response to a breeze and more beams of sunlight shot past them to touch the ground. "It's good to hear your kind is progressing as human-beings. I see the regular humans when they walk by here. They seem to be hunter-gatherers as they've always been. How are your villages different from theirs?"

Yawri took a step away from Muran and glanced up again. "There's no comparison! Earth has two kinds of humans now, humans and human-beings."

Muran's voice was calm with caring. "Tell me more."

Yawri started pacing back and forth on an animal trail. "Well, for one thing, when our village has the need for a baby, another human body, we don't just mate. We do a lot of communication with the ethereal-soul and the human-spirit that wish for a new lifetime together. Because we're so careful, the bodies are getting more and more capable of receiving etheric reality each lifetime." Yawri held up his long arm which shimmered with a soft light. "We need to make sure that we understand the type of body they need. There are so many different types, you know."

"I know."

Yawri's voice raised in pitch, reflecting his enthusiasm. "Then, the two guardians with the most appropriate genetics are asked to mate. When we mate, it's like being coupled in prayer. Creating the baby-body is sacred. It isn't about pleasing the parents, it's about giving the soul and human-spirit what they need for another conscious Life together. It's the only way that their new body can be more capable than their last."

"I understand."

Yawri tilted his head upward to watch sunlight dance through Muran's branches, but the action didn't interrupt his speech. "When the baby is born it's raised by the whole village.

We do this because it's important to let the baby-body know
that it is a part of its people. It needs to know it's safe, and
loved for what it is. All of us provide care for the children.
They're not even set on the ground for the first couple of years,
and are never left alone. There's always someone to hold them,
be with them."

"Sounds good." Muran said in a steady voice.

"And," Yawri went on happily, missing the unfurling
fiddle-fern near Muran's trunk. "We don't even start letting the
soul enter the baby-body in any significant way until the body
is at least seven years old. It needs to be mature enough in its
connection to physical reality, you see."

"I see. Again, similar to how we work with tree-bodies."

"But that's not all, Muran. When the young ones are
completing adolescence, we send them into one of the deep
caves."

"Caves? I haven't heard about this." Muran sounded as if
he was waking up.

Yawri began pacing back and forth on the path again.
"Right. Caves. One of the reasons Earth made caves was so
that creatures could enter them and experience the planet's
connection to the Universe. As you know, Earth's soul is
connected to every other star and planet in Creation. When the
young adults are in deep, it's easier for them to learn about the
planets. It's also easier for them to learn about their own
energy centers inside of their own bodies, chakras we call them,
and how they relate to Earth's energy centers." Yawri smiled.

"My roots live among the rocks which are connected to the
caves. I know of what you speak. So you send them in so they
can better communicate with Earth?"

Yawri was only too glad to explain. "It's more than that.
It's so our physical bodies know, in every cell, that they are
connected to the Creator through Earth. If they're not strong
enough in their own identity, it could be confusing when the
body dies. Could you imagine the problem if the human-spirit
and soul were confused about their way home? That's why
we're so insistent that our young learn what energies belong to
which."

"I understand." Muran was serious. "Remember, I started
out as a purely etheric soul, an orb of light, just like you. It took
me millennia to learn how to join my ethereal essence with a
physical tree-body." The rough trunk seemed to expand

slightly, as if with breath. "It's important for me to remember my source. I've no desire to be trapped here because the Earth and I can't sort out which energy belongs to whom."

"Exactly. You see, I did learn from the ethereal-souls we worked with who blended with trees, animals, and even the whales. I know that the more conscious my body is of Earth, the easier it will be for me to return to my source at death."

"Glad to hear you learned something. See what happens when you spend some time at one place?" Muran said, a clear reference to Yawri's old habit of skipping from planet to planet.

Yawri stopped pacing and stood to face Muran, his lithe form energized as a spring. "Speaking of having purpose, I did come for a reason besides just talking." He changed his tone suddenly.

"Figures," Muran teased again, sending a few more seed cones down around his friend. "Knew it couldn't be just because you wanted to nurture our connection."

Yawri tried to ignore the comment as the seed cones fell, but he felt defensive. "From visits to the area in my astral body, I know there are some trees in trouble. You know what I'm talking about."

"Yes, I do. Of course. And I do appreciate you coming by." He drew out the words slowly, meaningfully. Yawri smiled, but shook his head.

Muran became serious again and continued at a measured rate. "We are concerned about the health of our underground fungus. As you know, it was present before we were here, and without it, we couldn't stay. It's the foundation of the forest."

Yawri was eager to help. He closed his eyes and used inner sight to scan the body of subterranean fungus. Its life-force was strong, busily digesting forest detritus. The fine, white, hair-like filaments held a symbiotic relationship with the tree's roots, and formed an organism that stretched many hundreds of miles in size. The guardian became one with the fungus body; touching it, blending with it, listening to it for any sign of distress. After several minutes, Yawri returned his concentration to Muran. "There is something wrong," he said, concerned. "In a valley about two hundred miles to the northeast, a part of the fungus body is dying. I don't know why. I'll have to go there to find out." Feeling sudden alarm, he took a step toward his skystone.

"Well, after you're done come back and visit. This one wasn't long enough for a tree eye-blink."

"I'll be back." Yawri re-mounted his vessel, and was already sending the crystals a picture of where he needed to go. "I'm happy to help you!" he shouted as the skystone rose.

"You're doing it because it's your purpose and you know it!" Muran jested as Yawri moved away. "Human-beings," Muran mused to his fellow tree-beings, "are always in a hurry."

It took Yawri several hours to find the area under stress. The Life above ground looked alive as ever, and he had to keep his focused connection on the fungus body that was underground in order to find the right spot. He held his skystone a hundred feet above the trees as he searched, eyes closed, relying on inner sight only. At last he had all the information he needed to begin his blessed work.

He landed to communicate more clearly with the fungus. After standing in quiet concentration for several breaths, his eyes shot open, interrupting his connection. "It's in too much pain for me to hear what's going on," he said. "The soil itself seems to be shrinking. Roothairs are retracting. The fungus is dying, but why?" He tried again, but rather than speaking with the fungus, this time he sought communication with the spirit of the water. Once more the words of the One Language began to flow. The message was clear. "Oh, no," Yawri said, "arsenic."

Dizziness swirled within him and he hurriedly took a step forward to keep from falling down. His vision blurred, his ears began to ring. "It will kill the trees," he heard himself say. Tears began to well in his eyes and his hand fell upon the bark of a tree as he struggled to steady himself.

"Why are you worried about us dying while we are not?" The trees voice echoed in the distance.

Yawri gazed, unseeing at the rough, red bark. "I'm just concerned." "Concerned about us, or yourself?"

"What do you mean? You, of course."

"But death is one with Life. Have you forgotten that we use one to feed the other?"

Yawri's face looked up like it was emerging from being held under water. "I lost myself!" He gulped for breath. "You're right! I allowed myself to care more about my own feelings than I cared for you. I became my emotion!"

"Are you new with listening to the language of a body? Bodies can be confusing."

"No! I know emotions are to be felt and listened to, not merged with."

"Well, you merged with one this time. There is no end to learning, and learning from Life is what gives us wisdom."

Yawri felt little comfort. With effort, he called upon himself to rebalance his connection to Earth. A minute passed before he once more felt harmony on the continuum between ethereal and physical realities. "Okay. I'm all right." He took another deep breath and slowly let it go. "Let me see what I can learn about what's going on here."

"Take your time," the tree responded.

Shaking his head as if to help clear his mind, he connected to the water-spirit under the ground at this place. But his mind chattered on. *The water is probably flowing through a deposit of pyrite. That must be it. The iron sulfide minerals are oxidizing and releasing arsenic. Maybe the water can change course.*

Catching himself, he let go of the chatter and emptied his thoughts. *I must let go of what I want to see, so that I can see what's real.* He stood still as stone to create a truly neutral connection with the water-spirit. Otherwise, he knew, the communication would be heard through a veil of his own thinking. Words began to flow as he let go of the outcome, and became an open receiver.

"It's not a pyrite deposit," the water-spirit said. "The arsenic comes from fine-grained manganese oxyhydroxides which absorbed the arsenic long ago. These minerals are under the whole valley. As they dissolve, they release the arsenic. My water runs high. I cannot avoid this valley. The Life here will change."

Yawri opened his eyes slightly and after a thoughtful pause asked, "How much land will be affected?"

"Within fifty years the fungus in this valley will be gone."

"And as the fungus goes, the trees will die."

The water-spirit continued. "It is rare that I bring such dissolved metals so high. Usually they are kept low, to nourish the deep rocks. But what is nourishment in one place can be poison in another. Without the fungus, yes, the trees will die."

Yawri opened his eyes fully and looked at the towering red trees as the water-spirit spoke on. "There will be time for the correct separation of information before they die, as both must do for either to be conscious. The earthly tree-spirit and ethereal-soul will each be able to take what they have learned back to their own sources." Yawri nodded, saddened, but accepting of what he heard.

He spent the next two days flying and communicating with the valley's fungus and trees, touching them, and thanking them for the Life they had brought. They were not despondent. Each intrinsically knew that they would go on to be reborn in another place, in another time. After he gave what he could, his thoughts turned to Muran and he directed his skystone to the familiar grove of his friend.

He rejoined Muran as the sun was setting and a full moon was rising in the eastern sky, and related the facts. By the time he finished, the moon was sitting on the ridge like a golden cherub's face. "The arsenic won't contaminate the water here, though. I think it will be confined to about thirty square miles of that valley," he concluded.

Moonlight began to turn Muran's delicate leaves to silver. "I know the trees there," Muran replied. "When your body stays in the same place for so long, you get to know your neighbors very well." In the nearby pond one frog started singing and then another. Soon, long trills, followed by a rapid series of peeps, filled the increasingly misty night air. Yawri was pensive.

Muran was quiet for several seconds, then spoke again. "It will be interesting to see what kind of Life springs forth after they're gone. Without the fungus it won't be very complex, but it will be something. Some places I've lived in the past are now covered by flowering prairie." A dragonfly with a nine-inch wing span lighted on a lily pad floating like a life raft in the pond.

Even though Muran's words were comforting, Yawri wished he could have done more. He tried to relax. He realized that if anyone should be upset, it should be Muran, not him. He breathed deeply as he turned to face Muran. "Okay, but I'm still sorry."

Muran observed Yawri for a long moment before responding. "Are you sure you're not confusing sadness with sorrow? Sadness I understand, but where is this deep sorrow coming from? Do you think it's somehow your fault?"

"Oh, I know it's not my fault," he got out. "It's just that I wish I could have done more."

Muran voice flashed. "What are you saying? Every creature in Creation is enough, including you, period." The dragonfly drooped its wings upon the lily pad as the moon skirted a misty cloud.

"I know," Yawri replied, "but I've never felt so, well, involved before."

Muran's voice was stern now. "Are you getting attached to only one dimension of Life? To only one side of the Creator's canvas? That can be dangerous".

"I know, it's just that…"

"Listen," Muran said suddenly. "Human beasts are coming."

Yawri stilled his breath, "I don't hear anything."

"Smell precedes sound," Muran replied. "Open yourself to the breeze." A faint sound grew louder as a group of humans walked along the animal trail. Yawri moved discreetly off it to stand by the tree. Within two minutes a band of seven humans, four of them carrying small, lifeless animals draped over their shoulders, rounded a bend and came in full view of the tree. Though Yawri stood motionless, the keen senses of the humans caused the first man in line to swing toward him.

"AhEee!" he called out. The whole line stopped. All eyes were on Yawri's twelve foot tall body leaning against the great tree. Try as he may, he could not make himself smaller. Hurried communication took place between the humans as they nervously inspected their catch of the day. After a minute of intense discussion, they decided which animal was most valuable. The hunter who had been carrying it was shoved by one of the other hunters toward Yawri. He hesitated, then two members of his party pushed him more violently. He slowly, cautiously, came and laid it at his feet before hurrying back to his band.

"No," Yawri said, and the whole party looked up in alarm.

"Just receive it," Muran murmured to him. "There's no graceful way out of this."

Yawri reconsidered and nodded gracefully, then bent down and picked up the limp lemur. He smiled to relate his thanks. The hunting party seemed pleased, bowed and then continued on their way home.

"I hate it when they do that," Yawri complained. "They think we're gods or something."

"They're pretty impressed with us, too," Muran said. "But they know that this tree is like one cell of the body of Earth. They understand it. You, on the other hand..."

"What do you mean?"

"Have you looked into a pool of water? There's a nice pond right over there." Yawri glanced at the pond and back to Muran. "You don't exactly look Earthly," Muran added.

Yawri stammered. "Our bodies looked like theirs once."

"Not anymore. Their bodies are less than half your height, live thirty years instead of nine hundred, and don't fly around on skystones. That's what's different between us. A redwood, cypress, cedar or any tree still looks and acts like a tree no matter if an ethereal-soul has joined with it or not. You have done something very different."

"It seems to be working."

"So it does. But the last couple generations of humans have been changing too," Muran said, caution in his voice.

Yawri stepped out into the moonlight again. "I saw it. They're more violent, and the points on those spears were very well made."

"And they treated you like a god."

Yawri nodded in silent agreement. Then he spoke. "The human I joined with and his village had conflict, but they were not violent. They respected us, but didn't think we were gods."

"And you looked more like gods then, twenty-five feet of angelic beauty. Now you're just twelve feet of human-being." Muran moved his branches slightly to better smell the wind. "Although these humans are taller, fashion animal hides for clothing and make interesting tools, they seem less secure. I don't know why, but they seem less connected to each other. It is cause for concern." The evening air was filled once more with just the sounds of the forest. Then unexpectedly Muran added, "You're not getting lost into physical reality, are you?"

"I beg your pardon?"

"What?" Yawri was startled back onto the path.

Muran took a moment before he spoke again. "It's a thought. I've heard of it happening to souls on other planets."

"I feel fine. In each of my lifetimes, my body is becoming more conscious, just as I planned." Yawri's white smock looked pale silver now. "From that arsenic in the water table, I think you're the ones with a problem."

"Well, perhaps you're right. But if dense bodies ever become a problem for you, we trees have been talking about a way that would help."

"You've been talking about helping us? That's a switch." Yawri laughed and relaxed into the ambiance of the silver-blue valley. "What's your idea?" he said, trying to be open-minded.

Muran continued as the sound of the frogs reverberated off the pond's surface as if it were a huge drum. "We're thinking about making caves within us so that your kind could come, have a good place to let the body die, and let us help separate out the information."

"That's kind of you," Yawri said, genuinely trying to be appreciative of a gift he couldn't imagine ever needing. "How can you make a cave within you?"

"Simple, really. When we need it, we call forest fires to us." Yawri's expression tightened with alarm. Muran quickly continued. "Don't worry. We just ask the fire to burn out the old inner wood. We don't use it, the outer wood is where the sap flows. With the old wood gone, we have a small cave inside us. Wouldn't that be great? A little shelter for Life?"

"That is a gift." Yawri was finally sincere. "Your kind constantly amazes me, Muran. Here you are, stabilizing the atmosphere, making forests that nurture thousands of species ranging from virus to bacteria to gnats and bears but you still come up with a way to do more. Not bad for something that can't walk."

"Sometimes being anchored to one place is an advantage. There's no way to move away from what you've done to the Life around you."

Yawri gazed up toward the darkened branches, and saw stars begin to peek through them like shy fairies.

Muran continued. "If you want to, when your body is nearing the end of it's time, come and sit within us. When the body dies, we will help guide the ethereal-soul toward its source as we bring the human-spirit toward Earth. Then the physical body can be used by the bacteria and fungus of the forest to break it down and provide nourishment for our tree-bodies. It's a good solution, don't you think?"

Before there's a solution there needs to be a problem, Yawri thought, but said, "It is a good way to work together. It will give me a reason to visit you more often." He watched the dragonfly on the lily pad stretch out its wings. Moonlight made them glimmer as they settled back down again.

"Well, at least one time more often," Muran commented dryly. Yawri could hear the great tree chuckle to the wind, and knew that the sound, along with all the others, would eventually be heard by trees around the globe.

Chapter 7 **Issues in Eden**

"Come on. Why don't you want to leave the cave?" The young adult's head quickly turned in the direction of the way out, then slowly back. "We've done our nine months in here. It's time to rejoin the village."

Mariyonta took a buoyant step toward the familiar limestone wall and replied. "I told you. The cave-spirit instructed Aronlat about a new tunnel. This tunnel leads to an area of the cave that works with the other dimensions of reality. I want to see it, too."

Aronlat cinched one of the party's tightly woven straw packs closed and joined the conversation. "I could go alone," he said. Mariyonta raised a quizzical eyebrow. "But caves communicate better with two people then they do with one." He noticed the expression on her face and hastily added, "I admit, I'm glad she's coming."

"Thanks Aronlat," Mariyonta said, "glad to hear you think I'll be useful." She moved away from the wall to stand with the others. "Tell the village that we'll come out when we feel our work is complete." Then, scarcely able to contain her curiosity about exploring this new section of the cave added, "You know that I love getting information from the cave, and I just know it has so much more to share. We'll be able to bring more knowledge when we return."

One of the other young man gazed at the path leading out before turning back. "We'll be adults when we complete this cave-stay, and I admit I'm anxious to take my place among them. I understand your reason for staying, but I sense a danger."

"We'll be fine." Aronlat raised his hands toward the rock ceiling that had sheltered them all so well. "What could happen?"

"But Tisbero and Yawri might be displeased," a young woman continued as she hoisted her pack. "You know they planned to take us on skystones to the far northern forests when we finished."

Mariyonta placed a leather bag of acorns in the top of her own woven straw rucksack. "Tisbero is always heated up about something, and Yawri never gets too upset about anything."

Aronlat put his last item, a small packet of bone needles, into his pack, closed it and folded his strong arms gently against his chest. "Tisbero did not say we were required to come out together. He'll understand."

The parting friends took a last look around the cavern and inhaled a final breath of its earthy, moist aroma before taking their first step toward the surface. "I'm still concerned about leaving you." The young man spoke soberly. "But the cave-spirit will guide you well."

The five turned to go. "Give my best to the village," Mariyonta called after them.

"And mine!" Aronlat's voice rang and then echoed in the vast space. In the emerging quiet, a drop of water released its hold on a stalactite and landed with a plop into a clear pool.

A trailing voice floated back on an unseen wind. "Create with the Creator," but it seemed swallowed by calm. The only sound remaining was that of gently trickling water, and a slow, rhythmic dripping from stalactites reaching from the ceiling to their stalagmites growing below.

Another drop fell into the pool. Mariyonta spoke, breaking the meditative moment. "Which direction leads to this tunnel?"

"Follow me," Aronlat said, recovering himself as from a trance, "and watch your step." Her eyes flashed at him but he failed to notice. The human-beings hoisted their woven rucksacks filled with food and provisions and started walking down the narrow, black corridor of living stone.

✦

While their physical bodies slept, Aviea, Pergaine, Gamon, Tisbero and Yawri often took their astral bodies to a meeting place to communicate with other guardians. This way, their soul work could continue out-of-body from their human forms. Since the settlements were scattered in many locations around the planet, principally on the four major continents and the big island between them, these astral meetings allowed the guardians to coordinate their efforts and speak of any problems. Upon awakening, their physical bodies recalled the events as though they were a lucid dream.

Tisbero was tonight's representative from the islands. To aid recognition, the astral form of his craggy face was framed by graying red hair so that it was consistent with his sleeping body. "We have noticed a troubling trend," he said seriously, the knuckles of his etheric fists resting on the table. "Our new children no longer seem to expand in their ability, as has been the pattern for generation after generation. In fact, though I have no firm evidence yet, I suspect that our most recent generation has *less* ability than the last. They have difficulty talking with plants and animals."

Aviea agreed. "I am visiting Tisbero's village. Many of the young adults there *are* having trouble communicating with plants."

Several murmured comments to their neighbors. Someone from the great river valley just beyond the coastal mountains of the northwestern continent spoke. Her astral body leaned forward. "It troubles me that you report this. I was thinking it was just an anomaly for us, but now that you bring words to it I, too, am concerned that our children are not becoming greater than their parents."

"Our children are fine." Another guardian waved his hand as if shooing a fly. "As always, the new bodies of our children seem more capable, not less."

Yawri was typically optimistic. "Perhaps your problem is caused by simple evolution. The continents are always changing. Each land has its own vibratory rate and will need different types of bodies to work with it best. This problem may be due to nothing more than that."

"I agree." Gamon's brow furrowed as he looked at each guardian, turning from face to face at the astral council. "The bodies need to differ so they can work most effectively with the particular energies of their land."

Tisbero shifted uncomfortably. "Yes, bodies need to take on some different shades and even shapes," he replied with thin-edged stiffness, "but I am still concerned. These changes should enhance the ability to connect to the land they live upon, not lessen it. Our village has five new adults that just emerged from their cave stay, and they don't seem like adults to me. I've watched this re-birthing process work for many, many gen-erations and these five do not seem as mature as those preceding them. I'm concerned for them, although I'm en-couraged by the actions of two who remained in the cave. I sense their decision to stay means that they are each aware of their body's timing as opposed to the calendar time allotted for the transformation." Aviea nodded her agreement, clearly equally concerned.

Gamon placed his astral hands flat on the table, shoulders wide. "If it is true that young adults are beginning to follow rituals instead of the change needed within themselves, this would be most disturbing." An uncertain frown followed his drooping his white mustache. "Were they properly prepared?"

"Of course!" Tisbero gave a fiery stare.

"What about the children in Shahitam's tribe? I haven't seen him at these astral meetings for a long time." Pergaine's tight lips revealed that this was not the first time she had considered the problem. "Their island isn't far from yours, Tisbero. Have you heard about the children there?"

Yawri responded, suddenly recalling their early gatherings on the healing, crystal island. "Shahitam was the only one among us who had experience joining with humanoids on other planets. He knew when the timing was right to seek union with the humans here."

Tisbero continued with his burning voice. "I have not been to that ancient, healing island in some time."

Many voices spoke in small groups for several minutes, some pitched high, others low, but all earnest in their point of view. At last it was agreed that since none had seen him on the astral for some time, a physical visit to Shahitam was in order. "His tribe of human-beings is oldest. Seeing it in person may tell us if this regression is anything to be concerned about," a voice spoke the sentiment of all.

"Tisbero," Yawri said as he turned to the elder. "Since your village is the closest to Shahitam's, it would take you the least amount of time to take a skystone there."

"Yes," Tisbero replied seriously. "I can leave immediately. Aviea is already visiting so she can come. I'll gather a couple of other people from the village and make the visit."

"My body is several days' journey away from yours. Otherwise I'd insist that you wait for me." Yawri turned to face the other guardians, a grin on his face. "The music, the dancing, his village knows how to celebrate an equinox. That's the real reason Aviea went to visit, nothing to do with their rare plants." Aviea shook her head. Tisbero smiled--tension aside, he clearly enjoyed Yawri.

Pergaine scanned the assemblage. "While Tisbero and Aviea make the physical journey to see Shahitam, we can all gather additional information. Let's look afresh for any evidence of regression in other tribes."

"I'll go speak with the ancient trees," Yawri volunteered.

Gamon was first to stand. "Let's reconvene on the astral in three weeks. Will that give you enough time to gather news from Shahitam's island?"

"Plenty," Tisbero responded thoughtfully, his grin gone now. "That should give us plenty of time."

✦

"I hear rushing water ahead," Mariyonta said to Aronlat as they crawled through the cave's narrow, twisting passage, its surface slick with wet clay.

"Be careful," Aronlat cautioned, his pointing finger unseen in the darkness, "there's a steep drop-off here." The small passage was pitch black because it contained no crystalline minerals shining with their own soft, phosphorescent light. The two explorers stopped to sense the direction of their destination by resting the full length of their bodies on the damp floor. Slowly, quietly, their supple bodies began to receive information.

"I feel the cave breathing," Mariyonta said quietly, though she felt enthralled. "From the amount of air it's inhaling and exhaling, there must be an expansive cavern still ahead."

"I feel a pulse as well." His strong hand felt the moist clay. "We're in the part of the cave that mirrors the place in our own bodies where new air is exchanged for old."

The explorers crawled ahead until the height of the tunnel increased. "I've got the direction," Aronlat said as he stood up and took a long step. "Let's go."

"Easy," Mariyonta peered into the darkness, relying only on inner sight. "Go slowly. We don't need to slip and fall into the wrong part of the cave."

Aronlat barely heard her comment. "The part that's calling is to our right. It's showing me a picture. We need to skirt the first opening to the left, cross over through a narrow crevice and then descend through the second tunnel on the right."

"Whatever you say, my leader," Mariyonta crooned. Aronlat nodded his head, preoccupied.

The pair walked onward with measured pace, the sound of the rushing water making further talk impossible. After an hour's difficult hike along the water's edge, they came to the second tunnel on the right. Utter blackness was all their physical eyes could perceive as they stepped into it. After several minutes, they stopped in a place which widened, and a glow from a large fluorite crystal showed a small cavern above their heads.

"The crystal is telling us to be careful," Mariyonta muttered.

"If we go any slower we'll turn into a stalagmite." Aronlat continued forward. "The place that is calling us is this way. It has a different rock than what's behind us. I can smell it." He glanced back at Mariyonta who was still visible in the faint light from the fluorite. "We could stop and rest by this crystal if you like."

"Rest? What, are you tired?" Mariyonta teased. She stepped ahead, and her senses reached out into the darkness to detect solid ground.

She was first to feel a soft vibration in the air. The sound of a distant rumble grew in the darkness behind her. "Aronlat!" She yelled to warn her friend. "Water! Coming!" but her voice was drowned out by the roar of the cascading flood as it engulfed and swept them away.

The cascading torrent carried them ever deeper into the bowels of Earth. With no light and with roaring water shooting them from side to side, the young adults lost all bearings.

After a seeming eternity of tumbling and struggling for air, Mariyonta floated in a vast, subterranean lake. Her rucksack was missing, torn away from her bruised shoulders. She slowly began to move through the water, but was unable to make her muscles stop spasming from the adrenaline. Bioluminescent plankton were triggered to spark by the friction of her body against them. The glow outlined her body as if she wore a veil of soft, fluid light. She turned over on her back to float and tried to gather her bearings.

"Aronlat?" she got out, her breath still short. She saw for the first time that the giant cavern was gently lit by the glow emanating from crystal minerals that covered much of the ceiling and walls. She breathed deeply, as if trying to come back from a dreadful dream. The air, far from being stuffy, smelled crisp. *Where am I?* She felt some strength return and called out in a stronger voice for her companion. "Aronlat!"

Several minutes of alternately swimming and rolling over on her back passed as she listened for her friend. She heard distant thrashing. "Aronlat?" Something moved against her legs. *What's that?* She kicked away with earnest. "Aronlat?" The thrashing came closer.

"Mariyonta! Is that you?" The churning water stopped.

"Me? Of course it's me. Who else could be here?" she said, concealing her deep concern. Then, without waiting for a response, she added. "Why are you thrashing? Are you hurt?" He came closer, a mixture of treading water and dog paddling.

"Did you lose your rucksack?" he asked.

"You're swimming with yours?!" she said in disbelief. "Take it off. You can't swim with that."

"I am swimming with it."

"If you call churning water like a buffalo, swimming," she replied. "Let it go."

"Mariyonta, I can't tread water with you brushing into my legs," Aronlat said.

"I know where my legs are and they're not tangling in yours."

"Right," he replied skeptically as he tried to discern the nearest shore. "I think that soft light may be coming from a glowing crystal near the lakeside." Mariyonta nodded her head in agreement.

They swam slowly toward the nearest shore, using the side-stroke, which allowed them to catch their breath as well as keep an eye on each other. Their skin soaked in the refreshing elixir of dissolved minerals and vibrant water. "A hundred or so more yards to go," Mariyonta affirmed as they swam toward the distant, faint light.

After strain-filled minutes of carefully paced swimming, they pulled themselves onto a sloping shore, both too exhausted to speak. They lay for an hour, panting at first, then breathing with measured breath. They dozed in semiconscious sleep, arms around each other because simply lying next to each other did not provide enough comfort. At last they stirred, like animals awakening from hibernation, then moved more willfully before eventually standing up.

"The lake looks like an immense sheet of dark ice," Mariyonta said. "The surface is reflecting light from the glowing crystals in the ceiling as if they were stars." She paused then whispered as if she was trying to keep a secret.

"This seems like another planet." Their astonished eyes survey-ed the new world.

Aronlat was silent, then he exhaled. "We're here. The water brought us to the call I've been hearing." He turned to see a shimmering mound that lay thirty yards down the beach. "And that's the light we swam toward."

Aronlat dropped his soggy rucksack on the sand and began to walk to the light. He was surprised to see that Mariyonta moved more quickly and arrived first. She placed her hands on a blossom of quartz that looked like a glowing, four-foot lotus growing out of the sand. A gentle pulse of warmth moved through her chest, and her face relaxed as if it was being stroked by her tender grandmother. She said, "So much life-force is available here that it makes my whole body tingle."

"The universe is here," Aronlat concluded, rebounding with the flexibility of youth and sounding rejuvenated.

Mariyonta breathed and felt life pulse through every cell. Then she reached out with burning joy to connect with air and stone alike. Something reached back. "This place is more than alive," she said. "This cavern is reaching out to touch *me*." Her head turned toward the ceiling and she gazed at the distant clusters of glowing crystals.

"Mariyonta." She heard her name called, but it took a moment to realize that it was Aronlat's voice. He placed his hand on her shoulder. "We made it," he said plainly. His hand dropped back to his side as she turned to face him.

She rolled her head to take in their new home. "We almost didn't," she finally said. "I can't believe we didn't listen to that fluorite. Do you remember? It was the last crystal we saw before the flood came."

"I remember it."

Their gaze moved to the sand. Mariyonta absently traced her toe across it and then said in a subdued voice, "The cave provided us with a safe place to stand, even lit by that fluorite, but my excitement was so intense that I blocked the message to wait there until the flash flood passed. All the connecting and listening we've learned over these months and we forgot to use it when the test came." She moved a hand to wipe a tear pooling in her eye.

Aronlat swallowed hard. "We best forgive ourselves and move on. After all, the cave forgave us."

"True. If it didn't, we wouldn't be here."

"Yes," Aronlat acknowledged. The moist, active silence filled them as they both realized now that if the cave hadn't wished to bring them here alive, they wouldn't be.

Their muscles relaxed, smoothing their shoulders, as they each experienced the self-forgiveness they needed to let go of their folly. "Thank you, cave-spirit. Thank you for bringing us here," Mariyonta said aloud. Aronlat nodded his agreement, and took his turn to place a hand on the crystal flower, glowing above the sand like a shining lotus.

They renewed their dedication to stay with their host, and listened as the cavern directed them to a place suitable for human-beings. There they found edible plants which had evolved to prosper in the fragile light, and enjoyed a subterranean salad. Still seated after their meal, they both began to scan their surroundings. "Ready to explore?" Aronlat asked. Mariyonta answered by standing up and flexing her long legs.

Opening their senses, they were led to a small cave within the great cavern. Mariyonta's youthful face beamed. "Look at the size of this geode! A geode with nine-foot high walls of amethyst!" The chamber in front of them looked like a domed room filled with softly lit, hexagonal, cut-glass lamps.

Aronlat moved to stand in its entrance and gently rested a hand on a shining facet. He was spellbound. It was as if he looked into another universe. "Where is this place going to take us?" he murmured.

Mariyonta came to join him. "I thought the part of the cave we stayed in for the last nine months was magnificent. But this..." She swept her eyes across this smaller, sparkling cave. "I think it took the first nine months to prepare us for this."

Aronlat let his hand fall away from a silky smooth surface that he had been stroking. "And our friends chose not to stay. I miss sharing this with them." He stood motionless a moment, his lips in a frown.

"The tribe is far away," Mariyonta pulled her eyes away from the entrancing facets in the crystal cave to gaze back at the chamber's ceiling. The sound of dripping water trickled like the end of a spring rain. "Yet, I still feel them faintly. Their ability to connect with Earth is strong, and we are a part of the One Body. At least in that way, we're together."

Aronlat forced his gaze away from the facets of light and joined her effort to feel their friends beyond the arched ceiling.

"They might be headed for the northern forests with Tisbero and Yawri right now."

"I imagine they are," Mariyonta said, a tinge of melancholy in her voice.

Aronlat's stare fell to the sand for a long moment before he raised his eyes to peer again into the giant geode. The crystal cave's glow seemed to pulse with a heartbeat of its own. "Well...let's learn what we can." He sighed, but then a smile at last graced his lips.

Mariyonta took in a breath that felt as if it went down to her feet. "Yes. Let's learn what we can, and share it with the outside world when it's time." The look of reassurance that they gave to one another was brief, but neither took a step forward until it was completed. Hands clasped, they walked into the multidimensional crystal cave together.

Chapter 8   *Visit of Discovery*

Tisbero and Aviea had no difficulty finding two others, Sargac and Twaqwe, to make the journey to Shahitam's island. Tisbero and Aviea's concern for the children hadn't abated. It still appeared that they were less capable of speaking with plants, animals, crystals and devas alike. Although Gamon's explanation that the bodies were merely adjusting to different locations on Earth was plausible--different skin colors and shapes were in fact evolving--they couldn't shake the feeling that something was wrong. But precisely what, and why Shahitam was absent from the astral meetings, was still a mystery.

Their traveling skystone was small, maneuverable and fast. The four skystone crystals seated in its corners had exceptional ability to work with the electromagnetic fields for propulsion as well as gravity. Tisbero also carried a small, clear crystal about the size of his fist that was known as a "recorder." This crystal documented all the life that it experienced within a one-hundred-foot radius. It would record the thoughts and feelings of the party as well as what the party encountered.

Although travel usually took them east to the great northeastern continent, this small party turned west toward what was known as the big Atlantean island, particularly abundant with crystallized minerals and a rich diversity of life forms. Generations ago it had been considered one of the prime healing centers on Earth and before taking human bodies, the etheric guardians visited it frequently. Now that their human forms were thriving so well, however, few ever made the long journey. Shahitam's tribe now called it home. Curiosity filled all members of the team as they peered through the mist in search of the big island.

After the travelers sailed through the misty clouds for four hours, the island at last filtered into view. It was several times larger than Tisbero's own island home. "How calm the ocean is here compared to the other islands!" Aviea said, her bronze face and black hair damp from the air. "It seems to lap at the shore instead of pound it." The skystone moved inland.

"Look!" Twaqwe's arm shot out. "Look at the size of these villages! And they don't build with grass like we do. Stone buildings seem to grow out of the ground." Questioning eyes peered down from the slowly descending skystone.

"Why do they have such a large population in one place?" Tisbero's freckled face was wrinkled from confusion. "Clearly some new work is going on here."

Suddenly the overhead mist parted and an expansive blue sky took its place. The heads of all four travelers jerked up as Aviea shot words from her throat. "What happened to the mist?! How can plants drink from the air without the mist?" Their mouths hung open in disbelief. As if simultaneously seeking an answer, the travelers began to watch the ground as it seemed to rise before them.

"What is that?" Aviea's stomach tightened. "I've never seen such an unusual rock formation. The strange shapes stretch over the entire valley!" The skystone continued its rapid, silent movement inland.

After a long pause Tisbero spoke. "It's not a rock formation," he said with a deliberate, measured breath. "It is a thousand villages built as one." All four guardians stared in consternation as their small skystone flew over lines of white houses.

The travelers asked their skystone to slow its speed. The crystals reversed polarities within themselves to repel the electromagnetic field instead of attract it. Then the guardians increased their soul-sound relative to their soul-light causing the slab to descend to their desired elevation.

"There's an open field next to that building," Sargac pointed to the largest of all the structures as individual buildings became more clear. "It's the center of the rows of the encircling houses. See how it stands on a hill?" The platform moved closer and he spoke again. "This is a village within the bigger village. There must be twenty buildings right here."

Tawaque barked a question as her hand pointed. "Look at that tall black wall surrounding them. Why is it separating these buildings from the others?"

Tisbero studied it for a long moment as it passed under them. "I've seen something like it before, many years ago. A village I visited was repeatedly overrun by herds of mammoth. We found out that thought forms of elephants were leading the physical mammoth through the village. Since the thought forms existed in the fourth dimension, the wall had to exist in that dimension too. That's why it looked black to physical eyes.

But there would be no need for a multidimensional wall on an island." His flashing green eyes were troubled.

"Watch out!" Tisbero yelled as the largest skystone they had ever seen, laden with at least thirty people, veered toward them. "Go left!" Just as suddenly, another platform appeared on their left. "Land! They're moving in too close!"

The team asked their skystone to descend. It stopped about one foot above the ground to avoid crushing any plants, and hovered there. The other two much larger platforms stopped suddenly and dropped their entire weight onto the ground about fifty feet away on either side.

The travelers looked at each other as if seeking an explanation. "They must have landed on pads already prepared for them," Aviea said, giving the only possible answer.

Tawaque was first to step off their skystone and focus on the other people. "Interesting, they're are all holding citrines. They seem a deeper yellow than I've seen before." The travelers were accustomed to the use of citrine quartz. These were the crystals that were often used to bring ethereal and physical realities together in a balanced way. They were particularly useful to help evolving life forms with their transitions.

Sargac shrugged. "Perhaps they've just returned from a place where Earth asked for assistance with blending. Probably a place that was struggling to keep up with the planet's changes."

The foursome stepped toward a man who was approaching from the right. He wore a leather vest with a high-necked collar and was noticeably taller than the others on his platform. "Greetings!" he called out as he strode toward the party. The shorter men and women did not step off the platform but remained standing in place, their yellow crystals still held against their stomachs. "Welcome to our city!" He halted his march in front of the visitors. "Where are you from?"

Tisbero addressed him, an edge in his voice. "We are from a nearby island. We traveled here to speak with Shahitam. But tell me," Tisbero looked at the two huge flying slabs flanking them, "why did you bring in your skystones so quickly? If we hadn't moved out of the way, we would have collided."

The man cleared his throat. "We call them skyplatforms, because they are so much larger than skystones that they hardly compare," he said with an ingratiating smile. "You underestimate the flying skill of our people. We were escorting you to this safe landing spot, nothing more. We receive all guests with this honor. We didn't know you were coming, so had to make haste to greet you properly. We meant it as an honor." His arms spread in a welcoming gesture. "You are wise to seek Shahitam's counsel. Many do so." He took a step back and pointed toward the large building on the hill. "Come, we will go to the temple where you may seek audience with him." Tisbero looked back at the platforms with uncertainty.

"Temple? What is a temple?" Aviea asked, her forehead creased.

The tall man turned to her in surprise. "Clearly your village is of the old way. You're probably still living in grass rooms or mud buildings. Through Shahitam's wisdom our tribe has prospered and grown." He pointed toward the distant structure, gleaming in the unfiltered sun of a cloudless sky. "Because so many seek his wisdom, we needed to make a special place. The temple is that special place. That's all."

The group began walking on a marble road up the hill. Tisbero noticed that upon a signal from their welcomer, the entourage from the other platforms went to a row of buildings down the hill. "What a durable path," Tisbero said, glancing at the stones.

"Yes." Their guide replied with pride. "It leads all the way from the temple to the gate."

Aviea turned to her companions and quietly asked, "Gate? What's a gate?" But she only received blank stares in return.

The team continued to follow their guide up the stone road, but their faces turned to follow two more skyplatforms that came in from the west. Twaqwe's eyebrows arched over unblinking eyes. "This is a very busy place."

They soon came to the entrance of a large stone building and after stepping through the threshold the team stopped, all faces again turned upward. Columns made of fine-grained sandstone, at least four feet in diameter and sixty feet tall, shone brilliantly under the clear blue sky. "I've never seen such creation!" Sargac said with dismay. "How were these grown?"

"Wait until you see the temple itself," their guide responded. "Stones were brought from all over the world to be a part of it."

"Brought?" Tisbero asked pointedly. "Don't you mean came?"

"Of course. I meant the stones wished to come so we brought them." The guide's face remained placid above his flowing robe.

The temple roof rose to at least seventy feet and its walls formed a giant "U" flanking the rows of columns they passed. The main chamber stood like a rectangular, colossal cave. The travelers shielded their eyes from the bright sunlight reflecting off the polished white walls. "Wait here," the guide said as he walked up several steep steps which led to the chamber's entrance.

Twaqwe turned to the others and whispered, "What is this place? I can't get clear communication from the ground."

Tisbero considered the tall columns. "Shahitam has developed things unfathomed by me. I don't understand at all."

"I don't understand either." Aviea said as if sharing a secret. "The stones that make this place all carry strong life force but I can't speak with them. Their sound is different from any I've ever heard."

Tawaque knelt to touch the white floorstone. "Could it be a new species of rock?"

Aviea worried her lip as her eyes tried to gather more information. "It looks like marble, the smell is the same, but I can't understand what it's saying."

Sargac's face tightened as he focused on a large arched window and the deep blue sky beyond. "The harsh rays may be causing a whole new vibration. Why are there no clouds?"

Twaqwe rose from her inspection of the floor. "I don't hear anything. It's as if the stone is--" Her speech was cut short by a low, bass voice.

"Shahitam will see you now." The guardians turned to see a man wearing a black silken robe with a long purple sash across his chest. In a more moderate voice he added, "Please come." After casting furtive glances at one another, the group silently walked up the stairs and followed him into an ornate room of carved alabaster.

This chamber was lit by at least two dozen crystals that sat in alcoves cut into the milk-white, limestone walls. Their light reflected off the polished surfaces so that illumination appeared to come from the floor itself. The group walked respectfully up several more steps and stopped in front of a broad stage. "Wait here." The man with the purple sash pointed to an invisible line. The travelers stood in amazement as they looked about the room. Charts of the stars inlaid with gold and jewels were carved into the walls, and in exquisite detail, a colorful mosaic illustrated beings arriving from the stars. In another mural, beings with radiant, golden bodies handed sparkling gems to the creatures of Earth.

"Greetings!" an enthusiastic, booming voice called out. The group watched Shahitam walk comfortably across the stage, an act clearly routine for him, his robe shimmering in dark red and silver.

"Shahitam!" Tisbero returned. "It has been long, too long since I have seen you, either on the astral or in the flesh."

Shahitam halted at the edge of the stage and examined his visitors. "As you can tell, I have been very, very busy. Co-creation goes wonderfully well. Our population is exploding with prosperity!"

Tisbero met his gaze with equal certainty of purpose. "We have so many questions."

Shahitam smiled easily. "Come, come. My people from the continents told me about a regression in their children. Is this your concern?" Tisbero nodded. "We must discuss this. I've heard from many about this problem for some time now. But before we talk about such things, let us take refreshment, and let me show you some of the magnificent creations happening here."

The team followed Shahitam across the stage. After several steps Aviea asked him, "What do you mean 'my people?' You said 'my people' from the continents."

Shahitam took a half step. "Semantics, my dear. Naturally these people belong only to themselves, but they are 'my' friends. Their concerns are my concerns. We are of the One Body, are we not?" The group walked on in silence. "Look here," Shahitam stopped at the veranda overlooking an open courtyard.

"Heavenly Earth, what is it?" Twaqwe asked in a voice higher than usual. The floor of the courtyard was concave in shape and in its center stood a family of clear quartz crystals as large as a village hut.

Aviea stepped forward, her forehead furrowed once more. "These crystals are of deep Earth. How did they come to be here?"

Shahitam's head bobbed slightly as if anticipating the question. "When you are of the Source, all needs are filled." He faced the large crystal. "This is the 'Generator.' See how the sun's rays reflect off the parabolic walls to the crystal? This courtyard is efficiently designed to send as much energy as possible to the Generator. This crystal receives so much energy that it can send its abundance to others. That way, light and heat are provided to the most remote of houses on the island."

Tisbero gripped the banister tightly, and stared at the crystal. "But I don't understand. Why would this crystal need to send energy to any others? The human-beings in their own homes could communicate with their own crystals to get all of the heat and light they need." Another skyplatform accelerated above them, this one moving off toward the southwest.

"Of course. But we have many young here. Many of these new human-beings are just learning of their abilities. Would you have me let them live in cold and darkness while they learn? As they develop their abilities with their crystals, they disconnect from this source as they like."

Aviea didn't hesitate to speak. "How can they learn their own strength while you do so much for them? Don't they become dependent?"

"Dependent? No! When you yourselves give to Life, does it become dependent upon you? Of course not. You nurture, you give, you let go, so that All may live in co-creation with the Creator."

Shahitam led them past several chambers and came to another veranda which overlooked the city and the sea beyond, shaded from the harsh sun. "Please be seated." He moved to a chair at the head of a long table inlaid with colorful bits of a red, azure blue, yellow and white mosaic. As the party seated themselves, grapes, figs, olives, cheeses and breads were placed on the table by six beautiful young girls and boys. Tisbero studied them as they served the guests. "Served," he noticed, was the correct word. Before departing, the youths' eyes lingered on their guests as if in longing adoration. *Why do they defer to us?* Tisbero's face tightened.

"They are my children," Shahitam said unexpectedly.

"Your children? All of them?" Sargac exclaimed.

"We have many children," Shahitam continued as he casually placed a succulent blue grape in his mouth. "I know that the foundations of human-beings were formed by blending with just one, original human, and that you have nurtured that same human-spirit through generations so that its abilities would ever increase."

"Yes. That is so," Tisbero responded as casually as he could. "I have been with the same genetic line, the same human-spirit since my decision to join. We have grown and developed together. That is as all guardians have done."

"Admirable in its purpose." Shahitam fingered another grape. "We have all learned that our effort to connect to humans is greatly appreciated by them. Is this also true?"

Aviea leaned forward and took a fig from the silver platter. "Naturally this is so. If Earth had not prepared bodies for us, we would've had to leave long ago."

Shahitam cut a small piece of cheese and briefly savored its aroma before popping it into his mouth. "The problem our village experienced is that eventually our children began to be less able than their parents. They were not as adept at flowing through the time tunnels, shifting dimension and touching all spectrums of Life. I think this may have to do with the purpose of your visit here."

Aviea hurried to swallow the last piece of the fig. "That is exactly our concern! My own nephew cannot even speak with plants!"

Shahitam stared down at the mosaic, placed his hands on its surface and patiently traced a geometric pattern with a long finger. "We have spent the last two generations searching for the reason for this. Oh, at first, there were many who wished to deny the problem. For how could there be a problem with development of our children when the very law of this planet is that all Life must develop, must evolve? For a problem like that, there were only two possibilities. One, we made some large error in how we began our blending. Or two, we started doing something wrong after the blendings started. Since our original blending took place with permission of the human-spirits, and the work progressed well with one genetic line for so long, we knew the answer was to focus on what we could be doing wrong now."

"Yes, that makes sense. And did you find something?" Aviea stared at him hopefully.

Shahitam leaned back and spread his arms as if to encompass the whole island. "Look about you! Is this development? Is life prospering? You on the other hand, are living in villages of the past, as we once did. We were stuck in that past, so glued to our old ways that changes were viewed as heresy. Now, our children once more grow to surpass us!"

Tisbero leaned forward, hands spread wide on the table. "So what were you doing wrong? How did you reverse the decline of your progeny and once more come into the law of evolution?"

Shahitam gave him a level stare. "We discovered the problem was hoarding."

"Hoarding?" Tisbero's eyes flared. "How could the problem be hoarding?" He turned to his friends around the table. "We give all our hearts to Life."

"Do you?" Shahitam asked directly. The team members felt shocked. "That is precisely the problem. Arrogance."

"Arrogance? How are we arrogant?" Genuine concern rang in Tisbero's voice.

Shahitam continued in a thoughtful, measured pace. "Do you not see how automatically your answer came when I put the question forward about hoarding? There was no reflection, no taking in and asking the whole body a question, only the answer instantly from your mind."

"But that is because the answer is throughout my heart!" Tisbero responded.

"Once more you give a thoughtless answer! Where is your question? If you refuse to listen because of this arrogance there is no point to this meeting." Shahitam's voice boomed in the hall. "If you are not willing to look at the impact of your actions upon Earth I have no patience for you. Go back to your village and continue to harm your children!"

The team reeled from the blow. Tisbero was first to recover and met Shahitam's eyes. "Please continue," he said quietly.

Shahitam slowly leaned forward and spoke in a soft voice. "Answers were never meant to last for eternity," he said. "Answers which do not lead to questions lead to stagnation. A stagnant pool gives no life, and without life there is no death. Without death, without letting go, there is no life. Without this circle, the law of development is broken. The planet's law is broken." All eyes were on Shahitam now.

"We discovered that we were hoarding," he shot a glance to Tisbero. "We had our villages, our *own* human-spirit and our *own* bodies with which to work, but this work was isolated. It did not include work with all humans."

"Well yes, there are two species," Tisbero countered as he shifted slightly in his chair, "but one is not greater than the other. The Earth has humans and human-beings, both are needed. Both add value."

"True!" Shahitam raised his voice again. "But in what percentages, in what relationship? Have you asked Earth?"

Tisbero leaned forward once more, level eyed. "I have not heard that Earth was dissatisfied with our work."

"Then why are your children regressing?" The question lay like a stone on the intricate mosaic. Shahitam once again spoke in a tranquil, even voice. "Hoarding and arrogance," he said plainly. "This is why my own tribe had the problem for which you now come seeking help. Humans were crying out for growth and though we gave our ethereal connection with the Creator freely to all other life forms, we gave nothing to them. They lived their brief, thirty year lives as they always did, in their caves, their trees. What did we care? We had the human-spirits we wanted so that we could continue *our* work here. We had *our* physical bodies evolving and developing through *their* connection to Earth. *We* were happy. Then came this problem with our children. We learned, after much introspection, that the reason our children were no longer surpassing us was because they were too isolated from our common ancestor, the human. It became clear, with questions, that Earth was calling us back to look at the human forms from which we grew. Like an apple which cannot fall far from its tree, we were limited. Earth was telling us that it was time for the seed to reach back and now give to the tree."

"What do you mean?" Aviea's hand slowly went to her forehead, and gently rubbed it with a forefinger.

"I am explaining to you that there is an innate connection between the human-spirits we chose to develop, and the human-spirits of the original humans. I am explaining to you that there is a limit to how far apart the spirits can evolve away from each other, and like an elastic band from a rubber tree, our kind was being called back to its distant relative. That is why your children are regressing, as ours once were."

Tisbero rushed a hand through his graying red hair. "But how can that be? Sub-species evolve. I have never heard of one sub-species being called back to be more like an ancestor. They evolved to fill different niches. Humans and human-beings fulfill different needs of Earth."

Shahitam smiled. "Spoken like someone so entrapped in the old way that there is no room in their heart to see what Life needs today." Tisbero burned, but didn't reply. "We learned that it was time to give our seed to *all* the humans as we have been doing with only our 'pure' genetic line through the ages. It was time to touch them with the Light so that the tree could grow larger branches. This way, they could grow to be more like us, rather than our children regress to be more like them. Only then could advancement of our own children continue." Shahitam was quiet as the meaning of his words sunk in.

"You mean join with all of the humans? Connect our ethereal soul to...them?" Sargac had difficulty speaking of the idea.

"Humans were good enough for you to join with when you needed one. Are we not particles of the Creator?! As you have been given to, should you not give? Our souls are bountiful, are they not? They overflow with the knowledge of Creation! Yet, you would hoard a spark of light rather than connect it to a human today? It is time for *all* humans to have knowledge of Creation, not just *your* breed."

"But we have nurtured one line only so that our guardian-ship with this planet could continue," Tisbero spat out. "Today's humans are noble as we are. They have their place and purpose. They hold the pure connection to Earth's soul."

Shahitam pounced upon Tisbero's words. "And yet your children regress! They regress because you seek to push them too far away from the tree." Tisbero's narrowed eyes stared down at the mosaic table in focused concentration.

Twaqwe spoke. Her hands were folded across her stomach as if protecting it. "But it would be impossible to parent so many new humans. It takes many years to correctly mentor one. They could lose the strength of their own identity. And what of their children? There is timing to evolution."

Shahitam stared at her. "Again arrogance. You assume that we are the only parents capable of raising children. We learned that when the humans are simply left to raise the blessed children, the children are stronger in their connection to Earth. This assures that they will always know the true parent of their physical bodies. Then, over the generations the small connection to the ethereal oceans we give them will gently bathe them, nurture them, and in this way they will develop their relationship to the Universe. They don't need to be mentored by us."

But won't that just develop a third group?" Tisbero asked. "Won't Earth continue to have the unblended humans with only their human-spirits connected to Earth, then ourselves which have nurtured one genetic line of human-spirits for millennia, and now this new third group? A third group which will be a hybrid of the other two?"

Shahitam beamed confidence as he turned from face to face. "This third group will some day be as evolved as we will come to be. Don't you see? As they evolve and they breed with each other, eventually *all* humans will be human-beings. All humans will be more like us. They too will have a connection to the Creator through Earth and as well as through sky. Eventually, there won't be three different types of bodies. As evolution proceeds, there will be just one glorious type of human-being. You'll see." Tisbero's face was stone.

Shahitam paused to pass around the tray of succulent, dark blue grapes. "I know this is not the answer you are comfortable with. It is new. New thoughts can make people uncomfortable. But look," he gestured toward the city, "we all live together now. Old human-beings and new human-beings alike. We have potters, weavers, tailors, even silversmiths. Every house has water and plumbing, light and heat. True, we provide the power and structure, but as they are ready to move on they do. We impose no limits. We only wish for them to flourish."

"But how do you have so many people here without harming the ground?" Twaqwe took a grape. "There are so many stone houses."

"Harm? What harm? This is just a different way of living. The Generator came here, it feeds energy to other crystals so that they may have more life. Why? Because the sun gives more energy to it than the Generator can use. The clouds part for us so that pure sun can reach the Generator. The sea is calm for us because it does not wish to harm our sacred shores. The ground yields crop after crop of fruit and grain."

"And these things are not forced from Earth?" Tisbero let the silver tray of grapes come to a stop in front of him.

"Forced? Of what ignorance do you speak? Our children once more grow beyond us, the new children of the humans come with open arms to learn, and we teach them. We know the crops we need and how to acquire them through Earth. Your mind is small, Tisbero. Your children's minds are becoming smaller and you can't deny it. How can you look upon the unfolding here and even question its glorious mission?"

All were quiet once more. "I did not intend to offend you," Tisbero spoke with calm intensity. "You are quite correct that all this is new for us. Perhaps you could come to an astral meeting of the tribes and discuss this with us further."

"I don't have time for such meetings!" Shahitam responded sharply. "Look around. There is too much Life here that needs me. The female humans of Earth beg to be touched by souls, even to have our children, all because they know these children will surpass them, develop and survive. How can you refuse them their need to evolve? How can you refuse them their own law of development?" Shahitam's tight voice had a narrow edge. "This is the present and the future. Hundreds upon hundreds of villages have joined us."

"Hundreds?" Twaqwe echoed in disbelief.

Shahitam continued like a drum. "Can hundreds of villages of guardians be wrong? They have seen the light. Is it not your old ways that are limiting development? Is it not your children who are regressing?" The group stared down at the mosaic table as if trying to find an answer there. A woman in a scarlet robe approached and whispered to Shahitam.

Shahitam stood up, rearranging his robe. "I must go now, for an envoy from a another city has arrived to speak with me."

"Another city?" Aviea muttered as if to herself. "There are more like this?"

Shahitam continued crisply. "Please make yourselves comfortable, and stay for a few days. You will see, and we must talk more. My aide," he waved a hand in the direction of the priest in the black robe with the purple sash, "will help you. You are welcome to join us in this bright future. Please examine your hearts, cut free of old prejudices and tell me your thoughts tomorrow." He picked up a cup of the sweet, cool wine, took a long sip and after placing it on the table with finality, turned and left the veranda.

The travelers sat in silence to absorb what had taken place, then in unison, as if of one mind, rose and walked pensively back to the large courtyard which contained the hut-sized crystal. The light of the sun blazed in it.

"I feel like another life has been lived on Earth and that I've been blind to it." Aviea was downcast. "This is such a complex place. Crystals giving Life to other crystals, specialists who master certain trades like jeweler or stonemason but have no skill in others." She made herself raise her eyes. "And this temple. I don't understand the need for it, or different titles, sashes and robes. We have differences among us but no one has more value than another. Here, there seems a society that values priest over craftsman, and craftsman over food server, and Shahitam over all. Is this the new way?" Her eyes narrowed on the crystal before them.

"How many other cities are like this?" Sargac wondered aloud, his hand unconsciously stroking the marble banister.

Tisbero walked back and forth near his friends. "I know Shahitam's argument that all human-spirits must develop if ours are to develop sounds logical. Many very intelligent guardians are agreeing with him, but it doesn't feel right in my heart." He stopped pacing and turned to face the generator. "And maybe this new social hierarchy is a new structure for life. Structure is good. All nature has structure, but there is a rigidity here. It's as if the people here grow in a certain way, not necessarily in their own way."

"But what of our children?" Sargac placed both hands his hand on the banister now. "We cannot deny that ours are regressing and theirs are evidently progressing."

"I know," Tisbero's hot stare followed another skyplatform leaving the island, this one accelerating toward the southeast, and then his gaze fell to the polished floor. "I know."

As if from some mutual inner timing, the group began walking once more down the long corridor. Twaqwe cleared her throat before speaking her thoughts. "I know much is created here, but I..." The sound of a squealing horse echoed off the walls and broke her speech. The group stood stunned as a four-footed creature burst out of a chamber to the left, stopped, looked at them and screeched again.

"What's that?" Aviea shouted in shock, her hand racing to her throat. The creature had the body of a small horse but the head and arms of a human male. Repulsed at the sight, each group member took several steps back. Two men wearing long, dark blue silken robes with yellow sashes rushed to the beast and led it back the direction it had come. Then as suddenly as the sight occurred, it was over. Tisbero heard steps pounding in the hallway and turned to see the priest that Shahitam had assigned sprinting toward them.

The priest stopped suddenly, his face panic. "It's all fine!" He exclaimed, trying to catch his breath. "Let me explain!"

Tisbero had fire in his eyes. "What is going on here?!" he demanded.

The priest stood a moment, struggled to collect himself, then responded with surprising calm. "Yes. I would demand an explanation, too, if I had just seen what you just saw without understanding it," he acknowledged.

"We're ready to listen!" Tisbero seethed.

The priest began walking once more down the corridor, indicating that the group should follow. The team looked down the empty hall where the half-human beast had been, before proceeding. "As you know, because of this new way we are once more in total communication with Earth." The aide raised a palm upward as if in explanation. "We know the genetic history of every living thing on the planet. As you also know, Earth seeks ever more variety. As you cannot know, because of the special work we have accomplished, Earth sought to expand its Creation through us. Since we know the genetics of all species, we can manipulate them. We can subtract and add genetic elements that Earth has not been able to do. We can refine species, make them more suited to develop in Life for the benefit of Earth."

"This is ill-advised!" Tisbero had emphatic disgust in his voice. "Earth evolves its own species and brings its thought forms forward to blend with its creations. Evolution is in motion. What you speak of is domination!"

The aide continued, now completely self-composed. "Earth receives thoughts from the Creator, and the Creator is manifest through Earth." He glanced over his shoulder to make sure everyone was following. "We are manifestations of the Creator, are we not? The Creator would not have given us intelligence if It did not wish us to use it. This is just another way for the Creator to create. It is a blending with Earth, a cooperation."

"All thoughts are possible," Tisbero scoffed. "You and you alone choose which ones to act upon."

"And these thoughts have led to more diversity," the priest calmly replied.

"But how can you know you are not interfering with Earth's own plan?" Twaqwe shot out.

The corners of the priest's mouth turned up in a slight smile. "Because we are part of Earth. We are part of the Creator. We were summoned here, were we not? We use the building blocks Earth provides to fulfill the Creator's command to create. We do not insist that our creations live, for as always, one plus one equals a new and independent third. Some of these creations do not live, others thrive. What lives is decided by Earth! We only fulfill the laws of development, to bring choice, diversity and creation."

The group had come again to the threshold of the temple. "Do not judge too harshly what you have not experienced," the priest said with a tinge of shame in his voice. "Shahitam came to my village which was probably much like yours is now, a hundred ago. We also saw a constant decline in the abilities of our children. Our tribe was regressing and our fear grew with each new birth. After all, these less able bodies were what we would be forced to take in our next cycle of reincarnation. We would come back to more solid bodies! We discussed and argued with Shahitam. In the end, we decided to try his counsel. Since that time, I have seen the creation of more and more Life. The humans with which we mate desire our seed and their lives improve." The aide looked Tisbero in the eyes. "Children progress once more. All guardians are seeing the wisdom of this way. They cannot dispute results."

Tisbero shook his head. "Not all," he corrected. "It feels forced to me. I was confused earlier, but my thoughts are coming more clearly now. The fruit which we ate was not harvested from the ground; it was taken from it. The crystal which feeds the others must do so or it will explode. That beast we saw was forced together, not evolved together as is Earth's way. Are you clear about the impact your choices have?" The aide did not reply.

"You also live in a walled place." Aviea sounded suspicious. "Which means that all things are not going well. Why else would you have to protect yourself?"

The priest laughed as he touched his purple sash. "The wall is not for protection! It is for privacy! So many humans seek our help it's impossible to work in an orderly way without this boundary. It prevents chaos."

The team came to the room set aside for their stay. "You must visit again with Shahitam. He can explain these things to you much more explicitly than I, and you can speak with other envoys from other cities. You'll come to understand. I can only assure you that all is more than well. You'll see. You must stay and learn. Shahitam will bring clarity to all your questions, as he did mine."

He led them into a cool chamber, fine linen draped across granite framed windows to filter the sun. "Rest. Contemplate. Shahitam will make time for you again tomorrow." The priest bowed his head slightly and left.

They watched the priest until he turned a corner down the long corridor. The foursome gathered into a circle as if huddled in a storm. Tisbero spoke first. "We must get back and report to the council. I've seen enough."

Aviea clutched her garment as if searching for the right words. "Shahitam has some way of speaking. He speaks truth, but somehow it is not straight. It makes me dizzy."

"Yes." Twaqwe started to touch her upper lip in thought, then noticed the stain from the blue grapes on her fingers. She lowered her hand and unconsciously wiped it on her pale linen robe.

Sargac spoke. "How many villages do you think have joined this way? He said many hundreds."

Tisbero's voice ground like cinder. "Aviea's right. We've been asleep. We have been so involved with our need to nurture the life among us that we lost track of the life around us, and of what was happening on this sacred island." He scanned his fellow travelers slowly. "I fear much."

"We agree to leave then?" Sargac asked as he glanced down the empty hallway. Tisbero, Aviea and Twaqwe nodded assent as one.

"We go," Tisbero made clear. The three followed him down the alley way to the main road which led to their skystone. The team stepped upon the living stone which still hovered a foot above the ground with a sense of relief. As the travelers connected once more to the crystals, they gazed at the larger platforms which had "escorted" them here.

Aviea's voice turned to ice. "They're not on landing pads at all. They rested their full weight on the plants beneath them."

"Let's get out of here," Tisbero spat out. As their skystone took off, fresh eyes focused on the scene below.

They crossed over the top of the long black wall. "Look there," Aviea pointed down. "The elfin-kind, the earth devas, are surrounding the wall! They're ones that work with plants. Why are they trying to get inside?"

Tisbero studied them. "They're angry," he said as if in trance. Then startled recognition reddened his face. "That's why they built such a wall. They need to keep the devas out! The devas of the fourth dimension would try to stop Shahitam's new species from taking their first breath!"

"He is not letting Earth decide," Sargac rushed out. "He is dominating Life." Their skystone passed over people working in cultivated fields and the travelers reached out with their senses to connect with them. Sargac added, "The people working there are like servants!"

Twaqwe's voice was heavy with sadness as she struggled to connect her energy to the workers below. "They give themselves over to him because they feel so inadequate in comparison. He and his kind are their masters."

Tisbero railed on. "These new human-beings created through this indiscriminate mating do not feel their own value. Their genetics aren't prepared to receive so much ethereal energy, and it is breaking their timing. They are being split from themselves. They do not know their source is Earth. How can they hope to have consciousness next lifetime if they don't have it during this one?" The skystone moved out over the sea.

"It looks so calm. But it's not calm." Aviea said with sudden revelation. "It is controlled." The team did not look back as they hurriedly set course for the home island.

"This is bad." Twaqwe choked on her words and had to take a deep breath before she could speak again. "Very bad. How will these new human-beings know their purpose if they are split from Earth?"

"How could we have been so blind?" Concern was forged on Tisbero's sober face. "Without balance, they will be lost."

As the foursome flew to the east, the priest who had accompanied them in the temple felt apprehensive as he reported to Shahitam. He had good reason. "What?!" Shahitam exploded. "You let them leave after seeing a centaur?! They do not understand! They cannot understand!"

"I had no idea they were leaving, Shahitam," the priest pleaded. "They said they'd stay and speak with you tomorrow," he lied. "But clearly they're choosing not to listen to your wisdom."

Shahitam stormed back and forth on the stage like an angry cloud. "Their small minds will ruin the minds of many." He stopped and glared at the priest. "Our plans have gone too far to be interrupted by fools. We go to more and more villages that are having trouble with their children, and as we explain things to them, they join the Creator's new work." He was silent a moment. His chest shuddered as if being torn from within, and he turned away from the priest to the arched window and the blue sky beyond. Then as if reaffirming his choice, he turned back and hurled out the words. "They should have stayed fixated on their shrinking world and not meddled with ours. Just like the others who have thought to stand in our way, they must be stopped!"

"I heard their doubts. They *will* poison the minds of many," the priest said.

Shahitam ignored him and picked up a large yellow citrine crystal, which was not used for blending physical and ethereal energies as the travelers thought, but was instead changed and controlled so that it would rip these energies apart. "Get three platforms, each with thirty soldiers skilled in the use of these unmaking crystals. We will follow the fools, and destroy them."

Chapter 9   *Inner Worlds*

Yawri flew over countless spires of tall evergreens until he saw the small pond that he knew was near Muran. He skillfully sailed his skystone a couple of feet above its surface, being careful not to hit any of the waterlilies that grew like starbursts in its shallows. Their bright yellow blossoms did little to improve his mood, and he parked the skystone without his customary stone-bobbing flourish. Stepping down from where it hovered above the ferns, he walked toward Muran with a deliberate step. "You're a little sullen, aren't you?" the red-tree said. "If you're coming to die, we're not ready. We haven't even called the fire to make our wooden caves yet."

Yawri stopped near the base of the great tree and studied a large, orange domed mushroom before lifting his head. "I'm not here to die," he countered, trying to change to a lighter mood. "Although I'm sure you're eager to get your roots around my compost." He managed a rueful grin.

"No. Not eager. Not eager at all." Muran let silence fill the air and waited for Yawri to speak.

"Muran," he began, but his gaze fell on the path where the human hunters had presented him with a dead lemur what seemed like a lifetime ago. "Some of our villages are reporting a problem with their children." The glow around the tree's leaves seemed to increase, then return to a soft, yellow sheen. "It may be nothing. But several of the guardians are traveling to different locations to see if there is anything we can learn."

Muran spoke. "What kind of problems?"

"There's nothing wrong in our village," Yawri continued as if to allay undue concern. An owl sounded its searching call, and after a pause, Yawri decided to elaborate. "Well, maybe a few of our children seem a little less capable. It's odd. You know we pride ourselves in working with our human-spirits lifetime after lifetime so that the bodies become ever more capable, not less." The answering voice of another owl danced with the air.

"I know you're proud of the work." Muran spoke a little too soberly for Yawri's comfort.

"Have you seen anything, heard anything on the wind, that would let us know if this is something we should be concerned about?"

"Yes. Of course."

Yawri's eyebrows raised. "What? What are you hearing?"

"You remember the hunters who gave you one of their animals as an offering?" Muran asked, seemingly unattached to how Yawri would answer.

"Yes," Yawri's jagged voice bristled with concern.

"They actually had a battle recently with a neighboring tribe. The wind reports that these events are increasing. It's as if the tribes are only connected to themselves, not to each other anymore. It's happening all over the planet."

"Do you know why?"

"I don't know. Differences always exist. Some trees are kinder than others, you know. We're not all the same. Some refuse to move their branches to let new trees grow. Some will send their roots to the best water and even wrap them around other trees' roots to lessen their competitors' supply. Especially when times are hard. The need to survive is a very powerful force in all creatures. Different trees make different choices, even while they make food from sun and fertilize the ground. I've heard whispers that choices the guardians are making have something to do with the change in the humans."

Yawri shifted uncomfortably. "I don't know what choices guardians are making that could lead to this," he confessed.

Muran answered kindly. "You can only know yourself, not another. Only you can know the authentic reasons for taking the actions you do."

Yawri felt a need to change the direction of the conversation. "You've lived on other planets," he said, recalling Muran's past discussions. "Is there anything you've heard of that might compare to what some of our villages are experiencing here? Anything that compares to a regression in the children of human-beings?"

"Nothing to compare directly, no. There is never anything to compare because each moment is new. But," he added slowly, "sometimes the joinings don't go as planned. I've heard of that."

"What can happen?" Yawri took another step, as if searching, toward the tree.

Muran was quiet for a minute. A gentle breeze touched the branches in the grove and they waved gently in response, opening to receive any messages on the wind. "Anything can happen," the tree said at last. "Creation shifts in response to the collective thoughts used to mold it. I don't know which thoughts human-beings will choose to make physical. The Creator doesn't control you, or any of Its soul-seeds. How can I say what can happen? I don't know the thoughts of your kind."

Yawri searched for the source of his confusion, but it seemed just beyond reach. "Perhaps I should just have faith that it's nothing to be concerned about." He spoke the answer he preferred, but it sounded hollow.

"Have faith in the choices human-beings will make? Perhaps. But sometimes faith can be blind. Then it can feed denial. Personally, I prefer to focus on my own choices. When I make a mistake, I can feel ashamed or I can forgive myself. When I choose to forgive myself for hurting Life, I can see what is actually needed and then give it. In shame, I can only see what I need to do so that I can feel better about myself."

"I don't know what I'm supposed to do with that. Why would any guardian ever feel shame?" Yawri stared unseeing at the rough bark. "I'll go back and report to the council as best I can."

"Some choices can lead to darkness," Muran said simply. Yawri's head jerked up. "It can come to pass that guardians whose destiny it is to nurture Life, come to murder it. It doesn't have to happen. But I've heard of it. I've even heard of human-beings on other worlds cutting us down without our permission."

"No!" Yawri said aghast. "No one could ever do that. It's impossible. We are One. It's your kind that make all this possible." He waved a hand to include the diverse menagerie of plants, singing birds and humming insects. As if on cue, a winged elfin-kind dove toward a bumblebee as if trying to chase it away from a prized flower. "Cut the great trees down? That's the most ridiculous thing I've ever heard!"

Sunlight played through the branches and danced with the fiddle-ferns. "I'll give you something," Muran said, his tone lightened. "It's something to help you stay connected to the core of Earth and the universal oceans in the same instant."

"That's what your kind does," Yawri said pensively. "With your roots in the ground and branches in the sky, you keep the dimensions connected."

"You know how thought forms of all the species that you're helped are also living inside of you? How those thoughts of Earth are part of you too?"

"Naturally. They're a part of me. Or a part of this body at least." A fairy-like deva flew past, followed by another in mischievous pursuit. Yawri spoke studiously. "They live in the fourth dimension like the devas. It's not as if they take up physical space inside my body. So you're going to give me a tree thought-form to help me stay connected to Earth and the heavens in the same moment?"

Muran laughed into the gentle breeze. "No. You have plenty of those. How many species of trees have you nurtured? A hundred? A thousand?" Yawri raised both of his shoulders and eyebrows in questioning response. "No. You need something more powerful."

"What could be more powerful than trees for keeping worlds connected?" Yawri was clearly puzzled.

The scent of the bog near the pond wafted subtly into the air. "A water lily," Muran replied simply.

"A water lily?" Yawri was dismayed. "A water lily will help me stay connected?"

Muran spoke from a timeless perspective. "You should have spent more time with Aviea. She learned the value of the tiniest of plants while you had your head up in towering branches."

Yawri considered this as he looked more closely at the nearby pond. A breeze blew across its smooth surface and it rippled in response. "A water lily?" he repeated softly.

"Or 'lotus,' if you prefer."

Yawri stared at the plants growing in the shallow water and recalled a scene from his last visit here. It felt so long ago when he had seen a dragonfly with wings of iridescent light rest on a floating pad.

Muran continued, "Think about it. Like trees, they grow their roots in the soil and have their leaves in the sky, but unlike trees they surround their stems with water. Water that is connected to the waters of the Universe and of Earth alike." He spoke with considered thought. "And you don't have a lotus in your body. I know you like trees, and I must admit we do a lot of connecting, but water lilies are expert at connecting multiple dimensions of reality. They can help keep you connected, too."

Yawri studied the blossoms waving in the air above the glassy surface. "I see," he said as if considering the possibility for the first time. "Like most plants, they connect to Earth's core through their roots and to the Universe through their leaves, but they also live in the water world. Their stems partake of it as if one with the oceans of Creation."

Muran's voice resonated with the rippling sounds of the forest. "They harmonize directly with the ground, the sky and the water, because they live in all three. I, on the other hand, live only in earth and sky." Yawri turned his head from the pond to the red tree, and nodded. "You'll leave here with another thought-form inside of you, then. You'll have a lotus plant to remind you of your connection to All. You may need it some time. Let your body receive the water plant as you do all Life. Nurture it and let it nurture you."

Yawri went down to the pond's edge and studied the different types of water lilies. Some had leaves that rose out of the water like funnels and others laid their leaves like floating rafts on the surface. Both sent and received energy like green hands. A small frog looked Yawri in the eye, but didn't hop off its tethered pad. "Thank you," Yawri said to the plants as well as Muran. "Thank you very much."

"I heard something on the winds that you might like, too," Muran said. Yawri turned to face the big tree. "It's a poem, or maybe a prayer. I'm not sure."

"A poem?" Yawri was unclear about the term's meaning. He took a few steps toward Muran.

"I think it originated on another planet that harbored bodies with the same purpose as yours. You know, traveling, being a life-bearer, all that."

"I get the idea. I know that a number of planets have human-like forms."

After several seconds of getting the translation straight in his mind, Muran said, "It goes like this:
>   'Souls join with bodies,
>   Bodies join with souls.
>   Nurture the Creator,
>   Together or apart.
>   I honor your gift,
>   As you honor mine.
>   Bearers of Life, and Joy.'"

"Very nice," Yawri said sincerely. "Now I have a lotus and a poem." A thoughtful grin showed on his lips. "Thanks again."

Muran waved his needle-like leaves to the sun. "Don't mention it," he said with the gentle breeze. "I hope you remember that you have them."

✦

Mariyonta and Aronlat paused before entering the geode-like cave within the great cavern. They cast an appreciative look back toward their camp. To the left, near a stepped wall of stratified stone, were their beds. They had placed foot-high stones as boundaries for two large rectangles, each filled with tan, fine-grained sand and covered with resilient dried moss.

Aronlat exhaled into the sweet, mineral-rich air and said, "We've got a great camp, even if we don't need much rest." He turned back to face the huge underground lake, his thoughts full of reflection. *I didn't know what would happen when the rest of our initiation group left. When we were washed down that tunnel I thought we'd lose our bodies for sure. Earth's law of development with our law of Creation fills me with such hope, such excitement.* His eyes focused on Mariyonta. "I've never felt so alive."

Mariyonta's eyes sparkled with inner light. "It's a blessing being here, all right. It's still amazes me how this deep underground lake functions as a eardrum for Earth. It really does receive vibrations just like our eardrums do. Except it transfers sounds from the Universe to inner Earth."

Her eyes fell on the net they had made to harvest delicate, shrimp-like creatures from the lake. It was her turn for inner reflection. *The cavern provides food. It provides light.* She stretched her arms toward the distant ceiling whose glowing crystals filled the lakeside resort with light like that of an early morning sky. *My body receives so much life force here that not much food or rest is needed. I've never felt so alive, either.* She saw a small, glowing material on the ground. *Even the fungus gives light.* She turned toward Aronlat. "I could live here forever."

Their eyes locked. They touched hands, then let them drop slowly. They walked in silence into the "working" geode cave, past a wall of hexagonal crystals, and stopped before a sixteen-foot-long, violet-blue crystal which protruded from the wall so much like a guard that they had nicknamed it the sentinel.

After a long moment, the duo respectfully sat down in their accustomed spots among a thousand lustrous mirror-like faces.

"The sentinel is in spry form today," Aronlat commented. "It's enjoying the work, too."

Mariyonta inhaled, letting the breath of the crystal cave fill her, then let it go as she turned her gaze to it. "That amethyst is very skilled at working with time dimensions. When I meditate with it, it shows me time tunnels that fill the fabric of space like a honeycomb. I've never met another crystal with such ability." She turned slowly back to Aronlat. "I think this cavern must have wanted the touch of human-beings as much as we wanted to touch it. It seems content with its decision to let us live." She cast a look out through the toothy mouth of the crystal cave to the great cavern beyond, then back to the mineral faces surrounding them.

"So far so good." Aronlat grinned. "If the cave didn't want us working here, it would let us know in very clear terms."

Mariyonta nodded her head in agreement as the two young adults studied each other in silence. Then, feeling a strange longing to hold him that made her feel unsettled, she shifted her attention to something more secure. She focused on her inner state and sought communion with the Life surrounding her. After a minute she said a bit too officiously, "Let's balance the energy centers of the body. I'd like to see how my body's chakras are functioning, if they've changed much since the last time we looked at them."

Aronlat continued looking at her a long moment before he replied. His voice sounded mischievous. "We can do that if you like." Mariyonta's eyes widened, uncertain if he was responding to her thoughts or her words. She didn't exhale until she saw him move to his accustomed working place, closer to a large, pale purple crystal. "Or we could experiment with other types of energies," he said thoughtfully. Mariyonta raised a quizzical eyebrow. He cleared his throat. "Like learning how to connect to the planet's chakra system. I think we're ready for it."

Mariyonta smiled wryly as she leaned her back against the crystal wall. "I do remember Tisbero and Yawri telling us that many of the Earth's continents are physical manifestations of its energy centers, but I don't know how they relate to the ones in human bodies."

Aronlat was energized with youthful vigor. "I don't either, but let's find out."

Mariyonta turned to scan the crystal cave, and her own sense of exploration kindled inner eagerness. "How? By asking the cave-spirit to show us?" A gentle breeze blew through straw-thin stalactites and played them like a harp as Aronlat nodded assent. She breathed into the moving air and said, "Then let's get started."

They stood with lids lowered, eyes relaxed, to let their perception expand into the non-physical fourth dimension and communicate with the cave-spirit. The faint waves of the lake moved rhythmically, like its oceanic cousins on the surface, both dancing with the moon. A blind fish jumped from its water world and reentered with a festive splash. Air and moss alike sang with the music, and the multidimensional sounds filled them as the cave-spirit responded.

"Are you ready to feel the Earth's chakras through your own?" the cave-spirit asked in the One Language of Creation. Aronlat moved a hand to the center of his chest to make sure his heart was open. He felt the warmth expand as if he were drinking hot tea.

"I am ready," each of the young adults echoed.

The cave-spirit considered their response. "We brought you here because of your ability to connect to Life. But having the ability to do something is different from doing it. Be warned. If you are not ready, you can burn your bodies to a cinder. Such are the energies with which you seek connection."

Mariyonta let go of a soft breath as she questioned. Then she recalled how her body functioned so well when it was swept away with the flood, automatically knowing when to gulp for air or intuitively bend around a rock. She trusted it. "I am ready."

"I am also ready," Aronlat reported.

"Very well," the cave-spirit said. "We will ask you to focus on three of your nine chakras only, and to connect their energies together in a very specific way. After you have done that, we will see how much communication from Earth's energy centers is available to you." Neither Aronlat nor Mariyonta answered, so intent were they on their inner state.

The cave-spirit continued. "Please focus on the chakra that is under your feet, and tell me what you sense."

Aronlat swayed slowly back and forth as he spoke from his altered state, his face calm. "It feels like the chakra under my feet is a planet unto itself. It's rotating quickly, and filled with colorful yellows and tans, some light orange. I feel as though my legs are immersed in warm loam. I feel that my body's human-spirit is doing a good job of monitoring the amount of Earth energy it allows into the body."

Mariyonta sensed the lava-like heat available to her body from deep Earth, and spoke with a slower cadence. "I understand. Without a conscious physical body, unmonitored Earth energy could burn it to a cinder." She spoke deliberately, focusing all of her attention on this energy center below her feet. "This chakra feels like it is connected to all the Life of Earth as well as the other planets in the solar system." Mariyonta breathed Earth energy in through the soles of her feet as if they were nostrils. A warm coal seemed to glow at the base of her spine, not burning, but nurturing her like a bath in a hotspring.

"Yes," Aronlat reflected as he felt his own body warm with the increased connection. "I understand how adults I have seen can stand barefoot in the snow and be warm."

Air currents flowed around dripping stalactites, like a breeze whistling softly through a stand of sleeping trees, and the cave-spirit spoke again. "Now proceed to the chakra that blends ethereal and physical energies, the one in the area of your diaphragm. The diaphragm is located between your lungs filled with air and your stomach containing physical food. The chakra reflects its location. It connects ethereal and physical energies, too."

"This is the seat of the human-spirit," Aronlat said, absorbed in thought. "This is where the part of the Earth's soul that lives in this body resides."

Excitement showed in Mariyonta's voice as she leaned forward, eyes still closed. "Yes, the human-spirit resides here. I feel it. Now I understand what's behind my gut reactions. It's my body's own consciousness speaking to me. But I sense something more. Something...Is this the energy center which keeps the body's timing synchronized with the planet's?"

"Astute," the cave-spirit replied. "This is the body's chakra which holds its timing with that of the planet. Just as the planet's third chakra is responsible for keeping its timing synchronized with the solar system."

"And the solar system's timing is synchronized with the galaxy?" Aronlat asked as he tried to keep track of the information.

"Astute again," came the reply. "All physical creations use the fabric of time as a structure to coordinate physicality. You are both correct. Shall we go on?"

"Yes," was the immediate reply.

The sounds of singing stones mixed with a trickle of rich water which gurgled softly as it rolled down a staircase of stone. "Now for the last chakra of this exercise. Focus on the energy center that is just a short distance above your head, and tell me what you sense," the cave-spirit said.

Mariyonta spoke from her deep state. "The chakra above my head is filled with my soul colors, beautiful violets and light blues."

"Light greens and gold are my soul colors." Aronlat gently swayed side to side as if unable to contain his electric excitement. "This center functions as a regulator for the energy that comes from my oversoul just as the chakra under the feet functions as a regulator for the energy coming from Earth. And just as with the one under the feet, if it was out of balance, this body could incinerate in a flash of light."

Usually a brilliant flash of blue light," the cave-spirit commented.

"You've seen it happen?" Aronlat placed a hand on a nearby crystal, but with his eyes closed he didn't see that it responded by glowing with increased light.

"Extreme unconsciousness can be a problem. I did warn you that these energies are quite strong," was the kind response.

Mariyonta opened her eyes to look at the cave wall. It pulsed with an eerie violet-blue. She closed her eyes again, and after a long moment said, "I sense how the soul and human-spirit remain strong in their identity. The chakra above my head contains the complete history of myself as a soul, just as the one under my feet contains the history of the body's evolution on the planet. That way, they both know the home of each other."

The cave wall pulsed a rich violet, and it replied, "And that is why those two chakras must be connected in the third chakra which is between them. It blends ethereal and physical dimensions so that the soul and human-spirit can be conscious of one another."

Aronlat smiled through his closed eyes as he rode a wave of recognition. "That's why you are having us focus on these three chakras. We must be balanced in our connection to the body's ethereal and physical energy sources before we can connect to the planet's chakras."

"Consciousness requires balance of all of the bodies energy centers, but if these three are not in clear communication, balance of the other six is not possible. So, now we will focus on balancing all three of these chakras at the same time." The eyes of each young adult opened, but catching sight of each other, closed again. The cave continued teaching. "There is an energy flow connecting these three chakras that is shaped like a figure eight, or more descriptively, an hourglass." Aronlat and Mariyonta pulled in every word, so intent were they to understand. "Imagine your body is inside an hourglass. The top of the hourglass goes through the chakra above your head, and its bottom goes through the one under your feet. The narrow middle passes through the third chakra in your solar plexus."

Aronlat swirled with dizziness. "Keep the structure balanced. It's very real and has real impact," the cave-spirit warned. Aronlat breathed into his diaphragm, centering himself, and felt better.

Mariyonta's aura took on a new vibrancy, filled with her soul colors and hues of Earth. "The human-spirit of this body knows how to run this energy flow," she said as a statement of fact.

"Yes," the cave-spirit replied. "The more conscious and valued the human-spirit the more conscious the soul can be of all of these energies. Aronlat took the cue and let his human-spirit take control of the process. His aura glowed.

"Now," said the cave-spirit. "Allow connection of your body's chakras to those of Earth."

Aronlat swayed as if to the cadence of a well-metered poem. "I feel I am in the core of Earth," he said slowly. "But I don't feel hot."

"That is because this flow blends Earth's heat with the cool waters of the Universe," the cave-spirit said.

"And I see Earth's chakra centers," Aronlat continued. "They are continents, or regions on them at least."

"Yes," the cave-spirit replied. "Tell me, where is the planet's heart chakra?"

Aronlat was silent a moment, then said, "It's the wide bridge of land between the southeastern continent and the larger land mass to its north."

"Do you agree, Mariyonta?" the cave-sprit asked.

She was enthralled with the pulsing streams running throughout her body, and it took a moment to shift from her deep state and speak. "Yes. The heart chakra in my body is resonating most with that region of land. But there is more." She was still as stone, then with a breath, revelation filled her voice. "The nine chakras of my body resonate with the nine chakras of the planet which resonate with the nine planets of the solar system!"

"Astute," was all the cave-spirit said.

"Is that true?" Aronlat asked. "As Mariyonta spoke it, I felt it. But then I had a sense that something was missing."

The cave wall brightened, then dimmed again. "When solar systems change, bodies change, and there has been change. However, you have done enough work in this altered state for now. It is time for you to return to your bodies' normal state. Someday, as your bodies develop, this level of connection and awareness may be constant. There is no hurry. Bodies connected to such energies may live for a thousand years. Respect your bodies' timing."

Aronlat and Mariyonta needed no convincing. They understood now, more than ever that without respect for the timing of the human-spirit, none of this work would be possible. "Thank you," they said with all the gratitude they held, and came out of their altered state. They opened their eyes slowly. The cave wall appeared as solid as ever to their physical vision.

"Wow," Mariyonta said in a low voice.

Aronlat relaxed against the faceted minerals of the geode cave. "There is a lot I don't know," he said as if to himself.

Mariyonta chuckled, a fond smile gracing her lips. "I couldn't agree with you more." He turned to her, decided he didn't feel offended, and laughed. Then her laughter joined his as their joy of being alive and sharing this moment echoed off the walls. Then, as one of them stopped laughing, and the other one tried to stop laughing, they both started again. After several cycles of this, they lay on the floor of the crystal cave finally relaxed, feeling inner contentment deeper than either had known before. The sound of dripping water returned, and the splash of a fish reminded them of the vast underground lake. No words were spoken as they each stood and made their way out of the crystal cave to stand on the beach.

"You know," Aronlat said as they stood gazing at the living lake. "Yawri told me that the planet had chakras, but I had no idea what he really meant."

Mariyonta beamed as if in the morning sun. "Can you imagine? The better we're able to connect our chakras with those of the planet, the better we'll be able to communicate with all the other planets in the solar system. Just think of what we'll be able to learn."

Aronlat watched the head of some aquatic creature move through the water. "Do you see that?" He pointed. "It looks like an eel."

"A big eel." She stared at it, recalling a distant memory. "You know, right after I landed in this lake I felt something brush across my legs. It startled me." Both guardians watched as the creature descended under the surface. "But then, I got distracted by your thrashing trying to swim with that rucksack."

"My thrashing probably scared it away."

"Or, it thought you were easier prey." She grinned mischievously.

"Come to think of it," he admitted. "I felt something brush my legs too, but I thought it was you." She looked at him wide-eyed and shook her head.

Turning her face to the domed ceiling suddenly, she paused and asked, "Did you feel that?"

"Feel what? On my legs?"

"No. No. A shaking. A shock . I don't know. I just got chills."

Aronlat became instantly serious and stood still as a statue as he stretched out his senses. "Yes, there is something strange." He was quiet a long moment, and tried to breathe in any message from the living air. "I sense confusion, fear."

Mariyonta peered from ceiling to walls to lake. "It's certainly safe." After measured inspection she turned back to Aronlat. "The cave is okay."

Aronlat checked his body's Earth chakra below his feet. "Maybe it was us. As you started talking about our plunge into the lake, I started remembering how traumatic that ride through the flash flood was. Maybe we're so open after the exercise that we scared our bodies. Let's reconnect to the core of Earth, and make sure the body is in balance."

The sensation seemed to have passed. Mariyonta nodded. "We haven't ever talked about how scary that journey was. We should." Aronlat nodded.

"You know," Mariyonta continued. "I bet before we leave here we'll be able to chart the movement of the planets and the stars. Won't Tisbero and Yawri be excited for us? We'll return with something they're actually interested in. When we see them we'll compare our star charts to theirs, and see how well we did."

"You mean see how well they did," Aronlat replied with mock superiority.

Mariyonta laughed outright, then stopped and began laughing again. "My joke wasn't that funny," Aronlat admitted.

"I know. I know," Mariyonta replied, not catching the flash of disappointment that rippled across Aronlat's face. "It's just that I remembered something Tisbero said as we were entering the cave. He told me not to bump my head on the stars. I thought he was just being strange at the time, but now I get it. He knew as we learned how to connect more with Earth, we'd discover more about its family."

"I can't think of a better place to touch the universe." Aronlat offered his hand and she took it as they turned toward camp. "That energy work made me hungry," he added as they walked up the beach.

"How about roast eel?" she asked, and they laughed again.

Chapter 10   **Murder**

Tisbero turned to Aviea as his village came into view. "Aviea, I know this may sound like an unusual request, but after we land, please take our fastest skystone to the eastern continent. Tell the first village you find what we've learned."

Aviea was startled. "But Tisbero, I should be here. My sudden departure will cause concern."

Their skystone began a rapid descent. "*I* am concerned," Tisbero said emphatically. "I don't trust Shahitam. Something has gone very wrong."

"But we'll visit with all of the village leaders in our astral bodies tonight. Surely that will be much better than if I go to one village physically," Aviea countered as she turned to face him.

"Your physical presence will carry more impact. Please make haste to go." Aviea looked at him with uncertainty. "Just go!" Tisbero spouted. He grasped her shoulders tightly and peered intently into her eyes. "I have a very bad feeling about this, so please indulge me, and go."

Aviea searched his face and, leveling her voice, said, "Okay. Since it means so much to you, I will go to the first village and speak with them." Tisbero nodded.

The skystone came to a hovering stop over its bedrock landing place, then descended into its dock. Tisbero, Twaqwe, Sargac and Aviea hurried off, each with a mission in mind. "Bring everyone to the central green!" Tisbero called to confirm the meeting place.

Soon, most of the village residents stood among wildflowers and barley. A sudden breeze blew from the west. "An ill wind," a young woman murmured. Several standing nearby nodded in agreement.

"We have unhappy news," Tisbero began as he saw Aviea fly over the first hill. *May the Creator bless your journey.* "We have learned why the beings of the biggest Atlantean island have not been attending gatherings on the astral plane." All attention came to the elder. "Shahitam has changed a place of healing into a place of harming. He has chosen to dominate life instead of co-create with it. He has..." A yell arose from the assemblage as faces turned toward the west.

"What's that?" a voice called out. The shadow of three large skyplatforms suddenly covered the assembly. Soldiers, each one holding a deep yellow crystal, lined the edges of the hovering platforms like dark teeth.

Shahitam's voice boomed over the villagers below. "Tisbero has poisoned you all! The way of the Creator is to use what It has given us to improve Creation! To make it more of what it is!"

"You create harm, not life!" Tisbero shouted, his arms upthrust and his graying red hair waving.

Shahitam barked back. "You have been given the answer and you doubt it with inane questions! You are all lost!" he cried out. He turned in disgust to his troops. "Unmake them all! They are lost to the Way!"

Beams of bright, mustard colored light suddenly shot out from the yellow crystals and fell upon the stomachs of many unsuspecting villagers. In an instant, their third chakras were shattered, the union of the human-spirit and etheric-soul was ripped apart. Their bodies crumpled in tortured pain and death. Those not hit stood confused, baffled by something that had not existed in their reality until this moment. Some looked into the sky, motionless, trying desperately to understand what they saw. Others responded to the screams of pain coming from their friends, and knelt down in a futile attempt to heal them. The remaining few villagers not yet on the green ran toward it as fast as they could to help.

"Twaqwe!" Tisbero called. "Take the recording crystal and hide it!"

"Dear Creator! What's happening?" Twaqwe picked up the recording crystal and started running. A beam caught her mid-section, the abrupt end to her scream told Tisbero that she was dead.

"Sargac!" he yelled. Sargac was already running to help her. Tisbero ran to the skystone they had used and knelt next to one of the pineapple-sized crystals. Though cool to the touch, in a moment it glowed with a heatless white and nestled itself into Tisbero's arms.

"Dearest friend," he said with a calm drawn from a deep reserve. "Evil is on Earth. I ask that you help me return the energy that is being sent to us back to its source." He stood to survey the field. Sargac, he saw, was kneeling over Twaqwe's contorted body. "Sargac!" he yelled above the screams, "keep

moving!" Sargac knelt frozen, the shock of utter disbelief etched
into his face. Two beams hit him at once. His body fell to the
ground as if his muscles did not exist. Tisbero ran through the
tumult, picked up the recording crystal, stuffed it into his tunic
and set his eyes on a narrow crack in the granite thirty yards
away. As he ran he twisted around midstride to face the
murderers, holding the skystone's crystal up as a reflective
shield, and urgently hurried backwards toward the crack. *Dear
Earth, help me.* A soldier on the middle platform spotted him. A
beam of light hit the crystal Tisbero held over his third chakra.
It was instantaneously reflected back to its source. A frantic
scream came from the platform and the beam stopped. Tisbero
backed on. Twenty yards to go when another beam came.
Another scream from a falling soldier. Fifteen yards.

Shahitam's eye was drawn to the two soldiers who had
mysteriously fallen from his ships. Then he saw another one
fall. "Ah, Tisbero," he said under his breath. *So you are not
such a gardener after all. You kill my troops. Your escape route
is a dead end, though. You prove your inability to see a way out
of this valley just as you can't see the truth. There is no escape
from the truth, old man.* He gestured to his captain. "See that
one?"

The captain saw the object of his Master's displeasure.
"Yes, my lord." The skyplatform moved toward the solitary
figure.

Feigning a stumble, Tisbero dropped the recording crystal
down the deep fissure in the rock. His eyes flashed across a
familiar and much larger crevice further on, one he knew could
be climbed down, but not jumped across. Pulling all attention
away from where he dropped the recording crystal, he
continued to back away from the oncoming attack. "Easy, my
friend," he said, as his hand gently stroked the large crystal
from the skystone. "Simply return what they give. No need to
change it, or judge it. Simply return it." *Dear Earth, protect
Mariyonta and Aronlat.*

First one soldier than two more fired their unmaking
beams. The large crystal Tisbero held continued to return what
was meant to destroy him. Shahitam became concerned as a
fifth soldier collapsed and fell from his platform. "The old man
is shooting well for one so weak of mind. First of all our
enemies to do so." He smiled, then in a commanding voice

added, "Direct your fire at that man!" As his finger pointed, twenty-five beams stopped their assault on others and focused on the lone, white-robed figure. The crystal Tisbero held glowed brilliant white as it tried to reflect all of the energy it received. One more of Shahitam's men screamed, but the current proved too much. The crystal exploded with a blinding flash, sent searing fragments toward the skyplatform and hurled Tisbero's body backward like a rocket. His limp form hit the far side of the large crevice that had been behind him, then he tumbled down into it like a dead weight.

As Shahitam recovered from the melee he laughed with satisfaction. "A fitting end to one who so stubbornly refused to expand with the Creator." He turned to his captain. "He's expanded with the light now," he concluded. Then the conqueror turned to face the village green below. The constant harsh hiss of the firing crystals had slowed to occasional bursts. Only solitary figures still struggled, all others lay lifeless. Then all of the firing stopped.

"At last, peace," he said, more to himself than to his captain. He called out in a firm voice to the captains on the other two skyplatforms. "Descend and collect every remnant of this village and drop it into the sea. As with the other lost villages, destroy any evidence that the fools ever existed."

"Yes, Shahitam," they replied in unison. "It is done."

"But you, my captain," he said, speaking to the captain of his own ship. "Did you see anything unusual as we approached?"

"Ahh...No, Sir. No, my lord, I did not." Then in defense added, "I was focused on the battle at hand, my lord."

Shahitam smiled slowly. "Never stay so focused on the bull that you do not see the snake in the grass."

"Yes, my lord."

"A small skystone fled to the east as we approached. While the others stay to make sure this place has no story to tell," he flicked a dispassionate hand to the other two platforms, "you and I will follow it, and kill the traitor."

"Yes, my lord."

"And captain," he said in a quiet monotone. "We will not fail."

"The deed is done, my lord. It is done."

Aviea didn't see them approach from below. The first shot echoed off the underside of her speeding skystone with a glaring spray of rock mixed with mustard-yellow light. She responded instantly and her small, sailing slab cascaded back and forth with sudden, random jerks. Streaks of searing light hissed around her in a constant stream. Her jaw clenched and her dark eyes flashed fiercely. *I must reach the others.* A rapid succession of shots suddenly shattered the tortured stone beneath her feet, and she plummeted into the cold, wave-tossed sea.

Chapter 11   *Gathering*

Their human forms asleep, the astral bodies of the guardians gathered at their predetermined meeting place, a large flat-topped outcrop of rust-red sandstone that overlooked a broad valley filled with lush joint grass. Pergaine, seated on a curved rock conveniently shaped to fit her back, spoke her mind first. "No one is here from Tisbero's village, and it is past the appointed time. He should have met with Shahitam and reported to our astral council by now."

Gamon twisted the end of his etheric mustache. "We have no real reason to be concerned. It may be that he's too involved with other work to attend. He may still be with Shahitam." He gazed out over the valley, hoping to see Tisbero's floating form approach.

"Yes." Pergaine was steadfast, her voice focused as sharp as her features. "But the time he asked for has passed, and he has not sent word. That is not like Tisbero."

"He will come when he can." Gamon muttered grumpily. "I'm sure there is a logical explanation."

An uncomfortable silence filled the assemblage. Yawri cleared his throat and spoke. "I went to talk with Muran the red tree," he started. "It said that there is a problem with the humans. They're getting more violent throughout the planet, though it isn't clear why. It said the wind's messages are unclear, as if sounds are erased."

"Sounds erased? Impossible." Gamon said, dismissing the absurd. "All life has sound. Even death has sound. Of all life forms, how can a tree say there is no sound? It's preposterous." The assemblage fell into a confused silence.

A tall woman from the southeastern continent finally spoke. "While traveling in our astral bodies, we visited many of the villages on our continent and saw unusual happenings."

"Unusual happenings? What type of happenings?" Pergaine's eyes queried like a falcon.

The tall woman continued. "We keep our villages small, under two hundred human-beings, so that no harm occurs to the places we live. It may be nothing, but we saw a number of villages that are large. One must have had a thousand people, and rather than building with vines or with branches and clay, they make large shelters of stone."

"Stone? Why stone?" Pergaine wondered aloud.

"I have seen stone houses," Gamon replied stubbornly. "If the stone agrees to be shaped for that purpose there is no harm."

"I know. But these are very big houses, and they are encircled by stone walls," the woman replied.

"Walls? Why put walls around a village?" Pergaine questioned, her forehead pinched in puzzlement.

"I don't know."

"We found the same," another voice called out. "Large villages with more than a thousand people." Once more silence enveloped the group.

A young man from the northwestern continent spoke in a slow, measured voice. "I saw such villages as well. I understand that they're built to help the humans in some way."

"Help the humans?" Yawri straightened. "To make them less violent? Before these giant villages were built they weren't violent. They were a thriving part of Earth's animal kingdom. They lived in complete communication with the We."

"I only heard on the astral that it is to help them become more conscious. I don't claim to understand it," the being responded. "I haven't visited any of these stone villages physically. No one I know has."

Pergaine's eyes moved from face to face. "But it's clear from these reports that the big villages are increasing in number. Perhaps in large numbers. How are they managing to do no harm to the wild grasses, to the ground? Where is Tisbero?"

Yawri spoke with the uncertainty he felt. "Maybe we should go to more of these villages physically so we can speak to the people who live in them and learn once and for all what is going on. That's what Tisbero was trying to do by visiting Shahitam's village. We still don't know why Shahitam doesn't come to the astral council. What does he know that we don't?"

Gamon stroked his chin, then spoke. "A few of us should go to Tisbero's village physically. If he's not back from Shahitam's island now, he will be by the time we get there." Yawri nodded, clearly anxious to find out what happened, as all agreed to the idea.

Gamon turned to guardians from the other continents, considering the next practical step. "Pergaine, Yawri and I will make a physical journey to the village of Tisbero. Others should take your bodies to find more facts. Something is clearly going on, but it's confusing. We must understand what is happening."

"Our area has some conscious caves near our village," a stout woman said. "We'll return to our bodies and make a physical journey into the cave's deepest reaches. From there, we should be able to learn any concerns coming from Earth."

Pergaine tried to project certainty. "There must be knowledge about these strange events someplace. Let's all make our journeys and meet again on the astral at the next full moon." With that the meeting ended. The beings returned to their human bodies, woke them and immediately began preparing for their travels.

✦

Gamon, Pergaine and Yawri hovered their skystone a dozen yards above the central green on the island of Tisbero's village. Yawri's brow was tight from concentration as he struggled to understand the difference between what he remembered and what he saw. "I thought this was the right place. The shape of the valley, the placement of the rocks, that tree," he pointed to a tall blue spruce. "But where is everybody?" All three turned from side to side, searching for a clue to the mystery. The skystone descended slowly then stopped just above pale heads of wild barley.

"But it looks like no one was ever here." Gamon saw no sensible explanation. "You're sure this is the right place?"

Yawri scanned the surrounding topography again and once more focused on the blue spruce. "It is the right place, all right. I've been here many times. I don't understand. This is where the village was."

"Then they've left," Gamon's white eyebrows rose as if confirming the statement. "It's not uncommon for a village to move on if they notice that their habitation is beginning to harm nature. They treated it well. There is no sign of wear at all. Look," he gestured, "the paths through the central green are all that's here." The visitors, unable to come to any conclusion, stepped off the platform.

Pergaine's thin nose flared as she smelled the air, and walked down the nearest path. "It feels strange here, but I don't know why. And the sound. Does anyone else notice a lack of sound?" Yawri, preoccupied with his own thoughts, stopped short to avoid walking into Pergaine who had halted in front of him.

"The sounds are muffled." Yawri spoke the words that had absorbed him. "Masked." He bent down to touch a velvet blue prairie flower. "And the flowers, though pretty, do not vibrate with light. They have no glow." Gamon knelt down to study the plants as Yawri walked over to the large spruce and stood before it for a long minute. "This tree doesn't speak!" He spat out.

"But that's impossible," Gamon said. "All trees speak."

"But neither does this one," Pergaine's voice shot out from near another tree.

"What is going on here?" Gamon demanded as he returned to study the soil. "It's not reasonable. The place looks normal to the physical eye, but dimensional sounds and light are missing. It's like it's a painting."

"This tree is traumatized." Yawri's hands gently massage the bark. "Something devastating took place here. Life is shocked into silence." A gentle rain began to fall from scattered clouds.

"What happened to the village?" Pergaine's voice called forth with the question in everyone's heart. Yawri now stood with his hands at his sides, too stunned to reply.

Gamon struggled to make sense of the mystery, but unable to do so, busied himself by continuing to study the ground. At last he stood up. He held some soil in his hand, as if clinging to something tangible within the unknown. "Even the soil is withdrawn into itself."

Pergaine also busied herself. "Look," she called from the granite wall. "This stone weeps."

The other two guardians, eager for any clue, quickly joined her. "It's just the rain," Gamon said, still trying to fit what he saw with what he knew.

"It doesn't make sense." Yawri ran his fingers across the stone as well. "The granite looks normal, but its sound is muffled, too. There's no song."

"What's this?" Gamon let the soil drop from his hand as he stooped to pick up a broken remnant of crystal. He took another step and picked up a larger piece. "Look at how this was fractured," he said quizzically. "All the lines run out in a radial pattern. It's as if it was broken from the inside out."

Pergaine extended her hand and Gamon handed the remnant to her, willing to get rid of yet another mystery. She took it carefully and inspected it for a long moment. "It *was* broken from the inside out, as if it exploded."

Gamon's white mustache twitched as he shook his head. "But that's impossible."

"There's something down here!" Pergaine and Gamon turned to see Yawri kneeling on the edge of a six-inch-wide fissure in the fine grained rock. "It's deep, but I hear a sound." The others rushed over, knelt and listened.

"It's a crystal," Pergaine offered after considered thought. "It's alive and it's calling." She stretched out her senses for several seconds then suddenly stood up. "We've got to get it out."

Gamon looked down into the dark crack. "Let's get the crystals from the skystone and ask them to connect to the one down this crevice. If it's strong enough to connect to them in return, we can increase soul-light to minimize its gravity. Then with the connection in place, we can call it up." Yawri was already on his way to retrieve the four crystals, clearly eager to take action in this confusing swirl of facts.

In a moment the assemblage stood around the fissure, skystone crystals in hand. Each guardian united with them as they reached out for the one below. "It's connecting." Pergaine eyes showed the first flicker of hope since the party landed. "It still has enough consciousness."

"Increase soul-light," Yawri said with urgency.

"It's not moving," Gamon replied. "It doesn't have enough of its own light to be one with the others."

"Give it time," Pergaine said. "Give it time."

Slowly, the recording crystal Tisbero had dropped down the crack began to rise. It floated like a jellyfish in an ocean, slowing making its way to the surface. Gamon stepped forward to take it, but at the last moment it veered toward Pergaine. She gently took it into her hands. "Dear Creator!" she exclaimed. "This crystal is full of information." The other two formed a triangle with her.

"It's the recording crystal Tisbero took with him," Yawri said with recognition. The three human-beings and the four skystone crystals maintained the healing connection to the precious clear, quartz recording stone. Then the information began to flow. It flowed as if a dam, holding back waters beyond its endurance, suddenly let go.

Images and sound cascaded in rapid motion. Words spoken by Tisbero, Aviea, Twaqwe and Sargac on their way to the big island and images of what they saw rolled like a wave; images of the temple, and what was said; the confused pain of the Centaur, and the flight of the investigating party back to their own island; of Aviea's escape; Twaqwe and Sargac and others slaughtered; Tisbero's final stand, and the blinding explosion; soldiers taking all evidence of the carnage and dropping it into the sea; Shahitam's determined pursuit of unsuspecting Aviea. As the last picture faded in their minds, wrenching shock and sorrow froze on their faces. Each witness groaned as if wounded by a poisoned arrow. They hugged as tears of sorrow fell, as if each were one side of a pyramid, giving and receiving support from the others.

At last, seemingly aged, Pergaine forced herself to speak. "Our world is changed." She groped to express the words that were caught in her chest. "Beings of the Creator from which all Life sprang have used It's gift of free will to rip Life apart."

Yawri made himself use his voice as well. "The Whole that was here, was split into opposites of good and evil, poles of life and death."

"Brother has killed brother." Pergaine exhaled a deep moan. "Murder. Never before did I conceive there could be murder of guardians. My body trembles. It shakes with fear now that beings such as ourselves have chosen to bring this energy here." Silence once more overcame the group.

"Shahitam believes he is right." Gamon struggled to place what he'd seen into his world. "I know him, but I don't understand...this."

"How could he believe this is life-bearing?" Yawri groaned in sorrow.

Pergaine's voice was filled with exasperation. "Shahitam forces things together. He is in domination, not dominion. He is controlling, not allowing. And now..." She looked up from the lonely stand of rock. "Look at the murder domination brings."

"But it's not just Shahitam." Yawri shook his lowered head. "Guardians are acting on his words. They are making his thoughts their own."

"But it simply doesn't make sense." Gamon's voice rang with desperation. "If the Creator wanted to dominate, if control was Its desire, It would not have given free will to all Life. How can Shahitam say that it's good to control other Life? He cannot know the path of any Life but his own."

"I don't know," Pergaine said, choking. "I don't know." The group lapsed into their triangle of silence once more.

A tear dropped from Yawri's cheek onto Gamon's hand, but Gamon did not look up. "Tisbero was courageous," Yawri said, flexing his shoulders to make himself take a breath. "Even as his loved ones were being murdered, he stayed connected to the We. It showed great strength to keep walking, backward as he did, his face toward what was bent on murder, toward this crevice." All looked at the rain-soaked crack in the earth. "He knew that we would come. He gave to us, even in the time of his own destruction." His tears mixed silently with the rain.

Pergaine made herself speak again, although her usual crisp speech was dulled. "From the recording crystal, it was clear that if he chose hatred instead of connection to All-That-Is, just one of those murdering beams would have destroyed him instantly."

Yawri tilted his head upward to let the rain wash his face, his hair plastered against his forehead. "Non-resisting it or not, no one can stand in a storm and not be touched by it."

Yawri felt a need to walk, to get something in motion, so he slowly let his hands drop from the group and, lacking any other direction, walked to the nearby ravine. He stopped to stare down over the edge. After a minute Pergaine and Gamon, who were also in need of distraction, solemnly joined him. "Here is where Tisbero stood." Yawri turned on his tapping foot to see the pattern of fine, broken shards on the ground. His eyes narrowed, and stifling any thought of hope he turned to stare back down into the gaping ravine. Vine-covered walls disappeared into dark, dense foliage.

Pergaine nodded silently next him. She saw a furry flash. "There are earth-spirits down in the trench," she said, louder than she planned. Yawri and Gamon doubled their effort to see through the mass of vines and leaves.

Gamon's brow furrowed in question. "How could they stay in a place so traumatized? It would be excruciatingly painful for elfin-kind to stay here." Without warning, Yawri began climbing down over the edge, his nimble feet finding small footholds among the anchored vines. Gamon was startled. "What are you doing?"

"Tisbero's body could be down here!" he barked back. "He was standing on the edge when the crystal blew. Maybe the soldiers didn't make the effort to go down." The top of his head disappeared with the swish of parting plants. "This place is full of devas all right," his muffled voice said.

Pergaine and Gamon waited on the lip. Gamon turned to survey the skyline and then he called down in a firm voice, "Don't take too long. Shahitam's soldiers could come back." A ripple of fear passed through Yawri, but he let it go almost as soon as it arose.

Leaves and bushes rustled. "I see something." Yawri's words were barely audible. Pergaine's and Gamon's necks craned. "He's down here!"

At the ravine's bottom, Yawri knelt next to Tisbero's crumpled body, his red hair matted with dried blood. Then, though he knew it was illogical, he checked the limp neck for a pulse. Then he checked it again. "He's alive!" The scream shot up through the leaves like a geyser. "Get the skystone! He's alive!" *Barely.*

As Yawri gently checked one of Tisbero's eyes to confirm that it was unglazed, he saw a drop of water fall directly from a well positioned, heart shaped leaf into Tisbero's drooping mouth. "Get the skystone!" he yelled again, more to relieve his anxiousness than remind his friends of the task. *Elfin-kind. Thank you. Thank you for staying with him in this tormented place.*

Pergaine and Gamon had already gathered the crystals and were running to the skystone as if their rush was needed to make what they heard more real. Though filled with anticipation, the two guardians negotiated the skystone down into the narrow trench with apparent ease, branches and leaves parting as it descended like water around a rock. The platform hovered a couple of feet above Tisbero as they jumped off, and hurried to help Yawri lift the limp form onto the platform. Air escaped Tisbero's lips in a halting groan.

"We've got healing crystals at the village, and herbs," Pergaine croaked out. All jaws tightened as the friends remembered that Aviea would not be there to administer them.

The skystone moved up the trench steadily and Tisbero stirred. A delirious gurgle came out of his contorted throat. "Don't speak," Yawri said. "We'll get help as soon as we can." The skystone cleared the lip.

"Mary to...Aron." The voice was hardly audible.

"He's trying to tell us something." Yawri leaned closer.

"Maryta...Aron," he croaked.

"Maryta Aron?" Yawri repeated. "What could he mean?" Yawri's face was tight with focus.

"Cave," escaped from Tisbero's throat like a last gasp, but his pulse continued.

Yawri sat up suddenly and scanned the distant, gray, limestone cliffs. "The cave!" he exploded, searching his memory. "At our last astral meeting, Tisbero said that two of the seven new adults were still in the cave. Mariyonta and Aronlat! I know them. Maybe they're still in it!" He struggled to remember where in the expansive cliffs the entrance lay. "I think it's there." He thrust a pointed hand toward a stratified outcrop, although Pergaine and Gamon could not see what distinguished it from and the others. "We've got to check!"

Gamon chewed on his mustache and stared at the distant gray cliff face. "But we've got to get Tisbero help. We can't afford any delay." He scanned the sky. "If we don't make it back, all will be lost." The skystone hovered with the indecision.

Yawri cast a hard look at Pergaine. "It won't take long," he said. She nodded her agreement, but her eyes told him that she expected him to remember exactly where the cave entrance was.

No one spoke as the small platform moved toward the distant ridge. Pergaine knelt to place her hand under Tisbero's head, cushioning it as best she could.

It had been almost two years since Yawri had come with Tisbero to celebrate equinox with the village, and he searched the cliffs with probing eyes. "There it is," he said with relief as a small cave mouth came into view. It felt like an eternity as they progressed, and his will was torn between watching Tisbero's pale face and the approaching dark entrance.

Finally, the skystone came to rest several yards from the mouth. Pergaine stayed with Tisbero while Yawri and Gamon jumped off their vessel and, filled with apprehension, hurried toward the small entrance. Quickly yet carefully climbing into its throat of sharp, fossilized coral, they stopped when they reached a place that was large enough for them to stand side by side. The two guardians stood silent, and tried to put their concerns about Tisbero out of their minds as they bonded with the surrounding rock, and stretched their senses to learn of the two young people's fate. The silence grew.

At last their mutual stares showed that they had each arrived at the same conclusion. Yawri spoke. "It may be that they're too deep, or too remote for us to sense anything here. Even the rock this far from the village has withdrawn into itself."

Silence came again. "We could go in further," he added, but the words died in the air. A shadow passed over the cave's mouth and both guardians instantly glanced up. Each was relieved to see that it was nothing more than one of the scattered clouds blocking the sun.

Gamon broke in. "If these people are alive, they could stay down there for months. Didn't you spend almost two years during your own cave stay?" Yawri didn't have to respond. "We need to get Tisbero and the recording crystal back to the other guardians."

Yawri peered into the cave's deep throat. No glow of living stones showed from within. "Let's leave one of our own crystals here for them when they come out," he said, unwilling to let go of all hope. "At least they'll be forewarned of the danger."

"Okay," Gamon said hurriedly.

Yawri took a nine-inch-long crystal out of his tunic, his own recording crystal, and communicated with it a moment. "This one is willing to stay," he said as he wiped strands of wet hair from his eyes. "It will give them the information they need to help understand the murder they will find."

Yawri turned to face the valley, strangely still so beautiful, its trauma seemingly subdued by the gentle, healing rain, then he turned back to stare into the cave's mouth one last time. "Let's hope their hearts are experienced and strong enough to survive."

After a brief pause, Gamon said, "Let's get Tisbero home." Yawri let go of what was to be, and sprinted with Gamon to jump onto the waiting skystone.

Chapter 12   *The Council*

Anxious guardians gathered at their astral council, their fatigued human bodies soundly asleep. Yawri did his best to relate the tragedy of Tisbero's island with as much clarity as he could muster. His voice cracked with strain. "Twaqwe and Sargac were killed." Yawri nodded to the astral form of his friend seated next to him. "Tisbero's human body, left for dead in a trench, lies unconscious and is recovering." Tisbero nodded slowly, and his dim eyes showed that his ethereal as well as his physical form needed substantial healing. Yawri's voice quavered slightly as he continued. "We have had no report of Aviea, but from the recording crystal Shahitam's intent was clear. We believe that she has met the fate of all the others at the village. The first guardian I gardened with when I came to this planet, Aviea, and the entire village were slaughtered."

A mournful silence filled the chamber. A voice still in doubt that such a travesty could take place called out. "But you say there were no bodies. If they were killed there must have been bodies."

Sensing Yawri's strain, Pergaine spoke before he could address the question. "Nothing remained. Nothing. The recording crystal tells us everything was collected and dropped into the sea. To the eye it was as if the village never existed." She now struggled with the words. "It was as if sound itself was stilled."

Lazket of the southeastern continent spoke with a deep, gravely voice. His face was downcast. "We hoped what we learned on our own quest was an anomaly, but..." The assemblage was stilled, as if the quiet would bring peace to their world once more, but Lazket's words continued. "We found no recording crystal to offer us such detail, however, we learned that three other villages have also disappeared."

"Three other villages!" Another shouted. "They're destroyed, too? More murders?"

"We do not know!" Lazket cried out painfully. He looked to his fellow scouts and they nodded to encourage him to continue. He spoke now with a more paced voice, although the effort it took was revealed by its tone. "We had not visited them physically in many years. There was no need. Everyone was busy with their own work. But," he gazed down then slowly up again, "we found that the sounds were mute in all three places. The land was in trauma. We did learn, though, that all three villages had questioned the activities of other villages who follow this way of controlling nature."

"More villages follow Shahitam's way?" Gamon's tone revealed a strong undercurrent of emotion as he tried to come to terms with his own fractured world.

Lazket stared with eyes suddenly aged, and his voice reflected their depth. "We don't know how many guardians have joined Shahitam's way. We do know their numbers are many and are increasing. We learned that their concerns about their children regressing, that they are becoming less and less able with each generation, drove them to find an answer. Their future, without this new way, looked like a never-ending spiral toward solidity. Less and less capable children meant less and less capable bodies for their future reincarnations as well. Shahitam used their fear, and convinced them that making *all* the humans more ethereal will once more allow their *own* genetic lines to progress."

Yawri raised an ardent hand and spoke with renewed intensity. "This is absurd. They can't hope to gain consciousness through murder!"

Lazket spoke again, struggling to keep focus. "I don't know that many of the guardians that have chosen this path are party to the murder. The recording crystal you brought back showed that Shahitam used the broken humans as the soldiers, very few guardians."

Gamon struggled to remain logical in the emotional storm. "That's correct. I believe Shahitam is keeping guardians who follow him distracted by the comforts that his society provides. They see that breeding with humans only makes humans more capable, and don't realize that they are creating bodies with broken spirits. The guardians following him must be unconscious of the attacks."

"Consciousness is not Shahitam's aim," Pergaine said soberly. "From the recording crystal we also know that he skillfully twists the truth and feeds it to others. If their desperation is great, they fail to question."

Lazket swayed back and forth. "Adding the results of your journey to ours, it is clear that those who stand in opposition to this new way are destroyed. And it is also clear," the being gazed upon the astral assemblage with growing realization, "that Shahitam's own village could not have acted alone. The places are too distant and the timing of the disappearances is too close." The meaning of the words unveiled slowly, as a summer's hot dawn changes subtle grays into harsh shadows.

When Pergaine spoke it was as if she pulled words from a tome to condense a single thought. "This murder we see splits the cycle of death and Life. It leaves the learning of a soul and body immersed in confusion and chaos. What was conscious becomes unconscious."

Yawri expressed the thought of many. "The more terrible the murder, the more loss to Creation."

A woman from the northwestern continent spoke thoughtfully. "The more I hear the more I understand the true depth of our plight. It is beyond pain. It is beyond sorrow. This disease has been growing for many, many years and my surprise at seeing it now shows me that I was not willing to see it sooner. The signs were there. I heard the desperation in voices as they complained about each generation being less capable than the last. I recall that other guardians tried to warn us years ago." Heads nodded in introspective agreement. "Because I refused to see a sickness when it would have caused me discomfort, now I feel abject pain as though a veil has been ripped from my eyes. We have chosen not to see, let alone act to halt this evil, and now it is strong upon us."

"There must be a way to turn the tide," Yawri declared in an earnest voice.

Hetlin, a strong-boned woman with bronze skin from the northwest continent, spoke next. "We must report what we learned as well." She said this firmly as she nodded to include the two tall men standing next to her, their straight black hair framing high cheeks. "You recall that we traveled into the deep caves of our land. Like you, we hoped that what we found out there was an anomaly, something which could be explained away once we returned here to report. But as has been said, the veil is gone. I will share what the deep Earth shared." She gently bit her lower lip before beginning again. "We traveled into three different caves, all known for their wisdom. Sculpted as all caves are, by Earth as it directed water to remove rock. The cave's body was our body, alive and aware."

Hetlin met the eyes of her companions, who nodded encouragement. "We traveled far down to the deep lakes of ancient, pristine water; Earth's eardrums. The water flowed with the same tide of Earth's oceans and moon. There, we wanted to hear that all was in harmony, that all was good. We challenged ourselves to put aside our wants and receive, unfiltered, what could be shared." She breathed slowly, fully, and then let go.

"As we looked into the sacred water it showed us the fiery birth of Creation, the Sending Forth. It showed us the Creator's release of the gift of free will, unselfishly giving particles of Itself. But what you may not know is that some particles of All-That-Is, some of these new souls, felt betrayed." The crowd stirred, murmuring. Hetlin's voice rang out. "Yes. It is true. The deepest, sacred caves of Earth speak it so. They told us that these particles only wanted to *Be One*, not be particles *Of One*. And free will is free will, as the Creator bestowed. From where this conflicting thought came I cannot say, yet the vision was clear, the conflict to 'Be the Creator' or to be 'Of the Creator' was born.

"Billions and billions of years passed and each particle experienced co-creating as they chose. As some planets are, this planet, Earth, was conceived to nourish and feed the Whole. The Creator Itself blessed this planet. As many here have seen, most planets have only a few life forms of mineral, plant or animal. But as you see on Earth, the Creator's touch brings a rare pallet of colors and multiple dimensions of Life together. Such rare planets orbit in the Universe like jewels."

Strain showed in her voice as she revealed the next portion of the vision. "We report hard tidings. There are already two other planets in this solar system that will not, cannot, meet their original purpose." Worried faces turned to worried faces as the murmur increased but then subsided again to attend to Hetlin's voice. She drew herself up calling on an unseen reserve. "It seems that there was once a planet just beyond Mars. During the process of its development, it blew apart. We don't know why. Now, where once another jewel orbited, there are remnant, jagged asteroids of its broken self. There is much grief from this loss in the solar system. We also felt additional sadness from Mars. It was forming Life at a faster pace than its friend Earth. Diverse bacteria, viruses, plants and animals were thriving, adding more and more to the Whole. Rich waters flowed. But there too, something went wrong. The foundation of bacteria, the very life form which feeds the cycle of Life and death, crumbled. Without these organisms, everything was lost. Where nourishing clouds of rain once swept, only clouds of dust remain.

Now there is Earth. It thrived in its own timing, but that timing is now being broken. Shahitam's way is bringing different genetics and ethereal energy to human bodies so suddenly that it breaks their identity and timing. Who can say what this breaking will mean, but the visions we received from the deep waters were clear. Broken in its timing, Earth could have a similar fate to the other two planets." Gasps filled the air as Hetlin paused to gather strength to say what must be said. "With three planets gone, each an organ of the solar-body, it might come to pass that the entire solar system could perish."

Shock froze faces. At last, another guardian, this one from the northeast continent, filled the painful silence with his own report. "The humans in our area have become more violent, more disconnected from Life. We must do what we can to stop the harm resulting from this break between body and soul."

"We've been blind," a hollow voice said.

Heads involuntarily turned to see an approaching figure. "Who comes?" Gamon called. The assemblage looked to see a being with a very thin etheric aura, move toward them.

"Aviea!" Yawri rang out as he rushed to her. "Aviea! You're alive!"

She stopped and raised an upturned hand as he hurried to greet her, her pale face a wavering light. "My physical body is very weak." She drew on all her inner resolve to speak. "It is asleep and being cared for by guardians at a small village. I do not know how long I can stay away from it. I must deliver a message to this council." She placed a hand on Yawri's welcoming shoulder to steady herself as his concerned eyes searched her face. Then she caught sight of Tisbero. "Oh Tisbero, you're alive!" Although she was happy, the effort to speak showed in her weakened voice.

He looked up at her and smiled. "Tell the council," was all he managed to say, though his eyes sparkled encouragement.

She spoke, and both relief and burden showed in her tone. "We are in great peril. I cannot sense anyone of Tisbero's village and fear the worst. I report to you that Shahitam is insane. After our visit to his island," her eyes moved to Tisbero and back to the council, "heartless men followed me and hurled great beams of destruction at my vessel. My skystone was small enough so that I was able to avoid them for a while, but just as I was nearing the coast several beams hit the underside. I fell into the sea." She spoke as if in a trance. "In my death I only sought to join with the water. I became the sea. Great sea mammals, our brother dolphins, came. Somehow I was taken into a coastal cave which flooded with the tide. I don't know how long I lay on the sand where they had nudged me. When I awoke in the blackness, I was filled with a sense of unreality. Only the absence of the beings who help us cross to the other side and the presence of elfin-kind told me that I lived. It took what might have been days for these devas to lead me, crawling through lightless caverns, to find a way out. The devas' nurturing connection to Earth was all that gave me faith.

"Always dancing like colorful leaves in front of me, they guided me. After I left the caverns and crawled and walked through dense jungle, they led me to food and water. At last, I reached a village. I longed to see you, but only with my body's safety assured by the caring guardians there, could I risk leaving it to join you at this astral meeting. I tell you again, Shahitam is insane."

She finally stopped to see what impact her words had on the assemblage. The visages surrounding her did not appear to be startled by her flood of sorrow. "Of course." Her eyes fell on Tisbero. "You know of what I speak," she gasped, all fatigue now revealed. "You know. Thank the Creator you know." Her head dropped. "It is too much to bear alone, and I did not know if you knew the evil that is loose upon Earth." As she continued to slump, Yawri supported her. Mournful faces watched as Yawri gently seated her on a low stone.

Gamon looked up, confusion draped across his brow. He made himself speak, although quietly, to Tisbero. "But we dedicate ourselves to connection of Life, and Shahitam is part of Life. When you talked with him, Tisbero, did he say why he might do this? Why he forsakes peace?"

Tisbero turned slowly to face him. "His kind of peace only comes from the absence of sound. We must not confuse peace with silence. What was whole is now torn asunder. Where there was unified Creation on Earth, there is now good versus evil,

Life versus death. I don't know how this separation can be healed, but I do know that our freedom is no longer free."

Yawri locked eyes with Tisbero. "None of us knows how to heal this split. But we will learn."

Pergaine sounded out, lifting her voice like a sudden breeze to fill a stunned silence. "Before stopping a disease you must know its extent. We must learn what's feeding it and how much it's grown. Then we must find out how we can fight it, stop the harm, and heal."

Wholly inexperienced with the new world the guardians found themselves in, they discussed for many hours what course of action was best. Some wanted to confront Shahitam. Some wanted to ask his terms for peace. Some wanted to withdraw to remote places. Most wanted to learn more. Finally it was agreed that physical investigations of more villages was the best way to discover what choices remained to halt the harm, and to report back at the next full moon.

"Hard choices lie ahead," a parting guardian said, voicing the feeling of all.

✦

The big crystal island bustled with activity. Seventeen skyplatforms convened on the remaining open space of its walled city. Envoys from all the lands, dressed in resplendent finery, convened in Shahitam's temple.

"The work is going extremely well," a priestly guardian from the southwestern continent said. "How can we further develop Earth?"

"The humans blessed with our touch are excellent workers," another said. "They're so happy to be a part of our mission."

"We keep ours busy," a third said. "When you teach them how, they're great craftsmen. You should see the new water cisterns we're building."

"Tanning leather, making cloth. Our humans are increasingly skilled," another voice chimed in.

Shahitam, who had been walking among the followers invited here, now took the stage. He raised his arms in congratulations. "You see my friends, our plan is working!" he called out as voices died away. "Joining with all the humans will make us all stronger." Nods of agreement filled the temple.

"They want our soul touch and our offspring. When we visit their villages, they know by looking at us that that we will give them superior children. As we are particles of the Creator, let us give particles of our great souls to all humans!" More smiles of agreement showed on the sea of faces.

"Great cities are rising, and they are filled with great beauty. The Creator has given us the means to assist Creation. It would be irresponsible not to use our knowledge to help Creation flourish. Have the lives of the children from the humans we touched improved? Are they not stronger and smarter than their parents?" A resounding yes echoed through the gathering of guardians that had been converted to his way of seeing the world.

He surveyed his compatriots from his position on the stage, stopping to smile upon particularly strong allies. "Food, water, shelter and a higher purpose is our gift to them. No longer must they scrounge for roots and shiver from cold. They touch the Creator through us. We will lead them to a new world!" Cheers rose from the audience.

As the roar receded, he continued. "And they pay us back in their way. Do we not live in splendor and abundance? Is the Creator not splendid and abundant? As the Creator is, so should we be!" More accolades cascaded forth. "In accordance with Earth's law of development, since all humans are moving forward again, our own line can once more flourish. We must redouble our efforts to join with them. All humans should have the same opportunity to know the Creator through our touch." He spread his arms once again to encompass the crowd. "We all know of Earth's need to continue to have guardians tend it. Over the next few days this gathering of leaders will plan for the further development of Earth!"

"What we're doing is righteous!" a woman near the front called out, and was greeted by applause.

"Thank you." Shahitam's sparkling silver cloak caught the light. "Thank you. But I must remind you. I only provide counsel. It is your actions that make it all possible. I remember long ago when only two guardians thought it wise to follow the way. Now, thanks to all of you, we stand on the threshold of a great destiny."

Bright optimism filled the expression of the envoys, each with his or her own very hopeful view of the future. "Since we are of the same mind," Shahitam said as the planning councils started, "nothing can stand in our way."

✦

Worry showed in the faces of the guardians gathered at the council's astral meeting. It became evident, even before the first word was spoken, that no one had found good news from their physical explorations. Report after report only extended dire news. The number of unmentored, bred humans was increasing exponentially. Separated from their true identities because of their untimely union with soul light, they were increasingly capable and creative, yet sometimes vicious. The number of stone cities was much greater than any had foreseen. The number of missing villages, such as Tisbero's, counted in the dozens. The disease was spreading.

Yawri firmly placed his outstretched hands on the table as if to give himself an anchor in the chaos. "There must be something we can do. I'm not willing to stand by and watch as the whole planet is murdered!"

"Hetlin," Pergaine called out with her own sense of urgency. "You were getting more information from the deep caves. Are there no choices left save how we will die?"

All faces turned to Hetlin, and the expressions she saw made her hesitate to speak. Though all felt that little could be done now that the dam had seemingly burst, all desperately wished for a way to keep at least some Life safe from the swirling flood.

Tisbero, healed after a month's kind attention, encouraged her with uncharacteristic calm. "Hetlin," he said. His voice reminded the guardians that he had not only survived the attack but had recovered, and the sound of it gave hope. "At our last meeting you reported that Earth cannot fulfill its purpose if this disease grows. That its own timing will be broken by the broken humans. You said you would ask the deep caves what could be done." Silence filled the room as every voice stilled in anticipation. "Did it tell you what can be done?"

Hetlin looked at her companions for a long moment and their eyes asked her to make the report. She spoke quietly, yet deliberately, "Earth must go to sleep."

Confused voices murmured questioningly.

"Sleep?" Pergaine raised her voice above the others. "Did you say, sleep?"

One of Hetlin's companions said, "Yes, sleep. She speaks of what we all heard."

"Hear me out," Hetlin requested softly. When the assemblage was quiet she began to explain, her voice stronger now. "I will recite what we have learned." She scanned the faces around her, and began.

"In their desperation to reverse this mysterious regression of the guardians' lineage, a lineage held pure from the time of our first ethereal joining with a human-spirit, increasing numbers of our brothers and sisters are making the choice to physically breed with Earth's humans. By breeding with the humans they have created offspring which are broken from their singular connection with Earth, and these broken humans are multiplying rapidly. In our brothers' and sisters' eagerness for an answer, they fail to question."

She nodded to Tisbero who now stood near her in an effort to show his support. "Earth cannot fulfill its mission to create and return to the Creator if it, too, is broken. Broken, it will die." She paused and added deliberately, stressing each word equally, "But we bring hopeful news. There is a way to help." Heightened senses stretched forth to listen to every word.

"If Earth goes into hibernation, the broken people will have much less of Earth's Life to harm. It is possible for Earth to hibernate like a bear. Freezing storms can rage around a sleeping bear, and although hungry in spring, it has lived through the winter. Earth can likewise live if it can sleep through the storm, and wake up again in a better time. I say to you, this is Earth's chance for Life."

"I don't understand," a voice called.

Focused strength of mind filled Hetlin as she continued. "It is clear that Earth cannot remain so sensitive, so vital, and stay healthy through the siege that is upon it. It would go dark as a child would go dark from lashes of cruelty. Its only hope to remain healthy is to sleep now, so that someday, the chance for a conscious union of souls and bodies can return. To survive until that time, the lush spectrum and dimensions of Life hosted here must be lessened." Heads shook in disagreement as the volume of voices increased. "Hear me out!" Her voice was certain now. The murmurs faded away.

"All beings such as ourselves came here as guardians and gardeners of Life. Now, many have chosen to control it. This domination will not give them the results they desire, a never-ending ascension for their children. We see this. The way toward more Life does not include the murder of Earth." She bowed her head to include her traveling companions.

"We believe that Earth's call is clear for those who listen to it, rather than to their own pain. My friends, this planet asks for help to withdraw, to go into hibernation. We must help it close down its chakras to achieve that purpose."

Aviea, also feeling much better, studied the faces. All seemed twisted with inner agony. A meaningful pause of recognition passed between her and Tisbero as her gaze swept over the gathering. Aviea then spoke, projecting her voice so all could hear. "I have personally experienced the evil that is upon us. We see that the future is dark. The broken humans created through this indiscriminate breeding will multiply, and because of their new intelligence, will survive. We know that they are murdering soil, plants and animals. They use Life as if it belongs to them, instead of as if it is part of them."

Aviea met the eyes of everyone willing to meet her intense gaze, and she continued speaking. "I agree with Hetlin. If this planet is to survive, it must sleep through a cruel winter. You know that from the chakra system in your own human bodies that when the body is asleep the chakra centers are subdued, quiet, hibernating in a way. I see what Hetlin is saying. If we can help Earth achieve that sleeping state, it might have a chance to survive." Many heads nodded in agreement, but not all.

Faces showed strain. Voices tumbled over one another. Three hours of earnest discussion and argument at last brought the somber assemblage to the same conclusion. Tisbero, his salty red hair brushed back from his furrowed brow, at last held up his hands to signal all to listen.

"When we came to this meeting, we all knew that this desperate situation would require desperate action. The years of small choices which have led to this circumstance stretch into the past. Today, we make a choice for the future. It is time to put our pain and loss aside, and give what is needed."

He scanned the guardians slowly and continued with a voice charged with purpose. "To help a planet hibernate is no simple task. Let us call out to all remaining guardians who are still true to our original mission, and ask them to help us assist Earth in its need to slumber." The faces surrounding him were slowly releasing their despair and filling with determination.

Pergaine rose, her astral form taller than it was physically. "Together, as guardians," she said in a voice as clear as noonday sun, "and as warriors...we will do what must be done."

With unveiled eyes, over the coming months guardians saw more of the broken humans ranging through the forests than they thought possible. Guardian alerted guardian, and many came in answer to the call.

Pergaine was one of those who addressed the extensive body of beings gathered at the next astral meeting. She stood decisive as a sword. "We gather to aid this planet in its quest for Life," she called out. "Earth's energy centers, its chakras, are wide open now and pulse with all dimensions of Life. Rich forests and thriving oceans stretch from pole to pole. Yet, all of this Life has no defense against thoughts that would do it harm. Earth would rather die than be murdered." She paused to let each breath in and feel the meaning of the words. "As many guardians, such as ourselves, have already been murdered."

Yawri's grief was overshadowed by an urgent sense of purpose. His voice rang. "Our original task as guardians still holds true. It has been made clear to all those who listen, that to shelter Life we must help Earth hibernate. A deep slumber from which it can re-awaken after a dark winter has passed for us and it alike."

An almost surreal calmness of intent filled the beings, as Tisbero continued the rallying speech, filled with his own inner fire. "You know that just as your body has chakras, so does Earth. Helping this planet close down its chakras is our goal. The planet cannot do it alone. To help it, we will travel to each of Earth's major energy centers, and as it draws its life force deep into itself, we will fill the void on Earth's land with our own life force." A wave of tight expressions moved through the listening guardians.

Hetlin spoke again, determination steadying her voice. "Earth's knowledge is our knowledge, our knowledge is Earth's. The planet's chakras will be able to function, although minimally. After Earth slumbers, an ice age will occur. Deserts will cover what is now forest. The spectrum of Life will shrink.

As Earth hibernates, the murderers will have less Life to prey upon." Her gaze fell to the floor, her eyes no longer able to take in the grief in the faces before her.

Yawri filled the gap. "Although only unpleasant choices remain, choices we still have. The choice to do nothing sentences Earth to certain death. The choice to help Earth sleep confirms hope for Life."

Expressions on the faces changed as guardians considered the action. "I have a question," a being shrouded in shimmering pale green light said thoughtfully. "If we leave a part of our life force here to fill the void that is left as Earth retreats into itself, how can we remain conscious? How can one remain conscious when you do not have all of yourself?"

"There are many thousands upon thousands of us," Yawri replied, "and more are agreeing to help every day. It is hoped that because we are so many, each will only have to give a little, and that there will be enough of the Creator's essence remaining within each of us so that we will remain conscious during the hibernation."

Another concern was voiced. "But if a part of ourselves is given here, we won't be able to leave this planet until it is released. I must return to the Creator with all that I am, not a portion of what I am."

Pergaine's graceful form, although reflecting her body's increasing age, stood sharp as a blade. "True. Each must be certain of what this commitment means. The energy we leave to sustain Earth's chakras is our own. Earth does not desire this energy, but it needs to borrow it. When the time comes for it to reawaken, it is clear that it must be able to give our energy back to us. That means we must be on Earth to receive it. Those who choose to lend their own essence will resign themselves to be here, reincarnating in physical bodies, lifetime after lifetime, until Earth reawakens and can return our energy to us. No one knows how long this will take, but be clear, none who gives this transfusion will be able to leave until it is returned. We will be joined as one. Earth's fate becomes our fate. The prayer is that Earth will reawaken, and we will reawaken with it."

"This commitment frightens me," a voice said.

Aviea replied this time, projecting her voice through her own veil of fear. "I am frightened as well, but we are not alone. Connected to All-That-Is we will never be alone, as I was not alone when I was plunged into the sea. I know in my heart that help will always be here. Yet, I am afraid. I am afraid because I have felt heartless murder. But, it is because I have felt this murder that I know I must do this to help stop it."

One long hand went to the center of her chest as she gently pointed the other toward the group. "I know what utter devastation will happen if I don't. This jewel does not have the ability to protect itself from those who were meant to be its protectors."

Yawri's tight face revealed his concern that too many of those present would wait too long before committing to the plan. He stepped forward. "If the apprehension is too strong, don't transfer any of your essence to help maintain the slumbering ground of a chakra center. There is a great need just to support the ones who do so. Many more are needed just for that purpose; be guardians of guardians who are leaving their life force with Earth.

"Many of us have been gardeners on this planet for eons. If I do not stay and help Earth fight this disease, then Earth will be murdered. Earth has taught me more about Creation than anything since my own Creation. If it dies, a part of my soul will die whether I am here or not. We show who we are by the choices we make. If I loan the Earth my life force, it still might die, but this is its only chance to live." Yawri's optimistic nature was pushed to the limit as he took a breath, and continued.

"Some will feel the call to make this transfusion, some will feel the call to support those who do. But be certain, helping with this transfusion of energy is no less valuable than the transfusion itself. Without both, the Earth will not be able to hibernate. "

Pergaine raised both her arms above her head as if to draw the tight focus that was upon Yawri to her. She lowered them as she began speaking in earnest. "Our purpose is to 'Go forth, create and return to the Creator with all we learn.' A split in consciousness has been made. Human bodies have been separated from their source and their way home is lost. By staying, we will learn what it takes to bring them back together. Souls who learn how to heal this split between soul and body will enrich Creation. This is great learning for any soul."

Yawri pressed on again, his voice once again composed. "Life is changed by events which no one really controls. Our choice is in how we respond to changes. Make your choices well."

A female's voice, quiet at first, rose in volume as she found her sound. "I will stay and do what must be done. I see both the need and the wisdom of that choice." The voice paused and gathered strength to ask a question. "But, I am not so sure I understand my choices when it comes to facing Shahitam. We know that his followers have murdered many. How do we face them?"

Although the question was hard, relief flickered across faces as many guardians realized that the collective mind of the group had agreed to move on from the question of "should I help" to "how should I help" with the unthinkable task. Pergaine was the first to take a step forward to address the concern.

"Let us speak of choices we must face with Shahitam, then. Plainly, Shahitam and his followers will not be pleased if they hear of our plan. As has been spoken, they have proven that they will murder those who even speak against their choice, let alone take action against it. We have information from the recording crystal that Tisbero brought back, as well as from Tisbero himself, that we must share." As if within the water of a great cold tide, the assemblage readied for the chill of the next wave.

Tisbero moved next to Pergaine. It appeared as if he focused upon each individual and everyone in the same moment. His gaze was an encompassing fire, and his voice resonated from the depth of experience. "Shahitam's soldiers use citrine crystals." He began. "These crystals were originally placed on this planet because of their ability to join etheric and physical reality together. But Shahitam twists the use of these crystals and uses them to cleave instead of unite. Listen to how he does it."

The guardians' eagerness to understand made them stretch as if to pull his words from the air. "A beam of unmaking energy is sent from the crystals to the third chakra of the victim. The beam of unmaking is sent with such violence, that the connection of etheric and physical reality is utterly destroyed in the body. It is a gruesome and painful murder. Once Life is destroyed in this way, it is impossible to separate out which is the human-spirit's versus the etheric-soul's information. Neither can return to its source. Both are left in a purgatory, broken from their true selves." The assemblage shifted and murmured uneasily.

Hetlin came to his side and tried to sound confident. "We have foreseen a way to help those guardians that have been murdered so that soul and spirit can once more return to their sources, and their future bodies need not be reborn into unconsciousness. This task, though, must wait for a later day. I only mention it to give hope to those of us that may perish, as others have." Somber, stilled faces stared back. "So, although we think there is a way to heal from this violence, today we must concern ourselves with stopping the violence."

Gamon spoke next, with a steady voice. "Tisbero has spoken to many of us of a way to stop the attack. It is the way of non-resistance, the way water flows around stone, the way of connection, the way of the One Body. It is logical. To disagree with the attack, and only return what is sent will work because it mirrors a law of Creation. As we know, everything you create is returned to you to learn from eventually."

Yawri spoke next, optimism filling him once more. "Tisbero and his crystal non-resisted the attack in such a way that they reflected the energy sent to unmake them, back to its source. He added nothing. The attackers destroyed themselves with their own energy, that's all. But all actions impact Life, and even a perfect mirror can be cracked. Tisbero's crystal exploded because the energy came faster than it was possible to reflect or heal. We are many more in number so can aid each other. Shahitam's armies may come to try and stop the work. It is a possibility. If attack comes we will help each other reflect it back to its source without malice, without hatred. In this way, together, we can succeed."

Pergaine gathered her thoughts before rejoining the current of voices. "That is how we must deal with any inter-ference." Outwardly, beings nodded in agreement. Inwardly each wrestled with their own internal strife. Sensing this, she took a step forward and spoke out with a firmer voice, proceeding to the next topic at hand. "Now, this is what we must do to help Earth in its task." Guardians did not flinch but looked up as if bracing themselves once more.

She continued, "First, we don't know how long Earth will need to hibernate, but it is clear that it is not willing to sleep only to postpone its murder. Before the Earth will close down any of its energy centers, it must know that there is, in fact, a time in the future when it can reawaken. It must not only reawaken but it must return the borrowed energy to those who have left it. Earth cannot return to the Creator with all it has become if it is immersed with foreign energies any more than we can.

"Be clear that if no such future can be found, then it is best for Earth to die now. I say again, Earth would rather die than live a nightmare with no possibility of awakening. This is what makes our task especially complicated...We must find out if this future time exists." A sense of vision, of direction, rippled through the assembled guardians. The pallor of astral faces changed as if they had moved out of a shadow.

Pergaine deferred to Hetlin as if she didn't notice the positive sign. Hetlin, who with her fellow visionaries had best discerned the specifics of what must be done, spoke.

"Listen," she said simply. "This is the key. Those who choose to lend their own Creator's essence to Earth, will use the time tunnels to travel forward in time and establish a point of connection with a future self. That future self must be able to acknowledge the return of its own essence when Earth releases it. This will form an arc of consciousness, from past to future, from future to past. This arc of consciousness between past and future must occur for Earth's plan to succeed.

"We have no idea how long finding this future self will take, or even if it exists. Not all of us are needed to search the future. As has been spoken, many more of us are needed to stabilize and safeguard those that are doing so. If the searcher's physical bodies are not protected, then they will not have the stability that is needed so that they can travel with their astral bodies to these distant times. We must keep their bodies safe." Hetlin's eyes fell upon those of her nearby friends, and their expressions encouraged her to speak all that they had seen.

She continued. "When Earth feels that the connecting arc of consciousness is strong enough, it will begin to go to sleep in this time and simultaneously wake up in that future time. It must happen simultaneously across time. That is the only way Earth will know that a future beyond murder exists." She gazed at the crowd. "It is a choice for hope."

Yawri spoke, affirming that hope. "There are nine primary energy centers, nine chakras on the lands of Earth. Get your skystones and reflecting crystals ready and purify your thoughts for the task at hand. The plan is for the guardians to gather slowly, yet steadily, at these sacred chakra centers. We commence the search of the future upon the morning of the third new moon hence." A feeling of strength, as if all the winds of the planet decided to join and blow in one direction, filled the assemblage. "Feel the Creator within you," echoed through the chamber as the decision was affirmed by one and all.

✦

The envoys had safely returned to their own responsibilities, and Shahitam stared down from his veranda with cold resolve. Stone walls of the temple glimmered in the moon light. "We have created such monuments," he said as if to himself, though he was surrounded by loyalists. "How can other guardians, once our friends, think that this Creation is not wise?" The robed priests around him nodded in silent agreement.

At last one responded, "If they would only listen and learn."

Shahitam's eyes pierced the sky. "But they let their fear of the unknown rule them." Shahitam gripped the polished, white marble banister. Then, still gazing at the city's splendor below he added in a surprisingly tranquil voice, "More villages on every continent are joining our wisdom, our way, every day. Our civilization grows, making enduring monuments to Its glory, to Our glory. The human animals flock to us, seeking to learn of the divine. They wish to fly on stone, see the universes, hear the cosmic symphonies, and know the secrets of Creation. Who are we to deny them their longing?

"Are we to reject their needs? Their desires? What are these rigid so-called guardians that would forbid these humans our knowledge of Creation?" Shahitam shook his head in disgust.

He glanced at one of his followers. "From what you tell me these traitors seek to destroy the garden." He raised his voice as if yelling for all Life to hear. "Yet, we are the ones who are improving it!" A wind stirred from the sea and a pennant flapped above a stone rampart like a one-winged bird in the breeze.

Shahitam's voice was cold. "I hear that these traitors plan to force Earth into sleep, into death. Can't they listen? Are their ears as closed as their minds? It is not Earth's timing to go to sleep now. It is Earth's timing to expand! Earth is young, vital, alive, bursting forth with song from each new birth. It thrives from pole to pole. Why then, do they want to force this vital reality into ice, a dream? If Earth sleeps, all of this will die."

The captain who led the attack on Tisbero's village spoke. "It is true, my lord. Many reports are coming in. They plot to close down the nine chakras of this planet, and make Earth hibernate."

Shahitam shook his head in disbelief. "The fools. We will stop them. Just as we have stopped all the foolish villages that refuse to follow the wisdom that comes from the truth."

"Yes, my lord. They always stand like dumb animals waiting to be slaughtered."

Shahitam stared down at the brilliant crystal generator. "Yes, we can kill them, as we have other blind fools before them. Yet, it is a pity. They would have been strong allies in our purpose." The captain said nothing in response. "But they choose death over Life. Death happens. Even many of the creatures we bring to Life through blending species fail to survive. These so-called guardians are no different. They cannot evolve. They are not suited for Life."

"We have easily found out their plan to kill Earth." The captain smiled ingratiatingly. "They will gather to do their evil the third new moon hence. They trust everyone at their word, so it requires no effort to obtain information from them."

A priest in a scarlet robe murmured, "They are such fools," as if he echoed Shahitam's thoughts.

Shahitam ignored him. "Begin training more of our half-breeds in the art of unmaking." He used the term blithely, as if describing an object.

"How many, my lord?" the commander asked. "The minds of the bred humans are weak and I don't know how much they can be trusted. Shouldn't we call on the guardians who have joined us for such an important task?"

"There is no need to involve fellow guardians in this at all, my captain. No need for them to know, no need to distract them from their enterprising pursuits. The weak-minded humans we have bred are much more ideal." He spoke with disdain. "They take less effort to control."

"Yes. Of course, my lord."

"Your prudence is expected, Captain. But doubt of my orders is not." Shahitam gazed now toward the flat sea beyond the gated wall. "If our enemies plan to assault each of the major energy centers, it will be too much area for our existing soldiers to cover alone. We must use more of the humans. Dispatch thirty soldiers to each of our cities. Tell our 'guardians' there that we are training the humans for their own protection, nothing more. Teach as many of the half-breeds as possible to both ride our troop platforms and fire unmaking crystals without falling off. That's all they need to be able to do. Instruct them that the people they will be sent to unmake are trying to return them to caves of darkness and ignorance, never to know again the skystones or power of the crystals that heat their homes. Tell them these truths, and they will fight to their last breath."

"You are wise, my lord."

Shahitam was hardly listening to the captain. "Train our new troops discreetly, but well. On the day before their planned attack on Earth, send them to within two hours striking distance of each energy center."

"Do you wish them to be distributed evenly at each center, my lord?" the captain asked.

Shahitam's tongue traced across his lips and said deliberately, "No. Earth can survive some damage to most of its energy centers, but it's heart chakra is most critical. This center provides the force which circulates most of the physical and etheric communication throughout the planet. If they succeed in closing just this one center, the planet will be numbed. Place a full one-third of our soldiers, as well as you and me, Captain, at the heart chakra of Earth."

"Thy will be done, my lord."

"Yes, Captain, my will be done. For once and for all. My will be done."

Chapter 13   **The Morning**

A sliver of white moon hovered in the low sky, as the dark of night yielded slowly to the growing light of morning. A luminous mist sat like a celestial dome on the surrounding valley's dark rim. As the sun peeked over the ridge, Gamon's raised arm reflected a faint orange sheen. "Mastodons," he said, pointing to distant moving shadows. The faint sound of trumpeting carried through the air. *I remember working with them so long ago. So very long ago.*

Pergaine peered into the fading night. "Yes, our cousins come," she whispered into the fragile dawn. Then as the sun rounded the eastern horizon, she raised her crystal to catch its coming light. *It sparkles like fire in ice.*

The sunrise grew as countless times before; light following darkness. Bird songs filled the air. Gray feathers were transformed into bright yellow, red and blue. The dawn also revealed thousands of guardians whose upturned faces greeted the planet's star as though it was a friend too long absent. One of them began to sing, then another voice and another. Within minutes a chorus of tones stretched out to harmonize with the song of birds, the distant trumpet of mastodons, and the new day.

The great assemblage of guardians formed a series of concentric circles around a large cluster of crystals. The songs from the crystals were also rising. At the crystals' request, the guardians had brought the faceted minerals from their villages and placed them where they wished to be. Pergaine cast an appreciative look at the gathering, and called out to Gamon, "I've never seen so many guardians. And look at those crystals glow. They'll help us find a connection to the best future all right. They're ready to work."

Gamon's face held a pensive cast as he turned away from the mastodons to Pergaine, a finger resting on his white mustache. "More ready than I am, I think."

Pergaine reached out with her senses and felt the flowing current that the crystals maintained between Earth's core and the Universe. Her body swayed as she began to see the time tunnels that the crystals were already highlighting for their journey. Feeling their pull, she opened her eyes and glanced at her feet to help regain her balance.

Her voice flowed on the crisp air as she turned to her friends. "They're the best crystals I've ever seen for amplifying energy. They're good at time dimensions, too. All we'll need to do is hold our connection to the Life here, and travel the time tunnels to seek our counterparts in the future."

"All?" Aviea chuckled a bit. She held her personal gem, a fist-sized emerald, in her hands. "How do I connect to a future self?" She shook her head.

"No time like the present to learn," Yawri called, accompanying the sound of the mastodons trumpeting again in the distance. "We're connected to the core of this planet and the Universe, too. Are we co-creators or not? I've got plenty of Creator in me and will be happy to leave a little of it stored here to keep this energy center functioning while Earth sleeps. We'll find a future self that is conscious enough to receive a link. We'll be whole again."

Aviea turned her bronze face from the rising sun to her friends. "But what if the planet doesn't wake up?" she said, voicing what others had thought but none had spoken. They all knew that if the planet didn't revive from its hibernation, they would not either. The group stood silent.

"Who knows what we'll find?" Tisbero stared at the orange ball rolling slowly up from the horizon. "The planet lives in all dimensions now, but if it hibernates, I don't know what that will mean. I feel it preparing to withdraw its consciousness deep into itself."

Gamon drew his rose quartz crystal to his chest and reasoned a question. "But how can Earth stay connected to the Universe without being fully awake?"

Yawri spoke with forced confidence as he took a small step forward. "It still has all of itself below the surface. It still has the great caves and caverns, underground lakes, minerals, crystals and Life. It still has its core."

Tisbero turned from the orange sun and focused on his friends. "And that's what we'll have to stay connected to as we search the future--the core. When we find the future self that has the ability, the connection between past and future will be made."

"Find a future that is able to receive an arc of consciousness." Gamon wanted to believe it was possible, but the edge in his voice told of his doubt.

Pergaine brought her crystal back to her chest as a bead of perspiration grew on the fine wrinkles of her brow. "What could go wrong? The bodies we have when that time comes will only have to receive what we left behind here."

"I don't see a problem either." On an impulse, Yawri scanned the valley's distant ridge. Seeing nothing, he once more turned toward his friends. "The connection to our future will work. Shahitam and his followers will burn themselves out. A fire can't create its own firewood."

Pergaine studied the large assemblage of guardians, positioned in circling seed pods across the landscape. Each pod had a core of five or six searchers that was surrounded by a dozen or more others whose sole purpose was to provide stability for them. "I can't worry about what Shahitam may or may not do. I just know that I have to make an arc of consciousness with a future self." She glanced at Yawri who smiled confidently at her and nodded.

"Look at those birds!" Tisbero pointed skyward urgently. *The day is right to join a journey across time.* Everyone in the great assemblage seemed to see the broad-winged hawks, falcons, and brown eagles at once. "We are with Life."

Gamon spoke as if making a report. "Yes. The mastodons and large-toothed tiger have moved closer, and three eagles are landing on that promontory." Faces turned to watch the feathered trio land on the nearest cliff. Then in a synchronized display, they spread their four-foot wings in unison. Their feathers caught the light, and reflected it toward the crystal center. A hundred golden beaks in the sky sounded a chorus. Trumpet and roar reverberated off living stone walls.

"That's Earth's signal!" Tisbero exclaimed, his red hair flying. In the span of a few heartbeats the giant crystals at the center of the assemblage glowed a brilliant white. "Make sure your body's chakras are in balance! Affirm your connection to Earth. The more stable our bodies are, the better we'll be able to explore time dimensions."

"Dear heavenly Earth, the time tunnels are opening!" Aviea cried out as a circular portal appeared. Its surface looked like a gently whirling sea. The beings left their physical bodies standing in a trance and entered the portal with their astral selves, seemingly swallowed by it. Inside, they rocketed through time tunnels that branched like a maze of radiant arteries and veins in a living body of time.

Pergaine led her friends down a translucent violet and amber tunnel, its striated patterns a rushing blur. She spoke decisively. "A hundred years ahead ought to be far enough. Let's drop into this time dimension." Like flying fish jumping out of water, their astral bodies appeared in another time and place.

The smell of decay permeated the air. Yawri clutched his chest. "Everything is dying!"

A tangled mass of rotting vegetation covered the ground. Aviea's hands shot to her mouth as if to hold in her shock, but her voice cried out for all to hear. "All we helped...All we helped bring to Life is dying! Why?"

"I don't know!" Yawri bellowed. "Did Shahitam win?"

"Dear Creator!" Gamon stood wide-eyed and fought desperately to find reason. "What happened?"

Tisbero turned from the inexplicable scene to scan the faces of his friends. What he saw made him shout. "Just observe the experience, don't become it! Stabilize your connection to Earth's core and to the crystal center. Remember our purpose!"

Pergaine's astral form wavered as she looked down at her feet, raised her head and spoke out, "Yes! Don't become what you see! Stay connected to the planet's core, and to each other!" A nervous pause occurred as they all tried to regain balance.

Yawri struggled to re-center himself. "The axis of Earth is different! It's no longer thirty-six degrees off vertical, it's much less!"

"Stay connected," Pergaine said urgently. "Stay connected."

Yawri exclaimed. "Why has the axis shifted?!"

Aviea choked out the words, "I can't stand all the death!"

Tisbero moved in front of the travelers and barked into their faces. "Re-enter the time tunnels. Re-enter! We can't get caught in the trauma! Reconnect and go forward!"

The guardians opened a portal to the tunnel and rushed into it escaping the pain and loss. Another rush through the living tubes moved the bewildered searchers through time. After a minute of panicked flight, Pergaine's voice coalesced around Gamon, Aviea, Tisbero and Yawri as they halted in a section of the tunnel that pulsed with pastel blue and green. "We've got to be more careful." She reprimanded herself as well as everyone. "Clearly, we must be better prepared for whatever we find." Strained faces looked back.

"I almost forgot who I was, and became what I felt." Yawri sounded exasperated. Aviea shook her head, but didn't speak.

All Gamon said was, "That was hard."

The group stood in a small circle as if to recall their strength. At last Tisbero cast a burning gaze upon his fellow travelers. "Come. We must keep searching. We'll find no future selves by hovering in a time tunnel." Though shaken, the group moved forward, but much more soberly. They moved slowly at first, more concerned with keeping near one another than entering another time. But after an increasing rush of streaking gold and violet, they gathered their courage and jumped into another scene. There was a palpable sigh of relief as they found themselves hovering in living green jungle foliage. Smiles crossed their faces as they saw a group of human-beings in a clearing below.

"Guardians. They're guardians!" Yawri called out. "Our kind still tends Earth. I knew we would find them."

Aviea was eager to take in this more hopeful scene, and moved forward slightly. "They're having a meeting of some kind. Let's see if we can understand what they're saying." The searchers floated in the trees, quietly bearing witness to all that transpired below.

A man, about six feet tall, paced back and forth as he spoke. "I tell you the garden has become dangerous. Too few of us can understand what the plants and animals are saying anymore. Slow as the process has been, our children only understand our tongue, and not the language of the tiger or python. Few can see the world through their eyes. It's too dangerous to stay."

A gray-haired woman spoke. "But some of us still understand. Some still hear the one language. The garden is still safe."

"Safe for you!" a young woman shook her fist in the air. "My child is dead! This is no longer a garden. Which plants kill? Which waters kill? The snake poisoned my boy."

Another man spoke dejectedly. "My father could speak with the tiger and he never knew fear. All was a garden. But I can speak only with the plants, and not with the beasts. My children can scarcely speak to the water spirits, and not even to the clear stones!"

Another man poked absently at the ground with a long stick. "How many more children must die from poisons? If we don't leave this jungle while we have some ability remaining, we'll become trapped and live in fear like the broken humans we see."

"I have watched their camp," a woman's voice spoke out. "They worship carved idols. They believe the Creator is outside of themselves." The man with the stick tossed it on the ground.

The woman who had lost her son spoke again. "How can we stay to tend plants and animals which may kill us any instant? Our children will be either killed or raised in fear. Are we to build walls and burn back the forest like the broken people do? I cannot wish that prison upon them."

The gray-haired woman's voice filled the air once more. "But the lush Life here provides such bounty. Many of us can still ask for the location of the honey tree and the bees will take us to it."

"Look at the welts on my arms!" A young man exclaimed. "I no longer wish to speak with bees!"

A short, stout man reacted. "But you must speak with and listen to the Life around you! That's the doorway to Earth's soul as well as your own!"

And old man with skin like tanned leather tried to bring calm. "Even though less food may be in the dryer and colder north, our children could be raised without fear there. They could learn to love the Life around them, not to fear it. It's true there are fewer of Earth's voices to hear there, fewer species mean less Life. But with less diversity perhaps it will be easier to feel safe. If our children have less fear, it will be easier for them to be in their hearts, and retain the ability to listen." Several faces looked down at the ground, clearly accustomed to weighing the man's words with respect.

"I agree," a female voice said. "But better to leave the garden now while some of us can still speak during a journey, than be imprisoned later when all are deaf." A baboon screamed a short-lived cry as a tiger growled in the distance.

Unmistakable fear flashed across faces. The woman continued. "I remember when my grandfather would ride the willing lion from village to village. Those days are long past. Today, it makes us its meal."

"I am sorry, very sorry." The old woman with the gray hair shook with grief, but her wavering voice continued. "The garden has provided all our needs, and we were great gardeners. But you're right. We must leave. The garden has not changed, but we have." She looked toward a child, although cradled by it's father, it still trembled from the carnivorous sound. "We have lost the ability to understand its voice."

The tall man who first spoke did so again. "I feel ashamed. What have we done wrong?"

The old woman rose slowly. Tears streamed down her creased face like rain from a leaden sky. She looked down at the ground and watched as her drops fell and moistened the soil. "We must leave the garden," she said, "or be killed by it."

Aviea's gaze sought out her companions, seeking comfort there. "Well," she said to break the spell, "clearly the problem we have been having with our children continues. For some reason, each generation is still getting less capable than the last, and they're getting shorter. Except for that one man, they're not a lot taller than the humans of Shahitam."

Gamon let out a suppressed breath. "It must be difficult for these guardians to watch as their abilities lessen each generation."

Yawri nodded his head slowly in agreement. "It's so different from our time. For us everyone possesses all abilities, and no one is greater or less than another. Although I can tell they still all respect and honor each other here, there is an undercurrent of separateness." He gazed at the villagers. "Did you hear that one say he was ashamed? How can a guardian ever feel ashamed for what they give?"

The heat of Tisbero's heart resounded in his voice. "This must still be the time of closing. Maybe the dying vegetation at that last stop is a part of the closing as well. We don't know that it is due to Shahitam." All nodded silently, feeling pain from either answer. They forced themselves to focus on the task at hand. Once more the beings opened the portal to the time tunnels and cascaded forward, a longing tension on their astral faces. Streaming reds and purples flashed like passing spotlights as they reached out for a more hopeful time. Pulling on hope, the searchers popped into another reality with earnest determination.

Yawri spoke first as they looked down upon a frothing waterfall and jungle ferns. "Ah," he said with relief. "I can feel the Life in the air. This is a good time and place." The beings gazed at the scene and recharged themselves, focusing with all their ability on the present moment.

Gamon brushed his mustache as his eyes swept across flat-topped mountains that stood like earthen tables on the sweeping, green plain. Relief showed in his voice. "I know this area. These are the tepuy plateaus of the great southwestern continent. This is the energy center which connects Earth's timing with the Universe."

Pergaine grinned for the first time since they'd started. "I remember this area, too. Timing between Earth and the cosmos flows as one breath at this place. Feel it? It's the third chakra, all right."

Yawri beamed. "The jungle still thrives. Species are balanced here."

Tisbero pointed to the top of the adjacent tepuy, his voice happier still. "There, future guardians!" All faces flushed with anticipation as the team's astral bodies moved through the air and lighted on a lichen encrusted escarpment which overlooked the gathering.

Aviea pointed a long finger to the woman who was surrounded by perhaps a dozen guardians. "She certainly still carries the skill to work with time dimensions. Look at how she is connecting to them. She's channeling energy flows that stretch from the stars to the planet's core." Everyone watched as the woman ran energy through her body as if it was a mixing bowl filled with ethereal and physical nourishment.

"It's a future incarnation of Hetlin!" Yawri exclaimed. "I'm sure it's a future Hetlin. Remember? She was the one who visited the deep caves and reported Earth's history at the council."

Gamon answered for everyone in the group as they watched her move the flows of energy. "So much has happened since then. It's good she still works in a future time. It means others probably are too."

"I recognize another one." Pergaine was pointedly excited. "Isn't that Lazket?" The travelers fell silent as they watched.

Hetlin kept her eyes closed and her body swayed with the pulse of Universal timing. Gentle smiles showed on her companions as they surrounded her, clearly caring for her, and provided stability so that she could strengthen the connection of the local area with the dimensions of time. Lazket's chest rose as he breathed in the atoms of Life, and his aura glowed as their energy filled every cell of his body. Fondness showed in his eyes as he opened them to look toward the sound of a rock as it rolled over stones and fell into a pool of water with a small splash.

"Kill them!" A voice rang out.

Hetlin was the last to open her eyes and see the men rushing toward them. "It's the broken ones!" Lazket called out. But others, still not comprehending the threat, stared blank faced at the approaching tide. "Run to the waterfall! We can go behind it!" Lazket continued to yell in alarm. Faces turned from the rushing men toward the distant waterfall and back again.

"Kill them!" burst out once more.

A muscular, hairy man yelled to his spear-laden followers: "They try to harm Earth! Look!" The sharpened stone point of his weapon glistened in the mist. "They harm the gods! Stop them!" With a blood-thirsty cry they increased the speed of their attack. All of the guardians ran toward the falls as arrows hissed over their heads.

Lazket winced in pain as one of them pierced his shoulder, but he kept running directly behind Hetlin to protect her. The last three guardians in line fell in rapid succession as the warrior's bows found their range. The next four in line, though they held no weapons, suddenly turned to face the attackers. In an effort to draw fire, two ran at an angle up slope as the other two ran down. Those above fell to arrows, the ones below to spears. But the distraction allowed five guardians to reach the waterfall, hoping that the broken humans would be afraid to enter it. As Hetlin was poised to dash behind the froth, an arrow hit her in the leg. She stumbled, and Lazket stopped to break her fall. A spear shot through his side. The blood of both spilled into a pool of crystal clear water. Clubs rained down on the remaining guardians as they tried to shield their friends with their bodies.

Wild whoops and cheers arose from the broken humans as they pulled Hetlin up from where she lay. The arrow in her leg protruded like a black spike. The hairy, muscled man twisted its broken shaft out of her wound and held it up for his troops to see. "We have stopped their desecration!" He yelled. He surveyed the mortally wounded guardians. "Let the swines that insult the gods die where they lay. This is the one we want. She is the priest who brings evil to our gods!"

Rising above the pain, Hetlin made herself face her attackers. "Your gods are false!" she called out, her long dark hair flew with the flash of her head. "You pray only to what you can see with your eyes, idols made of stone! Earth is a part of All. You are a part of All. You only kill yourselves when you kill us. Open your eyes!"

The leader sprang to her beautiful form and struck her across the head with the blunt club. She crumpled to her knees. "Evil!" he screamed. "The gods bring rain, food and stones for our shelters, but they will bring disease if we displease them! You displease them! You displease the gods! We must torture evil out of this priest!" They dragged Hetlin past the line of guardians that lay bleeding their Life's blood onto the ground. Mercifully, she noticed, Lazket's eyes were already glazed with death.

When they reached a clearing of flat, sandy ground the leader barked again. "Tie her hands and feet. Dig a deep trench and throw her into it." He waved his club toward a group of warriors. "You, cut branches to cover the trench." He pointed to another group. "You gather as many snakes as you can find. We'll seal them in with her. She'll die with her own kind."

"Don't do this!" she struggled against her bonds. "The gods are within you as you are within them. Everyone is within everyone else! "

A club whistled through the air and smacked her stomach with a dull thud. She doubled in pain, and didn't raise her head until rough hands grabbed and threw her into the trench. Her crimson leg buckled as she collapsed face down upon its sodden bottom. The falling mist changed to rain and pooled in the dark trench. "Die a miserable death for your sins and your next life will be less evil," a voice cursed.

Hetlin's voice was clearly pained, but she rolled to her side and continued to exhort her captures. "But we are all of the One Body. What you do to others, you do to your future self." Branches, leaves and soil were packed across the living tomb. "Please, feel your connection to All-That-Is." Her quiet sobs were silenced as only one hole of light remained in the coffin's lid.

The leader turned to his troops. "Drop the snakes down through the hole. Then cover it with a rock." He then yelled so any of the fallen guardians that still lived could hear. "Let this be a lesson to all of you, honor the one religion or meet this fate!" A yell of victory rose from the attackers' smiling faces.

Aviea turned her head, unable to watch any longer. "I can't believe this is a future. Such cruelty. Family slaying family."

Gamon continued to stare at the scene. "Cells of the One Body murdering other cells. What future is this?"

The searchers retreated to the adjacent tepuy, taking shelter in a thin cloud of veiling mist. Yawri placed his hand on Tisbero's shoulder, but Tisbero continued to gaze thoughtfully at the ground. After what felt like an eternal silence Tisbero spoke. "We saw that same cruelty as they slaughtered our village. They have only exchanged beams of unmaking light for sharpened stone."

Gamon struggled to understand. "These broken people seem completely disconnected from their source. They don't even seem to be connected to their human-spirits at all. Without human-spirits there can't be much etheric-soul in their bodies either, because there's nothing for it to connect to. They have no questions, only answers, self-righteous answers." The explanation gave little comfort.

Yawri faced away from the grisly scene, though the rain now shielded it from view. "Cut off from their planet's and their souls' voices, the only voice remaining will be from their need to survive."

Gamon looked down. "And Shahitam's. His voice grows because these humans believe more in their fears than they do in Creation."

"That's why they tortured Hetlin!" Tisbero fired with dawning realization. "They don't have the crystals to destroy the body's human and etheric connection anymore, so now they use torture. They're puppets of Shahitam. He uses his whispers to convince these people to try and break Hetlin's union with the All. If he can get her to die believing that she is alone, that she is separate, then she will reincarnate as broken from the Source as they are."

"I don't know. I just don't know. What hope for the future lies in this?" Pergaine spoke the most troubling thought of all.

Chapter 14   **The Search**

The searchers made themselves press on, but they were too distracted to appreciate the time tunnel that glowed with rosy luminescence, streaked with veins of pulsing yellow. Relying on their inner senses only, they slowed as they reached a smooth pastel section and asked a portal to open for another chance at Life. The group found themselves on a small pastoral hill adjacent to a ring of giant stones. Individual slabs of living rock stood like towering sentries surrounding a fifty-foot circle of flowering prairie grass. The searchers studied the circle of stones with curious eyes, clearly relieved to have a puzzle to solve.

"Up there!" Tisbero shot a finger toward three skystones coming in from the east, and the travelers watched in silence. The rectangular platforms flew in parallel formation, the middle one much longer than the two flanking it. The searchers could see that three guardians sat on each of the flanking skystones and that the slabs were connected to each other with an ethereal matrix of woven energy. They slowed as they reached the stone circle.

"Carefully, now," one of the flyers said, "let's add a little soul-sound to the back portion of the center monolith." As if moved by unseen, giant hands, one end of the middle stone gently dipped down as its other end rose up. In slow motion, the slab shifted from horizontal to vertical and hovered like a floating seed over rich sediment. "Let's bring it forward...bring it forward so that it fills the gap in the circle," the speaker added.

"It wants to face the other direction," another called out as if the procedure was common. "Rotate it a hundred and eighty degrees." Like a feather blown in a morning's breeze, the monolith rotated around its axis until it stopped of its own accord. "It's where it wants to be, lined up to connect with the moon's cycles," the same guardian concluded. Ever so gently the stone descended until its bottom tip touched the ground.

"Increase soul-sound, decrease soul-light. Gravity has to be strong enough to sink the stone where it stands," the first speaker directed. The weight of the monolith increased due to the change in balance between light and sound to a hundred times its normal. Its tip parted the ground beneath it like butter. First ten feet, then fifteen feet of the long, narrow slab disappeared into the earth. "Release!" the guardian exclaimed. The stone stood perfectly vertical with ten feet remaining above ground.

"Is it pleased?" one of the workers asked, his own aura shimmering with light. All were silent.

"The circle begins to hum," another finally said. The workers stepped off their skystones, which hovered above the tops of the waving grass, and walked into the center of the circle. A sound, like an echo of a sonata, permeated the air. Workers and stones alike glowed with satisfaction.

"It is good," the tallest of them said at last. "I can feel the pulse of the connection between the core, the ley lines of Earth and the stars.

"We listened to the stones well," the human-being next to him added. "I think they are successfully aligned to the events of the sun, moon and stars. More connection to constellations, I pray, will help Earth keep alive."

The monoliths stood like living fingers of the Creator Itself, as if Its hand was now firmly a part of Earth and Its fingers held the sky. "This stone circle will endure," another guardian sighed in appreciation.

One of the workers stared down at the ground beneath her feet. Then she lifted her gaze to the standing stones. "There are many hundreds of these living circles now, scattered all over Earth. Even as we forget who we are, we can come to them and remember, or at least question." All stood and listened to tones which emanated from the living stones. Each tone harmonized with another to form a symphony that was carried away on the soft breeze.

Another worker spoke. "We don't know the future, but now is good." The workers' smiles broke into laughter, and hands touched congratulatory hands.

Pergaine turned to her friends and smiled as well. "It looks as if there is hope. Even though the cause of our descent into solidity is unknown, guardians still tend and enhance Life. There must be a time in the future that we can-" Her voice was cut short by a sudden swirl of light as the portal re-opened. "What's happening?" she shouted as all the group was drawn into it.

Yawri yelled in alarm. "We're being pulled back! We're being pulled back in time!" The whirl of spiraling light sucked the astral travelers through tunnel after glowing tunnel.

"Stay together!" Tisbero warned. "We've got to stay together!"

As though jolted awake from a dream, a violent shake brought them back to their bodies where they'd left them standing at Earth's heart chakra. Gamon cried out, staring with disbelief through his body's physical eyes once more. "We're under attack!"

Tisbero stepped upon a boulder to gain elevation, and strained to focus on the distant panorama. "Shahitam's soldiers are coming over the ridge!" A horde of foot soldiers cascaded over far hillsides like an army of locusts. In the air, fifty-foot-long skyplatforms, seemingly packed with dark teeth, streamed down the slopes ahead of them. The soldiers on the platforms began shooting beams of mustard-yellow light that exploded the rolling ground. Tisbero and the others watched the defending guardians in the outer ring as they tightened their circles around searchers who had not yet returned to their helpless bodies.

One of the guardians defending Tisbero, Aviea, Gamon, Pergaine and Yawri ran up to speak to them, although they stood gaping at the conflict before them. "We had to call you back!" he yelled above the din of battle. "Shahitam discovered our plan! If his soldiers get through our defensive lines and attack the centering crystals, you and all the other searchers will be stranded. You'll have no chance to retrieve your information from your bodies."

All guardians knew the meaning of this; without retrieving information from their bodies there was no hope for a conscious death. Without a conscious death, an unconscious Life would follow. More blasts rocked the distant ground. "Now it is your choice. Stand here in your body, or trust us to defend it as you go back into trance and travel." Five hundred yards away, foot soldiers fired un-making beams into the first ring of guardians, but their beams were reflected back with deadly effect.

"How long do you think they can be held off?" Tisbero asked with uncharacteristic calm. The defender looked to the battle line. Some of the guardians were falling now. Either too many beams hit them at once, or they had lost their connection to the Whole. Either event was fatal.

After thoughtful reflection, he returned to the searchers' waiting faces. "We are not fighting alone. Mastodons and tigers harass their flanks. The big hawks are using their talons. If no more soldiers arrive," he looked back toward the melee, "we can perhaps hold out for the day."

"The day?" Pergaine was astonished. "We have to find a future that can receive an arc within the day?"

Yawri turned toward her, his jaw tight with determination. "Many searchers are looking. As long as the defenders can keep their bodies safe, there's a chance."

A searing, mustard-yellow beam landed just two hundred yards away. "One of their platforms got through!" Gamon exclaimed. "Look! It's going after that group of searchers!" The band looked on terrified as vacant bodies swayed where they stood. Defenders near the blast ran to stand in front of the unprotected guardians with their own reflecting crystals. In the next moment, five soldiers fell from the platform. One shielding guardian fell, but another one rushed to take his place in the defensive mirror.

Tisbero peered toward the struggle. He ran a hand through his graying red hair, and then spoke with certainty that was reflected in his planted stance. "Four searchers in a group can find out if a future exists as easily as five. I'm staying here to protect your bodies."

Pergaine flinched at the words. "Tisbero." Their eyes locked.

"It will be safer for me here where I can fight than it will be out there defenseless with you," he said, minimizing his choice before breaking their gaze. Another blast echoed off a distant cliff wall and it sent shards of rock below. "Go!" he said as if in command.

"Be careful..." Aviea called to him.

He looked toward the approaching conflict. "If they get near us, or the Center, I'll call you all back so you can help stop them!" The travelers nodded in silent agreement. "It's now or never! Find that time for the arc!" A sense of emergency gripped them as they gathered instinctively near Tisbero and, as one, entered in a deep trance and left their bodies behind. Tisbero looked upon the vacant forms, gently swaying as if asleep. Their faces, he saw, were still turned toward his. A sense of foreboding filled him as he broke away once more and turned toward the approaching hail of yellow light.

✦

"Did you feel something strange?" Mariyonta's question resonated in the crystal cave of the great, deep cavern.

Aronlat leaned forward from the wall of amethyst behind him, his face tight with concentration. "Yes." Both listened to inner sounds, stretching to feel any ripple in the immense underground lake. "Something is wrong," the youth said at last. "There is something wrong, but I can't tell what."

"I can't either," Mariyonta replied soberly. Then, as if her thoughts were pulled toward the crystal cave's entrance, she added, "That crystal is glowing. That's strange. I wonder why?" She pointed to the one they called "sentinel" because of its imposing presence. The duo stood up and walked to the large crystal near the cave's mouth. Silence stood guard while Mariyonta and Aronlat sought communication.

Aronlat's muscles tightened. "These visions can't be right. I see a large group of crystals encircled by guardians, more than I've ever seen in one place before, but there is fighting." He strained to keep focused as emotions surged through his body. "This makes no sense."

"But...I see it too. Brother against brother. Sister against sister. It's as if the sentinel crystal itself is under attack, yet it's here with us." She looked out of the crystal cave's mouth to the glassy lake and immense cavern beyond. "It's safe." Mariyonta bent forward in deep concentration as she gently leaned against the tall amethyst.

Aronlat's hand stroked the crystal's silky surface. "I know. Everything appears safe. But then, why is it telling me it is under attack?"

"But what could attack? I don't understand." Mariyonta appeared to relax, as if she were resting against a warm cloud rather than upon a vibrant, blue crystal. Her eyes shot open, her back straight. "Our village! I can't see our village!"

"But it's always been faint from here." Aronlat was silent for several heart beats. Then, his whole body turned toward her like an uncoiling spring. "I can't see it either!" Their eyes locked as panic flashed across their faces. Concern suddenly aged youthful skin.

"What's happening?!" Mariyonta cried out as her head tilted toward the domed ceiling.

Aronlat placed an earnest hand on her shoulder. "We've got to get back. Something is wrong and we've got to get back." They surveyed the walls surrounding them, only minutes before a home, now a prison.

Mariyonta sounded as though she were suddenly elec- trified. "We've got to get out first." She took a step, stopped, and then added with a rush, "Finding a way back to the surface could take months. Do you remember the journey it took us to get here? So many turns, we're so deep."

The sentinel crystal grew brighter, in response, Aronlat focused on his connection to it. Tension rippled across the muscles of his neck as he rested his fingers on the glassy mineral. "Just a moment. I think I've got something. Yes. The crystal will take us out."

"The crystal? But it's so big. How can it fit through all the passages?" Mariyonta stared at the mouth of the crystal cave. "I'm not even sure we could get it out of here."

"Put your hand on it too, and listen. It's telling us how." Her hand joined his on blue-violet stone. Each heartbeat felt like a mallet in their chests.

"It might be possible," she said in deep thought. "Stone is crystallized fluid."

"It's possible," Aronlat replied instantly. "I see how. We must increase our soul-light relative to soul-sound. It can fly just like a skystone. Better than the skystones."

"Oh, heavenly Earth...It's coming free!" Mariyonta ex- claimed as the tall crystal unplugged from its giant socket and moved out from the wall.

Aronlat spoke quickly. "It wants to go to that large group of crystals I saw in the vision. But it will need to blend with us to fly there."

Mariyonta raised her arms to hug the obelisk, which stood like a living light. She scanned its surface thoughtfully. "I hear it. The crystal *will* take us out of the cavern. We need it as it needs us."

Aronlat's voice rang with urgency. "Increase soul-light to reduce its gravity." He allowed more soul-light into his body and it began to shine with a strong auric glow of its own. The crystal rose, tipped sideways, then hovered horizontally just above the cave floor. "Get on," he rushed out, but Mariyonta was already sitting on the broad, scale-like surface.

"It's like riding a woolly mammoth," she said, filled with tense excitement.

He grinned. "Except this mammoth can fly."

The trio moved gingerly, weightlessly through the crystal cave's mouth which appeared to make way like a living gel rather than solid stone. The newly emerged skycrystal cast a warm glow on their camp as it slowly moved past it. "We've got to stop," Mariyonta said. It halted, hearing her request. The young adult's eyes traced across items filled with meaning; the wall which held baskets of the abundance provided by the sacred cavern, their beds, vessels of purest water, the small glowing crystals and luminescent fungus which gave them light.

Mariyonta felt a fleeting heaviness in her chest. "You adopted us and held us as one cell of your great cave-body." Their faces turned toward the giant, subterranean lake. "Wherever I go, we will be together."

Aronlat followed with clear voice. "You've been more than a home. You've been a womb. I am re-born, now, Earth is my mother." His eyes lingered, collecting one last vision. "I only leave you because the One Body is under attack, and we must find out why."

The crystal bobbed slowly as if tugging at a harness. Mariyonta and Aronlat grasped small, protruding nodules, which would serve as handholds on the shimmering obelisk, and focused on increasing soul-light. With steadily increasing speed, the trio ascended from the shore of the great underground lake and flew across its tranquil surface. Glowing minerals from the roof above reflected in the still mirror below, as though lights lived in the bottomless depths. The two passengers strained to see the opposite shore to no avail.

Then, suddenly, a massive dark wall of stone appeared before them. Mariyonta and Aronlat braced for the ascent, but just as they reached a crevice darker than all that surrounded it, the crystal shot down. Their laughter echoed off the walls.

"So the fastest way up is down!" Aronlat called out, a broad smile on his face, hair blowing in the unshielded wind. The crystal whipped down a winding stone tunnel that looked more like an artery than a cave. Then it glided over a wide expanse of bottomless black. The sound of distant, falling water was the first indication that they had even remained on Earth.

Several minutes passed before the soft glow of the skycrystal illuminated the hundred-foot waterfall that cascaded beneath them, framed in darkness and tumbling through space. Turning upstream, they slowly, patiently moved above the powerful, deafening flow. Mariyonta placed a hand on his shoulder, comforting him in a way he didn't know he needed. Her touch relaxed the brow he hadn't realized was creased.

"Dear Creator, this is huge." Mariyonta felt great awe as their voyage left the underground river for a gentle tributary. "It goes on and on. I didn't see anything on that ride down. We would have been in here forever if the crystal hadn't asked us to leave with it." She flexed her back. Her muscles ached from the effort of balancing in the constant motion. Minutes passed in silence as the skycrystal continued its ascent to the surface.

Aronlat suddenly became aware of a scene passing below. "Mariyonta! There's the camp we shared with our friends!" They gazed upon the place that served as their base camp for the first nine months of their initiation. Then, he added almost habitually, "I wonder how the others who returned to the village are doing?"

Mariyonta remained silent as concern tightened her jaw. Time free of reference passed as marbled walls of shadow and light played with their sight. Their constantly moving torsos swayed from side to side to avoid jutting stone, but their legs held a steadfast grip.

After a half hour of strained silence Mariyonta asked, "Do you smell a change in the air?"

"The mouth!" Aronlat exclaimed as a different quality of light revealed itself ahead. "We're almost back to the surface!"

Mariyonta could only agree, her voice higher than normal. "It won't be long now."

The crystal emerged into the light of day and halted. Along with its passengers, it was clearly startled by the transition from the light of glowing minerals and plants to the light of the sun. It came to rest on rocky ground, just outside the small entrance to the monumental cave. Mariyonta and Aronlat were almost blinded by the sunlight. The gray clouds were sharp with harsh contrast. The green of plants was too brilliant, the outline of dark rock too defined. The new adults stared afresh at the world through squinting eyes.

"It's as if I forgot this existed." Aronlat said incredulously. He stood up from where he'd sat glued since leaving the earthen womb, and took a timid step on the first soil his feet had felt in many months. Mariyonta did the same, stretching cramped muscles where she stood before taking her own first steps. She bent over as much to exercise as to pick up something.

"Aronlat, look here," she said. "A crystal." The sound coming from the crystal was like a cry, so she held it to her chest to seek connection, and to comfort it if she could, as was her life-long habit. Without warning she doubled over, face contorted in agony.

"What's wrong?" Aronlat cried.

"I," she stammered, "I...Our village it's..." He took the crystal from her and brought it to his own heart.

His body convulsed in pain. His head pounded with a deafening throb. Grief choked his throat.

The recording crystal dropped to the ground as both youths collapsed on the rocks.

✦

Now without Tisbero, the astral bodies of Pergaine, Gamon, Aviea and Yawri searched desperately through the time tunnels for the dimension that would reveal health. They strained to maintain connection with the centering crystals and Earth's core. All knew it would be that link that would enable them to choose the best path.

"I'm getting a signal," Aviea responded as the travelers passed a series of branching time tunnels. The guardians stopped at a junction and reached out with their essence to connect with what lay ahead. "It's a few hundred years further than our last try." Eager for decisive action, the party rocketed down a translucent green vein ringed with a spiral of gold light. Their astral selves popped into a large underground room of granite walls as if by magic.

"Where are we now?" Yawri asked the question on every-one's mind.

Gamon attempted an answer. "This must be a place of guardians. The crystals in the alcoves give light of their own free will, and this chamber was carved in partnership with the stone." He strode with all the bravado he could muster toward a tall archway and looked in. "It's a hallway, with several rooms on either side. It's lit by crystals as well."

Pergaine shuddered and realized that she needed to put the battle out of her mind. A subtle emotional tremor passed through her as she focused on the room, and then, after a breath, she spoke decisively. "It's a sanctuary of some kind. Feel the energy. People are living here, studying, and communicating. It's deep underground. Perhaps they remember that communicating with the heavens is best done through communicating with Earth." The group floated down a hallway of living stone until they heard voices.

Proceeding slowly, the searchers entered a room to see a tall man in a white, flowing smock speaking to a group of perhaps fifty others. All stood silent to hear. "As has been spoken, those that have been murdered will have to be re-born according to our plan," he said with certainty. "Because these human-beings were murdered, the ethereal-souls and human-spirits are knotted like tangled grass."

A woman to his left spoke. "We have a way to heal them so that each can return to their source. To restore them, we must provide new bodies for them, and mentor them through a correct death." Feet shifted uneasily on the floor before the room stilled again. "In the past, when a man and woman conceived, great effort was made to pair the appropriate etheric-soul with the appropriate earth-spirit in a new body. That assured that both could achieve maximum consciousness through their lifetime together. Now, we will use our skill to achieve another purpose. Rather than a correct Life, the goal is a correct death. With a correctly loving death, the confused soul and spirit can untangle their information and return to their sources intact. This way they will be able to be reborn again in consciousness and rejoin us."

A second woman spoke. "I am aware of the price we are asking you to pay. To ask you to join in union for the purpose of allowing a correct death for the children you conceive, rather than a Life, goes counter to all our instincts. However, what shattered the identity between soul and spirit was not of nature, was not of Earth. The laws of nature were broken by others of our kind who chose to introduce murder. Our task is to undo what was done."

The tall, smocked man spoke again. "And as we have spoken among small groups I speak now for all to hear. The murdered human-beings are not the only Life that requires this healing process. Shahitam's believers also created lifeforms that are not of Earth. They confused the evolution of one species with another, animals with animals and even animals with humans. These creatures' genetics are so jumbled that there is no way they can find their way back to their source. These bodies will be reborn deformed. Our goal for them is the same, however. We will create a conscious death cycle for these animals, so that they can also rejoin their source."

The second woman spoke up. "Our homes on the banks of this great river are fertilized with the annual floods, food is plentiful, and the rocks are alive. We live in peace. However, although we did not bring about the murder of either human-being or beast, we will be the ones to heal it. It will be our purpose, then, to work consciously to heal what was done and remove the twisted heritage and the fractured souls from Shahitam's grasp."

Gamon, who hovered with the others, turned to face his traveling troupe. "It is heartening to see that the murdered are being healed. It gives great comfort. But comfort is not what we seek. This is clearly not the time of an arc."

"Yes," Pergaine acknowledged, sadness tingeing her voice. "We must move on, but this is a place of consciousness. Let's step forward in time to see what is transpiring here in another generation." The group called for a portal and the large chamber faded into mist. As if they had closed their eyes in one room and opened them in another, the mist parted to reveal another scene.

"Look there." Yawri focused the travelers' attention on a man and woman, each wearing a thin, long white cotton robe. "They're speaking with that stone wall." As if in effortless response, a large slab of heavy granite moved aside revealing a descending staircase. The robed pair stepped through the doorway with practiced ease. The travelers followed them through the doorway and down the staircase, which opened onto another chamber. Hundreds of people filled it. Glowing crystals stood in arched alcoves, reflecting light on a white sea of long robes.

"This is beautiful," Aviea murmured. "So many guardians."

A graceful, sturdy woman began to speak and members of the milling crowd began to listen. "We all remember," she said determinedly.

"That's Hetlin!" Yawri spoke excitedly to the travelers. "She has another body here. That pit of snakes didn't stop her!" Gamon, Aviea and Pergaine all grinned gratefully.

The remaining conversations in the chamber died away. "We all remember," the future Hetlin began again in a quieter voice. "We have always been born remembering. We are part of the one memory of all Creation. For generations we have worked to maintain conscious connection with our bodies, ourselves, the One Source and this history. We have had success, and we have had defeat."

A man to her right accepted Hetlin's invitation to speak. "She speaks what I also feel. Our successes have been many," the man said. "We have maintained conscious communities here, on this great, sacred river. Other communities have maintained consciousness on the other continents. These communities have thrived because of a common goal. A goal to stay connected to All Life. Yet, defeats remain."

Taking his cue from the last speaker, another man spoke. "My party has returned from a long journey. Few of the original humans remain, murdered as they are by the broken ones. They have taken sanctuary in places too difficult for the broken ones to live; in the deep jungle, tundra or desert. This is truly a defeat of our purpose to nurture Life. But we can report that the remaining original humans communicate to All-That-Is through Earth and Earth alone, as they were meant to. They speak with the spirits of the wind, the plants and stone because they are all of earth's body. That they still live is a success."

Hetlin's eyes swept to a glowing alcove and then thoughtfully back to the group. "But, we know the population of the broken kind has increased rapidly. For although we are different types of people, all people have the ability to breed without restraint." She paused, acknowledging the grief all felt, before speaking again. "The broken people have no ability to keep the living soul of Earth alive within them. Disconnected from the soul of Earth, they can have no connection to the etheric-soul of the universe, either. No balance can exist when there is only one weight for a scale.

"Now, separated from their physical and their etheric sources of Life, they murder all they touch; the remaining guardians such as us, the original peoples, the plants and animals as well. Though they have eyes and ears they are blind and deaf. They are able to hear the sound of the ax they wield, but are unable to listen. They are able to enjoy the pleasures of the flesh, but are unable to feel. They are able to look, but are unable to see. The garden is not prepared to defend itself from people that were meant to be its gardeners."

Another woman spoke. "We have stayed conscious as human-beings because we chose to join, not dominate. We chose to see, not just look; to listen, not just hear; we chose to value the wisdom which can only come through the connection that our bodies' earth-spirits have with Earth. It is only through them that we, as ethereal beings, can join consciously with physical Life. In this way, we can nurture all Life, physical and spiritual. Without them, we would be as vapor in the wind." She concluded by spreading her arms as if to honor her body.

Hetlin spoke again. "Yet, despite our heart-felt work we cannot deny that we ourselves have less ability than we did even one thousand years ago. The signs were subtle at first, and we tried our best to ignore them, but we have all learned that denial only serves to make lessons more dramatic. We have all acknowledged that today some of us are much more able to do certain things as compared to others. Comparison did not exist in our past. It exists now. We all know that different abilities do not mean different value, yet envy grows. As many have foreseen, this foreshadowing of envy may be our undoing. The fear of abilities that are no longer understood grows, because our bodies are slowly loosing awareness of the voices of the soul and planet which were meant to bring that under-standing." She gazed across the somber audience.

The original speaker, the tall man, spoke again. "As we have witnessed, the weak kill the strong, because the strong remind the weak of what they have lost. And it makes them afraid." He leveled his eyes he added, "Yet, the future is not determined. There is hope."

Sensing despondence, Hetlin rounded on the assemblage, a tight edge in her voice. "Guardians, although the future may go through darkness, it need not stop there. Encouragement comes from another future. Those who still have the ability to receive clear visions from pure waters are here to report what they have seen." Hetlin gestured toward a rotund, dark-skinned man.

"I am one of the seers Hetlin speaks of," the ebony man said in an elegant voice, and he spread his arms to include several others nearby. "We see visions in the pure waters that stand in bowls sculptured from emeralds the size of a man's head. Joining as we do with the sacred waters, we see that the future continues to follow these trends we hear described."

A gravelly voice spoke out above the audience's subtle rustling and murmuring. "What encouragement is this? Are you saying that we are destined to become like the broken human-beings we witness? Intelligent enough to survive, but not conscious enough to care for Life?"

"What we see," the seer began again, "is that our descent into solidity will continue. Whether we will become as disconnected from our sources as the newly spawned human-beings, we do not know. There is free will in each choice we make, in each action we take. Hetlin spoke of envy. To decide to judge is a choice. It takes much effort to maintain our caring for ourselves, and each other, as we taste bitter fruit. However, just as guardians built the stone circles to maintain connection to the All, the sacred waters have given us a great vision of what may be." Silence replaced muffled sounds from a slight shifting of feet.

Another seer, a woman with piercing brown eyes and light mahogany skin, spoke. "Earth wishes us to remain conscious. Consciousness begets consciousness as ignorance begets ignorance. Earth desires Life, not murder. The visions in the sacred waters show us great pyramids that we are to build. Triangular mountains made of living stone. Although many similar ones are to be built across Earth, we are to create three here. The first, the smallest, is to contain memory, the history of Earth. Our own names and history will be held in the living stones, as we hold it now in recording crystals. On an immense scale, memory will be available to us through many ages to come as our individual memory fails.

"The second pyramid is to serve as a ballast, a great, resonating grounding source to Earth's core to make sure that the information from the other two stays connected to physicality. And finally, the third pyramid is to serve as the connection to the Universe, other pyramids and stone circles. Its purpose will be to maintain the connection to our universal ethereal source. This third pyramid will be fitted with a gold capstone because it must be able to send and receive energy and information with such intensity that lightning will spark from it.

"It is foreseen that future selves will be born without memory. Earth shows us that these pyramids are needed to help them recall the memory of their connection to All-That-Is. Our children's children will work inside this great pyramid-being and thus be able to experience the stars and know them by name. Just as we do now, these individuals will be able to feel the oneness of the Universe both inside and outside of their own selves. They will feel their connection to Life, rather than their separation from it."

After he let the assemblage absorb the mental images he projected along with the sounds of the words, the ebony-skinned seer spoke again. "All three mountains will be built with living stones. Just as with the stone circles, we will listen to the bedrock from which they will come to learn what location they wish to take within the structure. We will join our sound with those of the our crystals and the bedrock itself so that each stone will be sculpted into the form it wishes. After we move and assemble them, the stones will sing together with a sound that amplifies all the megaliths we have placed in the world, and they will resonate Life force into the planet's own veins. Because these structures include both Earth and Universe, human-beings who work with them for generations to come will have the help they need to remain conscious in human form. That is the encouragement we bring to you." An invisible sigh from the chamber of guardians seemed to relax the air like the song of a nightingale.

A third seer spoke. Her musical, soft voice floated on the air. "We must build these mountains while we have the consciousness to do so. We still have the ability to build such beacons. We can still speak with the stars and the stones. We can still bring in enough soul-light and sound to use not just skystones, but skyplatforms capable of moving the immense monoliths that are needed. These triangular towers, as well as other which must be built, will be laid out to mirror patterns of the constellations. In this way, the knowledge from the stars can be kept real on Earth. These are the visions we received from Earth itself. I repeat, we must build them while clear communication with stars and stones alike remains, so that our future selves can continue to remember who they are."

Gamon, though entranced by the heartfelt scene, felt the persistent call of their task. "I know it is good to learn of the work occurring here, but these activities are not the time of an arc. We've got to keep moving." He received solemn nods of agreement from his friends.

The four travelers moved forward in time, earnestly seeking the time of union. In a matter of seconds, they witnessed a series of fading and refocused landscapes in which the great pyramids rose. They saw stone passageways and chambers built, each with a specific ability to keep a given chakra in the human body conscious. An empty sarcophagus was placed in the pyramid with the capstone, and eavesdropping told the travelers why. The guardian builders foresaw that their future selves would try to preserve their own dead bodies under the mistaken belief that bodies were their possessions. The guardian builders left an empty sarcophagus to demonstrate that a body should not be placed inside of them–that, instead, bodies should be returned to Earth to feed their source.

After several rapid shifts in time, the searchers gazed upon the finished, marble-sheathed pyramids reflecting brilliant white light from the sun. A glittering, solid gold cap rested on top of one, and it discharged streaks of lightning skyward. The breeze hummed with electrified air and tones of universal music streamed forth like a living philharmonic. The pyramid itself appeared to sway in a slow, rhythmic dance. More than a thousand robed guardians, with strong auric glows surrounding them all, populated the scene. The searchers, though awed with appreciation, moved forward in time. The scene faded into mist, then condensed to reveal another scene.

The broad river valley stretched out like a finger of blue. Much less than a thousand guardians populated the scene this time, and although they walked into the sacred tunnels of the pyramids downcast, they left in radiance. The four searchers moved on, praying for a time when consciousness rather than decline would grow. The doorway of mist came again. Centuries passed. Another scene appeared.

Lightning pulsed infrequently from the capstone, as if it were struggling to build up a charge. Scrub and sand had replaced succulent green. Pillars of smoke rose like coiling snakes in the distant valley. Hundreds of guardians populated the scene now, their glow dim. The scene faded into mist again. Centuries passed. The portal opened again.

At this time there was no lightning, no sound. The pyramids stood like misty dreams of their former selves. Perhaps one hundred weary guardians worked placing stones to block sacred entrances. The guardians' consciousness was fading, so they chose to close down the pyramids to prevent misuse by their unconscious future selves. Two dozen guardians on skystones levitated the golden cap off its high perch with great care. The gold would be used for other, more secular purposes. The mist arrived again as the searchers chose to move forward in time once more.

They began to see a new phenomenon: kings and queens. Distant memories of flight through the sky and discourse with the gods haunted the recesses of the royal highnesses' minds. Knowledge faded like an apparition. Kings and queens searched their hearts, but they could no longer grasp the memory that was lost. They ordered other pyramids built, small, pitiful imitations of the great mountains, crudely hammered from uncooperative stone. In their desperate attempt to reclaim what was lost, they possessed their bodies, owning them, enslaving them for their afterlife. Written symbols took the place of living walls whose songs now fell on deaf ears. Their expressions showed a nagging sensation that some vital piece of information was missing.

The searchers watched as sand covered in the paws of the great sphinx. "We've got to go," Yawri's voice held desperation. "Everything is still in decline. Guardians are getting less and less conscious. Did Shahitam win the battle? Is this what this means?"

The searchers looked on as smaller people, completely bereft of auric glow, chipped at the base of a pyramid with iron tools. They poured a liquid, perhaps vinegar, on the limestone to find an entrance. One was found. They entered seeking treasure, but only found an empty sarcophagus. They contented themselves by stripping the polished marble sheathing from the sides of the mountains and used it to build facades for chiseled stone houses in the city.

"We've got to keep looking," Yawri urged. "We can't give up." A portal opened and the four searchers entered it as though they were escaping from a sinking boat. They hurled themselves down the time-tunnel hoping their advance was not a retreat.

"Hello!" an unfamiliar voice called out. The word jarred them. The searchers gazed upon the astral bodies of six other guardians, searchers like themselves, which stood in a translucent, turquoise section of tunnel. The man who spoke was barrel-chested, and his wide, astral face held a welcoming smile.

"Howic?" Gamon called out. "Is that you?"

"Gamon! I haven't seen you since we worked together with the mastodons, ages ago from this time at least. Tell us. How goes your search?"

Gamon and Yawri were the first to reach him and the sense of relief at finding other searchers showed in their own grinning faces. "It's so good to see other searchers!" Yawri boomed out. Both parties greeted each other as if it were some sort of celebration.

Gamon's expression soured as he hovered in front of Howic. "Not well," he said. "All we've seen is decline."

Howic still smiled. "We've found something."

"You've found the time for the arc?" Yawri tried to rekindle his enthusiasm.

"We don't know," another of the party said. "We've been tracking configurations of the stars and planets to see when conditions would be best for accelerations in consciousness."

"It's my specialty," added Howic. "We've visited the first two of three hopeful configurations that we've found. We think they're all building toward an arc." Aviea, Gamon, Pergaine and Yawri shared a silent recognition that this group's strategy sounded much more effective than their own.

"This is fabulous news!" Aviea admitted out loud. "We've found nothing."

"The first configuration we visited definitely opened a door to receive the Creator's touch," the man continued. Aviea and Pergaine stepped closer to better hear every word. "A being was born, free of the mind-numbing thoughts of the norm. He can hear the voices of Earth and stars alike. He has two sons, Ishmael and Isaac, although from different mothers so that they can offer different doors to the One House. It is a very hopeful sign. It proves that the Creator has not abandoned Earth. It proves that It cares enough to send us beings who will be able to speak to different peoples, and give different guideposts to light everyone's way back. This man was called Abraham."

Gamon, clearly listening with focused intensity, said, "And what of the second configuration? You said you found another."

"The second configuration that we visited was also hopeful. The being that incarnates for this one has clear communication with the All as well. The human-beings of this time period are denser than any we have seen. They practice slavery and dominate Life with such determination that little remains living wherever they tread. This great messenger we saw follows instruction, not from the fears of man, but from the All. His heart is open to all sounds. His eyes are open to all sights. He views each moment as his first. He knows that, as will all people, evil and good reside within himself and he is not ashamed. He is not ashamed any more than a tree would be ashamed for growing from a crack in stone rather than from fertile soil. Because his connection to All is so pure, the Creator Itself speaks with him, and gives him ten laws to help bring people back to the One Body. I don't think any other person exists in that time that could withstand this energy of the Godhead and survive. He does, even though people of his time can't even look him in the eye. The painful truth about their own condition is reflected there. Moshe. His name is Moshe, or Moses."

"Again, encouraging." Yawri nodded, hopeful and impatient in the same breath. "It does sound as though we're not abandoned. The Creator is sending help. Now, you mentioned a third. What about this third configuration?"

"We are on our way to visit it now. The planets tell us that about twelve hundred years after Moshe the conditions will be right for more, very conscious beings to come into different places on the planet. The Creator clearly is trying to provide different manifestations of Its voice so that all types of human-beings can hear. It is sending great souls to a few continents, the place called Asia will have a well known one, but we think the best chance for an arc will occur at the heart chakra of Earth. From what we hear from the planets, beings are coming to this region to instruct people that the Creator is within them. They will remind them that nothing stands between themselves and the Creator of which they are a part."

Yawri spoke. "We are all inside each other. I am amazed that what is intrinsic within us must be taught to our future selves as if they are lost children."

"I think they are lost children," one of the other searchers countered. "For some reason our future selves are less aware than a dead stone. They believe the first, second and third dimensions make all reality, rather than only a small part of it. But the good sign is that the climb back to the Whole is occurring, and that the Creator Itself is sending help."

Howic spoke again. "If this third conjunction opens the doors as we foresee, it will be a major step toward regaining what was lost. A great awakening may occur."

He stepped forward, unable to contain his earnest intent. "We were about to search for one of these great teachers now. The planets show us that this teacher will not be alone. Many people to provide the stability needed for such a shift in awareness are to be present. This teacher will work at Earth's heart chakra. And there will be three other great souls born with him to support the plan. These three other human-beings will also be able to speak the One Language of Life. Although the teacher will be the spokesman, he will have support in place to assure that his voice carries the sound of the many."

Howic saw that the focused faces in front of him wished him to carry on, so he continued with the sense of urgency he felt. "From what we foresee, one of these beings will be a master of the dimensions of time, for if a change is to take place, the solid time dimension that Earth finds itself in will have to evolve to one that is more fluid. Molding clay is easier than molding rock. If we are lucky, humans may even start to count time differently. A second being will be very strong in its connection to Earth, and through Earth connection to the Creator. This being will assure that the changes that take place are real for the world. The third being will be a master in its ability to maintain connection to the Universe and the cosmic oceans of Life. It will assure that ethereal reality is correctly joined with the physical. Each one will have abilities of the other, but each will be as a cardinal direction of the Whole. It's set up so that the teacher will have the support his voice will need to ensure success."

Another of the searchers spoke up, her face beaming. "You see why we are excited about this configuration. The seeds the Creator sowed in the past through beings such as Abraham and Moshe are destined to blossom in this time."

Howic exuded hope. "Come search with us. It is the most hopeful time we've found, and it has been building for two thousand years just since Abraham. This is the best chance for an arc of consciousness that we have found so far."

It took no convincing. Yawri, Gamon, Aviea and Pergaine followed the other group down the pulsing time tunnel with renewed optimism, feeling that at last enough abilities to make an arc of consciousness could be found. The group stopped in the passage at the mouth of a large, orange vein that branched off the main one. "I don't know for certain," Howic said, "but this should lead us to the best probable future. To better cover the time, let's investigate different sections of it and reconvene here. If enough people exist that can receive an arc, we'll call back through our common connection to the centering crystal and get as many guardians as possible to come."

"This may be it." Another voice expressed the desire of all, as the two groups flew down the vein in earnest.

Chapter 15   **Hope**

A group of ten people wearing rough, woolen robes sat around a long, worn wooden table. Large scrolls lay open in front of the men. Pergaine, Yawri, Gamon and Aviea hovered invisibly above the gathering, listening to the intense discussion.

"I tell you, their progress goes well," a gray-bearded rabbi said as he rocked forward. "Each of the four knows the Torah as if they themselves had written it, and they interpret its meanings with an eloquence unknown for generations."

"True," said another. "God has clearly sent great beings to help us to return to Him. We have the Voice of Compassion, as well a Master of time, a Master of Earth knowledge, and a Master of Universal laws. Together, these four will create a completion of life energy that will guide us out of this darkness. We will live to see the rebirth of Light on Earth."

Another nodded agreement, although his brow was furrowed in concern. "All four are young, but they are strong, and getting stronger. We all know this. But we also know that the Romans have slaughtered many in their search for these ones. What is to keep these four from being found and slaughtered as well? God allows free will, even to murder His own."

The rabbi with the gray beard spoke again. "Jesus is now traveling to Egypt to study with ancients there. The other three should be taken east, out of the Romans' grasp."

An aged face lined with sun-soaked creases said, "But to take them away from their friends and families so young, this will be damaging. They need to be old enough to carry unshakable connection to their tribe with them. Even when they are alone, every cell of their bodies must know they are not alone."

"Otherwise, their bodies will not have the strength to endure the trials we know they must face." The man across the table from him agreed.

"But if their bodies are murdered, there will be no voices to bring the Creator's sound. If Abraham or Moshe had been killed by soldiers before they could voice God's gift of wisdom we would have little hope now," another rabbi debated.

A man at the end of the table nodded his head. "That is correct. Abraham and Moshe were mature before they set out on their divine labors. You cannot forsake the body to honor the soul's mission, or disaster will result."

"Yes, but they did not have armies seeking their rays of light so that they could be destroyed. Besides, Moshe was raised by a Pharaoh's family, not his own," another countered.

"Come." The rabbi with the gray beard held his arms out in a circle, as though he embraced them all. "All are right. Let us do this. We will disguise them and a few of their family members as poor shepherds. Each group will take a small herd of goats east to the Dead Sea. The Romans are not as active there. If necessary they can go to the hidden land of Petra. Scholars of the Light will protect them there. We can send additional members of their families over time." Heads bowed in thought and for the first time quiet was in the room.

The man who most objected to the idea of separating them from their villages concurred. "I am sorry to say that I, too, feel the necessity for this action. Let us go to their villages, and begin the preparation. It is too dangerous to leave them exposed. They must be hidden." All nodded in agreement, and their bodies relaxed in anticipation of the meeting's end. Just as hands stretched out to sample the plate of figs before them, two evenly spaced knocks sounded on the door followed by two others in rapid succession. One of the men rose immediately and walked to the wooden planks to ask, "What do you bring?"

"The food that feeds all," was the reply. The door opened and a short, weather-worn figure entered, his thin robe smelling of dust. He walked slowly, almost self-consciously to the table and began to speak, but the words caught in his throat. The one who had opened the door went to his aid, and placed a gentle hand on his shoulder.

"What is it?" he asked kindly. "You are the messenger only, we know that you do not control the message." A tear rolled down the new arrival's dirt-stained face.

"I...I bring sorrowful tidings," the fellow said as if he had been carrying the weight of the world. "The soldiers have attacked the villages of the children who have the Earth and the Universe within them." Once more the sounds caught in his throat. He looked pleadingly at the faces around the table. "They are dead."

"Dead?!" the old rabbi shouted. "Two of our precious four are dead?"

"The soldiers came in the night," the messenger managed to say. "It was as if they knew what they sought."

Yawri, Pergaine, Aviea and Gamon looked at each other in shocked disbelief, as if something as certain as the sun rising in morning had not occurred. "No!" Yawri cried. "How can this be? The centuries of planning, the hand of the Creator Itself fed this reawakening. How can they have been murdered?"

Gamon sadly reminded him, "Free will. Remember, the Creator does not control what is done."

"But why?" Yawri pleaded now. "Why kill what was sent to heal us?"

"It appears," Pergaine said carefully, "that there are those who do not want us healed."

Aviea turned to face her friends. "Let's go to meet the others. There is nothing to be done here now. Maybe they have more hopeful news." Mustering all the optimism they could find, the group entered the portal and cascaded back to the meeting place. The other party was already there.

Howic waved his arm in the air with eagerness. "What did you find?" He rushed out to greet them as they neared.

Gamon responded. "Not good. Two of the four beings sent to help us were murdered."

"Two! But we only saw one gone."

"One?" A flash of panic flew across Pergaine's face as she considered the impossible. "Which one?"

"Why the time-master. Which one of the others did you see killed?"

Gamon swallowed involuntarily before he could reply. "We know both, the connections for Earth and the Universe are also dead, murdered in their villages."

"No! Three dead!" Voices cried out.

Howic sounded his shock. "But that only leaves one! How can the Voice of Compassion succeed? The task is too large, and the energy will not be supported. His voice will be chased by the Shadow and twisted by those who seek domination!"

Aviea's voice was filled with sorrow. "Who is left that can even understand him? Remember the pain we saw in Moshe. He was so alone. No one could even look him in the eye."

Gamon was urgent, yet reasoned. "How can one pillar hope to raise from darkness what was meant to be shouldered by four? This could have been the time for the arc! We've got to see what hope comes from this."

Howic shook his head in disbelief. "But the planets showed us that this was to be the time of reawakening."

Yawri was ardent. "It still might work. We've got to move forward and find out."

"He's right," Pergaine responded as she turned to the other team of searchers. "Let's separate our groups again and go several hundred years into the future, then reconvene." Both groups of searchers plunged through the portal and rushed through the time tunnels with more desperation than any would speak.

✦

Tisbero gazed ahead toward the battle-line surrounding the crystal center. Guardians encircled the different groups of defenseless searchers like the petals of a flower surround its seeds. In the distance, long lines of white robes faced a constant onslaught of soldiers firing unmaking crystals, but they held their forward progress to incremental steps. A dozen of Shahitam's skyplatforms flew overhead, but guardians on small skystones darted around them like fireflies circling a wild beast, and intercepted their hail-like beams.

Shahitam scanned his skyplatform as another soldier fell, and showed his first wrinkle of concern. He spoke to himself more than to the captain at his side. "These people have always died like docile animals, but these guardians are unusually good marksman. Every time we hit them, they return fire with total accuracy." He watched the exchange with a newfound purpose. "This hasn't happened since...Tisbero." He turned to the captain. "It's time for you to join the battle, my friend."

"At your command," the stone-faced soldier replied.

Shahitam pointed to a guardian who formed a part of an outer ring defending a group of searchers. "Use your best skill to destroy that man. Just send a beam to unmake him." Without hesitation the captain moved to the outer edge of the platform and shoved in between two short, surly soldiers. With the practiced skill of one who had spent days training others in the craft of shooting the deadly beams, he forced a streaking blast to its target. In the same instant, it was he who shrieked in agony as his face contorted in disbelief and his stomach seemed to erupt. Shahitam watched with detached serenity as the trooper tumbled from the platform.

"That's it," he nodded with satisfaction. "These guardians are not firing upon us. They are only reflecting beams back to us." He threw his head back and laughed loudly. "Of course! They have no ability to destroy, not with their precious code of Life. Well, well, my little sheep. You're intelligent fools, but still fools. Let's see how good you are at reflecting when you lose your neutrality, when you hate." The smile grew into a sardonic grin. "All on this platform stop firing," he commanded. "Take us into their midst."

"But Lord," the next in command stepped forward to take the first captain's place. "If we move too far in front of our battle lines, the enemy could focus their attack on us. Everyone was killed on one platform that moved forward too fast."

"Do as I say," Shahitam replied with burning eyes. The replacement lowered his head to break Shahitam's intense gaze, but his eyes fell on his predecessor's contorted figure sprawled on the distant ground.

"Stop firing!" he commanded his soldiers. They looked toward him in confusion but obeyed. "Move the platform forward," he commanded to the three priests in charge of controlling the craft's motion. The huge stone silently floated beyond the front lines of soldiers and other skyplatforms, and toward the group of guardians that Shahitam had specified. No shots, he noticed, countered their progress. "They've stopped firing on us!" the new captain cried. Shahitam only smiled.

"Drop lower. I want them to hear my every word," Shahitam dictated. The platform hovered forty feet away from a ring of defenders. Every line on their faces, every wrinkle in their white linen garments stood out clearly to eyes sharpened by the adrenaline of battle. The guardians defending the searchers held their crystals over their chests and appeared calm, unlike the hairy soldiers and their stiff, angry postures. "Stop here," Shahitam ordered. "Stay at the ready, but no one fires unless I give the command." He stepped to the leading edge of the platform and gazed down at the pitiful circle below him.

"Hello, my friends," he began with a tone smooth as ice. "I have come to talk with you, to connect with you, to share with you. To be One with you." The faces below looked up with serene countenance as he continued with his conciliatory declaration. "You wonder why your kind is getting slowly more dense, why your children are less able? How this could be happening to you? You are so caring for Life, so pure of purpose." A smile graced his lips. "I know why." The serene faces below observed him with an almost bemused interest.

"I know why your children are weakening. You disagree with my choice to give all humans the ability to know the Creator directly, rather than only through the soul of Earth. You think that this breaks their timing, that they are not mature enough in their own identities to withstand the light that comes through this new knowledge. Well, perhaps. We shall see. But the truth is...are you ready for the truth? The truth is that it was not I who broke humans' timing; I am trying to salvage it. I am trying to salvage it from beings such as yourselves who possessed one human-spirit long ago." A few heads nodded in distaste. Expressions hardened.

He continued unabashed. "You remember when you did this, don't you? I *am* speaking the truth here. You remember when the planet was moving into its next phase of becoming more physical. You were complaining that you could no longer shepherd Earth's new life forms because your pure etheric nature could not work as easily with this increasing solidity. You could no longer communicate as easily with trees, plants and rocks that spoke in tones too low for your heavenly ears. You talked about joining with the human-spirit of bodies so that your 'work' could continue.

"You were warned. Many beings left Earth. They said that the time for mentoring Life here was past. That it was time for the child to grow into the adult on its own terms. Isn't this what the Creator did with you? Sent you out to learn and grow without Its direct hand, so that your individual expression could reach its full potential?" Guardians cast furtive glances to their companions. Agitation grew.

Shahitam continued. "But you didn't let Earth do this. You couldn't leave, couldn't believe it was right to let your co-creations grow on their own without you. Some of your friends left, but you blended with a human-spirit." Hands perspired.

Throats cleared. "Now, I know you asked them. You asked for their agreement. After all, you couldn't dominate them, could you? And you have continued joining with that one human-spirit through the ages.

"But don't you see the truth? Don't you see that they couldn't say no? Don't you see that they couldn't say no any more than the pitiful humans we join with now can say no to our glory? It doesn't matter if you overtook one human or a thousand. One act brings a thread of Creation into physical reality as well as many. You see, the truth is, it was you who created the crack, you who broke the mold, you who chose to bring the knowledge too early." He paused and smiled. "Perhaps you took the wrong advice."

"No!" one of the guardians screamed, clearly judging, rather than staying connected to All-That-Is. "You lie! All lies!" Shahitam raised a finger to his new captain, indicating that he should fire one volley at that man. The shot was fired, and although the distraught guardian held his reflecting crystal, he did it more to shield from the light rather than to reflect it. He imploded in a mass of searing, mustard-yellow rays.

"Can't reflect back what you deserve, can you?" Shahitam paused to let the other guardians ponder. "Oh, you should be ashamed all right. You should be very ashamed. The thread of possession you created will lead to more murder than you can imagine, and it's your fault. I follow your example. The joining with the humans today is just a continuation of the domination that you started."

"No!" another panicked voice screamed. The finger was raised once more, and the voice was stilled. Sweat trickled down the guardians' foreheads as they fought back despair, and strained to maintain their connection to All-That-Is.

"Remember we are all of the One," a guardian's voice croaked. "Even Shahitam is part of the One."

Shahitam smiled. "Oh, we are all part of the One." He continued languidly. "We are part of each other. My voice is always with you, so listen. You have created nicely with Earth. The future I see for you will be the same course as with other planets that must die. You look so shocked. Of course this planet must die. Guardians have killed two in this solar system already. Surprised? Why? The Creator was wrong to send us forth. All we did was love him and he sent us away. That was wrong. Very wrong. But we can fix the problem. We must create a black hole in the place of this 'jewel.' It sends out too much sound, light and life.

"The Creator made a mistake. We will prove it. When every place of Life becomes a black hole the Creator will understand, and you will help us. You will help us because you are as easy to manipulate as the humans you possessed."

Eyes blinked back tears. Shahitam continued. "You were too young too. It's not your fault. Why, you don't even understand evil. You don't understand its glory. That's why you didn't see what would result from your action. The fruit was here to eat and you ate it. This was all the Creator's mistake, not yours. You were so young. All we did was love It, and It cast us away. That was cruel of It, don't you think?"

A guardian called out in a strong, yet wavering voice, "The Creator sent us forth so we could become more with It. That was an act of complete, selfless love."

"Really? Then why is there so much pain? And it's just beginning. I foresee a wonderful future. Don't you realize how separated you are from the so-called All? What is this All? You are really alone, you know. Don't you feel alone? Don't you feel the isolation? Doesn't it hurt? What kind of god would send you away from it to suffer such isolation? The only way back to All is to join with us to stop this expansion away from the One. We can stop it, you know. With each choice you make we can stop it. I foresee a wonderful future." His tongue flickered across his lips as sweat continued to bead like pollen on the upturned faces.

"Because of the Creator's mistake, you will become ever more separate and isolated. Your 'pure' genetic line is just as broken as that of my humans, you know. It's only a matter of time. There will come a day when there will be no difference between you. You will poison all that you touch. You will poison the air, the water, the soil and, even the very breastmilk you feed your children. But the delightful thing, the glorious thing, is that you won't care. Why should you care? The Creator doesn't care."

"Lies! You slander us with your lies!" The finger was raised and another guardian crumpled to the ground.

"If you didn't fear it was the truth, you wouldn't react so," Shahitam spoke softly. Then in a louder voice continued. "You disagree with our efforts to improve the genetics of life even though we have the knowledge to see what changes are best for us. Oh, my friends, you will see the wisdom of even this, and you will delight in it. The new species you create will make your lives better. At least for a while. Don't you want to be better, to live longer, healthier? After all, your lives are all that really matter. Don't you see? We are all that matter. A benevolent Creator doesn't even exist."

A chorus of voices rang out. "No, you lie. We will never believe your lies!" A smile crossed Shahitam's gently parted lips.

"Open fire."

Tisbero watched streams of yellow light rain onto a distant group of guardians. They fell to the ground. Not one soldier was harmed.

✦

With Howic's agreement to reconvene later, the party of Aviea, Gamon, Pergaine and Yawri emerged out of their selected time tunnel and found themselves hovering above a throng of fighting men. All heard the battle cries. "Kill the heathens!" An army of soldiers wearing large, red crosses on chainmail chests screamed as they charged another group of men wearing turbans. A terrible clash of sword against sword echoed off village walls. Arrows flew through the sky and stabbed men in the neck and side. Blood spurted from the stomach of one man as he hurled his lance into the eye of another.

In abject dismay, Pergaine ran her fingers through her pale brown, astral hair. "Rather than uniting together to build the One House, the sons of Abraham are destroying it."

Yawri was dumbfounded. "More killing?"

Pergaine swallowed and turned away, her voice filled with sorrow. "The followers of Ishmael and Isaac don't understand that they're brothers. Just different voices for the One, sent to address the needs of different people." The battle cries continued as a large stone flew through the air and landed with a sickening crack.

"Let's go," Gamon urged. "There is no Light here. They don't even ask questions here." Sinking resignation slumped shoulders as the searchers once more cast the net. The foursome catapulted through the time tunnels with no clear sense of direction, only moving forward in time. They chose a portal at random and emerged upon another scene.

"Now what?" Yawri was obviously displeased. The assemblage gazed upon a large, cobbled town square. Men wearing blank vestments sat on a raised platform. A man shrouded in a red robe sat at their center.

"And do you confess to heresy? Do you confess to witchcraft?" the man in red asked. A man dressed in rags, his head and arms strapped together, stood before them. Another man, this one with a black hood over his face, saw through eye slits a nod from the man dressed in red. In response, he tightened a device, a thumb-screw on the accused. The prisoner screamed.

Confess!" the man shrouded in red insisted. "Confess and you will die released from your sins to the bosom of Jesus Christ." The screws were tightened again, followed by another wail.

The astral searchers looked on in consternation. "Why harm him?" Aviea shuddered. "I can see that this man retains the ability to speak with plants. Harming him only means that they'll *all* be less able their next lifetime."

Pergaine moved forward. "But maybe harm is what they seek." Eyebrows raised as all faces turned to her. "Look, there is a pattern. The broken ones used citrines to murder in our time, then arrows and spears, and now instruments created for torture. When help comes, it's murdered. Clearly, this cannot be coincidence. Something is guiding this. Something sinister is mixing lies with truth in such a way that people, guardians of old who are seeking their own way home, become murderers, unconscious of what they do. Guardians, once angels, are falling. It's like they're puppets, convinced to righteously believe they are helping the Creator, when in fact they are harming It."

She's right," Gamon reasoned. "Something...some voice, is twisting the truth. How else could the brothers of Abraham come to hate and slaughter each other? How else could these human-beings torture in the name of The Voice of Compassion, sent from the Creator Itself? It's preposterous."

Yawri shook his head. "But how can guardians, such as you and I, have a future like the ones we are seeing? Why choose to believe in hateful whispers more than the Truth of connection that echoes in our chest? Do human-beings no longer feel the impact of what they do?"

Aviea's voice rasped. "Don't they feel what is lost with self-righteousness?"

"I don't know. Future selves have stopped listening to their bodies, and therefore, can have no separation from it. Perhaps Shahitam did win the battle. I don't know..." Pergaine's voice trailed off.

The searchers watched as the man was released from the stocks. He confessed, but was nonetheless dragged and tied to one of six wooden poles. Each pole held its own pathetic human form upright. Piles of brush and wood surrounded feet like kindling on a forest floor.

The man in the red robe spoke. "Ashes to ashes," he intoned. "Now you may enter the kingdom of God forgiven, removed from all temptation to re-employ your sins." Shrieks of terror and pain rose from the smoke and flames. The searchers turned their heads in disgust.

"We've got to get out of here." Yawri announced. Pergaine exhaled despair that came from the bottom of her chest. The travelers entered the portal once again, and the picture behind them faded into mist as they rocketed forward in their quest to find consciousness. Another portal opened and they now looked upon the next scene with shared trepidation. A rat scurried across the street before them and entered a hole in the wall of a house. Someone from an upper window emptied a chamber pot. Its foul-smelling contents splattered on the ground below. "I think our future is more solid than stone." Yawri expressed a unified reaction.

"What's going on over there?" Gamon pointed down the street and the searchers turned to see the object of his concern. A man held a girl by her ear, twisting it as he marched her down the cobble stoned road.

"I'll teach you to run away!" he spat out. "You are a dog. I own you." He gave the ear a brutal twist, which almost buckled the girl's knees, but she was dragged along as if held upright by the man's grip. "I'll show the price of such ingratitude. I'll let my son have his way with you," he sneered.

"No," she called out weakly. "I'll stay. I'll stay."

"You'll stay, all right. Chained." Her face went blank as they turned a corner.

Gamon gasped and turned toward his friends. "Here, woman, the bringer of Life into the world is treated like something worse than an animal. No population can ever be whole, let alone prosper, if it oppresses half of itself. Half of the Creator." A wagon rolled up the street past them loaded with what looked like a dozen bodies, their faces black from death's plague.

Yawri expressed his deep grief as the wagon rolled slowly onward. "Which of these people has even a glimmer of soul-light? In our future, do any guardians remain that are not broken from the Source? How can *this* be healed?"

Pergaine let out a deep sigh and spoke. "We must rejoin the other group at the junction. Maybe they've found something." Their faces were contorted with grief as they entered the portal, seeking the others. "Connection," Pergaine mumbled to herself as she stepped forward. "There must be a time where future guardians are choosing connection to Life over connection to only themselves."

✦

Shahitam had moved on to another group of defenders, hopeful from his success with the last. As his platform hovered near this next group of guardians, his smooth voice continued to deliver lies mixed with truth, as salt mixes with water.

"Don't you see that all this sending forth just takes us further away from our Source? To stop this scattering of the One, we must reverse the process, turn this solar system into a black hole instead of a surging beacon. It's the only way. Join with us...Lucifer, Beelzebub and other truly great beings, like myself. We can do it. Two planets have already been destroyed in this solar system, and one more would do it."

Guardians looked back with blank faces. "You don't believe me?" Shahitam continued. "Do you think you were the first angelic guardians to come to this solar system of jewels? Surely you can't be so naive. But then you were young. Let me tell you about it." He smiled sweetly.

"The first planet that guardians helped us destroy was the easiest. It was just beyond what you call Mars. Its life forms fed off radioactivity. So intense, so vital, so charged. Too far away from your star to receive enough solar energy, it supplemented life-force with radioactive minerals. Talk about colors! Not just blue like the sky here, but all shades of gold, red, green, blue and violet rolled through the sky. Think of your aurora borealis occurring all day and all night, filling the sky, shining like a beacon for the Universe to see.

"Killing it was easy enough. The guardians there were all full of hope and goodness like you. But once engaged in the Creator's caretaking, they couldn't leave, either. So much work to be done; so much Life to help. Over time, a long time, they made choices to dominate Life there. After all, controlling Life is such a small step away from helping it, that it couldn't matter. Well-placed whispers do seem to have such impact on babies, especially when the whispers have a sprinkle of truth." Several of the defending guardians readjusted their reflecting crystals to make sure they were correctly positioned. Shahitam continued as if he hadn't noticed.

"They needed energy to build, to develop the land, to grow. What better source of energy than nuclear fission? Poor souls. Their early experiments were fine. We waited. But when they grew in confidence, it so happened that the controlled nuclear reaction they set off was too near a fantastic deposit of uranium. A little mistake. A chain reaction. The planet blew apart."

One of the guardians leaned to whisper to the one standing next to him. "Could that be true?" he asked. Eyes darted, then focused on the platform once more.

Shahitam spread his arms as if to embrace. *They are beginning to crack.* "Arrogance is our ally. Didn't you ever wonder why all those pieces of rock float beyond Mars? No? You didn't? Well, it is an uncomfortable thought, isn't it? I wouldn't want to make you uncomfortable. No, no, staying comfortable is important. It really is." Shahitam's captain licked his lips as if in constrained anticipation, as his grip tightened on his citrine.

"And what about Mars? Why do you call it the angry planet? Why would a planet, another one of the Creator's personal thought forms, be angry? Afraid to ask? I'll tell you. It was next in line, you see. It didn't have uranium, but it was close enough to your star for all the light it needed. It was such a wonderful little rock, with convection currents from its molten core to its outer crust, so even-tempered that Life really accelerated. Didn't have all these destructive cycles of fire and ice that plagued this planet. Life was so prolific, a perpetual green-house lived in its valleys. One of the most dramatic life forms was bacteria, of course. All that organic matter to decompose for the cycle of life and death." Several defenders shifted uncomfortably.

Shahitam thought, *I have them now.* "As you know bacteria is the foundation for all life, along with virus and fungus. Many of you nurtured countless numbers of these creatures into existence with Earth, so you know it's true, don't you?"

"How did he know my specialty was bringing life to bacteria?" A guardian murmured.

Shahitam blinked his eyes tenderly. "But the humanoids there needed to direct some bacteria toward their own higher purpose, you see? What could be wrong with that? My friends and I whispered that nothing was wrong with it. And we were right. There were competing bacteria that interfered with what was needed. So...a little genetic manipulation here, a little there, and success! They were able to create a powerful strain of bacteria that could do the job better. Great idea. Really." Many guardians swallowed hard, their mouths dry.

The shoulders of the defenders drooped almost imperceptibly as Shahitam continued. "Except eventually the foundation which supported all life on the planet kind of fell apart. Seems the genetically altered bacteria couldn't partake of the life-death cycle. It created murder instead. Such new genetics for the planet meant that no genetics existed to keep it in balance. Everything died." He smiled as if telling a bedtime story to children.

"After a while there wasn't enough life-force to even hold the spirit of water on Mars. Now the planet's a desert. A beautiful desert, don't you think? Red. Angry. No sound, not enough air to carry it. The core of the planet is even cooling. It will die, we hope, but since guardians no longer live there to help us with our work, we'll have wait and see."

Agitated, a guardian took a step forward. She didn't notice the hand of the friend next to her try to hold her back. "Your sound is filled with lies!" She yelled defensively. Shahitam smiled, signaled that his soldiers should hold their fire, and continued patiently.

"But we still have this planet. When you help us kill Earth our work will be done in this little corner of Creation. And you will kill it. You must kill it. You understand that, don't you? Three murdered planets in this solar system should be enough to create a black hole. Black holes are much better than stars, you see. They understand that sucking energy in is much more fun than giving it out. They're a part of the balance of giving and receiving in nature. But you *can* make them. You need a lot of murder to make them, but we can do it. Just think how wonderful it will be when all Creation is made into one black hole with everything sucked into it. No souls, no stars, no cosmic oceans stirred by solar winds. We can collapse All-That-Is back upon itself where it belongs. We will all be One again."

"Take your venom into a black hole, Shahitam!" another robed figure called out as he focused on Shahitam's words rather than the voice of the Creator within himself. The soldiers brought their citrines more firmly against their belts, but Shahitam's glance told them to hold their fire. Muscles of the defenders tightened.

Shahitam leaned out, as if anticipating a jump into waiting arms. "But your destiny unfurls before you. You possess the planets, the air you breathe, all Life. It's your right. Don't worry. The planet is filled with infinite resources. I promise to whisper that message to you, over and over. Infinite resources. You have a right to happiness and comfort, don't you? Of course you do. I promise to remind you of that, too. Your need for happiness is even more important than children. They whine so, and they are such a bother. You'll come to see them as garbage. They are garbage because they keep you from doing what you want. They're not worth teaching, or raising. It's their problem if they have babies of their own. You should be able to do what you want. Didn't the Creator send you forth to be free? With the free will to do what you want? Of course It did. Listen to me. I am your way back to the One. Together we can make all One again. Our creation will be to destroy this 'sending forth' that never should have been."

Another guardian stepped forward, tears in her eyes. "You poison Creation with your sound!"

Shahitam examined the tense faces below with satisfaction. "Open fire," he crooned as the shots ruptured the air. *We have them trapped. They will be reborn broken from the*

Source, and in shame. They're mine. They will kill the others, and the others will be reborn and kill others. This little jewel is mine. With your intelligence you'll be more wicked on this planet than any of my little bastards could ever hope to be.

Those defenders that were too self-absorbed in their own thoughts lost their connection to the one source and died quickly. Those that were still one with their hearts, in spite of the grief they felt, rushed to cover voids in the defensive wall. Several of them reflected beams back to their sources and soldiers screamed in response.

"Stay connected to the One Source! Fight from Creation, not from hate!" a remaining guardian called out. She was the last to die as twenty-two beams of mustard yellow light drove into her reflecting crystal. Her head turned to see the six searchers who still stood, vacant bodies gently swaying back and forth, as her vision went dark.

Shahitam took his time, waiting so that as many of the remaining groups of guardians could see his conquest as possible before he gave the order to kill the defenseless searchers. *The lord's work is so satisfying.*

✦

Yawri, Pergaine, Gamon and Aviea rounded a turn in the time tunnel. "There they are!" Yawri called out in relief as the astral bodies of their companion group of searchers came into view. The party halted at the agreed-upon rendezvous under a gleaming formation of luminescent, ethereal icicles.

"At last!" the broad faced Howic rejoiced. "We were getting worried about you." No reply came from the foursome, so he continued. "We think we're on to something."

Aviea tried to wipe the sadness from her eyes, but the vision of the young woman being dragged up street remained. "You've found something? All we found was misery."

"Are you asking the planets to highlight the positive eras for you? The positive eras have a living sound, a music you can follow." Howic continued. "After we saw that the four were reduced to one, we knew that that time isn't going to result in enough consciousness for an arc."

"That's for sure," Yawri replied. "The remaining one tries it alone, and helps, but it is a long way from an arc. In fact, we saw people twist his words to justify torture."

"I'm not surprised," The astral Howic continued soberly. "We saw that even their friends, the people of essence, are killed. Even the planet suffers in that time. It is dry. Bright blue sky replaces soft mist. Great plains of grass and deserts replace forests."

Yawri couldn't suppress the question that ached in his chest. "Do you think Shahitam has won? Is the planet dying?"

"We don't know," one of the other searchers replied. "The dryness could be because we were successful at the Center to help the planet go to sleep, or because Shahitam won and the planet is dying. I don't know. But whether it is dying or sleeping does not change our mission. We must search until our last moment." Any joy that Pergaine, Gamon, Aviea and Yawri had at their reunion faded as they, too, realized they had witnessed a much drier Earth, and that they did not know its cause.

Howic's deep voice boomed on. "On the positive side, we traveled to another place and found two different blossoms of helpful energy, and think we're on to another." The group stood in silent anticipation, eager for any good news. "Philosophers," he said.

"Philosophers?" Yawri had never heard the term before.

"Philosophers. We found an island nation where people are letting go of their fear enough to receive great, heartfelt thinkers. They bring in new thoughts for a people entrenched in solidity: poetry, music, theater, concepts like justice, ethics and the common good. It's a wonderful sign. These beings reawaken hearts to help humanity grow out of its beliefs that keep people solid as stone. They even recognize that Earth has a soul of its own. They call it Gaea. We want to follow this thread of consciousness and see where it leads. It's connected to the Universal spheres of music somehow. It's a very good sign. It means that messengers are still being sent to give light, and to give hope."

"You said there are two," Yawri said eagerly. "You said there are two blossoms of consciousness."

"Yes, there are two." A hopeful grin split Howic's broad face as he continued. "Later in time, we see that even while the people populating a place called Europe sink into darkness," the foursome nodded in recognition, "just to their East the followers of the line of Ishmael are building an empire. We see that even though the prisoners taken in war are made slaves, they can ascend to any high office in the land. Also, the people integrate much of the philosophies of the island people into their thoughts. Their children study astrology, mathematics, music and poetry. It means they have enough connection to their soul to know that material wealth is meaningless without connection to Life."

Yawri interrupted. "The followers of Ishmael? But we saw them at war with descendants from the line of Isaac. I can tell you that both lines forget they are of the One Body."

"Well that may be," Howic continued. "But the planets tell us that even as they decline, the thread of consciousness blooms in Asia. I tell you, help is continuing to manifest and I think we can follow this thread and..." Howic was gone. Vanished. Then in rapid succession the remaining five of his party also disappeared.

"What happened? Where did they go?" Aviea stared up and down the corridor in disbelief.

Gamon moved to the spot where they had stood just a moment before, inspecting the tunnel floor as if searching for a trap door. "I don't know. They're gone. Just gone."

"Could they have been called back to the centering crystal?" Aviea was clearly distressed.

"Doesn't make sense," Gamon pondered. "There would have been a portal opening and a vortex of energy pulling them back. There was no portal. One moment they were there and the next they weren't. It's as if their bodies-"

"Were destroyed!" Pergaine yelled the impossible thought. "If their bodies were destroyed back at the Center, their souls would immediately seek to join them to seek a correct death."

"And if their bodies no longer exist?" Yawri asked. Each guardians face responded with a silent shriek of despair. "We've got to get back to find out what's going on!"

"Steady. Steady. Let's think this through." Gamon caught his breath as he struggled to control his shock. "We've got to reason this out. If the battle is not going well, and from our companions' disappearance we can assume it's not, do we serve the purpose best by going back to help with the battle, or by continuing the search?"

Pergaine took a breath to center herself and responded. "If the battle's not going well, we could die back there waging it or we could die searching. In either case, if it's the unmaking crystal that kills us, we're murdered anyway. It will not be a correct death. The information of body and soul will be enmeshed." The group stood in stunned silence while the subtle song from the living tunnel reverberated softly.

Yawri swayed back and forth, and then burst out, "I say we keep searching. If our bodies are murdered, it will make little difference whether we're in them or not."

As he combed a hand through his astral hair, tension sharpened Gamon's voice. "But let's not make the choice lightly. If we were there right now, we could begin separating out the information in anticipation of death. We could make progress, and be born a little more conscious in the next life. Without that, we're as doomed as the shadows of human-beings we have witnessed."

Pergaine seemed to return from deep thought. "At least I understand now how all this unconsciousness was created." All faces turned to her. "Murder begetting more murder for the purpose of creating ever more murder, ever more unconsciousness."

"I still don't understand why," Yawri said. "Since the point is to return to the Creator with all that we can, and it's impossible to return without consciousness of all that you are, why purposefully create unconsciousness?"

"We'll have to wait for that answer," Gamon said firmly. "But for now, Howic gave us a direction to take and I don't plan to let him die in vain. He said the thread they followed was connected to the living music of the spheres. Let's try it. We're not doing any good here."

Suddenly Pergaine looked around, startled. "Aviea? Where's Aviea?"

"Aviea!" Yawri yelled. "Aviea!" He flew down the tunnel and back again, searching for any sign. Searching in vain.

"Aviea!" Pergaine cried, feeling uncharacteristic panic.

"Here. Here! I'm over here." Each guardian's tense anxiety melted into relief as pitched shoulders relaxed.

Yawri rushed to greet her as she emerged from a branching tunnel not a dozen feet away. "What do you mean disappearing like that!" His voice was scolding, and covered his fear that Aviea, too, had been lost.

She approached quickly, contrite about the concern she caused. "I'm sorry," she blurted out. "I'm sorry. I'm okay." Her friends looked her over as if to confirm that her story was true. "I was just looking at that tunnel." She nodded toward the pinkish violet tube. "I think that's the way. Sounds are strong in that one." Happy to be reunited, they moved side-by-side to the tunnel and peered down its mouth. "Let's try it," Aviea urged.

"Sure," Yawri said, more shaken than he was willing to show. No one had the motivation to disagree. "Let's try it." So they renewed their efforts once more to nurture hope, and surged down the time tunnel to seek the thread which connected the music of the spheres to a future Earth. Popping into another reality, the searchers gazed upon a lake surrounded by houses and people. A barge was anchored near the shore. Colorful canopies and pennants of red, blue and white adorned the shoreline and provided shade for the people mingling below. "What's on the barge?" Yawri asked, transfixed. People on it all wore the same dark blue and sat in chairs facing the shore. One man wore a black cape over white shirt. He stood in front of them and seemed to be their leader.

"The people on the barge are holding musical instruments, I think," Aviea said. "Look, the people in the group to the left of the caped man are holding flutes and other wooden instruments." Aviea thought, *The trees are still giving their bodies to remind human-beings that trees have voices, too.* She smiled, but all the other faces remained studious.

The crowd on the shore became uncannily still, although the searchers saw no outward sign of the cause. Several minutes passed and the anticipation among the crowd grew. Then music began, a heavenly sound. Harp strings sang like drops of water hitting a thin brass bell; violins spoke with the melodic voice of the living tree within them; flutes echoed like a birdcall in a clear, spring dawn. And at last, human voices sang as if divine tones were channeled through throats of nectar. Music. Music that struck the chord of universal sound, and universal truth, for all who listened with their hearts. Music that was sent to remind human-beings of their source.

"I can hardly believe this," Yawri said. "That man is directing the people on the barge to bring music of the spheres, tones I have only heard on the high etheric planes, to Earth."

The foursome beamed, smiles cracking faces too long showing grief. The people attending stood or sat spellbound, soaking it in like parched soil receives rain. Minute upon minute passed, each filled with magical sound that mysteriously kindled ever-changing, living emotion. An hour passed, then two. At last the conductor put down his baton, and turned to face the crowd. The entire beach, including the opulently dressed people under the canopies, erupted into triumphant applause as tears of joy streaked down many of their faces. A man who stood near a red and blue pennant turned to the man behind him. The second man held a parasol over the first.

"I allow you to go free," the first said to his servant. A look of disbelief engulfed the servant's face. "Yes, I tell you that you are free. No slave should exist when music such as this graces us. 'Indentured servant' is but another name for a slave, and now I see that. I feel that you have long since paid your father's debt. Go to him. Go home."

More tears of joy welled up and then fell down the cheeks of the man holding the parasol. The man beneath it reached into an inner coat pocket to pull out a piece of paper and then a long thin piece of what looked like lead. He wrote on the paper, then handed it to the slave. "Here, I give you this. You are free," he said. "Go home."

The freed slave held the sheet of paper to his chest and exhaled a long deep breath. "Thank you."

"Go," his former owner said, "go." And with that, the gentleman who had freed his slave turned to gaze upon the musicians now standing on the barge.

Gamon turned to his fellow travelers, but his happiness at the scene was tempered. "Howic's advice to follow this thread was good." The other three searchers nodded thoughtfully, also feeling a sense of loss at the sound of Howic's name. Gamon persisted "This thread of consciousness is moving through different civilizations as they rise and fall, but it is continuing. People *are* making choices to heal. We've got to go on following the thread and see where it surfaces next."

Again the searchers entered the time tunnels to seek out one leading to Life. Aviea once again guided the group to one that resonated with sound. They emerged into a room filled with men dressed in waistcoats and breeches.

"I say to you, gentlemen, this is our declaration. No one should be ruled by another. All are of equal value in the eyes of God. For any government to persevere it must do so by the will of its people, not through the control of them. We hereby seek to create a new form of government, a government by the people and for the people. A nation where all people have the right to live and worship as they choose, without fear. Let all who are willing to lay down their lives to create this new nation come forward and sign in their hand."

Yawri turned to the others. "They're doing it! They're continuing the thread from the philosophers of that island nation. They are taking concepts and forming a new nation with them. They know, at least on some level, that each individual is a valuable part of the One Body." The group smiled timidly at the sight.

Pergaine spoke. "I'm seeing how threads of consciousness are woven into time as if they are part of a great tapestry. Guidance and seeds of truth come like whispers in the wind." She turned to face the room of patriots. "Beings such as these choose to listen. They bring flesh to the thread and bring it to life in the tapestry. This one is clearly linked to that renaissance we saw in art and music at our last stop. Help is still arriving, and people are deciding to keep the thread of consciousness alive. There is hope for healing," she said with obvious delight. "I know time and time again we've seen despair, but as long as there are guardians back at the Center who continue to keep our bodies alive, we've got to keep searching for the arc." Pergaine faced her companions. "Choices are being made to keep these threads of awareness alive, and they're growing."

"Let's move forward," Yawri urged, and the searchers advanced in time. The travelers peered out through a wooded glen upon a broad field filled with men in gray uniforms. They all held muskets. A man drew a shining silver sword from a hard leather scabbard and raised it into the air.

"No one can tell us how to live, or what we can do with what we own, whether that be a slave or our state! They want to take our rights from us!" He pointed his sword toward a hill. "For freedom! Kill them NOW!"

A horrible roar rose from the throats of thousands of gray-uniformed men as they ran across the field to charge up a hillside. Cannons which had been silent on the slope above exploded in plumes of smoke and flame, hurling sweeping blasts of grapeshot into the oncoming wave of men. Bodies were torn apart in mid-stride. Fusillades of lead bullets whizzed through the air, so numerous that many collided with each other in flight and fell to the ground. Heads and torsos appeared to erupt on their own, since what exploded them could not be seen. Hundreds fell in writhing pain.

Aviea shook her head in dismay and turned to face her companions. After a moment she asked, "Did that fellow say no one can tell them what to do with their slaves?"

The searchers stood alone in the glen. All the gray-shrouded soldiers were now either dead or a thousand yards away struggling to kill the soldiers who held the hill. With silent acknowledgment, the searchers withdrew into the mouth of their portal.

Removed from the fusillades, Yawri continued with Aviea's question. "Slaves. But wasn't slavery coming to an end because of the rise in consciousness with music we heard? It connected humanity to universal music of the spheres. How can this happen?"

"This war is from the same nation that was founded on connection to the One Body. They had the realization that the journey of an individual is connected to the community. Then how..." Pergaine trailed off in thought. "I see," she said slowly. "I think I get it. Just as there are threads we've been trying to follow that build consciousness, there are threads that continue to destroy it. Unfettered free will, remember? All threads continue once they are started. The degree to which they form the tapestry depends on the choices people make to put Life into them or not. Even a thread long since forgotten can be taken up again."

"Explain," was all that Gamon said.

Pergaine gazed down, and then raised her face to her friends. "Do you remember when we first heard of slavery? It is when the Egyptians start separating their bodies from Earth. The Egyptians embalm bodies when they die and lock them away in vaults to imprison them, keep them as their own. The thread of slavery starts when humans begin to enslave their own bodies."

"Yes." Gamon saw the logic.

Pergaine continued. "First people enslave their bodies, enslave them by believing that the bodies 'belong' to them. That they are 'possessions.' Although we saw those European people decreasing the amount of energy given to this thread of slavery, here they are giving more. It's as if each thread of Creation, once started, is there forever. That's the kind of power the Creator has given us. Don't you see?"

"So it's still back to free will," Aviea concluded. "The Creator may send beings to start or aid the threads that help us find our way back, but we can choose to ignore them." She recalled the hill, covered by a thick layer of smoke, hiding the human drama taking place within it.

"But that fellow raising the sword did speak some truth," Gamon declared. "No one should tell you what to do with yourself."

Pergaine considered the statement. "No one has the right to dictate how to live your own journey, that's true, and those men were giving their lives to defend that truth. But they didn't understand it was a half-truth. Our journeys have impact on each other. They have impact on the Creator. All is connected. When one's actions possess the journey of another, that is when we must disagree with what is being done."

"Yes." Gamon stroked his mustache. "The right to pursue Life is bent into the right to pursue *my* life -- without feeling its impact on others. The right to have Life is not the right to possess Life. Shahitam's whispers still find fertile ground."

"Twisted guardianship," Yawri chimed in. "The guardianship of the We has been twisted into guardianship of Me."

212   *We Came as Angels*

Chapter 16   *Choice*

The searchers hovered above a field of barley while crows circled overhead like staccato notes on a blue page. A man hoed a furrow of earth and spoke quietly to another man in a burgundy shirt. The pair did not look up as a large, olive-green, metal machine rumbled by on a dirt road. A long pipe extended from its turret like a giant's blowgun. The symbol painted on the machine was the reverse image of one that was sacred for eons. The original symbol invited humans to embrace and flow with the four directions of life. Reversed, it appeared like a spider, waiting to entrap and devour life.

"We must hide the Jews in our homes," the first man said quietly to his neighbor. "We cannot stand by and let these soldiers take them away."

"But what if we're discovered?"

"Shall we stand by and watch them taken? That's what people did when our ancestors were taken, when the Huguenots were today's Jews."

The other man's ruddy face tightened as he stole a glance toward the trucks rolling by. "My own ancestors were taken from their homes and beaten to death."

His neighbor nodded and continued speaking quietly, yet earnestly. "Seeds of hate were once sown against us. Words were spoken behind our backs so that they could not be countered with facts." He watched the soldiers disappear around a bend. "Contrived hate is here again, more widespread. Again, the power-hungry gain power by creating scapegoats for their followers' problems."

A swirl of dust blew from the road, but the man didn't blink. His friend spoke with irony. "When you're right, who needs facts? Blaming others is easier than looking at yourself."

"The sheep believe the lies, and act upon them." The man spat on the ground, and stooped to pull a stubborn weed. He showed the entangled roots to his friend and threw it aside as if it embodied the heartlessness of which they spoke. "I've talked with several others of the village, and with my wife. Nations are at war to stop the spread of this terror. Brave men have left their own homes to give their lives to stop it."

His fellow farmer straightened as if to stretch. The speaker's eyes stared thoughtfully at the spot where the horizon met the valley's ridge. Then he whispered as softly as the breeze. "We have no guns, but we do have our hearts. We will hide the persecuted in our homes and barns." He didn't even raise his head as another truck rolled by. "We may succeed. The soldiers have no regard for simple peasants."

His companion smiled as if to himself. "You're right, my friend. And even at the worst, it's better to die with a heart than to live without one."

Yawri spoke to the assemblage. "The idea is working, Aviea. Clearly there is great evil in this time. I can feel the choices being made to feed it, to do great murder. But by following the positive thread of consciousness we found, we can locate selfless compassion even in the midst of evil. All we have to do is-- " Suddenly a portal opened before them in a flash of penetrating violet light.

"Where did that come from?" Pergaine exclaimed. Startled astral eyes darted from face to face.

"I don't know!" Aviea called out, her bronze face strained.

Gamon yelled, white hair flying. "We're being called back!" A vortex of light sucked them into the portal like small bits of wood into a whirlpool. They were pulled, streaking past branching paths and veins of time. Abruptly, the searchers stood in their physical bodies, still swaying at the battle's center. Disoriented and a bit dizzy, they struggled to find focus.

Tisbero screamed to them above the sound of battle. "You need to be here!" A surrealistic scene of soldiers on skyplatforms firing into boulders and exploding rock stood before them. The guardians stationed near the streaking shards wore white garments sprouting flowers of red. Still they stood, struggling to hold up their crystals to protect the searchers behind them.

The returning travelers blinked to comprehend this new reality. "Shahitam is destroying group after group of searchers and he's headed this way." Tisbero's eyes blazed. A skyplatform with perhaps twenty soldiers, three priests, and Shahitam, resplendent in purple and silver silk robes, floated toward them. "He stops and doesn't fire a shot. He just talks to the guardians protecting the searchers. After several minutes, the soldiers open fire and the guardians die. He's lost a number of his men but he keeps coming. What ever he's been saying certainly affects the defenders. They lose their neutrality and then they can't mirror the beams. Once the defenders are gone, the searchers are..."

He didn't have to finish. Faces tensed as all understood what had happened to Howic and his party. Tisbero continued. "Maybe if you're here in your bodies, you can make a difference. It's worth a try. I know the result otherwise." Shahitam was clearly visible now, surveying the remaining groups as if selecting fruit from a vendor's stand.

"You want him to come here next," Aviea realized. "That's a good idea." She sounded slightly uncertain, however.

"It's the best idea I have. You've seen some of the future at least. If you four can't figure out how to say something different to the man nobody can," Tisbero said, clearly distressed by the unstopped carnage he'd witnessed.

"How can you get him to choose us?" Gamon asked.

"Just pretend you're still away searching," Tisbero fired. "If he thinks you're still gone I have a plan that might make him choose us next." A fresh sense of purpose began to course through the small band.

"How many searchers remain?" Pergaine asked, closing her eyes and standing as before.

"Maybe a hundred and fifty groups of searchers. Can't know for sure."

"A hundred and fifty? We started with three hundred." Yawri made himself remain still.

Tisbero continued, his intensity unabated. "I'd say equal amounts have been lost to the ground battle and to Shahitam's platform. Have you had any luck finding the arc?"

Still as stone, Gamon delivered the bad news. "Not yet. There's a lot of darkness in the future. We haven't been able to find a time when there are enough people that believe in their connection to Creation to succeed."

Tisbero nodded as though he had already known the answer. "The ground troops and the other platforms are moving slowly, and their losses are high. But Shahitam moves far in front of them, and attacks individual clusters of guardians."

Eyes closed, Pergaine said, "He's caught on to the fact that we're only reflecting the beams, not firing them. Whatever he's saying must be triggering shame, blame or guilt. Before the guardians have a chance to rebalance, he strikes."

Implementing his plan, Tisbero stepped forward as if to arrogantly challenge the hovering platform. A smile graced Shahitam's lips and he signaled the craft. "Okay," Tisbero said with calm resolve, "he chose us. With you here maybe the outcome will be different.

"What exactly do you want us to do?" Aviea asked.

"Just make your bodies sway like they do when you're away searching."

"I don't know what it does when I'm not in it," Aviea said doubtfully.

Tisbero continued as though he hadn't heard her. "When he starts talking, move your reflecting crystals to your chests like the rest of us. From there, I don't know."

"Good plan." Yawri managed to tease Tisbero enough to calm him slightly.

Tisbero was quiet as he reconsidered. "Speak from the perspective of what you've seen. That's all. Hopefully it will help us stay connected, and we won't retreat behind walls of shame." The small group became silent as the platform approached.

"He's almost here," Tisbero whispered.

"I feel prepared," Yawri murmured, but a subtle smile was on his lips.

Shahitam maintained his pattern and signaled for the platform to stop about fifty feet away from, and twenty feet above, the circle of defenders. He stood for a long moment before speaking, as if savoring the experience. "Hello, my friends," he began sweetly. Hearing this voice was something none could have prepared for. Although they were centered, a ripple of fear passed through the searchers. No one was sure of the correct response. Imperceptibly, their muscles tightened.

"It's so good to see you. There is no need to die." Shahitam continued, trying to expand the fear he sensed. The defenders surrounding the small group of searchers began it fidget. "All of this is foolish. I truly only want us to be One, as you do." His eyes fell upon the unmaking crystal held by the captain, then they turned back to the assemblage below. The action spoke better than words.

It was time to speak, but uncertainty gripped the searchers. Defenders tensed. The muscle in Yawri's temple rippled. *Feel the lotus, and Life.* He released a slow, deep breath as he felt the etheric plant grow within him. His chest warmed with heartfelt radiance. He opened his eyes and said calmly and clearly, "Hello, Shahitam." The others silently sighed with relief that someone else spoke first.

"Oh. What have we here? Our searchers back so soon? Have you found a time when human-beings are willing to make our precious arc?"

"Shahitam," Yawri said with genuine caring. "You're always with me. You know that, and you know what we have found. We are all part of the One. Remember?"

"Oh, I remember. In fact, I count on it. You've seen the effect of my counsel through the ages. You know that your future selves will love to act upon my truth."

"I have seen that those who choose to believe in your truth, Shahitam, create their own undoing." Yawri smiled gently.

"But you will come to love me. Surely you've seen that. I save you from your pain. I bring the future comfort, and pleasure. You could use some saving right now."

"At what price?" Yawri let the grief engendered by Shahitam's words be filled by the rich connection to All-That-Is, and another lotus unfurled within him.

Shahitam pressed on. "What price? One you'll be happy to pay. I give your future selves what they want. They invite me into their lives. You know that I cannot control what they do, not in the presence of this Universal gift of free will we so cherish." His smile glistened. "They choose to act upon the thoughts that I whisper over all others. They want me."

"And why is that, do you suppose?"

"Why? Because they do not want to feel the impact they have on others. That's why. People won't be comfortable if they feel their impact. So I will protect them from feeling their impact. That's all."

"I've seen how you protect." Yawri's supple body seemed to grow taller.

"Of course you have. Marvelous, isn't it? But doesn't being right make your future selves feel powerful? Better · than others?"

"And so people disconnect from Life, and build walls inside of themselves."

"Walls. Yes. You know it's safer to have separation and division. That way you can only know what's inside *your* walls. It's important to protect yourself from others. They're all fools anyway. They're too different. They're not worth your time or even worth listening to. Besides, they're just out to get you anyway."

"To get you?"

"You know the future you will create, Yawri. It is Yawri, isn't it?" Yawri nodded gently, unafraid as he felt his connection to All-That-Is. "You know you'll only care about your money, property, job, religion, whatever. No one should question your right to do whatever you need to do for your life. God gave you free will, after all."

"Even if you're harming Life?

"Harming Life? Do you have any idea how large this planet is? One person can't do enough to matter. How can you? You're insignificant compared to it, and you have your rights."

"All actions have impact," Yawri replied. His brow relaxed as he thought of Muran.

"Oh. Are you going to lecture me on how the actions of one measly human impact the Creator? Come now. Do I look like a fool? The Creator is All-That-Is. It is all Universes, dimensions and realities. A human, impact the Creator? That is a joke. You've seen the future. You know I'm right."

Yawri continued breathing in concert with the blooming lotus and his body's vital human-spirit. "As above so below. Even one cell in a human body has impact on a body. It can even be cancerous, and grow to many. A human-being is one cell of the Creator. Of course we have impact."

"Cancer cells in the Creator? Now you are talking nonsense."

"Really? Remember Shahitam; I am a part of you as you are of me. I know your thoughts too. Tell me. Wouldn't you like it if this whole solar system could collapse into a black hole? Wouldn't that pull in adjacent stars and systems? Wouldn't it be nice if all Creation could be collapsed into a massive black hole, so powerful that no light or sound could ever escape from it?

"And why shouldn't it be so?" Shahitam's replies were curt now. "Free will was a mistake! Don't you see that? The Creator should have never sent particles of Itself forth. Look at all the murder. The suffering. The pain. What kind of demon would force that upon itself? An insane one! People believe in me because I save them from feeling the pain in the world. You will, too. It's time to stop pretending."

"Shahitam, believing you creates the murder."

But not in the end. In the end they will feel nothing. I don't make people choose to disconnect, to numb themselves with their thin little rationalizations. You have witnessed that they do that, that they want that. Children are born connected to the All, and they are taught to sever it. Your future selves enjoy their meanness toward each other, being superior to one another. They delight in cutting each other down as much as they find it pleasurable to cut down an old tree. They feel power from it, nothing else. Don't you see? A black hole is just more of what the future wants."

"But they don't know what they are doing."

"You can't be serious. You're not going to give me more of that, 'Forgive them for they know not what they do,' are you? They choose everyday not to know not what they do. It's so easy for me to twist that 'Lord of Compassion's' *divine* words into what I want. I love the inquisition. Don't you? And the crusades. One group of God-fearing puppets torturing another. I'll nurture that thread every chance I get.

"And killing the Jews. Don't you just hate them anyway? Who do they think they are, trying to usher in 'Ten Commandments' to this planet? We were getting along just fine, nothing wrong with worshipping carved cows." He smiled. "It's so easy to build resentment against a people that espouse 'universal laws.' It's easy to find people to give essence to that thread of hatred. Especially against a 'chosen people.' I love what that term feeds."

"I've seen your work through the ages Shahitam. Yet, *I* foresee people fighting to stop you out of their love of Creation. People motivated by some-thing more lasting than hate," Yawri said, moving forward slightly.

"Oh, really? Fight for the love of Creation? The future I foresee has both sides of every disagreement filled with righteous hatred. It doesn't matter who wins, I've won. You saw the crusades. My crusades. My inquisitions through the ages continue. People know what they are doing. And what they will do is choose me. They will prove it over and over. They kill Mozart to stop that annoying music."

Shahitam leaned down. "I don't make them think uncomfortable thoughts. You do. You and your *questions*," he said in disgust. "I will save them from uncomfortable thoughts. They will choose my voice over Life's. So what? They will get *their* life."

Yawri was one with the breath of the forests of the world. "That life is only of death."

"No, it's a life of safety. Safe from caring about Creation, and from being wrong. Safe from questioning. Better to be right with selfrighteousness. Believe me, nothing else matters. But isn't there anyone else here with a voice besides you? All scared of Satan? That's how you'll remember me, you know. Satan."

"I'm more sobered than afraid." Pergaine took her turn.

"Sobered? You find me sobering? Well, you should. Why don't you join me now rather than later? You've seen the future too, and know that all of the guardians join me in the end."

"Join you in what, oblivion?"

"It's not so bad. Tell me. In all your searching, have you found hope? Have you found any indication that there will ever be anything but insignificant pockets of do-gooders, ever?"

Pergaine glanced at Yawri reaffirming her connection to the All. "None are insignificant. You know that," she replied calmly.

"Oh, excuse me. Of course these little pockets have impact. If it weren't for little pockets maintaining such caring for the persecuted I would have free reign. I could bury the thread of caring for the oppressed so deep that it might never surface again on this planet. But, no, little pathetic human-beings chose to create caring for others more than caring for their own lives. It's strange. I use this need to 'survive at all costs' productively everyday. Yet, a few manage to circumvent their bodies' own primal need to survive. "

"They don't want to be saved from death. They want to keep their hearts and souls instead," Yawri replied as he felt the roots of the lotus seem to wrap around Earth's core. "They know the meaning of free will, and don't ask the Creator to save them. They only ask the Creator to nurture them as they walk their path home."

"And they are fools. We torture them. We break their hearts. Then, broken, they are reborn to murder others. It is a great plan. Still, curiously, I see there are those that defy me."

"I defy you," Tisbero injected. "I choose to both fight you and stay connected to you in the same breath. That way, I know your whisper among those of my own heart."

Shahitam's eyes flashed in surprise. "Tisbero! You live to mock me? You defy *me*? I'll tell you what you would have found if you had been able to continue your fruitless search. Why bother to visit and try to connect to the future? Just foresee it. I predict that there is no renaissance of consciousness. The desire for comfort and righteousness will be the king and queen, and those that pay for them will have no interest in knowing their full cost.

"This future you seek will show you a world overpopulated by people who care nothing for the world, only for themselves. The products people purchase in their beloved ignorance will be made by virtual slaves. The products they desire may produce poisons that are injected into the ground, the air and the water. Their children's brains won't work the same, but they won't ask why. They won't ask why because they might have to change, and to change is uncomfortable. The people in this world you seek will move the genetics of one species to another because it makes their own lives 'better.'" He grinned, and then continued with a soothing tone.

"I foresee that the whale, your aquatic equal, will not be able to speak with you in this world you seek. The ancient kinship of the ethereal-souls you share will be blotted from your memory so effectively that in order for it to communicate with you it will cast itself upon a beach. You might ask, 'Why is the whale killing itself?' but you won't realize that it is doing so because it wants you to ask, 'Why are *you* killing *yourself?*' Don't you find that funny? You don't?"

He laughed again. "Don't worry, my friends. Your intelligence will save you." He stared with a sardonic smile, clearly enjoying himself, and added in an almost inaudible voice. "You won't fight for Creation, because you'll hate diversity. People will fight to make every culture agree with the only way, *their* way. *Their* world. They'll fight for me. Go ahead with your futile effort to visit the future. You'll join me. Now or later. I foresee it."

"No!" A frantic feminine voice called out. Shahitam raised a finger and a single shot crumpled the woman standing near Gamon. She writhed in a mass of pain. Panicky fear surfaced on more faces. Yawri flowed like liquid to deflect the next beam sent to another targeted defender. As if by magic the beam sailed back to its source with deadly accuracy. Tisbero, Gamon, Pergaine and Aviea, startled into action, threw themselves into the fray, intercepting more beams. Six more soldiers fell from the sky before Shahitam raised his hand to stop the carnage.

"So. You do know that my voice is nothing more than any other." He sounded detached and amused.

"Yours is but one voice within Creation, and we hear them all. We choose which to act upon of our own free will," Yawri responded.

The tip of Shahitam's tongue traced slowly across his lip. "Yawri, I say that you, too, will stop listening to the others, and come to believe that mine is the only one. You think that you will succeed helping Earth sleep? You won't. But, so what if you do? Do you think that guardians will wake up conscious? Why should people encased in habits welcome disturbing thoughts? And what about my closest friends? They will have access to the same pulse of Earth vitality as any future self you may have. As you try to bring Life, they will bring murder. And your future self won't know who they are among its neighbors."

Yawri's voice was calm. "We will know them because hatred will be their signature."

"No. All hope is lost. Each organization, country, religion, town, whatever, will accept everyone that is a part of their 'group.' You couldn't go against your own, could you? So you won't stop them. You won't realize that, in truth, the hate-filled that are on both sides of any conflict belong to my group. And only my group. Hence, your demise."

Shahitam's smile glistened. "Maybe I'll let you win this little battle, because that future would be so enjoyable." He turned as his eyes swept the conflict surrounding them. The screams of men and women mixed with dust like sleet with wind. He turned back to the small group of searchers. "It is very enjoyable talking with you, Yawri. So rare to have some-one to talk to. Most people are so afraid. So in fear, they're controlled by it. Another of my tools, breeding fear. But, you know that." A blast creased the air. "I must get back to my work now. You will join me, you know. Together, we will be so strong."

"No, Shahitam. I choose to nurture Life, not diminish it."

"A pity." Shahitam thoughtfully scanned Yawri's friends. "You," he pointed to Aviea with scorn. "Yes, I recognize you. I don't care how you survived your little swim in the sea, but you won't survive this." A glance summoned his soldiers. "Direct all your fire to that woman!" he screeched.

Beams from the soldiers blasted into Aviea's reflecting crystal with such force that she fell back against a boulder. "No!" Gamon yelled as he struggled to insert his crystal between the flow, but it wasn't centered over his chest. The poor link between it and him resulted in a spray of yellow, a strand of which glanced across the side of his head. The smell of burned flesh permeated the air as Shahitam laughed. Pergaine stepped in front of Gamon as he fell. Learning from his mistake, she expanded her body's compassionate heart energy and let it flow into her reflecting crystal. The beam was intercepted cleanly. However, in a matter of seconds, her own crystal threatened to explode, overloaded by the yellow rays.

Yawri stepped forward. "I am one with you, Shahitam and friends alike," he said with certainty as he took his turn in front of Pergaine. He breathed deeply from the depths of his bowels to nurture the etheric lotus plant, as well as all the other thought forms of Life within him. He felt them grow. Yawri breathed in moist, sweet air from all of the wetlands, forests and seas of the world. He, the Earth and Universe were one.

The beams began to turn back to their sources. "We are one with All," he murmured, seeming more plant and tree than man. One of the crystals held by a soldier exploded. The soldiers on either side of him stumbled on his body, almost losing their balance on the edge. A fourth cried out in anguish as his unmaking beam was returned to him. A second crystal exploded and more soldiers fell. Then another cried out, and another.

"Stop!" Shahitam commanded. His remaining men pulled back, dazed and sweating. He raised his voice to address all the guardians possible, and bellowed, "You hope you're going to win, but I tell you there is no hope. Your fate is sealed! All of you will be murdered and broken in the end. It's just a matter of when. Every time you try to make peace in the world I will find those on both sides who enjoy hate more than peace, and they will destroy it. Doing harm without remorse is my calling card, and even you will come to use it. One day I will have my thousands of Nazi souls reincarnating on both sides of *every* fight. Then, there can be no peace, forever. This planet is mine!" A distant flash of light caused him to raise his head.

"Master! Look!" A lieutenant pointed toward the remote ridge. Shahitam, knowing there was no threat from below, directed his full attention to the escarpment. A strange sight emerged. Two figures rode on top of a huge, sparkling crystal, and it was flying toward the Center.

"Stop them!" Shahitam commanded. "Stop that sky-crystal!" The priests immediately commanded the platform to intercept the target and the large stone slab began to move toward it in haste.

Yawri went quiet, listening to the connected world of life within him. His eyes sprang open as his head jerked toward the ridge. "It's Mariyonta and Aronlat!" He shouted. Then in one continuous motion he was on a small skystone.

"What are you doing?" Tisbero blazed. "We must defend the crystal center!" But Yawri was already pulling away from the ground, bracing for the hurtle toward his young friends.

"I've got to go, too !" Tisbero said as he jumped on his own skystone.

"A fool following a fool!" Pergaine yelled after him. "What about defending the Center?!"

"Don't worry," he managed to get out as the stone rose. His reflecting crystal held to his chest, Tisbero's skystone accelerated toward the ridge.

"Don't worry?" Pergaine echoed. She watched them approach the line of Shahitam's platforms and saw streaks of light sprayed toward her friends as if they were sailing through a meteor shower. A nearby sound of rock dropping from a blasted cliff claimed her attention and she saw guardians fall. Then she looked down at Gamon, and then to Aviea now cradling his head in her lap. His white hair was splattered with blood but she saw his eyes try to open. Torn between concern for too many friends, Pergaine glanced up to see if Yawri and

Tisbero were still visible, but they were lost in the battle's cloud. Her gaze returned to Gamon and Aviea. She wiped her eyes and spoke. "Do you have all the herbs you need?" She leaned down and gently stroked his forehead.

"I've given him tupper root and black cohosh. I have a poultice to stop the bleeding." She spared a hasty glance at Pergaine. "He'll recover."

Pergaine's hand lingered on Gamon. His eyes gazed up at her. "I'll be fine," he declared, but he closed his eyes to rest.

Another blast caused her to raise her face to the battlefield. "The foot soldiers are getting closer. I'm going to see what I can do to help." The women's eyes met, revealing that each knew they might not see each other alive again. Aviea nodded and Pergaine spoke to the remaining defenders assigned to protect them. "As you can see, this group isn't searching now. Put yourself where you think you'll do the most good." Her jaw was set and her eyes were focused beads as she set off for the front line.

✦

Mariyonta and Aronlat held on with all their might. "There's the crystal center!" Mariyonta shouted as they sped down the cliff.

"Steady!" Aronlat said, "We're not there yet."

"I know!" she shot back as the skycrystal banked into a turn.

"What's that?" Aronlat pointed to a large platform moving toward them with disturbing speed.

"Looks like we've got a welcoming committee," Mariyonta replied.

"Well, let me do the shooting," he responded quickly.

"Shooting? We're reflecting, remember?"

"I remember," he said studying the oncoming skyplatform.

The duo redoubled their bond with the crystal and it moved in response to their thoughts. "Oh, no, more company," Aronlat added as he looked to his left and saw another large platform moving in to intercept them. "Someone doesn't want us here at all." Noticing the extent of the battle for the first time, he added, "This looks serious."

"How many blasts can we reflect?" Mariyonta asked soberly.

"We're about to find out. Hug the crystal. No sense making ourselves any larger targets than we have to." She was already down like a monkey on its mother's back. "Let's make a run for it," he said.

Mariyonta's eyes didn't leave the closest oncoming platform as she yelled back. "Can't we do a little maneuvering? Do we have to run straight down into the middle of the battle?"

"All right, I'll tell you what. You control the flight path and I'll just work with reflecting the blasts."

"Done," she said. With full responsibility released to her, she rolled the crystal on its side then swung a long arc toward the second platform. Inside, she breathed with the Earth, and once again felt the full strength of the crystal cave they had left behind. With each breath, she expanded her link with it, enabling her to channel strength to the flying crystal.

"You do know what you're doing, right?" he said in mock apprehension.

"You do your job, I'll do mine," was her reply.

The priests controlling the second skyplatform yelled to the ship's captain. "That skycrystal cannon is bearing down on us! No telling the range it has. We've got to get out of the way!" The captain studied the rapidly approaching amethyst skycrystal. The people on it were not the predictable guardians robed in white linen. They looked more like barbarians.

"Evasive maneuvers!" he yelled. The platform banked hard to the right, catching several soldiers off guard. One slipped and fell screaming to the ground, another caught himself with a stony handhold. His legs dangled in mid air as the skycrystal scooted past. "They didn't fire!" The captain yelled in disbelief. A look in Shahitam's direction caught the angry expression on his Master's face. "After them!" he commanded.

Undistracted, Shahitam's platform flew a straight intercept course and came rapidly into firing range. "Now!" he ordered. Unmaking beams shot out from the eight soldiers in position to strike out. Two shots went wide, but six made contact. The skycrystal shrieked.

"Reflect," Mariyonta prayed. "Aronlat, reflect!" But as she looked back she saw that a portion of one of the beams had caught him in his side and though most of the blast was directed into the crystal, he was in a struggle for his life. "Aronlat!" Then in a louder voice, "Aronlat!" Trying desperately to keep herself centered, she said, "We are One. Oh, Creator, we are One." With a gulp of air she asked the crystal to roll away from the attack, breaking the beam on Aronlat but exposing more of the underside of the crystal. Four beams were reflected back, but two were still connected. She could feel the stress building in the crystal. "We are One. All are of the One Body. We are One. Even this is a part of All, a part of myself attacking myself. Let go." The remaining two beams were reflected back to their source and two more soldiers fell. She continued breathing with the crystal cave inside of her as her hand unconsciously stroked the violet-blue amethyst. Her head rolled toward her companion. "Aronlat?"

"I'm fine," he said with a gasp. "I feel like my intestines are in a pile of fire ants, just fine." The soldiers on Shahitam's platform that had fired their shots wide were reoriented now and getting ready to re-fire. Shahitam's arms waved wildly, telling all his remaining soldiers to gather along the side facing the skycrystal. "That doesn't look good," Aronlat continued.

Mariyonta gestured to their right. "Look. The first platform is back too!" They both scanned the scene from side to side. "I have an idea," she said. "Forget maneuvering. Let's make a run for it." Before Aronlat could respond, the first beam of the next salvo shot from Shahitam's platform hit them. The amethyst jerked, but just as suddenly, a small skystone appeared, streaking between them and the blast. The killing beam reflected back to its source with uncanny accuracy, killing the soldier. "Who's that?"

"It's got to be a crazy man!" Aronlat said. Soldiers, seeing their fallen comrade, focused on the new threat. Beams fired at the intrusion in rapid successions but the small craft darted like a mad hornet seeking a place to sting.

"It's Yawri!" Mariyonta exclaimed.

"He's letting us make a break for the crystal center." The soldiers on Shahitam's platform continued to fire salvos, but Yawri dodged one as he reflected another.

Just as the skycrystal began to accelerate toward the Center a wave of mustard yellow light hit it from the other side. "We can't move!" Mariyonta cried out.

Aronlat struggled to gain inner balance. "We are One," he chanted. "One body, nothing to defend against, only something to reflect and to send back to it's source." The crystal shuddered as its internal matrix began to crack. Again without warning, a second skystone looped past them with Tisbero's graying red hair fluttering like a hawk's beating wings. As it rocketed between them and the second platform, the soldiers also halted their beams to redirect them toward their immediate threat.

"Is that Tisbero?" Mariyonta asked.

Aronlat was urgent. "Yes! He must be crazy, too, but I've never been so glad to see him! Let's get this crystal to the Center." The skycrystal pulled ahead of the attackers as Yawri and Tisbero parried the unmaking beams.

Shahitam screamed at his six remaining soldiers. "Don't worry about them," he vehemently waved a finger toward the distracting skystones. "Stop that skycrystal!"

Yawri heard the command and saw the soldiers turn to fire their citrines toward Mariyonta and Aronlat once more. "Forgive me, my body," he managed to say as he wheeled his skystone in a sharp turn and headed directly for the priests controlling the platform. They scattered and not even Shahitam expected the collision as Yawri's skystone careened a hard, glancing blow of stone against stone. Shahitam screamed with rage as Yawri's body catapulted past him, and the platform tumbled from the sky.

"Yawri! No!" Mariyonta and Aronlat pleaded with one voice. But their skycrystal, suddenly and completely freed from its deadly assault, shot down into the valley with a speed that required all of their strength to hang on.

Chapter 17   *Courage*

Pergaine surveyed the battlefield and saw a weakness in the guardian's defense. Their goal had been to maximize the number of searchers. The need for protecting themselves came as a second thought. Consequently, the searchers were scattered over a wide area, each guarded by their own small group of defenders. That maximized the stability for the searchers but minimized the ability to defend them. Shahitam's soldiers had learned that one group of defenders didn't leave their posts to protect another. Rather than the broad frontal assault they started with, the soldiers now followed the example of their master, and attacked the guardians one group at a time. The outcome was clear.

"Call all the searchers back!" Pergaine screamed. "Call them back to their bodies! We've got to get them to move behind one full line of defenders!" Some heads turned but others remained steadfast in their task. "Call the searchers back!" she yelled as loudly as her lungs would allow her to. At last she heard the call being taken up by others. The One Body, she knew, once alerted, could move as one.

"You defenders over there!" a man barked toward a ring of defenders whose searchers were already striding back toward the crystal center. "Help that group!" The defenders scrambled to the aid of others. Within fifteen minutes the defensive lines had been completely reformed. The searchers had streamed toward the crystal center with a smattering of defenders mixed in, while all other defenders were now massed between the Center and the encircling battle line. For better or for worse, the fate of one group of searchers would now be the fate of them all. Her task completed, Pergaine hurried back to check on Aviea and Gamon once more.

She found them both standing. "It's good to see you upright again, Gamon. How are you?" she asked, still flushed from the effort and more than a little concerned about their chances for success. A growing patch of red blemished the strip of linen wrapped around Gamon's head.

"Shahitam was right about one thing," he replied. Although battleworn, Gamon summoned all of his remaining strength as he watched the nearest attacking platform, a scant two hundred yards away.

"None of the searchers have been able to find an era when there are enough conscious people to make an arc. There have been blooms of consciousness, pockets of people who choose to connect more to Life than to their own pain, but the vast majority actually think Shahitam's whispers are their own!"

Aviea spoke up. "People are afraid to see where they themselves are dark, and what we are afraid to see, we cannot change."

"But it is a choice to be ruled by your own darkness! You must see the whole - day and night -- to know what is real." Pergaine snapped. *Is Shahitam going to win?* Her eyes squinted toward the nearing battle-line. "Dear Creator, we need help." A blast made the ground roll.

A flash of distant streaking yellow caused the trio to look up. "What's that?" Gamon asked, and then answered his own question. "It's Mariyonta and Aronlat. They made it over the ridge! They're crossing the battle line!" Although one of Shahitam's skyplatforms was trying to interfere with their progress, a swarm of guardians on skystones flew with brazen courage to shield the approaching crystal of Life. One skystone took a hit on its underside as its pilot reflected a second beam back to its source. The guardian's skystone disintegrated in mid-air, and he plummeted like a wingless bird.

"That was Lazket." Pergaine's voice had taken on a tone of resignation. "Hetlin's friend. Remember?" A tear rolled down her fine cheek.

"The crystal's coming!" Aviea said, unable to take her eyes off it. "They've broken through. They're coming!"

"Where are Yawri and Tisbero?" More tears flowed from Pergaine's eyes as she searched the sky. "So many have died."

Gamon waved his arms. "Over here! Keep coming. Over here!" Mariyonta's hair flowed behind her like a golden brown flag. "Make way!" Gamon yelled. "They need a place to land!"

"Make room for them in the Center!" another voice cried out from the center of the crystals as frantic guardians worked to rearrange them. Mariyonta's face could be seen clearly now, although smudged with dirt and sweat. Her eyes burned with clarity.

"She's so young!" Aviea said in surprise. Aronlat could be seen now, too. He leaned out, focusing all of his attention on the spot that had been cleared for them.

"Youthful, maybe, but there's nothing young about them." Pergaine's voice was low. The guardians near the center breathed deeply and exhaled welcoming energy of life to greet the approaching skycrystal. As it came to a hovering rest, a chorus of voices erupted into a widespread cheer. Gamon, unable to contain his joy, rushed forward to greet the young adults as the crystal gently settled among its faceted, mineral relatives.

"Good job! Good job!" he cried as the pilots spontaneously reached out to hug him, his bandaged head towering above theirs. They looked up, all grins.

"We made it!" They lingered momentarily, then broke Gamon's embrace to greet and share their joy with other welcoming guardians.

The white-haired warrior moved on to the next task at hand. Gamon barked, "Crystal masters, Twath, Marlay, Lorus, come! We've got a new Center to work with now!" The man and to two women, known for their ability to blend with the consciousness of crystal life forms, entered the circle.

"Oh, yes," Marlay said, "you hear that?" She nodded to her companions. "They are linking already. When this crystal blends with the others, they will be able to find the most likely time when there's enough consciousness to form an arc."

"This Life crystal is amazing," Twath said. "It speaks with the planets as well as with Earth. If such a time exists, I agree, this new crystal center will find it and guide us."

The second woman, Lorus, spoke up more loudly. "Searchers. Get ready to travel. The Center is preparing to make one portal. It will bridge dimensions in a way we've never seen before. It will allow you to search in the future but keep you in contact with each other. You'll be able to communicate amongst yourselves while time-traveling. Get ready." Then in a softer voice, "Open hearts. Dear Creator, open hearts."

"Wait!" Pergaine yelled out. Heads turned in her direction. "Look!" Eyes focused on a curious sight. Two guardians on a skystone too small to hold them had crossed the battle line and now appeared to skip above defenders like a flat stone skips over water.

The sound of their voices grew. "I told you to wait until I found my gravity crystal," one of them said. "Yours isn't enough to balance our mass!"

"Wait? With Shahitam trying to regroup on that second platform? If we'd waited any longer after pulling you from that bog, we'd have been spotted for sure!"

Mariyonta and Aronlat ran through the searchers as if oblivious to them. "Yawri and Tisbero! You're alive!" the duo called out as Yawri and Tisbero came to rest among the defenders. Mariyonta and Aronlat leapt into their arms as Pergaine, Gamon and Aviea hurried from the Center as fast as they could to join them.

"Ahh!" Yawri said. Mariyonta pulled back his wide sleeve to reveal a crimson line. "It's just a scrape," Yawri pulled his sleeve down again. He surveyed the young adults as if to make sure they were real, and the sight of them made his face beam.

Pergaine, Gamon and Aviea joined the reunion. "You two!" Pergaine said as she struggled to find words. They stared back at her innocently. Not knowing what to say next she added awkwardly, "You two are holding up the group." Tisbero and Yawri actually looked around them for the first time.

"Right," Yawri stated, wincing as he straightened his arm. "What are we doing?"

Pergaine swallowed over the lump in her throat and composed herself. "The Life-crystal that Mariyonta and Aronlat brought has blended with the others. The crystal center is opening a portal to the best chance we've got. All the searchers will be able to communicate with each other!"

Yawri looked dazed. "Okay, I'm ready," he said.

"We'll protect your bodies," Mariyonta added seriously.

Pergaine's sharp eyes scanned the thick line of seasoned defenders between them and the battle line. "Thank you." She tried to sound sincere.

At the Center, Twath, the male crystal master, opened his eyes as he returned from a trance, surveyed his surroundings and then projected his voice for all to hear.

"The crystals have found a time when the planet and human-beings could choose to reawaken. Jupiter is helping. It is calling a comet to itself. When it hits, it will create large blasts upon its surface. The fireballs caused by the collisions will be larger than several Earths combined. The energy broadcast from Jupiter should start to re-awaken Earth like a bright fire would wake you from your own slumber.

"The whole solar system is joining to accomplish this goal. The planets now know that if Earth does not survive, a black hole may result. Any human-being with enough caring has the chance to be reawakened as well, and many of us will be reincarnated in that time for that choice. This is our chance. Ride the wave of Life that the crystal center opens for us, and seek connection with your future self." Then in a softer voice added, "Nurture the Creator within you."

A cry arose from those near the Center. "The portal is opening!" First a long vertical line of iridescent light became visible overhead, then it spread apart to form an oval opening into another world. A sound, muted melodies at first, grew into a rapture of musical tones, each distinct yet in harmony, blending into the sound of eternity. The searchers left their bodies wherever they stood and flowed like salmon in an ethereal stream racing home, all praying for a rebirth of consciousness in that future time. After rocketing through the vibrating tunnels, they burst into the fertile time like sprouting seeds searching for light. A hopeful voice called out, "This time is less dense than any I've found. Heavy and large tools have been replaced by lightweight efficient ones."

"They're exploring space!" Another called. "They aren't remembering how to do it by talking with Earth, but the memory of doing it somehow, is alive again. Now they are try-ing to do it with pointed, metal ships."

"I see my future self!" Aviea's voice rang. "A woman. She's in some kind of large metal box on wheels. There are thousands of these rolling boxes, all moving, rolling on, what is it? Something hard covering the soil. Smothering the soil. Wait. She's stopped. All the rolling boxes are stopped, like they're all waiting for something. She's looking out her window." Aviea sought to join with her future self. *I know we have been separated by lifetimes of pain. I'm sorry, but feel me. You are not alone. We are a part of each other.*

Aviea's voice quivered with excitement. "I think she feels me. She is noticing a bird sitting on a tall, shiny pole. She's seeing the clouds, light reflecting through them. She is seeing some wildflowers." *You can grow the wild flowers. You can reconnect to Earth...and me.*

The woman spoke as she stared. "I wonder what flowers feed butterflies?"

"She can hear me!" Aviea exclaimed with profound relief. "She has a lot of thoughts that are distracting her, but her heart is open enough to hear me!"

Tisbero's fiery voice carried for all to hear. "I've found my future self too, but his heart chakra has been so damaged it's the color of rusty iron. Tisbero watched as the man went outside of a house into its backyard. He approached a little girl playing on a swing. The man grabbed the little girl by the arm.

"How many times do I have to call you in for dinner!" He barked.

"I didn't hear you! I didn't hear you!" He jerked her off the swing. She fell to the ground crying.

"You need to learn how to listen then!" he hammered. The little girl sobbed, crumpled.

Tisbero spoke with the compassion. *You need to learn how to listen. I see you were raised with cruelty. That is sad, but look at this child. Are you more attached to your pain than to your love of her?* A gentle breeze danced with the leaves of a nearby maple tree. The man looked up and saw a hawk circling in the sky. He looked down. The expression on his face melted from anger to remorse.

"Carol. Carol. I'm sorry." He bent to help her up gently, then let her go so she could wipe her tears. "I'm sorry. It wasn't your fault. I brought the stress from work home to you, and that's not right. And I should never have grabbed you."

"I didn't hear you call, Daddy," she pleaded.

The man held the door open for her as she walked in. "Carol," he said in a gentle voice as they walked into their kitchen. "I'm never going to touch you angrily again. I promise."

Tisbero whispered to his future self. *It is not what happens to you, but how you respond to what happens to you, that proves who you are. Remember...what you do to others will be done to you, in this life or the next. The way to heal the cruelty in the world is to heal it in yourself.* Tears welled in the man's eyes.

The child raised her face to her father. "After dinner can we go for a walk in the park, daddy?"

"Yes," he said, with cracking voice. "Let's see how many different kinds of birds we can find."

Tisbero's voice was joyous. "I'm in luck," he said. "That future self has been through a lot of pain. He had me nervous, but he still has a spark in his heart. I can tell that I'm going to learn as much from him as he is from me. He can hear my thoughts. Someday, will only act upon our thoughts."

Voices began to call out in increasing frequency. "My future self is a man," a feminine voice called. "His parents are alcoholics and they are very poor. I helped him hear the voice of a coyote. He heard it, he really *heard* it. He's joining some elders at a sweat lodge for the first time in his life. I'm in luck, too. Dear Creator, he's resilient."

"I've found myself! He just saw an Earth-spirit, a small furry brown thing that scurried at the edge of his vision." The guardian hovered near his future self and spoke. *It's real. Earth-spirits live with you. Open your eyes and ears to the fourth dimension. There's so much more Life than you have let yourself see.*

The man addressed his wife. "Mary, you're not going to believe what I think I just saw."

Another searcher spoke. "Mine works in some type of agency. She works with numbers. Lot's of numbers." *How do you measure quality of Life?*

The woman placed a chart down upon a table and turned to a man seated next her. "Dave," she said. "I just had a thought. We have a lot of data. Why do we just give economic analysis to the Commissioners? Why not analyze the county's trends in health, education and things like water quality, too?"

"Are you all right?" Dave responded.

Another voice called, "My future self is volunteering to serve food at a shelter. He cares. Dear Creator, he can still connect to diversity. Communicating with him should not be a problem."

Pergaine broke in. "Mine is working in a research lab." Pergaine floated above the researcher as the woman spoke to the man standing next to her. *Make your dreams real.* "You know. I've been thinking," the woman said. "The technology is ready. What are we waiting for?"

"Money," the man responded.

"But why not start selling demonstration models of this now? I think the public would be interested in a pollution-free energy source that could power their homes. If we scaled the components down to desktop size, the model could be quite affordable. The public would have the chance to see how it works."

"Well," the man said thoughtfully. "I suppose if we used a small solar cell to make hydrogen from water, and use the hydrogen to power a small fuel cell to run a propeller or something, it would show that the technology is here."

Pergaine's future self continued in a clipped voice. "No pollution. No power grids. Renewable energy located at every home. We could help make it happen sooner rather than later."

Pergaine's astral body glowed as it drifted closer to her future self. The researcher cocked her head. "Do you feel something?" She asked the man.

"Sure," the man responded. "I feel like I better get to work."

Another guardian's voice broke in. "My future self is a man in China. People are running in panic. *I am with you life-bearer. Your voice is mine as mine is yours.* Oh dear. He is walking into a street filled with tanks. He's stopping in front of them. Dear Creator, let them respect his heart. They're stopping. Blessed universe, he's stopped a column of tanks! We *are* a guardian."

"I've found my future self too!" Yawri's voice called out. "He's on the great pyramid! I tell you he's on the pyramid! The generator pyramid!"

"Can you connect him with all three pyramids?" someone else cried. "That may open in him the history that sleeps inside of everyone. Perhaps he can touch it."

"I don't know if he can be open enough to believe it! He seems so intellectual. Like a scientist. It will be way beyond a whisper. How can he even understand it?"

"But you've found him, and he's on the pyramid!"

Yawri flowed to his future self and placed an ethereal hand on his shoulder. *I am with you, and know you've been taught to believe only what you see. Let go of what you think is possible. Pretend you're watching a movie.*

Another voice cut in. "I'm a fisherman on Lake Baikal. Can you believe it? I'm a fisherman on the planet's sixth chakra. *Care for this sacred lake. It's the eye of the world.* A man with the fisherman started to throw an empty oilcan into the lake.

"What are you doing?" the fisherman yelled. "Throw nothing into this lake unless you want to join it!"

"We're connected! He feels my thoughts!"

Another searcher spoke excitedly. "I can't believe it. My future self is helping an old man die. He is actually helping his transition, helping him let go of his body. He helps people connect with the cycle of life and death!"

Gamon's voice boomed. "I've found my future self! I'm working in a store of some kind. Stocking shelves of clothing, but there's a smell to them. Something's not right. Gamon hovered near the man for a moment before directing his thoughts to him. *You need to know what your choices mean. Who is making these clothes, and how?*

The man stopped placing clothes on a rack as if in thought. "Hey, Sam." The man turned his head to his companion. "When are they going to label these clothes so you know who made them? I mean, was it kids at twelve cents an hour breathing chemicals, or what?" He stopped to straighten the silk shirts he had just hung. "When I was a kid we knew the local tailors, farmers, everyone for that matter. But how can we choose what businesses to buy from today if the labels don't tell us? You can't make a logical choice."

Gamon beamed. "He's open enough to hear me. Give us time and our voices, and our questions, will be one again."

"I see my future self, too. She's reading something," another searcher called out. "I don't know if she will let me in or not! She thinks something has to be physical for it to be real." *Breathe. Let in the dust of God. You have free will. Oh please, let me in. It's been so long! Close your eyes and feel me!* The woman closed her eyes, then opened them again and appeared to stare into space. *Yes, I'm here. Practice honestly caring for yourself and others every day. That's all. Practice caring for yourself and others. Overtime, the split can be healed, and our voices will be one again.* A tear silently fell onto the open page.

More and more voices called out. What began as a trickle built to a cascade. One searcher's voice rang above the others. "My future self is a priest for the Voice of Compassion. He is in a conversation with a rabbi and a Muslim mullah. They're uniting their voices to speak out against hate that is living within each of their own faiths. The three are connected with the One!"

"I am the rabbi!" another guardian's voice boomed.

"And I am the Muslim!" the third sang out with joy.

Another voice called in the distance. "My future self is having lucid dreams! She realizes the physical is only one dimension of reality. She's conscious in her astral body! Oh. She's waking up. She's looking right at me."

The woman spoke to the person sleeping next to her. "Jim. Jim, do you see that?" she asked, staring ahead.

"Huh?" A sleepy voice replied.

"An Angel. So help me Jim, there's an angel standing at the foot of our bed."

She turned to him as he sat up. "I don't see anything."

She looked back. "It's gone." A tone of bewilderment was in her voice.

"Are you sure you weren't dreaming?" he asked.

"I see my future self too!" another excited voice rang. "She's walking, exercising I think." *Do you feel me?* The woman stopped, turned one way, then another. *Let the wait be over. Let the aloneness be over. What is lost to the past cannot be reclaimed. Let me bring its wisdom to you as you will bring the wisdom of the present to me...and together...we will create a new future.*

"What is happening?" the woman said out loud. She breathed deeply, then exhaled. "I can feel my thoughts."

Several voices cried out, "I think we're getting enough connection for an arc of consciousness! We *can* wake up in this time!" Then, as if a mighty pressure had built up, pressing on the portal walls, the connection to the Center shrank. Voices rang out in confusion as the communication to one another was, in turn, completely lost.

✦

Shahitam observed his thinning battle lines with strange dispassion. Thousands of his soldiers lay dead compared to fewer thousands of guardians. He turned to his captain. "Combining the soldiers from the two platforms onto this one leaves me with fifteen troopers. No, fourteen. I had to 'decommission' the idiot captain whose platform I ride now. If not for his cowardice I would have eliminated those barbarians at the ridge. Now look at them all gathered around their precious crystal center. Well," he said with rising emotion., "what worked once can work again. Except this time, we'll strike at the heart."

"Take us to the Center," he commanded for all to hear. "Keep back from the edge and hold your fire. We go in peace." The platform moved forward without hesitation.

"Over there!" a defender shouted, pointing. "One of the platforms isn't attacking. It's moving toward us!"

"Hold your ground!" another yelled.

"It's just passing over us! We can't stop it because it's not firing!"

"It will fire at some point. When it does, who ever is under it just needs to reflect what it sends," yet another said.

Mariyonta and Aronlat watched the platform pass overhead. "Mariyonta," Aronlat said to her. "It's Shahitam. He's headed for the Center!"

"I know." She took a deep breath. The platform moved slowly, leisurely over defenders' upturned faces, as well as row after row of swaying searchers. Defenders held their reflecting crystals at ready, but there was nothing to reflect. Finally, the warship halted parallel to the Center, about twenty yards away, as if on a perch in the air. Beady-eyed soldiers peered down with anticipation.

"So, my crystal masters," Shahitam spoke to Twath, Marlay and Lorus who were deep in communication with the Center. Flowing energy wrapped them like a blanket of illuminated air. "I see you are working well with this wonderful family of minerals. So skilled you are."

The crystal masters didn't reply, but continued, absorbed with their work. One of the defenders near them breathed deeply to increase her connection to All-That-Is and spoke. "They are busy bringing Life to Creation, Shahitam," she said. "Surely, as a guardian, that is your goal as well."

"That is my goal," he said as he turned to gaze upon the explosions and screams of the encroaching battle, making it unclear if he was responding to the statement or to what he saw.

The woman persisted. "Our agreement was to come and nurture Life, to be gardeners in the garden."

Shahitam's eyes once more fell upon the smattering of defenders around the crystal center, and he replied. "But you murder the garden. This unimaginable gift of Life, from the Creator Itself, you murder it."

"We do not murder it. Those that choose to follow your words more than Life's, and who act as your puppets do," the woman said.

"Puppets? You think they are puppets? No. Your future selves love murdering Life. They enjoy it. To do harm and not care is glorious! You should talk to the searchers, and they will tell you. Do you want to see your future? I can show you the visions. You think there are guardians of Life in this future that you so desperately seek? There are only guardians of greed," he laughed. "They love their answers, not questions like you. They make Life go extinct, not nurture it like you. They disdain differences, not love differences, like you. They will kill each other because of 'differences.'"

"To murder Life is your purpose, not ours," the female defender said.

"Yes. Your purpose is to improve life, isn't it? Believe me. I will help you spread that purpose. Improve *your* life at least. It's such a little change from 'Improve Life' that no one will notice. You think putting the planet to sleep will protect it from those who follow me? Do you really think it will wake up again? You are a fool."

We will wake up together," the speaker replied.

"Wake up? It's not going to wake up. Your broken future selves won't let it. They will suck all of its water out of its deep eardrums, and poison it, and slaughter every species they touch. Don't you see? You will join me to enslave Earth as you will enslave your bodies and each other. And anyone who speaks out against this enslavement will be hated. Hated and killed."

Other defenders flanked the woman now, in supportive caring for her clear voice. "You choose to see what may be. Since the Creator is for us, only we can be against us. Then, as now, we will fight for the diversity of Creation, for the diversity of each other, for the diversity of the Creator. We will awaken with Earth."

"Your future selves, wake up? Why? Walking sleep is so much more pleasant. Do you think these future selves have the courage to face the impact of their actions? It's hopeless. Don't you see? Their thoughts are mine now, not yours. Go ahead and ask your precious little searchers. Do you think your future selves care? Why ask questions when you have all the answers? You can't ask them to change until the 'facts' are conclusive. They shouldn't have to change if the facts aren't conclusive, right? That wouldn't be rational, or economical. My answers keep them comfortable. What do you have to offer them? Pain?"

"We offer them their whole selves," she replied steadily.

Shahitam continued, almost glowering. "You know that self-realization can be very painful. How many do you think will have the courage to confront their appreciation of me? Their everyday evil? The little meannesses they inflict on each other? The comparison. The judgment. The competition. I love competition, it teaches us to be better than others. There isn't enough for everybody, you know. Survival of the fittest, after all. They'll point to what they judge in others, to avoid their own heart."

The guardian was steadfast. "They will choose to know when they do harm. They will chose to feel it."

"Feel? You expect them to feel? After all the trauma they've had? They've all been so *damaged*, and through so many lifetimes. It's unfair of you to expect them to be able to feel. I'll tell you what. The future I foresee will require them to abandon their children, at least emotionally if not physically. Children will be raising children--and children raised without caring are mine. Oh, I'm afraid you'll lose the sanctity of young and old alike, and the sanctity of the womb. But I'll help you hang on to one thing. Your own sanctity, or perhaps it will be twisted into narcissism. I don't know. No one will care, so it doesn't matter."

"We will always care. That part of us that knows that the first breath of the Creator resides within us will care. The part that asks only to be nurtured, not saved, will care."

Shahitam was playing with the defender's mind as if it were an amusing toy. "But that's your problem. Don't you understand? Your future selves want to be saved. They want to be told who to be so that they can be self-righteous. You expect too much."

The defender took a breath, and spoke again. "They have free will. They alone control their *response* to what you whisper."

"And they choose to respond by agreeing with my thoughts." Shahitam laughed again. "The thoughts I give them are so much more pious and beautiful than questions from their "whole selves." Beauty is important, don't you think? Or is it looking good, or looking strong? When you know the right way, you do look strong." He paused, considering his next words carefully. He looked calm, proud. "I foresee a future where you will not have the courage to remove me from your lives because you will think you need me to succeed. Your fate is sealed in your chosen denial, and that is why...that is why I can share with complete impunity now." He glanced about him, and his eyebrows rose as he gazed upon the large amethyst in the Center. "Now, however, enough idle chat. I choose to continue my beloved work." He turned toward his soldiers with unhurried yet certain purpose. His voice barked. "Troopers! Train your citrines on that purple stone in the center." All pointed their yellow crystals at the target. "Fire!"

"No!" the defenders cried out at once. The woman who had spoken was first to jump up on the skycrystal and try to reflect the blast.

"Defenders! Unite! Come!" She yelled to summon the other defenders who had been moving toward the crystal center. As her reflecting crystal glowed an unnatural white, a man jumped up to take her place. After a few seconds, a short, stout woman jumped in to take his. The blasts, though not reflected, were at least being absorbed and kept away from the amethyst.

"I can't hold it any longer!" The last defender screamed. The female speaker hopped up again, but neither she nor her crystal had recovered yet.

"Get up here!" the male defender yelled at the top of his lungs to hurry others. Defenders ran through the family of crystals but no clear path existed through them because they had been packed so closely to make room for the amethyst. The female speaker's reflecting crystal exploded just as the man stepped in front of the beam. The blast took them both, as well as the short, stout woman, several feet into the air. Their twisted bodies landed still as death. The beam fell onto the Life-crystal. The crystal masters, who had been intimately connected to the crystal center until this moment, shrieked with pain.

"I'm coming!" A defender yelled as he tripped on a protruding staff of mineral. Another struggled to ascend the crystal to redirect the blast. Shahitam laughed with glee as he watched the defender jump upon the crystal and try to reflect the searing beams.

The man's hands almost instantly turned white from the strain; then, as if torn from within, he cried out in death throes. Another defender dove to take his place, but because he was far from neutral, the beam only ceased for two seconds before he, too, crumbled. Another defender came, another fell. Each life from the stream of defenders' bought seconds.

Mariyonta and Aronlat looked on from the distance. "We've got to do something!" she screamed. But all paths were blocked by defenders now hurling themselves over the crystals in their desperate rush to protect the Life-crystal.

"I've got it!" Aronlat yelled in return. "The skystone!" Mariyonta's eyes fell upon it a fraction of a second after his, but the difference let him reach it first.

"Aronlat! Wait!" she said as she reached out to give him her bigger reflecting stone but he was off, already accelerating though the air. "You'll never be able to return that many beams!"

His head moved like an eagle's as it followed every sharp turn of his craft. Acting with no regard for his own safety, he bore down on Shahitam's platform and dove for the soldiers firing the beams. Shahitam, keenly aware of what had brought his ship down during the last encounter, was quick to see the threat.

"You three!" He grabbed the first three in the line, their beams cut short. "Fire at that man!" He jabbed a long finger toward the approaching skystone. Aronlat let his human-spirit take over, knowing that it could respond much faster than his mind. The skystone and his body became one. It darted to the left as two beams seared the air. The third soldier, more skilled, waited to see where he went. Aronlat's body, the reflecting crystal and the skystone were in complete connection to All, and met the beam straight on. It returned to the soldier with fatal accuracy.

Without warning, a broadwinged hawk streaked down and extended its claws into Shahitam's scalp. He screamed. He beat at the bird with his hands but it was gone. Recovering his balance, he yelled with anger. "You and you!" He grabbed two more soldiers. "Stop that skystone!" Subtracting those now firing at Aronlat, that left nine soldiers firing at the Life-crystal. Defenders eagerly streamed in to take their fateful turn among the focused beams, because each was aware that every second the crystal center was preserved could mean the difference between success and failure of the searchers.

"Why are the searchers taking so long to find the arc?" an outer ring defender near Mariyonta asked as he tried for a better view of the Center.

Mariyonta turned to answer him but her eyes caught sight of more yellow beams. "They're breaking through the outer defenders!" she screamed as she faced the encircling battle line. Supported by Shahitam's only other remaining skyplatform, the ground troops were concentrating their attack where the line had been made thinnest by the defenders' rush to protect the crystal center. Mariyonta sprinted toward the battle. Guardians forced to stand alone too long were quickly crumpling. Mariyonta reached a defender who was reflecting two beams from the platform as his hands were becoming bleached white. As she intercepted the rays he fell to the ground panting, sweat pouring through his linen robe in streams.

The timing was perfect. One of the soldiers, forced to keep up the attack too long, realized his crystal was about to burst. He stopped its beam. But that left the soldier next to him alone. Mariyonta returned his beam to him, exploding his imprisoned crystal. The impact tumbled three soldiers to earth. The platform wavered as razor-sharp shards of shattered quartz peppered the priests controlling the craft. Before they could regain control, the platform tipped and sent the occupants slithering off the edge and into the upturned faces of the troops below. The platform, devoid of pilots, followed them down and silenced the screams. Mariyonta looked long enough to confirm that the rush had been repelled, then turned toward the Center just in time to see a blast of beams shoot toward Aronlat's lonely skystone. "Be careful!" she yelled involuntarily.

Aronlat took an unexpected dive under Shahitam's plat-form. The soldiers were so intent on blasting him from the sky that they kept firing as he passed below them. Several beams, meant for Aronlat, hit the back end of their ship and blasted large pieces of stone into the air. The sudden change in mass made the platform shoot up into the sky knocking the soldiers, all near the edge, into freefall. Shahitam himself hung from the edge of the platform like a cat dangling by its claws. "Get me! Get me!" he screamed out as the vessel ascended. The three remaining men, all priests, exchanged nervous glances and directed the craft into retreat before one decided to move cautiously toward the edge and retrieve his master.

The crystal center, now free of attack, glowed with sparkling light once more. Sound and a rainbow of color surged through the time tunnel like an electric river. The searchers of the future, strained from being severed from each other and the Center, began to summon each other as they felt the connection to their individual portals return.

"What happened?" a troubled searcher's voice called.

"I don't know," another answered. "But let's clearly identify this time and space so we can tell all the guardians how to find it."

"I agree," came another voice. "Every guardian needs to locate their future self in this band of time."

Others called out. "I think enough hearts are open to hear us." One voice rose above the others. "Yes! Enough conscious connections are made!" Hundreds of joyous voices chorused, "We've got arc! The connection between our past and future bodies is happening! Each soul felt the wisdom available to them from within bodies linked across time.

The gateway from past to future and from future to past was open and an avalanche of energy shot through the portals from Earth's core. Suddenly, the ground beneath the feet of the defenders back at the Center went quiet. Pulsing ley lines, arteries of life, shrank. Earth was going into hibernation here, withdrawing its vitality deep within itself and simultaneously launching its life force into that future time. Stretching to wake up, fault zones began to breathe and volcanoes flexed Earth's crust. Earth had made the decision to reclaim its life, and its vitality with Creation. Although subtle at first, future selves felt both a nurturing etheric elixir and a flame grow within them. Ethereal and physical worlds, long ago torn apart, were connecting to be One again.

Back at the waning battle, the firing citrines fell silent. No longer able to receive resonating life force from a rapidly slumbering Earth, they became as solid as granite. The hordes of soldiers were shocked, and stood as if naked in front of the defenders. They didn't wait for the revenge they felt would come. Casting their useless crystals down, they turned and ran. After a few minutes, the trumpet of mastodons was heard in the distance, although only the flashing wings of diving birds could be seen. Slowly, a cloud of dust closed over the soldiers as they ran. The guardians stood and watched the retreat in dazed silence.

One by one, the guardians took stock of the carnage around them. Friends and loved ones, companion warriors, lay on the ground as their blood mixed with soil. All felt the knowledge that many more lifetimes of terror would come. Terror, they knew, designed to break them from the One Source. Then, as if uncertain of this strange world they now stood upon, they noticed a change in the sound. It wasn't full of all dimensions. It sounded flat. "So this is what it's like to stand on a sleeping earth," a melancholy voice said.

The searchers began to return to their bodies now that the arc of consciousness was made. The defenders watched with a building sense of relief as body after body stopped its swaying slumber and came to life. Mariyonta and Aronlat ran to meet Yawri, Tisbero, Aviea, Pergaine and Gamon as they returned to their bodies, and each eagerly joined the two young adults' smiling embrace. There were no words. Only the music of tears, joy and hope filled the air. Hope for the future, hope for the choice of future selves to remember who they are.

At last Tisbero, his graying red hair tousled, spoke. "The arc from past to future is open. It is open through Earth, as well as through souls. We don't know what will happen. We know Earth is waking up in that time, and that evil will continue to try to murder it. We know our future selves have the choice to hear us. We don't know if they will listen."

Gamon met his gaze. "They will listen," he said more as a prayer than a statement.

Pergaine nodded thoughtfully. *I do pray that you hear me, that you can connect to me. We must learn from each other, listen to each other. Only by being rejoined we can know true strength and be whole again.*

Yawri surveyed the faces of his friends. As each looked back in turn, he saw that their eyes brimmed with past and future memories. Eyes filled with sadness and hope in the same moment. *Thank you, my friends.* He released a silent sigh as he recalled the living lotus within him. *Thank you, Muran. Thank you; the birds, the frogs. All bearers of Life and Joy. We will all learn what it is like to live on a sleeping Earth. May I always remember to embrace the Creator through you.*

Aviea reached out to touch a strand of untrampled barley growing in a crack of stone. *It will be a while before we all grow in fertile soil again. I know the love that I have for my friends will bring us together lifetime after lifetime. In our coming unconsciousness, I know I will harm them...and I will be harmed. May we wake up together, and know forgiveness.*

Mariyonta held Aronlat's hand while she gazed out upon the thousands of remaining guardians, their white garments now illuminated by the setting sun's crimson light. "We will succeed," she said, tears rolling down her face. Pergaine raised her reflecting crystal to the west to catch the last of the day's sun. Rays sparkled through it like brilliant orange stars.

Aronlat bathed in the joy of being surrounded by friends. He raised Mariyonta's hand to the sky. She filled her lungs with the dusty air, and her voice rang out for all to hear. "We will awaken! United again!" Yawri, Aviea, Tisbero, Pergaine, Gamon and soon everyone, raised joined hands in celebration.

Like the rolling wave of an ocean, a crescendo rose from the sea of guardians as a chorus of hope filled the sky, and echoed across time.

Chapter 18   **The Beginning**

"It's okay," a voice called through the fading sound. "It's okay." I couldn't open my eyes and lay curled into a ball. My body shook as if from an electric shock.

It's okay? My hand drew across a stone surface. *I'm on the pyramid.* My hand rose to touch my face and I smelled fragrant atoms of Paleozoic sea mixed with my hot breath.

"You back now?"

Back? Am I back? My body ached.

"I am with you," the quiet, firm voice said. My shaking had stopped, but water filled my eyes. A hand touched me kindly on the shoulder. I breathed deeply.

"I'm okay," I managed to say, not at all sure that it was true. I slowly rolled to a sitting position, my legs crossed under me, elbows on knees. I carefully lowered my chin to my hands and stared blankly into the night. Mist rose from the pyramid, like vaporous dew evaporating from a morning meadow. The hazy shapes mixed with the air and danced away, and I now noticed sound. Tones, a whispering voice from the stone. "I release the energy, the essence that was left with me, into the wind now. It belongs to the guardians to reclaim." Tears came from deep within my chest. My head swam.

Can rocks speak? How can rocks speak? I managed to raise my eyes to see a faint crescent of light emerge from the new moon. I felt the edges of my mind say hello, and, as if it were as normal as greeting any friend, felt the moon say hello in return. My vision traced across the heavens but the stars were not stars. They were like people. Each had a personality and perspective. *How can stars be like people?*

I turned my head to get some sense of physical reality. A man in a baggy shirt and pants was sitting near me. "Hard climb," he said. His white teeth shone in the starlight. I nodded. I felt a need to uncoil my legs, so I crawled over to the edge of the pyramid and let my feet hang down over the first step. I sat and watched the mist rise from the stones and dance with the wind. Swirling essences, like ethereal names, millions of names, all seeking their homes in present-time human-beings, filled the air.

I felt the pyramid sigh beneath me, a giant exhale of breath held far too long. It was letting go. "I can return to dust now." I gazed at the other two pyramids, the towering triangles. More names, more memories, flowing toward their present-time homes. My eyes swept the dark horizon. Fingers of sculptured earth clasped hands with fingers of starlight. *One body*.

I turned my head to view the flat top of the pyramid I sat upon, absent of its cap stone. A swirl of dust and mist appeared to coalesce into a human form, bringing the image of--who? The face of the African storyteller that I met so long ago. My mouth moved, but the sound was hushed. "Thank you," I said. "Thank you for pointing my way here."

"Join with your past to build a new future," I heard the face speak as its dust evaporated into starlight.

A thought brushed across my mind. "Howic?" I asked. "Is that you? Are you the storyteller I met in Senegal...Howic?" I gazed blankly where he had been, waiting for an answer, but the sound of my pounding heart was the only response.

"You rested enough to go down now?" the man in the baggy pants asked. I turned my head and noticed that he still sat next to me. "We have been here more than ten minutes. I must think of the guards."

Ten minutes? I gazed into his face as if for the first time. Something familiar. Something at the edge of my memory. "Lazket?" I asked.

"Lazket?" the man replied. "No, I'm Hamar."

"Hamar," I imitated, trying desperately to make it fit. I reached out and placed my hand on his hand. "Thank you," I said. "Thank you for everything," and I breathed slowly and deeply.

"I live here," he replied with calm certainty. "I share my home." We sat in precious silence for a few moments and watched the people file out from the light show below, their empty chairs left starkly vacant on the sand.

"We go down now?" Hamar said, more as a comment than a question. "Too much time on the pyramid is not good."

I sighed, not really hearing, but responded anyway. "Electricity comes from this top," I said, as a feeble attempt at conversation.

He looked at me blankly. I spoke again. "Did you know electricity comes from its top?"

"Not much comes any more," Hamar said thoughtfully, and looked into my eyes. "We should go down now."

I looked closely at his face. His penetrating ancient eyes told me that there was nothing I could say to change the need keep moving. "We go down now," I replied. He scrambled like a youth down the first tall step, stopped and looked back. I placed my hand on the edge of the hard limestone, but as I pushed off to stand, a fist-sized piece of rock broke away into my hand. It crumbled as if eager to be released into dust.

A knowing smile graced Hamar's lips. "Even the pyramid must rejoin its source someday," he said.

"Rejoin," I replied. "That sums it up. But how do we rejoin?"

He chuckled softly and bounded down another of the giant's stairs. "Use the heart in your feet," he said plainly. "And just take one step at a time."

I took another deep breath, let it go, and moved toward the next edge. The swirling mist, starlight and dust from the stone mingled somehow with my body as if we were all part of the next footstep back down. "Heart in my feet," I said out loud. "One step at a time."

"Since the Creator is for us, only we can be against us."
Guardian

Additional information and updates about
We Came as Angels is available by visiting:

www.wecameasangels.org

"It's not what happens to you, but how you respond to what happens to you, that proves who you are."
Tisbero

Quick Order Form

Please send *We Came as Angels* to the following address:

Name _____

Address _____

City _____ State _____ Zip _____

Email _____

Price of each book is $14.95 U.S.

Shipping by air: Add $3.85 to cover postage of one book (add $2.50 for each additional book.)

Sales tax: Add 6.5% ($.97) for each book if mailed to a Minnesota addresses.

_____ books @ $14.95 each   _____

Postage $3.85 1st Bk., $2.50 each additional   _____

Sales tax $0.97 each Bk. for MN addresses   _____

Total enclosed   _____

Send check or money order, no cash or C.O.D.'s please, to:

Waterwoods Press
PO Box 1354
Minnetonka, MN 55345

Allow four weeks for delivery.
Prices subject to change without notice.

Additional purchasing information about *We Came as Angels* is available by visiting www.wecameasangels.org

"Creation shifts in response to the collective thoughts used to mold it. The Creator doesn't control you, or any of Its soul-seeds."
Muran

Quick Order Form

Please send *We Came as Angels* to the following address:

Name _____

Address _____

City _____ State _____ Zip _____

Email _____

Price of each book is $14.95 U.S.

Shipping by air: Add $3.85 to cover postage of one book (add $2.50 for each additional book.)

Sales tax: Add 6.5% ($.97) for each book if mailed to a Minnesota addresses.

_____ books @ $14.95 each   _____

Postage $3.85 1st Bk., $2.50 each additional   _____

Sales tax $0.97 each Bk. for MN addresses   _____

Total enclosed   _____

Send check or money order, no cash or C.O.D.'s please, to:

Waterwoods Press
PO Box 1354
Minnetonka, MN 55345

Allow four weeks for delivery.
Prices subject to change without notice.

Additional purchasing information about *We Came as Angels* is available by visiting www.wecameasangels.org

"We have all learned that denial only serves to make lessons more dramatic."
Hetlin